ABANDON

Also by Blake Crouch

Desert Places

Locked Doors

ABANDON

BLAKE CROUCH

Minotaur Books New York

This is a work of fiction. All of the characters, organizations, and events portrayed in this novel are either products of the author's imagination or are used fictitiously.

ABANDON. Copyright © 2009 by Blake Crouch. All rights reserved. Printed in the United States of America. For information, address St. Martin's Press, 175 Fifth Avenue, New York, N.Y. 10010.

www.minotaurbooks.com

ISBN-13: 978-0-312-53740-1
ISBN-10: 0-312-53740-9

First Edition: July 2009

10 9 8 7 6 5 4 3 2 1

This book is dedicated to Aidan Crouch.

ACKNOWLEDGMENTS

It's been a long trek to reach the end of this book, and I owe a lot of people my gratitude. Rebecca and Aidan, for sharing me with this story. It isn't always honeydew and sugarcanes living with a writer, but you guys are troupers and you're my people. I love you both so much. Linda Allen, for your friendship and endless support when I needed it most. Michael Homler, for pushing me in the right directions and being as much of a perfectionist as I am. Anna Cottle and Mary Alice Kier, for your priceless insight in the final stages. Joe Konrath, Gregg Hurwitz, Marcus Sakey, and Scott Phillips, great writers and greater men, who gave me diamond-hard feedback and support when things were looking insurmountable. David Morrell needs his own page, but this will have to suffice: you're a gentleman and an inspiration and I'm blessed to know you. Everyone in my local writers group—Suzanne Tyrpak, Terry Junttonen, Doug Walker, Shannon Richardson, Dinah Swan, Cacy Alexander, Gail Harris, Nina Moats, Haz Said, and Adam Watson. Early readers: Sandi Greene, Jordan Crouch, Clay and Susan Crouch, Judy Johnston, and Anne Marquard. Sally Richardson, Andy Martin, George Witte, and Kelley Ragland for making all this possible and putting me in the best of hands. Jeroen ten Berge, for your amazing creativity and love of books. Michael Richard, Joe Foster, Duane A. Smith, Marianne Fuierer, Art Holland, Karen Sway, and Clyde Gibbs for providing answers to questions I couldn't hunt down in books. Diane Cerafici and Beverly Coleman at Rocky Mountain PBS for tracking down the quote. Carol Edwards for your virtuoso copyediting. The awesome baristas and kickass coffee at the Steaming Bean in Durango, Colorado, where much of this book was written. And finally, group hug with the Jordans—Jon, Ruth, and Jen—thanks for having my back and for your friendship.

In the West, the past is very close. In many places, it still believes it's the present.

—JOHN MASTERS

Thursday, December 28, 1893

W ind rips through the crags a thousand feet above, nothing moving in this godforsaken town, and the mule skinner knows that something is wrong. Two miles south stands Bartholomew Packer's mine, the Godsend, a twenty-stamp mill that should be filling this box canyon with the thudding racket of the rock crushers pulverizing ore. The sound of the stamps in operation is the sound of money being made, and only two things will stop them—Christmas and tragedy.

He dismounts his albino steed, the horse's pinked nostrils flaring, dirty mane matted with ice. The single-rig saddle is snow-crusted as well, its leather and cloth components the mochila and shabrack—frozen stiff. He rubs George's neck, speaking in soft, low tones he knows will calm the animal, telling him he did a good day's work and that a warm stable awaits with feed and fresh water.

The mule skinner opens his wallet, collects the pint of busthead he bought at a bodega in Silverton, and swallows the remaining mouthful, whiskey crashing into his empty stomach like iced fire.

He wades through waist-deep snow to the mercantile, bangs his shopmades on the door frame. Inside, the lamps have been extinguished and the big stove squats dormant in the corner, unattended by the usual constellation of miners jawboning over coffee and tobacco. He calls for the owner as he crosses the board floor, moving between shelves, past stacked crates and burlap sacks bulging with sugar and flour.

"Jessup? It's Brady! You in back?"

The twelve burros crane their scrawny necks in his direction when Brady emerges from the merc. He reaches into his greatcoat, pulls out a tin of Star Navy tobacco, and shoves a chaw between lips and gums gone blackish purple in the last year.

"What the hell?" he whispers.

When he delivered supplies two weeks ago, this little mining town was bustling. Now Abandon looms listless before him in the gloom of late afternoon, streets empty, snow banked high against the unshoveled plank sidewalks, no tracks as far as he can see.

The cabins scattered across the lower slopes lie buried to their chimneys, and with not a one of them smoking, the air smells too clean.

Brady is a man at home in solitude, often spending days on the trail, alone in wild, quiet places, but this silence is all wrong—a lie. He feels menaced by it, and with each passing moment, more certain that something has happened here.

A wall of dark clouds scrapes over the peaks, and snowflakes begin to speck the sleeves of his slicker. Here comes the wind. Chimes clang together over the doorway of the merc. It will be night soon.

He makes his way up the street into the saloon, still half-expecting Joss Maddox, the beautiful barkeep, to assault him with some gloriously profane greeting. No one's there. Not the mute piano player, not a single customer, and again, no light from the kerosene lamps, no warmth from the potbellied stove, just a half-filled glass on the pine bar, the beer frozen through.

The path to the nearest cabin lies beneath untrodden snow, and without webs, it takes five minutes to cover a hundred yards.

He pounds his gloved fist against the door, counts to sixty. The latch string hasn't been pulled in, and despite the circumstance, he still feels like a trespasser as he steps inside uninvited.

In the dark, his eyes strain to adjust.

Around the base of a potted spruce tree, crumpled pages of newspaper clutter the dirt floor—remnants of Christmas.

Food languishes untouched on a rustic table, far too lavish to be any ordinary meal for the occupants of this cramped one-room cabin. This was Christmas dinner.

He removes a glove, touches the ham—cold and hard as ore. A pot sits there, the beans frozen in their broth. The cake feels more like pumice than sponge, and two jagged glass stems still stand upright, the wine having frozen and shattered the crystal cups.

Outside again, back with his pack train, he shouts, turning slowly in the middle of the street so the words carry in all directions.

"Anyone here?"

His voice and the fading echo of it sound so small rising against the vast, indifferent sweep of wilderness. The sky dims. Snow falls harder. The church at the north end of town disappears in the storm.

It's twenty-seven miles back to Silverton, and the pack train has been on the trail since before first light. The burros need rest. Having driven mules the last sixteen hours, he needs it, too, though the prospect of spending the night in Abandon, in this awful silence, unnerves him.

As he slips a boot into the stirrup, ready to take the burros down to the stables, he notices something beyond the cribs at the south end of town. He urges George forward, trots through deep powder between the false-fronted buildings, and when he sees what caught his eye, he whispers, "You old fool."

Just a snowman scowling at him, spindly arms made of spruce branches, pinecones for teeth and eyes, garland for a crown.

He tugs the reins, turning George back toward town, and the jolt of seeing her provokes, "Lord God Amighty."

He drops his head, tries to allay the thumping of his heart in the thin air. When he looks up again, the young girl is still there, perhaps six or seven, apparition-pale and just ten feet away, with locomotive black curls and coal eyes to match—so dark and with such scant delineation between iris and pupil, they more resemble wet stones.

"You put a fright in me," he says. "What are you doin out here all alone?"

She backpedals.

"No, don't be scart. I ain't the bogeyman." Brady alights, wades toward her through the snow. With the young girl in webs sunk only a foot in powder, and the mule skinner to his waist, he thinks it odd to stand eye-to-eye with a child.

"You all right?" he asks. "I didn't think there was nobody here."

The snowflakes stand out like white confetti in the child's hair.

"They're all gone," she says, no emotion, no tears, just an unaffected statement of fact.

"Even your ma and pa?"

She nods.

"Where'd they all go to? Can you show me?"

She takes another step back, reaches into her gray woolen cloak. The single-action army revolver is a heavy sidearm, and it sags comically in the child's hand, so she holds it like a rifle. Brady is too surprised to do a thing but watch as she struggles with the hammer.

"Okay, I'll show you," she says, the hammer locked back, sighting him up, her small finger already in the trigger guard.

"Now hold on. Wait just a—"

"Stay still."

"That ain't no toy to point in someone's direction. It's for—"

"Killin. I know. You'll feel better directly."

As Brady scrambles for a way to rib up this young girl to hand him the gun, he hears its report ricocheting through the canyon, finds himself lying on his back, surrounded by a wall of snow.

In the oval of gray winter sky, the child's face appears, looking down at him.

What in God's—

"It made a hole in your neck."

He attempts to tell her to stable George and the burros, see that they're fed and watered. After all the work they put in today, they deserve at least that. Only gurgles emerge, and when he tries to breathe, his throat whistles.

She points the revolver at his face again, one eye closed, the barrel slightly quivering, a parody of aiming.

He stares up into the deluge of snowflakes, the sky already immersed in a bluish dusk that seems to deepen before his eyes, and he wonders, *Is the day really fading that fast, or am I?*

2009

ONE

Abigail Foster stared through the windshield at the expired parking meter. Her fingers strangled the steering wheel, knuckles blanching, hands beginning to cramp. This had all seemed like such a good idea a month ago back in New York when she'd pitched the article to Margot, her editor at *Great Outdoors*. Now, on the verge of seeing him for the first time in twenty-six years, she realized she'd done herself the disservice of glossing over this moment and the fact that she'd have to walk into that building and face him.

Her watch showed five minutes to seven, which meant it was five to five, mountain time. She'd sat in this parking space for twenty minutes, and he was probably about to leave, thinking she'd decided not to come.

The hostess showed her toward the back of the brewpub, which at five in the afternoon stood mostly empty. Peanut shells littered the floor, crunching beneath the heels of her black pumps, and the reek of brewing beer infused the air with a yeasty sourness. The hostess held the back door open and motioned to the only occupied table on the patio.

Abigail stepped outside, smoothed the Cavalli skirt she'd paid way too much for last year in Milan.

The doubt resurfaced. She shouldn't have come. No story was worth this.

He sat alone with his back to her at a west-facing table, with the town of Durango, Colorado, spread out before him in its high valley, specked with the icy yellows of cottonwood and aspen, enclosed by pine-wooded hills and bare shale hills and, farther back, the spruce forests and jagged peaks of the San Juans.

The sound of the patio door banging shut caught his attention. He looked over his shoulder, and at the sight of her, slid his chair back from the table and stood—tall, sturdy, wavy silver hair, dark blues, and dressed like something out of *Backpacker* magazine—plaid Patagonia button-up shirt tucked into a comfortable pair of jeans, Livestrong bracelet, Teva sandals.

She felt that knot constricting in her stomach again, noticed his left hand trembling. He seized the chair he'd been sitting in to steady it.

"Hi, Lawrence."

She knew he was fifty-two, but he'd aged even better than his photo on the history department's Web site indicated.

No handshake, no hug, just five seconds of what Abigail ranked as the most excruciating eye contact she'd ever held.

Easing down into a chair, she counted three empty pints on the table, wished she'd had the benefit of alcohol to steel herself for this meeting.

She rifled through her purse, found her sunglasses. It was Halloween, and though the air carried a chill, at this elevation the intensity of direct sunlight made it pleasant to sit outdoors.

"I'm glad you came," Lawrence said.

A waiter costumed as a hula dancer approached the table.

"Want a beer, Abigail?"

"Sure."

"They have a bunch of different—"

"I don't care. Something light."

He said to the waiter, "Bring her a Rock Hopped Pale."

"Right on."

The whistle of a steam-powered locomotive blew somewhere up the valley. Abigail saw the plume of smoke in the distance, heard the chugging palpitations of the valve gears as the train steamed south through the heart of town.

"I don't have any backpacking gear," she said.

"Scott will outfit you."

"Who's Scott?"

"Our guide."

The silence, uncomfortable as it came, crawled under her skin.

"Pretty town you have here."

She couldn't help thinking this didn't feel anything like she'd imagined it would. Having run countless versions of this moment through her head, they'd all carried more gravitas. She would scream at him. She'd hit him. They'd break down and cry together. He'd apologize. She'd accept. She wouldn't. Now she understood none of that would happen. They were just two people sharing a table, trying to limp through the awkwardness.

"I'm curious," she said. "All this time, and now you contact me."

"I've followed your journalism career, subscribe to all the magazines you regularly contribute to, and I thought this . . . expedition . . . might be good fodder for your—"

"But you haven't been interested in helping me since I was four years old."

Lawrence slugged back the rest of his dark beer, stared at the mountains, wiped the foam from his beard.

Abigail said, "That came out more angry than—"

"No, it's fine. You've got standing to be as angry as you want."

"I'm not, though."

The patio door opened and the waiter returned with Abigail's pint and another round for Lawrence.

When he'd left, she raised her glass.

"Lawrence," she said, "here's to our past. Fuck it."

He grinned. "That easy, huh?"

"We can pretend."

They clinked pints and Abigail sipped her golden beer.

"So why'd you come?" Lawrence asked. "To be honest, I never expected a response to that E-mail."

"Funny, I was just sitting out in the car, building the nerve to walk in here, and trying to answer that question for myself."

The sun ducked behind the mountains and Abigail shivered, the rocky slopes and snowfields blushing with alpenglow.

TWO

At 4:30 the next morning, Abigail hurried across the parking lot of the Doubletree, moving toward a big Suburban, where four figures stood in the diseased light of a flickering streetlamp. The air was perfumed with wet sage and resonant of the jabbering Animas River, which flowed behind the hotel.

They all turned at the sound of her footsteps, her eyes gravitating first to her father, then to the man standing beside him, who came only to his shoulders. His head was smooth-shaven and his beard, just beginning to fade in, matched the gray of his deep and thoughtful eyes.

"Emmett Tozer," he said as they shook hands. "Guess you could say we're responsible for this outing. Lawrence was nice enough to agree to take us out, share his expertise."

"Abigail Foster, freelance journalist." She turned to the woman holding Emmett's arm. "June Tozer?"

June's face lighted up and she took Abigail's hand in both of hers. "Pleasure to meet you, Abigail." She stood just over five feet, with a streak of white running down the middle of her chin-length brown hair. A sweet energy seemed to exude through June's fingers. It made Abigail's arm tingle, as if a gentle current were passing through.

"And I'm Scott Sawyer. I own Hinterlands, Inc. I'll be your guide for this trip."

Abigail shook the calloused hand of the beautiful man in a Phish T-shirt and torn khakis, instantly liking what she saw, a feeling she sensed he reciprocated. He was young, his hair bleached, probably just shy of thirty, and she discerned beneath his faded clothes the body of a seasoned outdoorsman.

They rode up toward the mountains in the dark, and Abigail was dreaming again before they left the city limits of Durango.

She slept soundly, and when she woke, the Suburban was ascending a steep, rocky road. Scott and Lawrence talked in the front seat, but their conversation seemed muffled. She swallowed. Her ears popped. The sounds of the straining engine and tires crunching over rocks came rushing in. Abigail sat up, rubbed her eyes. The dashboard clock read 6:01 A.M. The sky had lightened into dawn, and they were climbing through a canyon, the one-lane road following the path of a stream.

Scott finally pulled over onto the edge of a meadow and parked beside a dinged and rusted Bronco that had long ago ceased to be one discernible color. But despite its state of disrepair, it had somehow managed to drag a trailer up the road. Abigail climbed outside after Emmett and June, heard the chatter of a stream.

They huddled between the vehicles, their breath steaming, the air redolent of spruce.

The driver's door of the Bronco squeaked open, and a man stepped down into the frosted grass. He was tall, his beard thick save for a few bare spots, his walnut hair drawn back into a ponytail.

Scott said, "Meet Jerrod Spicer, my trustworthy assistant. He's an excellent outdoorsman, so you should know you're all in capable hands."

Jerrod let slip a yawn, said, "Sorry. Still waiting for the coffee to kick in." He walked to the back of the trailer, unlocked the doors. "Gunter, Gerald, time to go to work."

Abigail smiled when two llamas stepped down into the meadow and began munching on the grass. She approached them, reached out to pet the black one, but it pulled away, affronted by the familiarity.

"I'd rethink that, Abigail," Scott said. "Gunter spits." He opened the back hatch of the Bronco. "Now if you'll step over here, we can start getting you all fitted for your packs."

As Abigail watched Scott cinch down the llama packs, she heard a car coming up the canyon. A moment passed, and then a hunter green Ford Expedition appeared around the bend. It veered off the road and pulled up onto the meadow, a rack of sirens mounted on top, SAN JUAN COUNTY SHERIFF'S DEPARTMENT emblazoned on the driver's and passenger's doors. A woman climbed out and approached the group, which had gathered by the llama trailer. She was petite and pretty, with bright, friendly eyes and long brown hair split into braided pigtails.

"Morning," she said, and tipped the brim of her Stetson. A sheriff's star had been embroidered into her black parka. "Y'all about ready to shove off?"

"Yep," Scott said, pulling the strap to tighten the hip belt of his pack.

The sheriff pointed to Scott, said, "I see you're taking a fly rod. You wouldn't mind letting me have a peek at your fishing license?"

"Not at all." Scott walked down to the sheriff and pulled his wallet out of his fleece pants. He flipped it open. She nodded.

"Y'all look like you're headed in for the long haul."

June said, "Well, we've got a ways to go. . . . How far did you say, Scott?"

"Seventeen miles."

"Yeah, a seventeen-mile hike into this old ghost—"

"What's your name, Sheriff?" Lawrence asked. "I feel like we've met before."

"Jennifer. And yours?"

"Lawrence Kendall. Get down to Durango much, Jennifer?"

"Not if I can help it." She cocked her head. "Where'd you think we'd met?"

"I don't remember, but you look familiar."

"Don't think we have, and I'm pretty good with faces." She addressed the group: "Well, I assume you all purchased backcountry insurance."

"They did," Scott said. "I'm the guide. I insisted they buy it."

"Where you taking them?"

"Grizzly Gulch."

"I thought she said you were headed to a ghost town. There are no ruins in Grizzly Gulch, at least that I know of." She leveled her gaze on him, unblinking.

Abigail watched Scott. His Adam's apple rolled in his throat.

"Actually, we're going to Abandon," Emmett said.

Without averting her eyes from Scott, the sheriff asked, "And what are you planning to do there?"

"Take some pictures. My wife and I are paranormal photographers. Depending on what we get, we may do a show in San Francisco this winter."

The sheriff said to Scott, "No call to lie to me if all you're gonna do is take pictures."

He nodded.

"That is all you're planning on doing?"

"Of course."

"And you've got the permits to visit Abandon?"

"They do."

The sheriff looked at June and Emmett. "Could I see them, please?"

Emmett reached into his jacket and pulled out an envelope, which he handed to the sheriff. She thumbed through the papers.

"Wow, a group permit. They don't give out many of these."

Emmett said, "We've been trying to score one for three years."

The sheriff gave the envelope back but lingered a moment longer, her brown eyes passing over each member of the group as if taking some kind of mental inventory. "I hope y'all have a real safe trip," she said, then tipped her hat again and strode back to the Expedition.

As they watched her climb in, crank the engine, and continue on up-canyon, Abigail caught something, but it was subtle, and she instantly let it go. In a day and a half, she'd remember this moment, wish to God she'd paid it more credence. What she saw was a glance between Scott and Lawrence—just two seconds of eye contact that looked something like relief.

THREE

They spent the first two hours climbing out of the canyon on a trail that switchbacked through a forest of old-growth Engelmann spruce. Abigail found herself near the back, between Emmett and Lawrence, trying to come to terms with the emaciated air.

At a break in the trees, she peered down and saw the road they'd taken out of Silverton, just a twisting brown thread eight hundred feet below. The sound of the stream had faded into a sustained hiss. The next time they stopped to rest, she'd lost the stream altogether and there was no wind, only the thud of her oxygen-starved heart banging in her ears.

At midday, they crossed a stretch of open country, the grasses dry and yellowed, littered with achromatic midsummer blooms of columbine, lupine, and Indian paintbrush. Abigail could see a subgroup of the San Juans—the mountains tan in direct sun, gray in the shadow of clouds, with rags of old snow high on the peaks. The sky shone neon blue.

Scott led them to the entrance of a broad valley. They came into a forest of ponderosa, plenty of space between the trees, sunlight pouring onto the pine-needle floor of the forest. As they climbed, the occasional spruce appeared among the ponderosa. The pines dwindled. Then they moved through a pure stand of spruce again. Abigail realized they hadn't been following a trail since breakfast.

In the early afternoon, they arrived at a small lake, and Scott told everyone to shed their packs. Abigail leaned hers against a rotten stump. Without the weight, she felt like she might float away. She knelt down on the shore and splashed water in her face. The arctic shock of it stole her breath. She sat on the grassy bank and drank from her water bottle. Tall spruce trees rimmed the bank, and the surface of the lake sent back a perfect reflection of the trees and the sky. The water glowed a deep green. She looked through it down to the lakebed, saw a cutthroat motionless among the pastel-colored stones.

Jerrod came over and brought her a bagged lunch—sandwich, apple, Clif Bar.

"How you holding up?" he asked.

"Feel like I'm breathing through a straw, and my hips hurt from the pack."

"I'll adjust the straps again before we leave. You're doing very well."

She shielded her face from the sun and looked up at Jerrod. She liked his face. She could tell that beneath the beard he was handsome, taller than Scott, even more well built. But she wondered about the scars, two bare patches curving up from the corners of his mouth in the shape of crescent moons. Staring at him, she wished she could see his eyes again. They seemed different—she'd noticed it at the trailhead before the sun came up and drove everyone into sunglasses. They reminded her of something she couldn't quite put her finger on, their density and depth, like they bore some great burden beyond the intake of the present.

Jerrod left to take Emmett and June their lunches. Abigail unwrapped her peanut butter and grape jelly sandwich. She ate, watching the llamas graze the bank.

They made camp at eleven thousand feet in a glade just spacious enough to accommodate five tents. They were only a few hundred feet below the timberline and the forest had transitioned into a withered-looking collection of blue spruce and alpine fir, crippled by years of extreme winters. Scott insisted that everyone change out of their wet clothes to avoid hypothermia. Within half an hour, they raised the tents. The guides showed everyone how to inflate the Therm-a-Rests and arrange their gear inside the vestibules.

With still a few hours of light left, Abigail emerged from her tent, bundled in long underwear, fleece pants, a vest and parka. Emmett and June stood watching Jerrod construct a campfire ring from a pile of rocks. Lawrence snored in his tent. Scott dug through a giant compression bag filled with what Abigail could only hope was real food, not that granola-bar shit.

She walked up to him, said, "I need to use the ladies' room. What do we do about that?"

"I haven't unpacked the toilet yet."

"Really? You have a portable—" His grin stopped her.

"You've never spent a night out in the woods have you, Abigail?"

"No."

"Well, no worries. There's a bathroom behind every tree."

She smiled seductively and raised her middle finger.

Abigail found a bit of privacy behind a blue spruce. The air nipped her bare ass. The ground steamed. She glanced at her watch—6:30 P.M., still on Manhattan time, and it made her homesick to think of Viv and Jen. Any other Sunday, she'd have just finished working out and showering, in a mad rush to meet them for cosmos at the Zinc Bar. But so far, this trip had been nothing like she'd expected. The thin air, the cold, ten fucking miles, and the hardest still to come. She thought she'd be in her element out here, but she hated everything—the Clif Bars, the smelly, bitchy llamas. And there was something about the light beginning to fade and no warm bed to climb into that depressed the hell out of her. *I'm a city girl. If there was ever a question.* While she squatted there, she gazed back down the valley. That open country they'd crossed several hours ago lay golden in the late-afternoon sun, and as she pulled up her pants, she saw it. A few miles below, perhaps at the lake where they'd stopped for lunch, a column of smoke rose out of the forest. As she walked back toward their campsite, she felt glad to have seen it, relieved to know they weren't completely alone out here.

FOUR

Abigail leaned against a fir tree. Down in the gully, Scott worked his way upstream, just past a fork in the channel. She watched him sidearm cast, the bright green line sailing in an S over the rocks, glistening like a spiderweb in the late sunlight, delivering the fly into a small pool. He'd hiked up his fleece pants, and he fished shirtless in a fly vest, knee-deep in the water. Abigail descended quietly to the bank, stood for a while listening to the stream's drowsy prattling.

"Aren't you cold?" she asked.

"Yeah," he said without looking back. "But there's a secret to it."

"What's that?"

"Not caring." He suddenly raised the rod. It dipped. A trout shot out of the pool and splashed into the main current, Scott holding the rod high now, the line taut, the bamboo arcing toward the water. He brought the fish out of the stream, a twelve-inch cutthroat, its crimson gill slashes palpitating in the fading light. Scott carefully unhooked the fly, then swung the fish against a rock. It shivered out. He slipped it into a canvas bag.

She said, "Correct me if I'm wrong, but didn't you jerk on the rod before it moved?"

"Yeah. I'm impressed you noticed. See, by the time you feel the tap, it's too late. He's already checked it out, realized it's bullshit."

"So how'd you know?"

"Caught him rising to my elk-hair caddis, saw it vanish, pulled to set the hook."

"No idea what you just said, but it was a lovely thing to watch."

Scott climbed onto the bank, sat down on a carpet of moss. He opened a small box containing an assortment of flies, Abigail now close enough to read the tattoo that wrapped around his arm above the bicep: MARIA 2.11.78–5.15.04 R.I.P.

She bent down to the stream, cupped a handful of freezing water, and as she brought it to her mouth, Scott yelled, "No!"

She glanced back at him, letting the water run through her fingers.

"Notice something about the rocks along the bank below the fork?" he asked.

"You mean how they're covered with orange algae?"

"That's not algae. It's a mineral deposit, a visual marker for streams with high metal content—zinc, aluminum, lead."

"So this water's toxic?"

"Yep. That's why I'm fishing upstream from that tributary. It probably runs out of an old mine." He lifted the rod. "So, you wanna give it a shot? See if you can hook one?"

Five minutes later, they stood casting together, Abigail thinking this was like those cheesy scenes in the movies when the guy shows the girl how to work a pool cue. But she didn't care. As their arms moved together, his body against hers, she thought of her recent string of New York men—beautiful metrosexual train wrecks. Scott didn't strike her as one of those superficial predators she always seemed to be falling for, and for the first time since leaving New York, she didn't want to be home.

They sat around a fire, eating trout that had been seasoned with fresh spices and seared on a stone among the embers. There was vegetable soup and a baguette, and over the flames, Lawrence roasted whole green chilies stuffed with cheese. He'd also smuggled in a case of Pabst Blue Ribbon. They all agreed—one of the best meals they'd ever had.

After supper, everyone washed their dishes in the stream until their hands had gone numb in the icy water. By the time they returned to the fire, Jerrod had stoked the flames into a big blaze. Abigail leaned back in her camp chair, noting the ache in her legs, the blisters on her hips. When she looked up, she saw the cinders rising out of the flames and through the spruce branches toward the night sky.

Lawrence pulled a flask from the pocket of his fleece jacket and offered it to June. She unscrewed the cap, took a swig, passed it to her husband.

A cloud of smoke gathered around Scott's head, and he asked, "Anyone else want dessert?"

The whiskey burned Abigail's throat. She took another sip, sent up a prayer of thanks when the glow settled in, dulling the pain ten hard miles had inflicted on her body.

Lawrence got stoned and slipped into his professorial tone, going on about the history of the ghost town, even reading from the diary of someone who'd lived in Abandon, a woman named Gloria Curtice. But Abigail was too beat, and her mind wandered for the next half hour, only perking up when he told the story of the vanishing, how a man had ridden into Abandon in January of 1894 in search of his missing younger brother, a mule skinner named Brady Sykes, only to find the town empty, not a chimney smoking, the stamp mill silent.

"I'm not talking about empty homes where people packed all their belongings and left. This town of a hundred and twenty-three souls just up and disappeared on Christmas Day."

Emmett asked, "So what happened to the mule skinner's brother?"

Lawrence expelled a lungful of smoke. "Did what any of us would've done. Hauled ass out of there. Few days later, he did an interview with the *Silverton Standard and Miner.* Said the whole ordeal had really spooked him, that the town felt strange, haunted, like the devil had been there. Everyone assumed they'd find the remains of Abandon in the summer, when the snow was gone, but they never recovered a single bone."

"That's fucked-up," Scott said.

"So what do you think happened, Lawrence?" Emmett asked.

"To the town?"

"Yeah."

The professor sighed, seemed to reflect on the question for a moment, then said confidentially, "I've never shared this with anyone"—Emmett and June imperceptibly leaned forward—"but I think a big spaceship came down, abducted the whole lot of them."

"Really?"

Lawrence smiled.

"Oh, a joke," Emmett said.

"Sorry, but you have to understand—I've been asked what happened to Abandon probably a thousand times, and I just don't know the answer. There are some loony-tunes out there who believe the town was taken by aliens or that something supernatural happened."

"What about a virus?" June asked.

"Bad ones were around in the 1890s, but lead poisoning would've been a greater threat to Abandon than an epidemic, what with their drinking water flowing out of the heart of these mountains. But assuming some supervirus struck the town, where are the remains? In the absence of any bones, I guess I can see how a person might look to supernatural explanations."

"Even you?" Emmett said.

"In all honesty, I do have a theory, but it's, well, personal, and I haven't shared it with anyone ever, and don't plan to now."

Scott stood, took the water bag hanging from a knob on a tree, and doused the fire.

It hissed, bellows of steam lifting into the trees, cold rushing in.

"Sorry, folks, but tomorrow comes early."

The others said their good nights and lumbered off to bed. Then just Abigail and Lawrence sat across from each other in the darkness.

She got up as soon as she realized it, said, "Night."

Lawrence stared at the last unyielding coal, scratching his gray beard.

"Sit out here with me awhile," he said without looking up.

"I would, really, but I'm cold and tired."

"Abigail."

"What?"

"I just wanted to—"

"I know, but I can't do this right now, okay? I'm not there yet."

Their campsite glade stood fifty yards through the trees. Abigail had to pee again, but the thought of squatting out here in the dark seemed worse than the pressure in her bladder. She climbed into her one-man tent, her sleeping bag freezing. She crawled inside the down bag and zipped herself up, pulled her long black hair into a ponytail. It reeked of wood smoke. The walk from the campfire to the tent had set her pulse racing, and she listened to the throbbing in her head. When it eased, the hush came. Even on weekends in New York, lying in bed in her studio apartment, the nearest thing to silence contained the noise of sirens and central heating, her refrigerator cutting on and off in the predawn hours. Here, the silence was a vacuum, a total absence. It made her uneasy.

With no threat of rain or snow, the guides hadn't stretched the rain flies over the tents. The ceiling of Abigail's was mesh. She reached up, unzipped it. A section of the ceiling fell away and she gasped. Through the opening lay a rectangle of night like none she'd ever seen, powdered with stars that dimmed and brightened, so the entire sky seemed to smolder with the embers of a cosmic fire. She couldn't remember the last time she'd seen stars, had no idea of their profusion.

Footsteps swished through the grass nearby—her father stumbling to bed— and as Abigail lay there on the brink of sleep, she puzzled at this life he'd fashioned for himself. He'd certainly aged well, but she wondered if he was happy, what kind of friends he kept, what sort of women he'd been with. Prior to coming to Colorado, she'd finally Googled him, but aside from a brief bio on the Fort Lewis College Web site, Lawrence's Internet presence was light.

Exhaustion set in, her sleeping bag warm, her ears detecting the murmur of the stream.

Nine meteors flared across her skylight before she succumbed to sleep, and despite all the campfire talk of the vanishing of Abandon, there existed no greater mystery for her than the man who snored twenty feet away, alone in his tent.

FIVE

Abigail opened her eyes. A film of ice had formed on her sleeping bag where her breath had misted and frozen during the night. She could hear some of the others stirring in their tents and, farther away, the crackling of what she hoped was a fire.

She laced her boots and climbed outside—8:23 A.M. by her watch, which meant 6:23 here. A heavy frost had blanched the tents and meadow grasses. The llamas grazed nearby. The air tickled her throat going down.

She relieved herself behind her favorite blue spruce, then made her way through the trees to the fire. Only Jerrod was up. He handed her a mug steaming with coffee.

"Take it with anything?"

"Black is bliss."

The coffee tasted strong and rich. She stood close to the flames, watching Jerrod light another camp stove. His long hair was down. While the water heated, he poured packets of oatmeal into plastic bowls and mixed in dried fruit and chocolate chips.

"Where's Scott?" Abigail asked.

"Helping Emmett. He started throwing up around three this morning. Probably altitude sickness. Scott's giving him some more Diamox right now. Making sure he stays hydrated. Emmett'll be okay. This kind of thing usually clears up pretty quick."

"Can I help with anything?"

He glanced up at her, their eyes connecting.

"No, I've got it. Thanks, though." Jerrod peeled two bananas and began to slice them into the oatmeal with a Swiss army knife. As Abigail watched him prepare their breakfast, she noticed the dog tags dangling from a chain around his neck.

. . .

Within the hour, they broke camp, Emmett weak but on the mend, the guides having distributed the weight of his pack between them. As they climbed, the firs grew scrawnier, these dwarfed banner trees limbless on the windward side.

The forest dwindled into alpine tundra—shrubs, grass, and rock crusted with black and yellow lichen.

They proceeded in a tight line, Scott and the llamas leading, Jerrod bringing up the rear.

Now well above timberline, rock walls ramped up steeply on either side.

They climbed a boulder field toward the pass. No grass, only large broken rocks that shifted under their weight, filling the upper regions of the cirque with a strange tinkling. Some had been gouged with potholes, filled with standing water. Black spiders scampered under their boots.

Abigail was thinking how these mountains reminded her of Gothic cathedrals, with their towers and chimneys, when somewhere high above, a boulder dislodged, dividing into pieces as it plunged toward them.

Scott yelled, "Everybody down! Shield your heads with your packs!"

They all crouched as the rocks hurtled toward them, bouncing and breaking and multiplying. Abigail shut her eyes and she whispered, "Please, please, please."

Most of the rocks shattered against a bus-size boulder just fifteen feet away.

Silence returned. The air smelled of cordite.

Scott called out, "Everybody in one piece?"

Abigail looked up, Jerrod beside her, his eyes still closed, teeth gritted, body quaking.

The boulder field steepened near the pass. Abigail used her hands to climb now, the weight of the pack disrupting her balance, feeling envious of the llamas' surefootedness.

They came to a series of ledges.

"Take your time!" Scott yelled. "This section is very sketchy, and the rock's rotten. If you start to freak out, let us know. We'll talk you through it. Focus on what's above you, and don't look in the direction you don't want to go. Namely, down."

The ledges ranged in width from four to six feet, contouring up the rock face. Abigail focused on putting one foot in front of the other and dragging her left hand along the rock to maintain her balance. The others had gotten ahead of her.

At the third switchback, she made the mistake of glancing down, had no idea they'd climbed so high above the boulder field, the exposure overwhelming, waves of dizziness engulfing her, filling her stomach with razor-winged butterflies.

Her knees weakened. The world tilted. She stumbled toward the edge.

Jerrod grabbed her arm, pulled her back.

She crumpled down on the ledge.

"Abigail."

"I can't breathe," she gasped.

Jerrod knelt in front of her. "You're okay. You're just hyperventilating. Close your eyes and take deep breaths."

She did what he said. Soon, the dizziness had passed and she could open her eyes without the world spinning.

"You saved my ass," she said as Jerrod pulled a climbing rope out of his pack. "What's that for?"

"I'm gonna short-rope us together until we reach the top. Can you stand up now?"

Abigail got to her feet and Jerrod reached around her from behind and began to wrap the rope around her thighs into a makeshift harness.

"Can I ask you something?" she said.

"Sure." He cinched the rope around her waist.

"How old are you?"

"Thirty-seven."

"Were you in Iraq?"

He stopped midway through his knot, turned her around so they faced each other.

"Yeah, actually. How'd you know?" His voice had tightened.

Abigail looked back over the boulder field at the glint of the lake where they'd stopped the previous afternoon. "Your dog tags," she said.

"Oh, right."

Other things, too. Especially the way you reacted when the rock fell. A couple years back, she'd written a piece for the *Times* about soldiers with post-traumatic stress disorder, interviewed dozens of vets with PTSD. No question, he had it. She saw the damage in his eyes.

At noon they crested Sawblade Pass, just a wind-ravaged thirteen-thousand-foot notch in a cirque of spires, ridden with old snow, sun-cupped and brittle as salt crystals.

They dropped their gear, took shelter from the wind.

From Abigail's vantage point, she could see down the other side of the pass—a two-thousand-foot drop into a box canyon. At the close end, she thought she saw the ruins of a mine. Farther on, perhaps a mile away, rows of dark specks peppered the timberline forest.

Emmett yelled, "Dr. Kendall!"

Lawrence had been exploring a recess in the rock at the end of a nearby ledge. He poked his head out. Emmett waved him over and Lawrence came and squatted beside him.

"What are those specks down there?" he asked.

"That's Abandon."

Abigail took out her cell phone. It roamed for a moment, got a signal.

She called her mother to tell her how beautiful it all was.

SIX

They spent the next hour descending a talus slope, and by two in the afternoon, they had reached the remains of the Godsend, Bartholomew Packer's mine. The stamp mill looked to be one winter away from collapsing. Boards bowed and splayed out on all sides, and amid the wreckage of the mill stood one of its indomitable cast-iron rock crushers.

They followed an old wagon trail as clouds filed in from the west. Pockets of snow clung high up the canyon walls and snowmelt bled out from them in streams down the rock face and into the ruts of the trail, making their boots squish in the mud.

Ahead lay a grassy lane, lined with rows of weather-beaten structures—all that was left of Abandon. Main Street ran for two hundred yards down the middle of the canyon, and the party walked six abreast between the false-fronted buildings. Many had collapsed. Lawrence pointed to a structure with six little balconies.

"This was Abandon's red-light district. Those were the cribs. Prostitutes would stand on the balconies and try to entice potential customers who were passing by."

"How'd this town get its name?" June asked.

"It was originally named Hope by Bart Packer, but as a joke, one of the better-read miners, who was none too fond of this high, remote canyon, started calling the town Abandon. Name stuck."

"What's that?" Emmett asked, motioning to a building across the street that had long since collapsed. "See that big metal thing in there?"

Lawrence walked over and peered into the rubble.

"This was the assay office. Assayer would evaluate samples for prospectors and the mine, tell you if your ore was high- or low-grade. That hulk of metal is probably the furnace. Bet if you poked around in there, you'd find some old crucibles, too."

They passed the blacksmith's shop, identifiable only by the anvil sitting amid the rotten boards, then the dance hall and the general store, where a faded sign had fallen onto the porch. It read ESPECIAL ATTENTION GIVEN TO THE COMFORT OF LADIES. Lawrence pointed out the drugstore, meat market, bakery, and harness shop, though they resembled little more than board heaps to Abigail.

Midway through Abandon, he stopped them in the street. "Most important place in town." He gestured to a building whose entire frame slanted to the right. "The saloon," he said, eyes lighting up. Abigail was thinking how in his element Lawrence was, thrilling people with what had happened in the past. She felt envious of the childlike joy he'd found in his career, wanted a little of that for herself. "I have to tell you about the woman who was tending bar in 1893. Name was Jocelyn Maddox. She was drop-dead gorgeous, sassy, and a black widow.

"By twenty-five, she'd been married three times to rich men, all of whom had died mysteriously. Her last husband's family got wise, proved she'd slowly poisoned him with arsenic. She fled Arizona, ended up, of all places, here. Made a big impression. Men loved her. She was one of the guys—funny, raucous, horribly profane.

"In November of 1893, someone came prospecting from Arizona, recognized Jocelyn, and reported to Sheriff Curtice that there was a murdering fugitive tending bar in his town. The story checked out and Ezekiel had no choice but to arrest her.

"Everything had been arranged to extradite her back to be hanged, but the snows came. It was decided she'd winter in Abandon, be transported to Arizona in the spring. Since half the town was in love with her, instead of just letting Jocelyn rot in jail, they chained her up in the saloon, with a deputy to keep watch, and let her go on tending bar. Of course, she never had her reckoning in Arizona. Jocelyn vanished with everyone else that Christmas Day."

They walked to the entrance of town, where the buildings ended. Off in the distance, set up on a slope in the spruce, stood a church. Its roof had caved in everywhere except in front, where a tiny bell tower dangled in the rafters. Atop the tower, a crooked cross stood silhouetted against the darkening sky.

June stopped.

"Honey?" Emmett said. "What is it?"

"Nothing, just . . . very similar energy to Roanoke Island."

"What's that?" Abigail asked.

"The Lost Colony, that settlement that vanished from the North Carolina coast in the late 1500s, where the only thing left behind was CRO carved into a tree. People thought CRO meant the Croatan Indians, that maybe there'd been an attack. We did some work out there a few years ago. Energy's even stronger here."

"What kind of energy?" Abigail asked.

June turned toward her, and those eyes that had seemed so kind just the day before at their first meeting in Durango had taken on a disturbing intensity. "Something awful happened in this place."

Abigail couldn't stop the smile from escaping.

"What?" June asked.

"I'm sorry." She chuckled.

"Oh, we have a skeptic."

" 'Fraid so. Look, it's nothing against—"

Emmett said, "No, least you're up-front about it. I respect that. Most people just patronize us and pretend to play along. But since you are writing an article about what we do, I hope you'll keep an open mind."

"You have my word."

They camped on the edge of town. Abigail climbed into her tent and fell asleep, and when she woke, it was evening and cold. She found a pair of gloves in the top compartment of her pack and crawled outside. Low, dark clouds scudded across the peaks. She saw Scott lying in the grass with the llamas, listening to a radio. Lawrence was sitting in the open doorway of his tent, thumbing through a tattered notebook by the light of his headlamp.

As Jerrod fed a piece of clapboard into the flames, she sat down across from him in the grass.

"Jerrod?" she said. He glanced up. "You think it's a load of shit?"

"What?"

She cocked her head toward Emmett and June, who were a little ways off, on their knees, facing the ghost town, heads bowed in meditative poses.

"I don't know. They aren't quite as kooky as I imagined they'd be."

Abigail pulled off her gloves and extended her hands toward the flames.

In the distance, the outline of Abandon formed an eerie profile in the dusk.

Scott walked over, followed by Lawrence and the Tozers.

"What's up?" Jerrod asked.

"I was just listening to the latest report on my weather radio. . . . Doesn't look good."

"You're kidding," Lawrence said.

"This early-season storm was supposed to plow through New Mexico, and now the track is farther north. Not particularly cold, but it should be all snow above nine thousand feet. As you know, Abandon sits at eleven."

"How much they predicting?" Lawrence asked.

"One to three feet. Winter storm warnings are already up. Supposed to start late tonight."

"So what does this mean?" June asked.

"Means we should pack up our shit and make a beeline for the trailhead."

Jerrod looked up. "You aren't serious."

"Actually, I am."

"Hike back in the dark?"

"Maybe we get only halfway. Be better than postholing all seventeen miles in a meter of powder."

"You don't know that it's gonna be that bad."

"Don't know that it isn't."

Jerrod looked at Emmett. "You paid a hefty chunk to come out here and shoot this town, have Lawrence give you the rundown—"

"What do you think you're doing?" Scott asked.

"I'm talking to our client. Maybe he should make the—"

"*My* client. Don't know if you forgot, but you work for me, bro."

Emmett said, "We have to leave?"

"If this storm really winds up," Scott said, "hiking out will be a bitch. We didn't bring snowshoes or skis. You ever tried to walk in three feet of snow?"

"Let them decide, Scott," Jerrod said.

Scott shot him a glare, then turned back to the Tozers.

"Look, I suggest we get the hell out of here, but if you want to stay, see what happens, I guess that's an option. What do you think, Lawrence?"

"Their dime, their permit, their choice."

Emmett glanced at his wife, then back at Scott. "This is our last chance to shoot Abandon this year?"

"Yeah, it's late in the season and a miracle there's not more snow already. We don't do it now, you won't be able to get back here until next June or even July, depending on how bad the winter is. And that's assuming you get another permit."

Emmett said, "Honey?"

In the silence, Abigail watched dark billowy clouds spilling over the top of the canyon, sweeping down into the ghost town like an avalanche.

June looked at her husband, nodded.

"We'll take our chances," he said as Abandon vanished in the fog.

1893

SEVEN

Bartholomew Packer pushed open the door and stepped out of the storm. He brushed the snow from his wool overcoat, hung his derby on the coatrack. The floorboards creaked under the substantial load as he waddled toward the potbellied stove.

While his fingers thawed, he surveyed Abandon's only remaining saloon. The light was poor. It disseminated in a smoky dimness from three kerosene lamps suspended from the ceiling, never reaching the corners of what was little more than a thin-walled shack.

There were only four of them in the saloon tonight. He saw Lana Hartman across the room, seated at the upright piano by the front window, playing "O Little Town of Bethlehem." She was always here, as much a part of the place as the bar stools. He'd never seen her in this dress—dark green, with red piping on the collar and cuffs.

Jocelyn Maddox sat on a stool behind the bar, watching Lana play, a cigarette burning in her hand, eyes glazed with boredom.

The young deputy tasked with guarding her had passed out in a chair beside the stove. A raging high lonesome, he snored, a line of tobacco-colored drool creeping down his chin.

Bart stepped to the bar, said, "Evening, Joss. Lively tonight."

"Merry Christmas, you big fuckin walrus. Come to wet your dry?" She smiled and hopped off the chair, dressed tonight, as always, like a man—high-back canvas trousers and a cotton dress shirt with suspenders. The disparity between her masculine outfits and the pitch-black hair that fell in waves down her back and the dark liquid pools of her big eyes drove men mad. She looked Spanish, exotic. The chain between her leg irons dragged across the floor as she set up a glass and uncorked a bottle of whiskey, poured Bart a full tumbler.

"I'm afraid you're drinking with me tonight," he said.

"That so?"

"Reckon Miss Hartman would hoist a glass with our ilk?"

"I never seen her take a drink," Joss said, "and as you well know, many a man, present company included, have sent a whiskey over to that piano."

"How about our man by the stove?"

Joss's dark eyes cut to the sleeping deputy, then back to Bart.

"Let that coffee cooler alone," she whispered. "And keep it down. He sees me drinkin, I'll hear about it all fuckin night."

She got a glass for herself, and when she'd filled it, Bart raised his, said, "Joss, here's how. May the coming year—"

"For Chrissakes." She swallowed her whiskey—one long, deliberate tilting of the glass. Bart drained his. She poured again.

"Joss, love, wish you could've seen Abandon when it was a roaring camp. In '89, night like this, there'd of been fifty men here, miners coming off shift, card games, whole flock of whores."

"It's all over now, huh?"

"Yeah. All over. All gone. The whores, the opium, the fun." He clinked his glass against hers and they drank. He replenished their tumblers and they drank and he refilled them again. Soon his face had flushed and gone blotchy and the burst capillaries stood out like tiny red worms, so that his nose resembled a rotting strawberry. Lines of sweat rolled down the dome of his great bald head.

Bart was not a man to stand when there were chairs on the premises. He installed himself on a bar stool and he and Joss worked their way through the bottle while Lana played Christmas carols and the deputy snored. He said things he'd already said ten times before on nights just as quiet, about the town in its heyday, the art of following a rich vein deep into a mountain, and how he meant to close the mill next year and make a new fortune in Montana.

"Hey, how 'bout shuttin the fuck up for a spell? You're makin my head hurt."

Bart attended to his whiskey. Looking through the window behind the bar, he could see it snowing harder than before. The walls strained against the wind.

After awhile, he got up, staggered over to the piano. He stood beside Lana, watching the spill of her blond hair, her tiny gloved fingers moving across the keys. The piano had been out of tune ever since a miner had shot it two years ago in a fight, mistaking it for an adversary. When she'd finished the song, he said, "That was very pleasant, Miss Hartman," and reached into his pocket. He withdrew a burlap sack that fit in his palm and placed it on the piano.

Lana picked up the sack, her hand dipping with the weight. She untied the string and peeked inside, saw the dull gleam of dust and tiny slugs, probably two hundred dollars' worth.

She looked up at Bart and shook her head.

"Oh no, it has been my greatest joy this year to watch you play. You're too good for this deadfall." He started to lay his hand on her shoulder but then stopped himself. He'd never touched her. Instead, he allowed himself a long drink of what he thought was far and away the softest face ever to grace the streets of Abandon.

Bart returned to his seat at the bar. "One more for the cold road home," he said, and Joss poured the last of the bottle into his tumbler. Lana had begun to play again.

When he finished his whiskey, Bart dropped another poke on the bar. "And a merry Christmas to you, Joss," he said. She weighed the sack in her hand, as if it might not serve, then smiled and leaned across the bar.

"You love her, don't you?" she whispered.

"Excuse me?"

"You're a seldom fuckin hombre. Come in here ever goddamn night, skip your own Christmas shindig just to listen to her bang—"

"Well, that don't mean—"

"Calm the fuck down, Bartholomew, and listen. You never know when it's your time. Mine's comin in the spring, and I guess this is just the long way around the barn a sayin I hope you won't leave this world with any regret."

"I don't understand what you—"

"Before you hive off, do what you been meanin to ever since you laid eyes on that filly."

"What in hell are you—"

"I want you to kiss her."

"I couldn't."

"What's the worst she'll do? Slap you? I'm sure you been slapped plenty. Hell, you ever tried somethin like that on me, I'd fuckin shoot you, but that's neither here nor there. I reckon you love her, and this is my Christmas gift to you. Kiss her on your way out."

Bart stepped down off the stool and walked toward the door. He put on his overcoat and his hat and reached for the doorknob.

He stopped. He walked back to the piano. His weak heart pounding, he leaned down and kissed Lana on the cheek.

She stopped playing and bowed her head. They both trembled.

"I apologize," Bart said. "It's just that . . ."

He hurried outside and shut the door.

Lana took a deep breath, then looked out the window, up to the second floor of the hotel across the street, at the woman sitting in the bay window.

You could hear the noise from the dance hall down the street, where most of the town had gathered for Christmas Eve. She started "Silent Night" on the discordant keys.

Joss took a candle out from under the bar, went over to the stove, opened it, and held the wick to a flame. She set the burning candle in the windowsill behind the bar, stood there watching torrents of snow fall through the darkness, wondering if they could see her signal in the blizzard.

EIGHT

Stephen Cole buttoned his black frock coat and stepped onto the musicians' platform, tall, pale, thin to the brink of fragility. His brown hair, parted down the middle, fell in greasy strings to his shoulders, and the only facial hair he could grow was a lean mustache more befitting a teenager than a twenty-seven-year-old man. It wasn't the snipe-gutted appearance people noticed, however, but his large eyes—brown, gentle, occasionally radiant.

"Let us pray," he said. "Dear Lord. Redeemer. Maker of all that is good. We thank You for the bounty of that which we are about to eat, for the hands that prepared it, for the generous Mr. Packer, who allowed his boarding-house cooks to make this feast for the town. We thank You for Your perfect and loving Son, Jesus Christ, Who You sent to save this despicable world. Let us remember the Child born in a manger as we celebrate His birth this night and on the morrow.

"Finally, dear Lord, I ask that You pour out Your protection upon Abandon. Protect us from the cold and snow, the deadly slides, the beasts of the mountains, the heathens, and, above all, from the wickedness in our own hearts. Kyrie eleison. Amen." As Stephen stepped down from the stage, the fiddlers took up their instruments and plucked at the strings, turning the tiny hardwood pegs.

Two years ago, this hurdy-gurdy would have been lined with whores of every make and model in threadbare peignoirs, bright stockings, some only children, others topless, a handful naked entirely, all painted up like lewd clowns, and the miners staggering drunk through the horde of dancers, the room redolent of a foul ambrosia—whiskey, sweat, and tobacco smoke commingling.

But the mine had pinched out, the revelers departed, though their nights in the dance hall stood memorialized in the bullet-holed walls, stains of vomit, tobacco juice, and blood on the floorboards.

This night, half a dozen tables had been arranged in the center of the room, decorated with ribbon, spruce saplings cut from the hillsides above town, and a whole multitude of candles.

Ezekiel and Gloria Curtice sat at the end of the table nearest the sheet-iron stove, a silence descending as the residents of Abandon filled their plates from the pans of corn bread, vegetables, fried potatoes, sop, and whole roasts. The hanging lamps did little to illumine the hall, the faces an indistinct canvas for shadow and candlelight. Gloria sat across from Harriet McCabe, watching the little girl devour her supper, dripping sauce on her white pinafore.

"Are you ready for Santa Claus?" Gloria said. "I hear he's on his way to Abandon this hour." Harriet glanced at her mother, as if to confirm the validity of the claim. Tears slid down Bessie McCabe's face. "Bessie?" Gloria whispered. "What is it? Are you poorly?"

Barely twenty, Bessie's pink cotton work dress was her best, stained and torn across the front from countless trips to the woodpile, hardly warm enough for a Rocky Mountain winter. Bessie had come from Tennessee ten months ago to join her husband, found him quite changed from the fifteen-year-old boy she'd married. She carried the dull burn of poverty in her eyes, and the stress of living this high in the dead of winter, with a man losing his mind, was causing her straw-colored hair to fall out in clumps.

"It's Billy," Bessie whispered, covering her mouth with her hand to mask rotten teeth.

Gloria reached across the table and held Bessie's hand. "Where is he?"

"Where you reckon?" Bessie's voice broke on the last word.

"With Mr. Wallace?"

"Sometimes, I suspect they go to the cribs."

"Mr. McCabe loves you," Gloria said, then felt a pinch under the table.

She turned and met her husband's disapproving eyes.

"So, Mrs. McCabe," Ezekiel said, "how's Mr. McCabe finding his job at the mine?"

"Still just a mucker, but him and Mr. Wallace been dirt washin on Billy's day off. Lookin for someone to grubstake 'em."

"Well, here's hoping he sees some color in his pan." He raised his glass of water, and when he'd taken a sip, turned his attention to the little girl. As he quizzed Harriet on her studies, Gloria nibbled on a piece of corn bread and stole glances at her husband. She was still wildly in love with him, this solid, gorgeous man with a thick mustache, long sideburns, and the most ardent eyes she'd ever seen, especially when in a state of passion—anger or otherwise—as if there were lava at his core. She'd convinced him to wear his four-button sack coat for the occasion, an outfit he despised, and which, in his words, made him look like "a feathered-out got-damn banker."

At length, Gloria's attention drifted away from their table, and she picked out pieces of other conversations about towns that were booming, towns that were busting. As she eavesdropped, she noticed the table closest to the musicians' platform. Ten people occupied one side, but at the far end, a woman ate by herself, completely ignored. She estimated the woman to be in her mid-forties, and even from across the room, Gloria could tell that she'd been striking years ago. Now she just looked tired, ragged out in a burgundy bustle ball dress with white lace at the ends of the sleeves and intricate beading of a style fashionable in the seventies.

"Would you excuse me?" Before Ezekiel could reply, she was on her way, stopping finally across the table from the woman in the outdated dress. "May I sit here, Rosalyn?" Gloria asked. The woman smirked, her hair pinned up in a mass of garnet curls, her cheeks rouged.

"If you don't care what all these hypocrites think, I sure don't." As Gloria set her food on the table and pulled out the chair, she couldn't help but note the thrill of hearing a woman speak her true mind again.

In proximity, Gloria saw that the woman was even more striking but even more ruined. It broke her heart. She thought of her mother, what she might have become had the syphilis not claimed her. "How are you likin the—"

"I don't do pity too well. What possessed you to come over here?"

"I seen you around."

"So've half the men in this room. And they feign outrage that I dare partake of this feast in their presence, laughing up their sleeves. You know I used to be *loved* in this town? Like royalty."

"Look, I just saw you were alone."

"Well, you done your good deed, so why don't you head back over—" Rosalyn stopped herself, reached out, touched the long blanched scar under Gloria's bottom lip. "Where'd you work, honey?"

Gloria flushed, took a sip of water. "I don't . . . anymore."

"I said when you did."

"Leadville."

Rosalyn smiled. "Hell of a place. You're stunning. Bet the men loved you. What happened to your chin?"

"I had a customer who went insane. Thought we were married, and that I was cheatin on him."

Rosalyn laughed out loud. Heads turned.

"This town's in high water," Gloria said. "Don't mind my asking, why've you stayed? Thought you might've gone to Cripple Creek."

Rosalyn smiled, wisdom and a lifetime of buried rage in her eyes. "Been a whore all my life. I'll finish out in Abandon and, when it goes, take what money I got, go somewhere where nobody knows me. Where it don't snow. Buy a house. Tend a garden."

"Marriage?"

"I'm afraid man's a species that's been ruined for me."

Gloria sliced through a piece of roast.

"How'd you become so respectable?" Rosalyn asked.

"Fell in love with a good man."

"Not many a those left, are there?"

Now they Black Hawk waltzed, the fiddlers sawing away, the clack of high-top lace-ups and stovepipe boots slamming the floorboards. Looking over her husband's shoulder, Gloria saw Rosalyn sitting by herself in a rocking chair beside the stove.

"It's shameful," she said to him.

"You know who that woman is?" Ezekiel spoke into his wife's ear.

"Wipe that feature off your face. She's a human being."

"Would you have people unriddle your past?"

"Would you have people treat me like I didn't exist?"

They bumped into the Ilgs. "Excuse us, Sawbones."

"Merry Christmas, Sheriff. Look at you in full war paint. Ma'am." The doctor doffed his bowler.

When they'd broken from the crowd, Ezekiel said, "That woman ain't my concern."

"Is decent human behavior? You're gonna dance with her."

"Damn if I will."

"Zeke!"

He glanced over her shoulder, whispered, "God bless that man."

Gloria turned, saw Rosalyn rise to accept the hand of Stephen Cole. Soon the preacher and the whore were stomping together.

NINE

Ezekiel and Gloria walked down the plank sidewalk. It had been shoveled that morning, but a foot and a half of powder had fallen since then. Gloria tucked her gloved hands under the wool of her hooded cape. Aside from the ruckus of the dance hall, Abandon stood in that kind of mad silence that set in during the worst of blizzards. There appeared to be no one else out, and the snow fell so hard, they could see only the nearest streetlamp. Beyond lay only faint suggestions of lantern light.

They arrived at the entrance to the hotel, the door starred with snowballs—the handiwork of bored children. Across the street, there was light in the saloon and they could hear the sound of Christmas carols being played on a broken piano. They entered the dark lobby. There hadn't been anyone at the front desk since the owner had left town three months ago. Gloria brushed the snow off her cape and followed Ezekiel up the staircase.

The corridor was empty, completely dark. They stopped at number six, the only room with light sliding under the door.

Ezekiel knocked. They waited. He knocked again.

"I don't reckon she's gonna answer," Gloria whispered.

"Mrs. Madsen," Ezekiel said through the door. "It's Zeke and Glori Curtice. We're leaving something for you. Merry Christmas."

Gloria set the basket on the floor. It contained two oranges, a can of sardines, and a piece of chocolate cake from the town feast. On a scrap of parchment, Gloria had written, "Merry Christmas and a happy New Year from your friends the Curtices."

They went back outside and trudged on through the snow.

"Saw Oatha Wallace today," Ezekiel said. "He was in the benzinery this morning. Told him my brother's over two months short now."

"What'd he say?"

"What he says every time. That Nathan and the others decided not to go last minute, since the weather looked ominous. I called him a black liar."

"What do you think happened?"

"Don't know, Glori, it's past me, but that man's bad medicine. Snaky."

"What if it turns out Nathan was with him?"

"I may be sheriff, but it won't be settled in no goddamn court a law." They turned onto a side street and followed a path beaten down in the snow, saw families huddled before fireplaces in those cabins on the hillside that were still inhabited—tiny islands of warmth and light in the storm.

"Need to warn you, Ezekiel," she said. "I wanna say something about our little whistle."

Ezekiel stopped, faced his wife. It was so dark outside, he could only make out the whites of her eyes.

"Told you. We don't talk about it." The tremor in his voice was grief, not anger, and it made Gloria's throat tighten.

"I just need to say something, Zeke. You don't got to talk—"

He grabbed her arms. "Said I don't wanna hear it."

"But I need you to," she said, and her eyes burned as they flooded. "I can't go on tonight and tomorrow pretending it's like it's always been. Only been a year, and I miss him. That's all I wanted to say. That I miss Gus so much, I can't breathe when I think about him." Her husband's eyes went wide. He turned away from her, his nose running. "I'm empty, Zeke, 'cause we don't talk about him. That don't make nothing better. Just makes us forget, and do you wanna forget your son?"

Ezekiel sat in the snow. "I ain't forgot Gus. Ain't nothin in this whole goddamn world make me forget my boy."

She knelt behind him, Ezekiel wiping his face and cursing.

"You reckon we'll see Gus again when we die?"

"Glori, if I believed that, I'd a blowed my goddamn head off a year ago. This is above my bend. Why you doin this to me?"

" 'Cause I don't remember what he looks like! He's just a blur in my head. Remember that day I wanted to get our picture made and you wouldn't?"

"Yeah."

"Well, goddamn you for that, Zeke."

The wind had changed directions and the snow needled Gloria's face. She turned her back to the barrage of ice. Ezekiel was saying something, but she couldn't hear. She moved forward, their faces inches apart. She asked him what he'd said.

"Said he came halfway above my knee. Close your eyes, Glori, maybe you can see him. His hair was fine, color a rust, and his skin so white, we used to say it looked like milk. He had your eyes." Ezekiel cleared his throat and wiped his face again. "And when I . . . Jesus . . . when I kissed his neck, my mustache would tickle him and he'd laugh so hard, scream, 'No, Papa!' "

Gloria had closed her eyes. "Keep going, Zcke."

"And he called my knee his horsey, and he named it Benjamin."

Ezekiel had stopped. Gloria opened her eyes. Her husband was shaking. He leaned forward into her cape and wept.

"It's okay," she whispered. "It's all right."

"Naw, it ain't," he said. "I lie in bed sometimes and try to picture what Gus would a looked like at ten or fifteen or thirty. I imagine him turned out a man. We was robbed, Glori. It ain't never gonna be all right again."

Ezekiel picked himself up and then lifted Gloria in his arms, both covered in snow. She bawled as Ezekiel carried her up the hill toward their dark cabin in the grove of spruce.

TEN

Bart Packer glided through the darkness in his sleigh, the whisper of the runners drowned out by the clinking of chain loops and the singletree groaning in the cold. A half mile south of town, and with the snow blowing in every direction, he could hardly see beyond the horses.

He'd have missed it, but the horses knew the way, making the turn just past the grouping of snow-loaded firs. They pulled the sled up a series of switchbacks and after awhile slowed to a walk, their legs punching through the snow, their nostrils flaring like bellows, Bart slapping the reins against their rumps, hollering, "Get up there! Go on, girls!" They climbed several hundred feet above the floor of the box canyon. The trail leveled out. "Now get on!" he yelled, and he worked the reins furiously until the horses trotted in the powder.

He wasn't rushing them out of meanness or impatience. Nothing riled Bart like the mistreatment of horses, but they were approaching the most dangerous section of the ride home, where the trail passed through a gap between steep slopes that produced slides every winter. If caught in an avalanche tonight, he'd have almost no chance of survival.

When the sled had passed safely through the gap, Bart drew up the reins and brought the horses to a halt. He stepped down into the snow. It rose to his waist. He unfastened an ax from the side of the sleigh and waded over to a pool of ice the size of a wagon wheel. He hacked at the mouth of the spring, chipping away the ice until he could see water flowing down the rock. He let the horses blow. While they drank, he climbed into the sleigh and pulled a flask from a pocket of his wool overcoat, then leaned back, wrapped in the buffalo robe, sipping brandy, listening to the pair of horses slurp the icy water.

Maybe it was the alcohol, but he imagined his lips tingled from their contact with Miss Hartman. He replayed the kiss. Why had he waited so long? *'Cause of your pride, man. Your fucking pride.*

The horses lifted their heads and neighed. They backed away from the spring and stomped their hooves. Bart grabbed up the reins.

"What is it, girls?" His first thought was they'd sensed a slide. He peered up, listening for the rumble of snow raging down through the darkness above him, heard only the horses nervously clicking their teeth on the steel bits. He took a final swig of brandy, stuffed the flask into his coat, and had just lifted the reins to put his team into motion when one of the horses snorted.

Bart cocked his head, strained to listen. He heard the whoosh of animals struggling through deep snow. Two riders appeared twenty feet up the trail, their horses buried to their stomachs. It occurred to Bart that they resembled phantoms in the snow.

He blinked, half-expecting them to have vanished when his eyes opened, but they were still there, and close enough that he could see the clouds of vapor pluming from their horses' nostrils.

"Evening!" Bart called out. There was no answer, and he thought maybe they hadn't heard him, so he yelled, "Merry Christmas!" The rider on the left said something to his companion, and Bart heard the click of tongues. The riders came up on either side of the sleigh. They wore wide-brimmed hats topped with several inches of snow, had draped themselves in blankets and wrapped their faces in pieces of a torn muslin shirt, so that Bart could only see their eyes. Those belonging to the rider on his left exuded a cold focus. The other pair of eyes were wide and twitching with fear and nerves.

"Merry Christmas," Bart said, more cheer in his voice than he felt, and wondered if he was facing a couple of road agents. "Hell of a storm. Ain't on the prod. Just trying to get my ass to a fire—"

"I'd appreciate you shuttin that fuckin hole in your face." The rider on the left had spoken, his voice low, metallic.

Bart said, "Sir, I'm sorry, I don't understand what the problem—" The business end of a double-barreled scattergun peeked out from under the rider's blanket. "You shoot that gun, sir, you're liable to bring a slide down on us all."

"Didn't you hear what he said?" Bart looked at the rider on his right. He was smaller than his partner, much younger, barely a man, if that. But what struck Bart was his accent. Pure Tennessee.

"I don't understand," Bart said. "You work for me, son."

The boy's eyes darted to his companion, then back to Bart.

"N-n-n-n-not no more I don't, Mr. Packer." Bart saw the six-shot Colt patent revolver trembling in the boy's hand, a huge sidearm, decades old, a relic from before the war.

"Easy son," Bart said, and though his intoxication had faded fast, he was far from clearheaded. He thought for a half second that maybe he'd been caught in a slide and was lying packed in snow, suffocating, hallucinating this nightmare. "What in holy hell are you doing? I don't under—" The other man put his horse forward and rammed the barrel of the shotgun into Bart's face. Blood poured through his mustache, between his teeth, down his chin.

Bart pulled off a glove and cupped his hand over his nose.

"Goddamn you, it's broke!"

"Now go on and drive the sled up to your mansion. We gonna follow behind. Don't know if you got a shoulder scabbard, but I wouldn't advise reachin into your coat for any reason. Rest assured I'll err on the side a blowin your goddamn head off. Savvy?"

"What do you want? I'm a rich—"

"You remember what happened last time you opened that mouth? Now go on." Bart lifted the reins and urged his team up the trail, his nose burning, tears running down his bloodied face. The riders followed close behind, and they hadn't gone fifty feet when one of them retched into the snow.

The other muttered, "Christ Almighty." Bart didn't dare look back, but he figured it was the boy, wondered if he'd gotten sick because he was going to kill his first man tonight.

ELEVEN

It was almost ten o'clock, and Joss figured she'd seen all the customers she was going to see for the evening. But in no hurry to return to her cold jail cell, she didn't disturb the deputy, who still snoozed comfortably beside the stove.

Lana had gone home for the night, and Joss hated to own up, but she missed the piano, sick as she was of the endless rotation of Christmas carols. Noise drowned out the hush of loneliness, though even loneliness was preferable to listening to that deputy blather on about what big shit he used to be down in Ouray. Joss had given serious consideration to cutting the young man's throat while he slept—one deep swipe with the bowie she kept under the bar. She could picture his eyes popping open, him reaching for the revolver that she'd already slipped out of its holster, the puddle of blood expanding on the floorboards, sizzling where it touched the base of the stove. But that would just fuck everything up. Besides, where would she go, with Abandon as snowbound as she'd ever seen it? What was another twelve hours?

Joss smiled at the thought of Lana. On her way out, she'd actually bowed her head and mouthed "Merry Christmas"—by far the most verbose that pretty mute had ever been.

The front door swung open and the preacher walked inside and dusted the snow off his frock coat. Stephen Cole glanced around the dead saloon, then walked up and rested his forearms on the pine bar.

"Good evening," he said.

"Evenin, Preach. Finally come to bend a elbow?"

Stephen smiled. Apparently, he'd left home without a hat, because his hair was wet with melting snow.

"Could I buy you a drink, Miss Maddox?"

"It's Joss, and yes, always. You off your feed?"

"No, why do you ask?"

"You're all gant up, just about the palest thing I ever saw." She placed a new bottle on the bar, withdrew the cork, and set up two tumblers. "Pinch a cocaine with your whiskey?"

"No thank you."

"Don't reckon I ever got booze-blind with a man a God. Here's to you—is it Reverend or Preacher or—"

"Stephen is fine, actually. Just Stephen."

They clinked and drained their glasses, Stephen wincing.

Joss went to pour again, but Stephen waved her off. "No more of that snakehead for me, but you go right ahead."

"I'll mix you a cobbler." She smiled. "Ladies seem to like it."

"No, I'm fine."

"Well, I'm gonna get a little more fine."

Joss filled her glass. The preacher pulled two bits from his leather pouch, set it on the bar, but he made no move to leave.

"There somethin else I can help you with?" she asked.

Stephen pushed his hair behind his ears.

"Actually, I did have ulterior motives for coming here tonight."

"And what might those—no, wait. Please, please, tell me you ain't here to make some half-assed attempt to—"

"Save you? No. God saves. I am a very small part of that equation. Besides, it would be an insult to your intelligence for me to think I can convince you of your need for God. You're a smart woman. You've lived many a year in this world and have certainly heard the Gospel at some point. You've chosen not to accept Him. It saddens me, certainly saddens God, but you have free will. I respect that."

"Well, that's a relief to hear. I didn't relish the idea a throwin a Gospel sharp out on his ass, but I was prepared to."

Stephen smiled. "I understand you're to be sent back to Arizona in the spring to . . ."

"To be hanged. You ain't gonna hurt my feelings sayin it."

"Miss Maddox. Joss. I was walking home tonight from the Christmas Eve dinner, and I saw the lamps glowin in your saloon, and God put it on my heart to come in here."

"He did."

"I would like to pray for you, Joss. Right now. It's Christmas Eve. You're chained up behind a bar. I can't imagine the fear you face at having to go back to Arizona next year. I thought I might say a prayer with you. If it could bring you any comfort at all, I would be most—"

Joss leaned toward Stephen. "You think I rejected God?"

"I just—"

"You said *I* had chosen not to come to God."

"I just assumed—"

"You wanna hear a story about rejection? The cunt bitch who birthed me abandoned me in a alley in the California goldfields when I was a day old. Man who found and raised me put me up for three dollars to any son of a bitch who had a taste for ten-year-old pussy. Ever husband I ever had beat me. Now the way I figure it, God either approved or couldn't be bothered to give a shit, so *don't* come in here talkin to me about *my* rejection a God. I'd say He's had His back to me ever since I took my first breath." A vein had risen on Joss's forehead and her big black eyes shone.

"You think God hates you?" Stephen asked.

"I stopped caring what He thinks or don't think a me years ago."

"Well, I can assure you that He loves—"

"Look, you don't gotta come down here, hat in hand, makin amends for God. He knows where I live. He can come Hisself or not at all. Thanks for the gesture, Preach, but you're barkin at a knot, and prayin with you ain't exactly on my wish list this year. Now, I gotta close up." She looked at the deputy. "Al! Get your ass up!"

The deputy startled into consciousness, instinctively touched the revolver at his side, his words slurring. "What's wrong? What happened?"

"We're done for tonight," Joss said. "Take me back to jail."

"But it ain't but—"

"Al, goddamn it, contradict me one more fuckin—"

"All right, Joss, you ain't gotta yell."

Stephen took a step back and regarded Joss with his sad, sweet eyes.

"Merry Christmas to you," he said, and started for the door.

Stephen Cole stood under a streetlamp, watching the wind build snowdrifts against the storefront of a vacated barbershop. Across the street, on the second floor of the hotel, Molly Madsen sat in the bay window, looking down at him, her face weakly illuminated by the candle in her hands. He waved, whispered a prayer for her.

He followed the plank sidewalk for several blocks, then turned up the side street that led to his cabin.

His mind brimmed with thoughts of his home in Charleston, South Carolina—the palm trees and live oaks and saltwater marshes, the ocean at sunrise, the faces of his father and mother.

He had come west three years ago because he believed it to be the will of God, had felt compelled to minister to those who lived in these harsh environs.

What he had found were a thousand little towns high in the Rockies, built upon debauchery and greed.

I've accomplished nothing, he thought. *God, show me one life in these mountains that has benefited from my presence.*

Overcome, he knelt in the empty street and prayed until his face had gone numb and his body shook with cold.

Stephen rose to his feet and wiped the snow from his hair.

He'd taken two steps toward home when he heard it.

He froze. Forgot that he was cold. Forgot his loneliness.

He just stood there in the darkness and falling snow, a strange warmth spreading through him. Having now heard it, he knew with certainty that all the other times, kneeling at the foot of his bed, sometimes hours in the silence, had been imagination and hoping.

It was simply his own name that he'd heard, but it filled him with such blinding peace that he didn't question for a moment the source.

When God speaks to you, His voice is unmistakable.

2009

TWELVE

Six tubes of light swung through the fog that had settled in the canyon—a colony of headlamps moving toward the ruins of Abandon. The air carried the steel smell of snow, though none was yet falling. Night had arrived moonless and overcast, with a darkness Abigail had never imagined possible out-of-doors, like they'd all been locked into an immense, freezing closet. She walked between Emmett and June, with Lawrence a few yards ahead, the two guides relegated to the back, with orders to stay close but quiet. Abigail had brought along her tape recorder and was collecting background information from the Tozers when Lawrence said, "Hold up!" They stopped. Lawrence shone his flashlight into the darkness ahead, the beam passing over a grove of spruce. "Can't believe I found it in this fog. Here's what's left of the cabin of Ezekiel and Gloria Curtice."

Abigail followed June into the grove. The small woman, swallowed in a red ski jacket, aimed her light at the rubble. Abigail saw a cookstove, cans, rusted bedsprings amid the detritus. Emmett slipped off his camera's lens cap and began to circle the homestead.

Abigail said, "June, while Emmett's taking photos, could you tell me how you two got involved with paranormal photography?"

June led Abigail away from the remains of the cabin. They stood apart from the others, separated by a lightning-fried spruce, headlamps off. "Ten years ago, our son, Tyler, was out riding his bicycle in the neighborhood. He was hit by a van. Died in the street." Abigail found June's hands in the dark. "Night after the funeral, Emmett and I were in bed, holding each other. We were talking about taking some pills. It's a pain like you cannot . . .

"So we're in bed, it's two or three in the morning, and all of a sudden, I just feel this calm engulf me, like the rush of some incredible drug. The air was thick, a living thing, and I felt like I was being wrapped in it. That's the only way I know how to describe it. Most intense and unconditional love I've ever felt, and I was smiling, and I looked at Emmett, and he was, too. We were experiencing it together, and we both knew exactly what it was. Ty had come to us. I felt my little boy's presence just as strong as I feel you standing here in front of me, even though I can't see you. He saved us, Abigail.

"Next morning at our local coffeehouse, Emmett saw a poster for a paranormal-photography slide show. We didn't even know there was such a thing, but having just had our experience with Ty, we felt this conviction to go. Unfortunately, the photographer we went to see was a fraud. I could tell that right away. Most people who claim to be psychic are delusional. The stuff they shoot, it's camera malfunctions, flash problems, dust particles on the film. But Emmett and I were inspired to buy a camera. We shot four rolls in our room that night—infrared film in total darkness. In the corner above our bed, we captured this fantastic pool of light, like this energy was watching over us as we slept."

"Your son."

"Emmett and I had always been artists. It's why we lived in San Francisco. We threw ourselves into paranormal photography, never looked back. And it's such a beautiful medium—a perfect intersection of art and history and service."

"What do you mean by 'service'?"

"See, it isn't just about taking photographs of paranormal activity for the aesthetic value. These are suffering spirits who, for whatever reason, haven't passed to the other side. Most important part of our job is helping them move on. It's not about the thrills for us, or 'ghost-busting.' It's our calling. If Ty hadn't died, we probably never would have come down this road. Isn't it beautiful and sad how these things work out?"

June placed something in Abigail's hand—a small plastic cylinder.

"What's this?"

"Emmett shot a roll of film on the hike in."

"Of me?"

"Of you and Lawrence."

"Well, that's . . . Thank you, but to be honest, I don't know that I want this."

June squeezed her hands. "Do as you see fit."

When Emmett finished shooting the Curtice homestead, the party moved on, six pairs of boots brushing through dry autumn weeds. They came down a slope, Abigail feeling guilty, convinced the death of the Tozers' son had turned them out of their minds, yet knowing their story would make the heartbreaking core of her article.

Shapes took form out of the fog. They stood in the grassy lane, Abandon's ramshackle buildings on either side, tendrils of mist drifting among them through the blaring silence.

"Let's start in the saloon," Emmett said, and Lawrence led them across the street, hopped over a few planks—all that remained of the sidewalk—and stepped gingerly into the shack.

"I haven't been in here in awhile," he said, "so I'm not sure how sturdy everything is. We'd better just start with the Tozers going in."

Emmett and June joined Lawrence inside. After a moment, Emmett appeared in the doorway, said, "Would everyone please turn off their headlamps? I don't want any outside light getting in here, interfering with the shots."

All the headlamps went dark except for Emmett's. Abigail stood on the threshold, watching them explore the interior, the beam of Emmett's light grazing the listing walls and a gnawed-board floor, littered with pieces of broken whiskey bottles, rusted tin-can scraps. The pine bar had toppled over and punched out a section of the back wall, through which the fog crept in, giving the saloon a natural smokiness.

"You can come on in," Lawrence whispered to Abigail. "Just be mindful where you step and don't go near the stove. If you look up, you'll see a hole in the roof. The boards underneath get rained and snowed on. Amazing they haven't fallen through yet."

Abigail walked inside, the floor bowing beneath her weight. It smelled of mold and marmot urine and whatever the fog had carried in from the canyon. Emmett and June stood together by the wall opposite the potbellied stove, near an upright piano, half of the ivory keys missing, the rest cracked and jagged, like broken teeth.

Emmett turned off his headlamp, the darkness filling with the click of exposures.

While he shot the saloon, Abigail whispered to June, "Are these spirits ever—"

"Mean?" June laughed. "We get that question a lot. In all our years of work, we've encountered only one aggressive spirit. Ninety-nine percent of the time, they're just confused, lost, and consumed in their own grief. It's funny, because once you're dead, all the beliefs you subscribed to while alive don't mean a thing."

Abigail turned on her tape recorder. "Tell me about this aggressive experience."

"Few years ago, we got a call to clear a church outside Monterey. This spirit had been locking doors, moving furniture around, just making a nuisance of itself. So we showed up, and the preacher was there. This hard-core, fire-and-brimstone type of guy. He said, 'You tell me when you feel the presence, and

I'll get rid of it, show you how it's done.' I told him, 'Well, it's here right now,' and he said, 'By the power of Jesus Christ, I command you to leave.' A chair went flying across the sanctuary, shattered on the pulpit. That preacher ran out the doors. Scared the hell out of him. He quit the church and everything."

"What do you think it was? A demon? Do you even believe in angels and demons?"

"Angels, yes. Demons . . . I'm not sure. Come to find out, this church had been converted from a nursing home. This spirit was probably tied up from whatever trauma it had experienced there when it was alive. But it certainly didn't like the church."

"How do you think it managed to throw a chair?"

Emmett piped up from across the room: "These spirits, when they die, become pure mind. You know what we could do if we had access to even eighty percent of our brain?"

"You talking about telekinesis?

"That's right."

"Have to say, I'm surprised by the lack of equipment you guys brought. I did some research before I flew out, expected to see you using thermal scanners and—"

"Geiger counters, ion detectors, an EMF alarm. Let me tell you something," Emmett said. "That's a bunch of garbage. All you need is a camera and film, because if you can't walk into a room and feel it in your bones, you're in the wrong business, wasting your time."

When Emmett turned on his headlamp, Abigail noticed that June had been drawn over to one of the windows, where she stared at something across the street.

"Lawrence," June whispered. "What happened up there?" They all walked over, peered up to where June pointed. Without light, they could barely make out a bay window on the second floor of a building across the street. "Did something happen in that room?"

"Not that I know of. It was just one of the nicer rooms in the hotel. Why?"

"Someone's watching me from that window." Even though she knew it wasn't real, a subtle chill moved down through the vertebrae of Abigail's spine.

"Can you get us up there?" Emmett asked.

"Never been, but we can certainly try."

THIRTEEN

One hundred and nineteen years of rain, snow, and high-altitude sun had bleached the block letters on the side of the building, so all that could be seen by the light of the headlamps was a faint OTEL. Excluding Bartholomew Packer's mansion, it was the largest, most resilient structure in the ghost town, a two-story brick building with what had once been a lavish dining room on the ground level and seven suites on the second floor. The middle of the three rooms that faced the street was the "Presidential Suite," identifiable by the large bay window that loomed over the entrance to the hotel.

Lawrence walked through the tall door frame, the others following, and soon the party had gathered in the lobby, a long but narrow room with two archways opposite each other, a front desk, and a wide staircase that ascended into darkness.

"This was the only brick building in Abandon," Lawrence said, "built when the mine was still producing and people thought this town was going to last." Abigail stepped through the archway on her left, her headlamp sweeping over the shambles of a lounge strewn with Victorian-style furniture and a long-dormant hearth. Draperies hung in shreds from the windows, and a billiard table stood at a severe slant, one of its legs having snapped off.

Abigail drew in a quick shot of oxygen.

Eyes shone back at her, illumined in the beam—the head and rack of an enormous elk, fallen from its mount above the fireplace, stared at her, mottled with mold and decay.

She returned to the lobby, where everyone had gathered at the other archway, this one opening into the dining room. It might have been the best restaurant in Abandon in the early 1890s, but tonight it lay before them in a mass of mangled tables and broken chairs. The three chandeliers had pulled out from their fixtures in the ceiling and shattered on the black-and-white-striped hardwood floor, the tiny shards of glass and crystal glittering under the lamps, as if the party had stumbled into an ice cave.

"Anyone care for a glass of hundred-year-old bourbon?" The headlamps converged on Scott, who stood behind the mahogany bar, a dusty bottle in one hand.

They made their way back through the carnage of furniture into the lobby.

"Here's the deal," Lawrence said. "I've never explored the second floor, so we're gonna take these stairs one person at a time. Be alert, be careful, and walk softly if you can."

His right hand glided up the rickety banister as he climbed. The first four steps were fine, but they grew progressively creakier the higher he went. The last three made no sound at all, and then he stood at the top, just a moon of yellow light fifteen feet above.

"Who's next?"

June went up, followed by Emmett. Abigail took the path Emmett had chosen, straight up the middle, her headlamp trained on each step.

"You're doing great," June called out as the fifth step creaked loudly and she felt the wood give beneath her. The next three were even worse. She could feel her pulse accelerating and a shortness of breath brought on by the first stage of panic. Abigail climbed the final steps faster than she should have, but as she neared the top, Lawrence and Emmett reached down, each taking an arm, and pulled her to safety.

"That was sort of terrifying," she said.

Abigail stood with Lawrence at the edge of the steps, watching their guide ascend. He climbed toward them, a model of patience and confidence, a man at home on dangerous terrain, even when he crossed the noisiest steps.

He was almost to the top now, and Abigail could see him grinning. He winked at her as he put his weight onto the last step. Then came a dry crack, and he simply disappeared.

The staircase collapsed in a fanfare of splitting wood, dust everywhere, people shouting in the darkness. Coughing, Abigail aimed her headlamp down toward the lobby, half-expecting to see Scott sprawled across the wreckage.

At first, she mistook it for a cry of pain, but then she saw the gloved fingers gripping the edge of the second floor and realized that Scott was laughing, even as his feet dangled seven feet above the fallen staircase.

"He's right here!" she yelled. "Help him up!"

Lawrence and Emmett dropped to their knees, grabbed Scott's arms above the elbows.

"Maybe I should just drop," Scott said. "It's not that far."

"Bad idea," Abigail said. "I see nails sticking out of the boards underneath you."

"Abigail," Lawrence said, "my grip's slipping! Get him under this arm!" They strained to lift him, inch by inch, sweating, groaning, swearing. Finally, Scott's knees cleared the ledge where the staircase had broken away and they all fell back into the corridor.

Jerrod yelled up to them, "Everybody in one piece?"

"Yeah, we're cool," Scott said. "Why don't you come stand underneath us. I've got rope in my pack. We'll hoist you up."

"I think I'll just wait down here."

Lawrence helped Abigail and June onto their feet, and soon they were all moving down the second-floor corridor, testing with each step the fidelity of the floor. At last, Lawrence stopped at a closed door with a tarnished number 6 hanging upside down from a rusty nail.

FOURTEEN

The five of them filed in, their headlamps making swaths of light across the room, showing where the gingham wallpaper had peeled so thoroughly from the walls, it resembled the curling bark of aspen trees. Aside from the broken bedposts and an upturned writing desk, the furniture had been well preserved. Water had damaged the ceiling and the south wall, and picture frames lay on the floor, their canvases gone or destroyed.

On the door frame, Abigail's headlamp fell upon some tiny scrawl that she wrote off as graffiti: *Something awful happening.*

"Honey, can you get over the heaviness?" Emmett said.

"I know. It's much colder in here. Room's really sagging."

"Why are certain places paranormal hot spots?" Abigail whispered.

"Usually because of intense, unresolved emotion," Emmett said.

June had wandered over to an enormous wardrobe, which she opened. Inside hung petticoats and evening gowns, so eaten by time, they'd have evaporated in a gust of wind.

In a corner near the bed, Abigail gazed at a collection of porcelain figurines on top of a bureau, wondering how they'd remained untouched all these years. Beside them, facedown, lay a small frame, its picture gone.

Lawrence came up behind her, whispered, "Do *you* feel anything in here?"

"Loads of bullshit."

They turned and watched June approach the bay window, where, remarkably, only one pane of glass had been busted out. A divan stood in utter disintegration in the alcove.

"She'd sit here," June said quietly, as if to herself, "watching the world go by without her." She crumpled down on the floor and rested her head between her knees. After awhile, she rose into child's pose and bowed her head.

Abigail muttered "Jesus Christ" under her breath.

Emmett walked over to Abigail and Lawrence. "You really don't know anything about the history of this room? Even the smallest detail might help."

Lawrence shook his head. "I'm sorry. I know a lot about Abandon, but there are gaps."

"Why don't you two go ahead and turn off your lights. I'm gonna take some photos." They all turned off their headlamps. The room went dark, Emmett just a shadow now, quiet save for the floor creaking beneath his footfalls, the clicking of his camera, and the deep rhythmic breaths June emitted as she knelt motionless before the bay window. Abigail's eyes had just begun to adjust to the darkness when Emmett finished.

"I can't wait to process this film," he whispered. "I think I got something."

"What kind of camera are you using?" Abigail asked. "I'll need to get all the technical information right for my article."

"This is a Minolta X-700. Only reason I use the older stuff is because it doesn't have all the electronic hardware, so it doesn't fool with the film. Infrared is so sensitive, you can't even shoot it in most of the newer cameras."

"Now, what exactly is infrared? It keys off hot and cold, right?"

"No, infrared is just outside the visible spectrum of light, so our eyes can't see it."

"She hears a church bell," June whispered. "She watches them all move past, but she won't leave."

"Any special lens?"

"This is a twenty-eight–seventy. Sometimes, I'll use a fifty-millimeter, depending on the conditions. Here, take a look." He lifted the strap over his neck and handed the camera to Abigail. She brought the viewfinder up to her left eye.

"I can't see anything."

"Lawrence, turn on your flashlight." Lawrence flicked it on. "Cool, it's red," she said.

"Yeah, that's the number twenty-five filter."

June got up suddenly and went back to the open wardrobe, began fingering one of the evening gowns, her face still radiating a blank, trancelike intensity. With June out of the way, Abigail took the opportunity to walk over to the bay window. From the vantage point, she could see down through old glass onto the street below.

She lifted Emmett's camera and stared through the viewfinder.

"Lawrence, can you give me some light, please?"

He came over and shined his flashlight at the saloon across the street.

"You know, I want to apologize, Emmett," Lawrence said. "For fucking with you last night about the spaceship and Abandon."

"It's all right."

"No, I was being a dick. Let me share with you my theory on what happened."

"You sure?"

"Yeah. Now, I'd have been laughed out of academia if I'd ever published this."

Where the beam passed, the night glowed in deep reds, and Abigail suddenly knew she would write about this moment, what it felt like to gaze into the viewfinder, through the number twenty-five filter, searching for lost spirits in the sea of red. Maybe Emmett wasn't actually looking for spirits when he snapped his photos, but she could embellish. Make his whole bizarre profession sound sexy and strange. She had the first inkling that this could be a phenomenal piece.

"But because of the way the town disappeared—everything abruptly abandoned, no record of what happened, no bones . . ."

Something stepped out of the saloon and ran up the street. She lowered the camera.

"I came to the conclusion that—"

"Lawrence, you see that?"

"What?"

Emmett came over. "What's wrong?" he asked.

"Something just came out of the saloon and ran up the street."

"Probably a deer," said Scott, who'd been leaning against the wall by the door, quietly observing. "Tons of wildlife out—"

"It didn't move like a deer."

"How'd it move?"

"Like a man. You didn't see it, Lawrence? It moved right through where you were shining the flashlight."

"I didn't see a thing."

Abigail handed Emmett his camera and walked through the suite and out the open door, moving quickly down the hallway to where the staircase had previously merged with the second floor.

"Hey!" she called down into the dark lobby.

Jerrod had extinguished his headlamp. Abigail turned hers on, directing her light across the collapsed staircase, to the front desk, where he'd been standing several minutes ago.

"Did you see something out there? . . ." Her words trailed into silence.

She swept her beam of light at each archway.

"Jerrod?" she called out. A shadow moved down the corridor toward her. "Scott?"

"Yeah."

"Jerrod left."

Scott came and stood beside her, flipped on his headlamp, moved his light across the lobby. "Jerrod!" he yelled, then cupped his mouth, shouted again, "Jerrod! *Where'd you go?*" Abigail heard the others emerge from the suite.

"What's wrong?" June asked as they approached.

"Jerrod's gone."

The five remaining members of the party peered down into the lobby, listening.

Lawrence finally said, "You think something happened?"

Scott knelt down, unzipped his backpack, and dug out a climbing rope.

"I'll see what's going on." Standing there, watching Scott unspool the rope, Abigail realized the soberness in his voice unnerved her. He jogged into the nearest suite, wrapped the rope three times around a heavy chest of drawers, and tied a knot. Then he came back out into the corridor and kicked the pile of rope. It dropped fifteen feet into the lobby. He got onto his knees, worked himself over the edge, his gloved hands gripping the rope. He slid carefully down onto the wrecked staircase.

"If you guys just want to wait up there, I'll be back in a minute."

"Hold up," Lawrence said. "I'll go with you."

The older man didn't make lowering himself look as effortless as the guide had, but he got down safely, and the two men disappeared out the front door of the hotel.

June, Emmett, and Abigail sat down in the corridor.

"I hope everything's all right," June said.

Emmett looked over at Abigail. "You got extra batteries for your light?"

"Back at camp. Why?"

"Yours is dying."

Abigail pulled off her headlamp just in time to watch the bulb fade out.

FIFTEEN

Abigail pressed the light feature on her watch: 9:59 P.M.

"They've been out there ten minutes," she whispered.

June and Emmett had turned off their headlamps to conserve the batteries, so all she could see of them were the white pairs of facing crescent moons that framed their irises.

From one of the rooms on the second floor came a sound like a shutter slamming against a window frame.

Emmett said, "Wind."

They sat awhile longer in the corridor, listening to the shutter squeak on its rusted hinges and bang into the window. Finally, Emmett struggled to his feet.

"Okay. I'm gonna go down and see what's going on here."

"No," Abigail said. "We'll all go."

June went first, Emmett and Abigail helping her to ease over the edge, her hands trembling as she cursed quietly to herself while her feet dangled above the lobby. She slid slowly down the rope and whispered "Thank you, God" as her feet touched the staircase.

When Emmett and Abigail had lowered themselves into the lobby, the three worked their way over the staircase debris, past the front desk, to the hotel entrance.

They moved through the threshold and out into the misty street.

The loose shutter had gone quiet, and Abandon stood in perfect silence save for the occasional creak of a teetering building bracing against the wind.

"Where'd you guys go?" Emmett shouted. No answer but that of his own voice resounding in fading refrains through the canyon. He shouted again. Echoes again. Silence.

Abigail felt something soft and cold on her face.

Snowflakes passed through the beam of Emmett's headlamp.

"Well," he said finally, "I'll walk up the street toward camp. June, you and Abigail head the other way. We have whistles in our emergency kits, so I suppose we should blow on those if we find the others."

"I think splitting up is a horrible idea," Abigail said.

"All right, then which way do you—" Emmett stopped mid-sentence. "What the hell?"

He looked past them now, his brow deeply furrowed, his mouth dropped open.

Something staggered toward them down the middle of the street, and it occurred to Abigail that the way it moved through the fog, in slow, exaggerated steps, resembled something from a horror movie—a zombie or some demon that had just crawled out of its own grave. It was close now, within ten feet of them, dragging its right foot and clutching its side.

Their guide collapsed in the hotel doorway, Scott's yellow fleece slicked with blood, and down blowing out of a gaping tear in his vest.

Abigail felt her stomach lurch, something rising up her throat. Her mouth tasted of salt and metal.

Emmett was already on his knees, cradling Scott's head.

"What happened?" he asked.

Scott moaned, his face so drained of color that it seemed to glow in the dark, his body quaking with the onset of shock. "I wanna see it," he gasped. "Lift my jacket."

Emmett unbuttoned Scott's down vest and unzipped his fleece jacket, Abigail at his ear, whispering to him that everything would be okay. Emmett peeled away the layer of thermal underwear and they all stared at the black hole in his side, blood sheeting down his pale abdomen into a widening pool on the old boards.

"Fuck!" Scott said. "Fuck, it hurts!"

"What do we do?" Abigail asked. "You're our guide. You know first aid, right? Tell us how to help you." Scott's eyes rolled back in his head. She slapped his face.

He came back, his eyes only slits now. "Run," Scott hissed. "They're coming."

"Who?" Abigail asked.

"We aren't leaving you," Emmett said, but Scott's eyes had already closed. "Scott! Scott! June, keep pressure on the wound." She pressed her palm into Scott's side, blood leaking between her fingers.

A scream blasted through the canyon.

Abigail whispered, "Turn off your headlamp, Emmett."

He did, everything still, and, for the moment, quiet.

A snowflake landed on Abigail's eyelash. She blinked it away and rose to her feet. "We need to get out of here," she said.

"There," June said. Abigail saw it, too. Fifty yards ahead, at the north edge of town, something sprinted toward them, arms pumping.

"It's Jerrod," Emmett said.

Abigail had begun to backpedal even before she saw the shadows emerge out of the fog behind Jerrod. The one in front slipped something out of its belt. As it reached him, it placed a hand on the back of Jerrod's head, jammed something into the base of his skull.

Jerrod dropped without a sound.

June released an involuntary whimper.

Emmett said, "Oh my God."

Abigail thinking, *This is not happening. This is not happening.* But it was. The shadows had passed Jerrod's body and were now closing fast on the hotel.

"We need to split up and run," Abigail said. "Right now."

SIXTEEN

The ghost town screamed by in a blur of fog. Abigail glanced over her shoulder, saw movement in the mist, though she couldn't tell if they were still chasing her. She had put a hundred yards between herself and the hotel when she veered off the main street and bent over. Having come from sea level in Manhattan, the thin air of Abandon crippled her lungs. She crawled through a hole in the side of a building, tried to turn on her headlamp, then remembered the bulb had burned out.

It took a moment for the faintest suggestion of shapes to appear—a table, dismembered chairs, tall windows, remnants of a stove. Abigail stood in the dance hall.

At the far end, the ceiling had collapsed and crushed a small stage.

Footsteps approached from outside. With quick, careful strides, Abigail traversed the rotten floorboards. Some creaked under her weight and she couldn't help but think of the staircase in the hotel, how suddenly it had given way. She stopped where the floor had fallen through, looked back toward the double doors that opened out onto the street. Abigail couldn't hear the footsteps anymore, only her accelerated breathing. The sound of whispering passed through the broken windows and something ran by on the street.

She dropped down through the hole in the floor, a nail catching on her parka, ripping through the sleeve, her pink fleece jacket, her long johns, all the way to her skin.

With less than three feet of space between the floorboards and the ground, she crawled away from the hole, through puddles of freezing water, until she found a dry spot. Crouched in the darkness, shivering under the floor of the dance hall, she felt a warm trail of blood meandering down her right arm.

Her breathing still sounded deafening, but she couldn't stop herself. The darkness sparked with her own dizziness.

What happened to Lawrence? She wondered what had happened to her father.

The floor creaked above her. Abigail held her breath, her pulse thrumming against the back of her eyes. The floor moved again. She raised her hand to see how near it dipped to the top of her head. Her fingers passed between the boards, touched the tread of a boot.

She froze. For a full minute, no movement, no sound. Her quads were cramping. *They're listening. Did I make a noise? Can they hear my heartbeat?* The cut on her right arm stung. Sweat ran down into her eyes, and she shut them tightly against the burn.

This made her think of growing up in the suburbs of Baltimore. She'd been a tomboy, and on Friday nights, in the summer of her tenth year, she would meet the neighborhood boys at a city park to play something they'd invented, called the "Dead Game." One kid was named the "killer," and everyone else had one minute to run and hide. The killer would then go hunting, and if he touched you, you were dead and had to lie on the ground until he'd caught everyone. She recalled hiding under a sliding board one night, watching the killer pass by, and the exhilaration, the pretend-fear that had flooded through her.

The boot lifted and she listened to the footsteps trail away.

As she huddled in the darkness, trying to fathom what was happening, she heard June's voice at the other end of Abandon, shouting her husband's name. For a moment, she considered hiding there indefinitely, days if she had to. *But what if they've seen me? What if they know I'm somewhere in town? In daylight, it won't take them more than a few hours to search every structure. Safer to escape now, in the dark.*

Abigail remembered her cell phone, which was sitting in the top compartment of her backpack in the vestibule of her tent. She probably wouldn't get service in this canyon, but earlier today, when they'd crested the pass, she'd gotten a signal, even called her mother.

Abigail crawled back through the puddles and the dirt to the hole in the floor, rising up slowly, until only her eyes peeked out.

The dance hall appeared empty. June's screaming had stopped. Even the wind had died away. Abigail scrambled up onto the floor. She felt safer, less exposed on her stomach, so she crawled along on her belly back to the hole in the wall she'd come through.

She peered through the busted clapboard out into the fog. It would be too dangerous to run back to camp through town. She'd have to follow the side street, climb the slope, and stay above Abandon as she worked her way up-canyon. Then she could go straight down the hill into camp, know before she arrived if anyone was there. Her battery was charged. If she had a signal, she'd call 911, but assuming she didn't, it might be an hour up to the pass.

Abigail took a moment to calm herself, filling her lungs with oxygen in preparation for the run. She tried to ignore it, but the thought forced itself on her: *They see me, I'm dead.*

Abigail ducked through the hole and stepped outside.

She jogged down the side street. Five more seconds and she'd be out of the ghost town.

Something darted out from behind the dance hall. A hand covered her mouth.

"It's me, Abby." Lawrence's voice. He pulled her down behind the building.

She said, "Jerrod's dead, and Scott's hurt bad."

Wood creaked in a structure across the street.

"Listen," Lawrence said, "there's a house up that slope, with a bay window in front. I want you to go there, hide inside, get out of the open."

"My headlamp's out."

"Take my flashlight."

"What about you?"

"I tweaked my ankle. You'll move faster without me. Here." He handed her his day pack. "There's a gun inside and a box of rounds."

"I can't."

"You can if you want to live. There's a button on the left side of the Ruger. Press it. Cylinder flips open, you put the shells in. It's double-action. No safety. Just squeeze back the hammer and fire. Now listen. When I say 'Run,' you go and you don't stop and you don't look back, no matter what happens. I'll go a different way, try to meet you in the house. We'll figure something out." Footsteps moved toward them up the side street.

"What's happening here, Lawrence? Who are these—"

"I don't know, but you have to get going. Now run."

Abigail scrambled to her feet, shouldered the pack, and took off.

Soon she was passing wiry firs and vacant cabins, dreary and haunted-looking in the freezing fog, fighting with every step the urge to look back. She suddenly emerged onto a long, narrow glissade, lost her footing on the old ice, and slid upside down on her back, racing toward the bottom. The ice ended, but she still tumbled through the scree, finally crashing into a boulder. Blood streamed down her face from a gash above her left eyebrow. Down in Abandon, someone screamed. She got up, pushed on, nearing the timberline, with the ghost town a hundred feet below, scarcely visible through the fog.

Just ahead was the house with the bay window—two stories, still intact. She glanced back. Too dark and foggy to see a thing. She came up on the house, saw a doorway toward the back of the old structure, slipped inside, scrambling over a pile of boards into a large empty room. She could see the bay window—four glassless rectangles with a view of the ghost town. She dropped the day pack on the floor and glanced through a window frame on the side of the house, spotted movement at the base of the slope she'd just climbed—two black specks slinking through the shrubs. She lost them amid the ruins of a homestead, then picked them up a moment later, larger and close enough that she could see their deformed eyes, protruding long and sharp, like fangs. *Night-vision goggles. They know I'm in here.*

Abigail knelt down in the corner and unzipped the day pack, shone the flashlight inside, saw the dull gleam of the revolver.

She didn't realize how badly her hands were trembling until she tried to grab the gun.

Holding the flashlight between her knees, she tore open the box of .357 Magnum rounds. Hollow-point shells spilled across the floorboards, most of them disappearing into a hole. She felt the button on the left side of the frame, pushed it. The cylinder swung open. With her hands shaking, it took her three tries to get the first round into the chamber.

Footsteps approached. Abigail pushed in three more shells, wondered if she'd even loaded them correctly, having never held a gun until this moment.

With the six chambers loaded, she pushed the cylinder back and stood up. Through the window, she saw it was snowing now, and the two shadows were much closer, less than twenty yards downhill. They moved up a steep section of the slope, climbing on all fours, like spiders, up the mountain. She turned off the flashlight, hunched down in a corner, knees drawn into her chest. Thumbed back the hammer, total dark save for the faint outline of night through the bay windows. Blood running into her eyes. Outside, rocks shifted. She couldn't slow her breathing down, her chest heaving, hyperventilating. *You have to be quiet. You* have to.

She closed her eyes, stilled her mind. Her heart followed. Then came the awful silence. No more whispering voices or clandestine footsteps or distant screaming.

Ice pellets ticked against the house, pinged on the tin roof.

She waited. A minute passed, and the image took hold again—that shadow thrusting something into the back of Jerrod's head. It wasn't just the brutality that horrified her.

Why is this bugging me? She remembered. *Oh Jesus.*

One of the interviews she'd conducted for her article on PTSD vets had been with a colonel in spec ops. They'd stumbled onto the topic of the silent kill, and he'd told her that, contrary to common belief, slitting a throat wasn't the quietest way to kill a person. He'd explained that when Force Recon or SEALs wanted to kill instantly and with minimal noise, they'd jam a combat knife at a forty-five-degree angle through the base of the skull, where the bone was thin. It scrambled the medulla oblongata. Instantly wiped out all motor control.

That's what happened to Jerrod. Are these guys spec ops?

In the darkness several feet ahead, someone exhaled.

The floor creaked.

Liquid fear, pulled the trigger, muzzle flash burning her eyes, ears ringing, and in that light splinter, she saw the rotted interior of the ghost house and two men garbed in night camouflage and face masks, suppressor-fitted machine pistols slung over their shoulders.

They stood by the bay window, one of them kneeling, hit.

As she thumbed back the hammer, she heard the hiss of compressed air. Barbed electrodes clung to her parka. Then she lay twitching and screaming on the floor.

1893

SEVENTEEN

Molly Madsen sat in her bay window, watching snow pour down onto Main, sipping from a bottle of wine of coca. It had stormed all night. She'd even startled from sleep once, awakened by a slide razing the forest below town.

An untrodden lacquer of powder lay between the buildings, and on the hillside, she could see the cabins—stoves and hearths aglow, smoke trickling out of chimneys. Here came the first passerby of the day, a petite blonde plodding through the snow. *That pretty piano player.* Molly had grown accustomed to staring down into the saloon, watching the young woman play. Sometimes, late at night, with the street gone quiet, she could even hear the music from the hotel suite.

Footsteps approached from behind; strong hands settling on her shoulders. She finished peeling one of the oranges from the basket Ezekiel and Gloria Curtice had left at her door the night before, offered him a wedge, her suite redolent of citrus.

"I was thinking, Jack. Could we take a trip to San Francisco in the spring? I'm so tired of all this dreadful snow."

"That's a lovely idea."

She squeezed his hand. Jack gazed down at her, eyes luminous with adoration, said, "Remember the first time I saw you? I was walking down the street on a San Francisco evening, when I passed this spectacular creature. I doffed my hat, smiled."

"Did she smile back?"

"Oh no. This was a lady, by every account. She simply nodded, and I thought, I have to know who that woman is."

"So what did you do?"

"Followed her to a ball."

"And then?"

"We danced. We danced all night."

"Do you remember what she wore?"

"An evening gown the color of roses. You were the most exquisite thing I'd ever seen. You still are."

"I'm so happy, Jack." Molly rose from the divan and stepped around to her husband. Even after all this time, he seemed utterly unchanged from the man she'd married in 1883—short blond hair, boxy jaw, ice blue eyes, even that same spruce tailcoat he'd worn the night of their first encounter. "Let me show you what I want for Christmas," she said, reaching back to untie her filthy corset, letting it fall to her feet. She pulled her chemise over her head, tossed it at the wardrobe, and climbed into bed. "Jaaaaack." She whispered his name like a prayer, fingers already fast at work in that swampy heat between her thighs.

EIGHTEEN

On their way to Packer's mansion for a Christmas brunch, Ezekiel and Gloria Curtice eyed the steep treeless slopes that swept up on both sides of the trail, listening for the first hint of the breaking snow that would precede a slide. Lying in bed in their fire-warmed cabin, they'd heard them going throughout the night, like the thunder of distant cannons. Stephen Cole sent up a prayer for protection as they moved into the treacherous gap between the mountains, their webs sinking through a foot and a half of powder with every step. When they emerged from the avalanche path, the party stopped to rest near a spring that erupted out of the rock.

Ezekiel and Stephen packed down an area of snow so they could sit without sinking. Then the preacher dipped an Indian earthenware vessel he'd brought into the spring, offered the first sip to Gloria.

"No thank you. I'm afraid it'll chill me down even more."

"Zeke?"

"Naw, Preach, you go ahead."

They sat in the cold and awesome silence. Ezekiel pulled off his fleece-lined gloves, took out a hip-flask tin of Prince Albert tobacco, set to work loading his pipe.

Ahead, the terrain flattened into a high basin, with a lake in the middle that in the summer turned a luminescent green, as though the lakebed were made of solid emerald, with the sun underneath it. Even then, no one could stand the water for more than a minute, leading the residents of Abandon to bestow it with the most extreme temperature designation in their arsenal—*"fucking* cold."

Gloria tucked in the blond curls that had escaped from her sealskin cap, shivering despite having bundled herself in two petticoats, two pairs of stockings, one of Ezekiel's heavy woolen jackets, and an enormous pommel slicker.

"Mind if I ask you something, Stephen?"

"Gloria, you can ask me anything anytime."

Ezekiel blew smoke rings, watched the snowflakes cut them down.

"If I tell you this, can it stay between us? 'Cause nobody else in Abandon knows what I'm about to say."

"What do you think you're doin, Glori?" Ezekiel said.

"Trying to ask the preacher something."

"Don't go botherin him with—"

"Zeke," said Stephen, "let her say what's on her mind. I'm here to help if I can."

"Glori, wish you'd let it lie," Ezekiel said, but she ignored him.

"There's no easy way to say it, Stephen. I used to be a whore."

"Aw hell," Ezekiel said.

"And Zeke used to be a outlaw. Killed a few men in his time. We each did enough sinning for ten. We changed. Not perfect by any means, but we're decent folk now, or try to be at least."

"I believe that," Stephen said as he brushed the snow off his visored felt hat.

"Reason I'm telling you this is 'cause I wanna know about God's punishment."

"What about it in particular?"

"Something happened a year ago—"

"Ain't gonna listen to this," Ezekiel said, and he struggled to his feet and webbed a ways up the trail, where he stood with his back to them, smoking his pipe, watching the basin fill with snow.

"Go on, Gloria," Stephen said.

"Last January, we were living up in Silver Plume. Had a son, name a Gus. Him and Zeke went out together one morning. They were waiting to cross the street, and somehow, Gus's little hand slipped out a Zeke's. Our boy walked in front of a hansom. . . ." Stephen reached over, touched Gloria's arm. She wiped her eyes. "The horse stepped on Gus and one a them big wheels . . . rolled over his neck. Weren't nobody's fault. Not the driver's. Not Zeke's."

"Not yours."

"Gus died right there in the street."

"I'm so sorry, Gloria."

"Now I want you to tell me something, Stephen."

"I'll certainly try."

"I just told you how Zeke and I used to be a wicked pair a souls. There's this little voice been whispering to me ever since he died, saying that God took Gus from us as punishment for all the bad things we done. That ain't true, is it? He ain't that kind a God?"

The preacher's calm brown eyes seemed to darken. He looked away, and when he spoke again, his voice took on a harder, bitter aspect.

"You're asking me if we worship a vengeful God?"

"Yes."

"I don't think I'm the person to answer that for you."

"Why not?"

"What if I were to say that that voice in your head is right? That it's entirely possible He took your son from you?"

"If that's the truth, I hate myself and Zeke for what we were. And I hate God for what He is."

"Then perhaps we shouldn't continue this conversation, Gloria. I'll not be responsible for turning someone from their faith." Stephen used his walking stick to boost himself onto his feet. "I'm sorry I can't be of more comfort to you."

"But just last week you preached about God's unconditional love."

Stephen reached down, extended a gloved hand to Gloria, helped her stand. "It's what people need to hear. They want a version of God as benevolent father, ready to protect, eager to provide, but to hold no accounting. I don't believe in that God anymore."

"But you did last Sunday, so something changed your mind?"

"Not something, Gloria. God Himself." And there were sparks in the preacher's gentle eyes—deep loss and rage at that loss—as he turned away and trudged up the trail.

NINETEEN

Emerald Lake lay ten feet under the snow beneath their webs. The storm eased as they hiked across, and through a hole in the clouds, a shaft of sunlight passed, firing into blinding white a piece of the serrated ridge that enclosed the basin.

A mansion materialized in the distance, ensconced on the edge of the lake. "Ever time I see it," Ezekiel said, "I can't get past what a load a burro's milk that thing is."

"It does look misplaced in these environs," Stephen said.

Packer had named his estate Emerald House—four symmetrical wings of opulence that met in a central block, crowned by a cupola. The top floors had been cedar-shingled, the ground level constructed of stone. Numerous brick chimneys soared from the gabled roof.

"Well, that's strange," Ezekiel said. "Ya'll see even a whisper a smoke rising from a one a them chimneys? Why you reckon he'd let his fires go out in a storm?"

There were drifts to the second-floor windows, and a snow tunnel with fifteen-foot walls had been shoveled to the portico of unbarked Douglas fir trunks.

They arrived at a pair of oak doors and Stephen rapped the knocker three times. They untied their webs, waited. Stephen banged the knocker again.

Gloria glanced up at the long overhanging eaves, said, "You don't think he forgot?"

The preacher speculated. "Perhaps he stayed in town last night, not wanting to chance getting trapped in a slide on the way home."

"Well, we just hoofed it through a blizzard, and I'm gonna by God walk in there, find out if we're gettin breakfast for our trouble."

Ezekiel grabbed one of the large iron handles, tried the door.

It opened.

"Think we should walk in unannounced, Zeke?" Gloria said.

"Yeah, I do." He stepped through.

Gloria sighed, followed him in with Stephen, and closed the door.

Every kerosene lamp had burned down save for one at the far end of the first floor, in the kitchen—just a wink of fire from where they stood. Soft gray light slanted through the tall windows that framed the foyer.

"Hello?" Ezekiel shouted. "Anybody on the premises?"

His voice resounded through Emerald House.

They made their way through the foyer and up a cascading stairway, beneath rafters of fir timbers. At the confluence of the four wings, a staircase switchbacked up the heart of the mansion. Between the stairs, a rectangle of weak light fell upon the marble floor, having passed through a skylight fifty feet above.

"Cold in here," Stephen said. "Hasn't been a fire in awhile. And shouldn't there be some servants? If I'm not mistaken, Bart keeps a staff of four or five ladies through the winter."

He walked to the north wing, peered through French doors into a **great** room furnished with a chaise longue, sofas, parlor chairs.

The opposite wing encompassed a dining room on a par with a feudal banqueting hall. Ezekiel looked in but glimpsed only the chairs and the long, broad table, naked of tablecloth, silverware, china.

"Our breakfasting prospects ain't appearing promising. Let's check Bart's room. You remember where it is, Preach?"

"I believe it's in the east wing of the next floor. Overlooks the tarn."

"What do you bet he bent a elbow in the saloon all night, came home roostered?" Ezekiel said. "Hell, might have to wake him."

They took the steps up to the second floor, calling out hellos as they started toward Bart's wing, not a single lamp in operation to illuminate Packer's extravagance.

Ezekiel suddenly stopped. "Might want to step back there, Glori."

She looked down at the hardwood floor, saw that her arctics stood in a gooey puddle of blood. She leaped back toward her husband, brought her hand to her mouth to stifle the scream.

"Well, that's an empty saddle," he said. "Look. More." Faint tracks of blood led back to the staircase, up the next flight.

"Bring your revolver?" Stephen asked.

"'Fraid not. Didn't think I'd be needin it of a Christmas morn. Tell you what. I'm gonna go see what in hell's goin on here."

"Zeke, no—"

"Glori." By the way he said her name, with a gravity she'd not heard in years, Gloria knew better than to push the issue. "Ya'll don't move from this spot. Savvy?"

As Ezekiel ascended toward the servants' quarters, he filled with an exhilaration he'd not experienced in some time. It wasn't fear—he couldn't recall ever having been plagued by that emotion, even as a younker in Virginia—but an airiness in his stomach, birthed by the anticipation of something he'd always had a taste for, and still did. It reminded him of the rough old days, helling around with the boys. In all honesty, he had to own up to missing aspects of his former self. Much as he loved Gloria and his life with her, he couldn't recall the last time he'd felt this alive.

Ezekiel reached the penultimate floor, but the blood continued up, sticky little pools of it on the steps and banister. He climbed on, following the drops and spatters to a small cupola that Bart had transformed into a library, the first seven feet of each wall lined with books, the last five sloping up to a hipped roof.

It made no sense. Blood on the floor, on the spines of books, entrails draped across the back of a leather chair, but the library was empty, its two hearths fireless and this top floor cold enough to cloud his breath.

Then he noticed the ladder tucked under a long bookshelf, glanced up, saw a trapdoor beside the skylight in the ceiling, almost smiled at the needles in his stomach. Using a shiny eight-foot brass pole with a hooked end, he reached up and unlatched the lock and pushed open the hatch. Then he stood the ladder up, bracing it against the opening, snow already falling into the library.

He climbed fifteen steps before emerging onto a small open veranda, the highest point of Emerald House. The panoramic eyeful of the four wings and chimneys and the surrounding basin distracted Ezekiel for a split second before he saw them—five figures near the wrought-iron railing on the east side of the platform.

Bart Packer and his servants.

Three had slumped over, face-first and half-buried in the newly fallen snow. Two still sat upright, Bart one of them, his face black, purple, and distended beyond recognition from what looked to have been a merciless beating. Their throats had been opened, the snow in the vicinity stained with great quantities of blood. "Son of a bitch," he whispered. "Son of a bitch." It snowed again, but the wind whipping across the roof kept the platform mostly bare. He heard approaching footfalls, spun around.

Stephen climbed through the trapdoor onto the roof.

"Goddamn, son," Ezekiel said, shouting to be heard over the wind. "Lucky I didn't have my gun. You'd a been belly-up, coming up on me like that. What'd you leave my wife—" He saw Gloria coming up the steps behind the preacher. Ezekiel rushed past Stephen, stood blocking her view of Bart and the servants.

"You seen it?" he asked her.

"Seen what?"

"Oh sweet Jesus," Stephen said.

"Glori. Glori, look at me. My eyes. They're up here."

"Dead?"

"Had their lamps blown out, I'm afraid, and trust me, 'less you alkalied to it, sight like this, you'll spend the rest a your life tryin to forget."

"But you seen it."

"Awful to say, but I seen worse." *I done worse.* "Now I'm madder'n hell you came up here when I said stay put, but I can probably let that slide if you listen to me." He held her face in his hands. "Look here, Glori. Go on back down now. Go on."

He watched her descend back through the trapdoor, then walked up to Stephen, said, "Man, where the fuck is your head? My wife almost saw this. Got half a mind to throw your ass off this roof."

But the preacher stood stone-faced and glaze-eyed, staring at the stiffs and all of that red snow surrounding them. "Who do you reckon would do a thing like this?"

"Bad men," Ezekiel said. "Looks to have been done with a couple a Arkansas toothpicks. Nasty work. They were probably worried about gunshots settin off a slide, blockin their way out a the basin."

Stephen started toward the dead. Ezekiel grabbed him by the shoulders, drew him back. "Best to let 'em lie for now, Preach. What can you do?"

Stephen nodded. His hands shook. He tried to steady them.

"Is it any wonder, Zeke, that He hates us?"

"Who?"

"God."

"Wait. You sayin God hates His own creations?"

The preacher gestured at the carnage. "Wouldn't you?"

TWENTY

When she opened her only Christmas present of 1893, Harriet McCabe ran shrieking in circles around the ten-by-ten cabin where she lived with her parents. It was by leaps and bounds the most extravagant gift she'd ever received, her mother having skimped on their family's last three food orders so she could purchase the doll from the general store's window. Samantha was sixteen inches tall, came with two dresses and a little comb to brush her luxurious red hair.

"Now I understand why we been eatin pooch and splatter dabs for supper, 'stead a meat," Billy grumbled, still stretched out and hungover on the lumpy straw-filled mattress.

Bessie said, "I's fine to make the sacrifice. Look at your daughter, Billy. You ever seen her so happy? Don't it warm your heart even a little?"

Harriet sat on the dirt floor by the sink—just a washbasin on an upended packing crate—whispering secrets to Samantha.

"Fire's gettin low," Billy said. "Go on, bring in some wood from the porch. This shithole's drafty as hell."

"Billy! That mouth! It's Christmas mornin, and your daughter—"

"Get goin, I said!" So Bessie wrapped every available blanket around her underpinnings and stepped into Billy's arctics. When she'd gone outside, Billy sat up in bed and raised his arms over his head. At twenty years, he was small and looked young for his age, with jittery eyes that caused most men to treat him like a boy. He was handsome until he opened his mouth. His front teeth had resembled jagged canines ever since his father had broken them when Billy was nine. He got up, the dirt floor freezing, his head pounding. He could feel the morning cold slipping through his stained and threadbare long drawers.

He staggered to the table, covered in oilcloth and a few airtights of rarities they'd saved for Christmas. Billy pried open a tin of mustard sardines, crammed a handful into his mouth. He went over to the cabin's only window and swept back the curtains Bessie had sewn out of an old lace-edged petticoat—nothing to see of the outside world, condensation having frosted the inside of the glass.

A whiskey bottle filled with tiny seashells sat in the windowsill. He ran a finger across the glass and thought of his big brother, Arnold, missed him so much in that moment, he felt his throat close up, went short of breath, like someone had punched him in the gut.

Billy turned around, looked at his daughter.

"Merry Christmas, girl," he said.

The six-year-old glanced up at her father, and he saw the wariness in her eyes, and it shot him full of sadness and vexation.

"Got a present for your mama," he said, and he reached under the bed and lifted something the size of a small loaf of bread, packaged in newspaper. He walked over to the spruce sapling they'd uprooted from the hillside above their cabin. Bessie had potted it in a lard bucket, kept it watered, but the needles had begun to brown at the tips. Billy placed the package on the flour sack wrapped around the base of the Christmas tree.

"Y-y-y-you like that doll?" Billy asked, blushing as he always did when he stuttered, no matter that he was conversing with his six-year-old. He'd never had a speech problem before coming to Abandon.

"Yessir."

"That's good. It cost a damn sight more than we can afford."

He lifted the lid and peered into the graniteware pot on top of the stove. The snow had finally melted, tiny bubbles rushing up from the bottom. He took his tin cup down from one of the newspaper-lined shelves above the washbasin and poured the hot water over the old Arbuckle's grounds. "Christmas mornin, ain't even got a decent cup a coffee to sip. This is belly wash." The front door swung open and Bessie stumbled in with two arm-loads of firewood and a draft of bitter cold. She dropped them on the floor, opened the iron stove, shoved in three logs. "Guess it's still snowin," Billy said, noticing the streaks of white in Bessie's yellow hair.

"Comin down like it got no mind to stop. Dust me off, will ye?"

Billy walked over, brushed the snow off her blankets.

"W-w-w-well, looky what's under the tree," he said.

Bessie saw the small package on the flour sack and smiled. "I didn't think you'd got me nothin." Bessie draped the blankets over the rocking chair beside the stove and approached the dying spruce.

She lifted the present. "Heavy."

"C-c-c-come over to the bed." Bessie sat down on the mattress. Harriet crawled over, crouched at her parents' feet.

Bessie ripped off the old newspaper.

"Holy God, Billy." What lay in Bessie's lap amid the torn newspaper was inconceivable, a dream.

"I weighed it," Billy said. "Twenty-two pounds."

"Mama, let me see."

Bessie hoisted the bar of solid gold, the metal freezing cold to the touch, marred with scrapes and tiny chinks, a dully gleaming bronze.

"How much?" she asked.

"Gold's at twenty dollars and sixty-seven cents a ounce, so you're holdin more'n seven thousand dollars right there."

It was more money than Bessie had ever heard of. She began to cry. Billy put his arm around her.

"Where'd you get this?" Bessie asked.

Billy sipped his coffee. The grounds had been used and reused so many times, they barely even colored the water.

"Look at this place." He waved a hand at their shanty. "We live in squalor," he said. "Ain't ye tired of it yet? This floor turnin to mud ever time it rains? Chinks fallin out. They's goddamn drifts in the kitchen from snow blowin through the walls."

"Where'd you get it?" Bessie asked again.

"I-I-I-I don't think ye need to know. We're rich, Bessie. Concern yourself with that. Oh, and this ain't the only one."

"What do you mean?"

He grinned. "That bar's got a whole mess a brothers and sisters."

Bessie dropped the bar on the bed and stood up. With her hands, she framed Billy's acne-speckled face. He'd been trying for a mustache the last six months, but it looked patchy and ridiculous.

"I need to know right now what you done," she said.

He swatted her hands away.

"What you mean, what I done? I'm providin for my fuckin family."

"Billy, when you brought the high-grade home from the mine, I didn't like it, but I let it go. Next thing I know, we got a half ton a ore in the root cellar. I said nothin. But that." She pointed at the bar of gold. "You take it from the Godsend?"

"What if I told you I found it and—"

"I'd call you a black liar." He jumped to his feet and grabbed Bessie's arms and shoved her toward the kitchen.

She crashed into the washbasin and the shelves. A can of condensed milk fell on her head, jars of sugar, long sweetening, flour, and salt shattering on the dirt floor. When Bessie looked up, Billy stood over her, eyes twitching, face bloodred.

Harriet had disappeared under the table, but her crying filled the cabin.

Billy ripped the oilcloth off the table, glared at his daughter. "Now you shut that fuckin yap, Harriet! I'm speakin to your mother, and I don't wanna hear peep one out a you!"

The little girl buried her face in her dress to muffle her sobs.

"Your daughter, Billy!" Bessie screamed. "That's your—"

Billy grabbed his wife by the ankles and dragged her toward the bed. He picked her up and slammed her onto the mattress, climbed on top of her, pinning her underneath his weight.

"L-l-l-l-listen, you ungrateful cunt," he whispered, straining to hold her down. "By God, I'll make you be still." He slapped her twice. Bessie quit struggling. They lay pressed together, panting, Bessie trying not to gag at the fishy reek of Billy's breath.

"It's Oatha, ain't it?" Bessie said. "He got you into somethin. You changed since you taken up his company." Billy pressed his forearm into his wife's neck and leaned into her windpipe.

"M-m-m-m-make no mistake," he whispered. "One word, I'll fuckin kill ye. Simple as that."

"And your daughter, Billy?" she wheezed. "Gonna kill Harriet, too?" Bessie saw it happen. The madness spilled over in Billy's eyes and she knew he would suffocate her. "All right, baby. All right." She'd been digging her fingernails into his biceps, but now she let go and ran her fingers through his greasy sandy-blond hair. "Billy." She couldn't produce anything louder than a whisper. "Billy, I can't breathe."

It passed. He let up on his wife's neck, but he still lay sprawled on top of her as she coughed and gasped for air.

"You gonna make me kill you one a these days," Billy said.

All Bessie could do was stare into his twitching eyes. It wasn't anger she felt toward him. Not anymore. Only fear and profound sadness, because so little about him resembled the person she'd married in West Tennessee at fourteen. That sweet and tender boy felt as distant as her father, long dead from stone on the chest.

Her eyes caught on the bottle of seashells in the window. She thought of that happy summer in '89 when they'd taken a steamboat down the Mississippi to visit Billy's brother on the Gulf Coast. It was the first and last time she'd seen the ocean, but she'd never lost the smell of it or forgotten the cool shock of salt water running under her feet that morning she and Billy had walked the beach together collecting those shells.

Billy rolled off of her and sat up.

Bessie touched the swelling knot on top of her head.

"You never beat me in Tennessee."

"When'd you give me cause? Now . . . this gold. We got a problem?"

"No, Billy."

"W-w-w-w-well, all right, then."

He sighed and got up from the bed, walked back over to the table, knelt down. Harriet still had her head buried in her gingham dress, so all he could see of her was a battery of black curls.

"Come on out a there now, girl. Me and your mama is all right. Sometimes adults have to talk things out, find a remedy for a situation." The little girl lifted her head, eyes still brimming with tears. "Come on now, honey. Your doll's over there on the floor all alone. She's upset, too. What's her name?"

"Samantha."

"You just gonna leave Samantha over there to cry by herself? Ain't you her mama now?" As Harriet crawled out from underneath the table, Billy said, "Well, how's about we crack open a can a oysters. It's Christmas after all, ain't it?" And Billy flashed Bessie his broken-tooth smile, Bessie thinking, *I don't know if it's this town or Oatha that done it, but you ain't the same. This thin air's poisoned you. Ain't my Billy no more. I've lost you.*

TWENTY-ONE

Christmas morning, Oatha Wallace slung his oilskin slicker over the coat-rack and breathed in the smell of Joss Maddox's cigarette.

"Comin down, huh?" she called out from behind the bar.

Oatha removed his slouch hat, beat the felt brim against his leg to dislodge the snow, and replaced it on the tangle of wavy black hair that fell to his shoulders. He strode to the pine bar, where Joss had already poured two tumblers of whiskey and uncapped a bottle of Pabst Blue Ribbon.

"So," she said. "How merry of a Christmas is it?"

He opened his coat, reached into the inner pocket.

"We got there with both feet."

When Joss saw the bar of gold, she went moist between her legs, reached out and touched Oatha's hand. He drank both tumblers and took a long pull of beer. "Tell me, Jossy—"

"Joss."

"Damn, you're snorty. Who's the woman across the street, sittin up in that bay window? She watches me ever time I pass by."

"Molly Madsen, and you ain't special. She watches everyone."

"What is she, a lunger, up here for the rarified air?"

"No, ten years ago, her husband sent her out here to set up a home. He knew Bart somehow, was gonna assay for the mine. Well, he never came. Never wrote. Just up and quit her." Oatha smiled.

"Bart felt awful about it, put Molly up in the hotel when she finally ran out a money. Been supportin her ever since. What I've heard, Molly went crazy as a sheepherder over it. Hasn't left that room in five years. Still thinks her husband's comin for her."

"Had a feeling she was sent for supplies." He pointed at the tumblers. She filled them. He drank again, then stepped quietly over to the potbellied stove, so as not to rouse Al, the deputy, who'd once again drunk himself into an unconscious stupor. Oatha warmed his hands, which were heavily calloused and perennially black with mine dust and grime. He wore thirty-year-old garments from his stint fighting for the Confederacy—gray trousers and a matching double-breasted frock coat with pewter buttons. There was a single row of braids on the left sleeve, denoting his rank as junior officer in the infantry. He'd long since ripped off all other insignia. Old wax drippings marred the shoulders of his frock coat, a telltale sign of his employment with the mine.

Lana sat at the piano, having come to the saloon at first light.

Oatha walked over, stood watching her play.

When she'd finished the song, he clapped, put his hands on her shoulders, said, "Merry Christmas, Miss Hartman. You sure do a beautiful job fillin out that corset and camisole, if you don't mind me sayin. I was wonderin if you'd take a walk across the street to the hotel. Thought you and me could exchange presents. I'd sure fancy a trim—"

"Oath." Joss said his name softly, but her voice cracked with rage, her black eyes smoldering. "Come here. Quit pirootin—"

"I'm talkin with Miss Hartman at the moment. I'd extend you the same opportunity, but seein as how you're presently chained—"

"Son of a bitch. Put this plain. I'll cut off your grapefruits."

Lana fixed her gaze on the yellowed ivory keys, paling, trembling.

Oatha sidled back up to the bar.

"Why you so knotted up? You her fuckin madam?"

Joss smiled and made a move so deft and graceful, the next thing Oatha knew, the right side of his face had slammed against the bar, Joss cradling his head, a cold knife point digging into his left ear.

"Swear to God," Joss whispered, wisps of her black hair tickling his mustache, "I'll jam it straight through whatever brains you got left in there. Go on playin now, Lana. It's all right. You won't be bothered no more." Oatha chuckled, though he didn't dare move. From his tilted vantage point, he could see Al, a half grin on the lawman's face as he shaded in oblivious repose beside the stove.

"Joss, would you accuse me of exaggeration if I said that is the most useless cocksucker I ever laid eyes on?"

"Al?"

"Yeah."

"No, I wouldn't contradict that statement. Now I'm gonna let you up, and you and me is gonna come off the rimrock. Behave yourself."

Joss released him, shoved the bowie back into its leather sheath under the bar. She set up two tumblers while Oatha retrieved his hat. They raised their glasses.

"To your impending release," Oatha whispered.

They clinked and drank. Joss glanced at the sleeping deputy, then whispered, "How'd it go last night with ol' Bartholomew?"

"It went."

"Smoothly? Without incident?"

"Well, by the end of the proceedings, Bart sure as shootin wished he'd never yapped to you about them bars."

"What I mean is, you did it quick, right? There weren't no need to drag it out, make things any harder on the man than necessary."

"Billy fucked it up."

"How?"

"Particulars ain't important. It got done what needed to get done."

"You sayin the boy was rough on him?"

"Well, Billy hadn't never done nothin like it before. He got carried away, but—"

"That little shit." Oatha withdrew a scrap of paper from his flap pocket, slid it across the bar. Joss unfolded it, saw where Oatha had scribbled something on a torn-out Montgomery Ward page advertising hobnailed miners' boots. "Fuck is this?"

"Wrote it last night. Notes for what you need to do tomorrow when I come back for you."

She lifted her suspenders and slipped the paper into the patch pocket of her plaid dress shirt. "What of the boy? You trust him?"

"Shit no, but what other choice I got? Can't play a lone hand, haul it all up there myself, can I?"

"Oath—"

"It'll get taken care of. You just worry about them notes I made for you. We do this right, everthing'll work out. Now this child's gotta haul out. This ain't gonna be easy in a blizzard."

"Know this. When the time comes, I'll be the one to take care a that hobble-tongue chore boy."

"Joss—"

"Ain't arguin with you about it. He gave Bart a rough shake, boy gonna by God learn somethin about pain on his way to hell."

Oatha headed for the coatrack. He'd just done the last button on his slicker and reached for the door when Joss called his name. He turned back. She held up the piece of paper he'd given her.

"Before I say this," she said, "let me warn you. If I see a grin, a smirk, a eye roll, one fuckin hint a condescension—"

"Jesus Christ, chew it finer. I gotta go get Billy."

She shook the paper. "Can't use this."

"What does that mean?"

"It means I can't *use* it, Oatha."

"Oh." He started back toward the bar.

"I said, not a fuckin word."

"I just said 'Oh.' It ain't a judgment. Why didn't you tell me this when I give it to you in the first place? Think I give two shits whether you can read or not?"

2009

TWENTY-TWO

Abigail returned to consciousness, aware of only two things—the staggering pain in her head and the echo of voices, one of them her father's.

"Don't say that to me again, Lawrence. You know exactly why we're here. And now that your partner's out of commission—"

"I swear to you, I—"

"Ain't believing this. Motherfucker *wants* me to take him apart."

"Put away the knife, Isaiah. He's gonna talk. I can feel it."

"That true, Larry? My man Stu know some shit I don't?"

"This is just a huge—"

"Misunderstanding?"

"Yeah, a huge—"

"Oh no, no, no. All right, Lar. After I slice off your thumbs, we'll continue this—"

"Okay, I'll—"

"No, I think I better go ahead—"

"We have to go to Emerald House."

"Big mansion up the trail?"

"Yeah."

Abigail opened her right eye. It took five seconds for the darkness to sharpen into focus. She sat with Lawrence, Emmett, and June inside one of the ghost town's structures, her hands bound behind her back. It all looked familiar—the archways, the collapsed staircase, the climbing rope still dangling from the second floor. Three men—she assumed they were men—dressed in night camouflage and face masks busied themselves packing an assortment of equipment into black backpacks.

Under the archway leading into the lounge, Scott lay holding his abdomen, moaning softly. She wondered if Jerrod's body had just been left in the street.

Didn't I shoot someone in that old house?

She leaned into Lawrence, whispered, "What's happening?" As he turned, she saw that his right eye had been closed from a vicious blow.

"I don't know yet, but . . ." One of the men finished zipping his backpack and walked over, crouched down in front of Abigail.

"Dirty Harriet," he said, grinning a big mouthful of straight white teeth through a slit in the face mask. She recognized his voice. It belonged to the man who'd threatened Lawrence. Isaiah. "Bad with that little Ruger, ain't you? You'd have killed my man, Stu, if he hadn't been sportin Kevlar. Nasty cut over your eye. Needs stitches." He pulled a roll of medical tape from his pocket, tore off a strip. "But this'll have to do." She groaned when he pinched the gash above her left eyebrow closed and slapped on the tape. Then Isaiah and his partners donned black parkas and trousers over their coveralls, each man also wearing black neoprene gloves and Gore-Tex-lined leather combat boots. One of them pulled a fifth of Ketel One out of his pack, unscrewed the cap, took a long drink.

"Stu, what the fuck?"

"You want my hands to shake? Besides, my ribs are killing me. Might be cracked."

"So take a fuckin aspirin."

Isaiah came and squatted down, facing June, Emmett, Abigail, and Lawrence.

He looked them over, said, "In a minute, we're gonna cut your nylon restraints. You'll be free to move, but I would advise you to follow my orders. To. The. *Let*. Ter." He held up a machine pistol. "Let me tell you about this work of art. Custom Glock Eighteen. Automatic. Supressor. Aimpoint. Thirty-three cart mag. We each have one, and we won't hesitate to aerate your ass if you deviate one millimeter from our directives. Ain't gonna be no love tap from a Taser, you fuck up again. You feel me?" Nods. "Can I get a 'yessir'?"

He pointed the machine pistol at June.

"Yessir."

Then he aimed it at Emmett.

"Yessir."

"What about Scott?" Abigail said, nodding toward the archway.

"Motherfucker look like he can walk to you? He had a seizure before you woke up." Isaiah leaned in toward Abigail, their faces barely an inch apart. His breath smelled of cinnamon chewing gum.

Two years ago, while waiting to catch a cab after a Christmas party in the East Village, she'd felt something push into her back, followed by low, menacing words in her ear: "Wanna die tonight, bitch?" She'd never seen his face, just listened to his footsteps running up the sidewalk thirty seconds later. He'd taken her purse, earrings, necklace, and left her with something that ruled her even to this moment—the ever-present knowledge of how fast a normal day, a normal evening, could turn into her being raped and bleeding out on the sidewalk. No such thing as safety or control. The worst moments of your life you never see coming, although she had to admit something had seemed wrong about this trip since the previous morning at the trailhead, when she'd caught that look between Scott and Lawrence. Had they known this was coming?

The man called Isaiah still spoke to her.

"That your boyfriend? Y'all fucking? What?" She shook her head. "I poked him in the gut. Be dead in an hour. Maybe less. Painful way to go. But if you'd rather stay with him"—he slid a Fairbairn-Sykes from an ankle sheath and pressed the knife point under her right eye—"I'll be happy to leave you here, because the truth, bitch, is that I don't need you."

Abigail stared into his large white eyes through the holes in the mask. They reminded her of eggs. She felt his sweet breath on her mouth, the cold of the blade against her cheek. She shook her head again.

"That's what the fuck I thought. Now, I didn't get my 'yessir' from you."

TWENTY-THREE

The orders were brutally simple. Walk. Keep quiet. Step out of line, you get shot. Lights on at all times. They'd even given Abigail fresh batteries for her headlamp.

Isaiah led the way, the four captives following single file, his partners bringing up the rear. Abigail walked between Lawrence and June, snow already accumulating in the grass and on Abandon's splintered remnants. With her hands free, she'd managed to scrape the dried blood out of her left eye. She could see now, but her head still throbbed like hell and her bones felt weak and jittery, her nervous system torqued from the Taser.

They passed their campsite on the outskirts, the llamas huddled between the tents. Abigail lusted after the cell phone in her pack.

Soon they'd left Abandon, gotten a half mile up-canyon, the ruts of the old wagon trail filling with snow and nothing to see but the flakes passing horizontally through the headlamps' beams, tiny planets of light in that galaxy of darkness and wind. Abigail heard June struggling to stifle sobs. She reached back, felt June squeeze her hand, tears gliding down Abigail's face now as she tried to comprehend the murder of Jerrod, Scott tied up alone as he bled to death in that degenerated hotel, and how in God's name she was walking at gunpoint through a snowstorm in this secluded canyon, too horrified even to contemplate what their captors intended to do with them.

Isaiah veered off the main trail.

They climbed narrow switchbacks up the hillside.

Soon the procession was four hundred feet above the canyon floor, scrambling over scree. Through the gap between the mountains, Abigail walked so close to her father that the steel toes of her Asolo boots occasionally banged into his heels. She thought she heard the trickle of running water—a stream, a spring perhaps.

. . .

Another half mile and they'd come to the edge of a lake. It stood mostly un-
frozen, the wind pushing ripples that lapped at the fragile ice extending out
a foot from the bank. Isaiah had started in the direction that would take
them around the north side when Lawrence said, "That's not the best route."
Isaiah stopped, looked back. "There's a rock glacier on that end, a quarter
mile ahead. Drops right into the lake. It's steep. Very dangerous. Our party
had a near miss yesterday with this type of situation."

"You know I trust you, Larry, but do you know why?"

"No. No, sir."

"Because I know that you know I will fuck your ass up if you give me bad
information."

They followed the south shore around Emerald Lake. Deep in the basin,
the wind had died. Snow fell vertically again, and aside from the whisper of
its collection, there was no sound save for the labored breathing of the party
and the squeak of boots in the inch of new snow. Across the lake lay the rock
glacier—boulders shifting, smashing into one another. From several hundred yards away, their collisions sounded like small-caliber gunshots.

Stu yelled suddenly from behind, "Hey, what's . . . what was that? You see
that?"

Everyone stopped.

"What you got?" Isaiah said, reaching for his machine pistol.

"I saw a light."

"Where? I don't see anything."

"Straight ahead." As Abigail stared into the distance, she didn't see a light
either, only the hulking shadow of Emerald House. "I'm telling you, Isaiah, it
didn't last long, but this light or candle, whatever it was, just winked on and
off."

"What floor was it on?"

"I don't know. It happened so fast."

"Anyone else see this light?" No one answered. "Larry? You the expert."

"No one's lived there in a hundred and sixteen years."

"I'm just telling you what I saw," Stu said. "Maybe I'm a little—"

"Fucked-up is what. You got every other day of your life to be a drunk
motherfucker. I need you to hold your shit together tonight. You do that for
me?"

"Yeah, Isaiah. Sorry."

Abigail filled with apprehension as she walked the last hundred yards to
Emerald House. She'd never seen anything like it—this rambling edifice enveloped in darkness and silence and ruin, the corpse of what it had once
been.

Wet snow clung to the facade. Windows busted out. Shingles peeled off. Four-story chimneys toppled into piles of rock. The north wing was a shambles but intact, its southern counterpart long since collapsed on itself, the winter snows crushing it through the years, until all that remained was the foundation and a small mountain of demolished framework.

Isaiah followed the stone pathway up to the portico, passing between the massive rotting Douglas fir trunks. Yellow notices had been stapled to the oak doors—Forest Service warnings regarding the instability of Emerald House, threatening all trespassers with aggressive prosecution. A feeble attempt had been made to chain the iron handles together.

Isaiah called out, "Bolt cutter," and Stu came forward with his pack, unzipped it, and produced the requested tool. One easy snip and the chain fell onto the sandstone. Isaiah grabbed the door handles, hesitated. "Larry," he called out. "It would be awfully tragic if some heavy shit was to fall on my head. Why don't you come do the honors?"

Abigail watched her father walk under the portico.

"Your show now," Isaiah said as Lawrence pushed open the doors and led the way inside.

TWENTY-FOUR

Jesus, this place is huge." Isaiah let the beam of his headlamp pass through the foyer. "My light doesn't even reach the far end. We safe in here, Lar?"

"No, but this is the most stable part of Packer's mansion."

The foyer smelled dank, redolent of mildew and wet wood. From her spot in line, Abigail shone her light on the cracked marble floor, saw piles of scat, puddles of ice. Through a hole in the roof, snowflakes drifted down. She removed one of her mittens, let her fingertips graze the stone wall—cold and soft and wet, carpeted in dead lichen.

"There's a journal in my pack," Lawrence said. "I need to see it."

Isaiah unzipped it, pulled out a black spiral-bound notebook. As Lawrence took it and sat down on the cascading staircase, Abigail couldn't stop herself. "What's going on here, Lawrence?"

Isaiah grinned. "You don't know?" He laughed, his southern-tinged voice reverberating through the foyer. "Nice, Larry. Very nice. More I get to know you, more I like you."

When Abigail aimed her light in her father's face, she recognized the guilt and the circuit closed, connecting on some primordial level to that girl who still inhabited her, and a subconscious memory, twenty-six years old, of that exact look of shame when her daddy had slipped into her bedroom one night to say that he had to go away.

"What have you done?"

"I'm sorry, Abby. I'm so sorry."

"For what? Tell me." Isaiah's hand passed through the beam of light. She fell. The darkness tingled. Emmett started forward, but his nose ran into the barrel of Stu's machine pistol. He held up his hands, retreated.

Isaiah knelt down, grabbed Abigail's ponytail, lifting her head so their eyes met. "My man's got some serious shit to attend to. Next time, the fist will be closed. You'll lose teeth. Now get the fuck up." He jerked her by her hair, pulling her to her feet. "And shut the fuck up."

"That isn't necessary," Lawrence said, his voice trembling.

"Tend to your notebook," Stu warned.

Abigail touched her cheek. The bruise burned.

"All right, Lar. Where we going?"

"I'm not a hundred percent sure, since I haven't actually seen it. This is all theoretical, based on my research. I was gonna try to find it on this expedition."

"You bullshitin me, Larry? Don't make me—"

"Will you give me two damn minutes here? I'm not saying I can't take you to it. I just need more time." Lawrence studied his notebook, flipping through several pages.

Somewhere nearby, water dripped, followed by a faint and distant scratching. From high above, came the chirp of a pika. Lawrence finally closed his notebook, stood up. "Bart's wing."

"Lead the way."

Lawrence guided them out of the foyer, toward the staircase that rose up the center of Emerald House. "Last one of these we went up collapsed," he said to Isaiah.

"You haven't been up here?"

"Not since last summer. I'm sure it's weakened."

"Then you best tread lightly. I'll be behind you."

Abigail was third in line, and to her relief, this staircase felt much sturdier than that flimsy death trap in the hotel. Part of the banister was missing, but none of the steps creaked.

As they reached the next floor, Stu whispered, "Isaiah, hold up. I hear something."

Their beams of light swept through what remained of the second level—tall door frames and window frames, three wings still intact, the south reduced to a hole so gaping, you could drive a bus through it, snow blowing sideways into the mansion and slowly rotting everything it touched. Another winter or two, the water damage would reach the stairwell.

"Stu, I don't know what I'm gonna do if this is another false—"

Isaiah suddenly lifted his machine pistol, motioned for his partners to do the same. Abigail heard it, too—the rapid patter of footsteps. Isaiah and Stu moved soundlessly, side by side, away from the stairs, toward the west wing.

Twenty feet in, Isaiah stopped and held up his hand, pointing at a closed door a little ways into the passage. Isaiah looked at Stu, counting down from three with the fingers of his right hand. He kicked the door, which exploded back off its rusted hinges.

The mansion filled with earsplitting shrieks, like those of women being murdered. A host of shadows flew out of the room, toward the stairs. June screamed, and amid blinding muzzle flames, Abigail heard panting and the muffled clatter of machine pistols.

A half dozen coyotes blitzed past Abigail, heading down the stairs and into the foyer, their yaps at once jovial and demonic as they escaped through the oak doors into the night.

TWENTY-FIVE

Lawrence led them to the east wing of the second floor. Abigail's head was killing her, and the left side of her face was hot, swollen. Her headlamp revealed a place of absolute decay, the wood-paneled walls warped and blackened with mold. They passed through a small sitting area and arrived at a pair of French doors. Lawrence pushed them open, the hinges grinding rust into rust.

As they entered a short hallway, Lawrence pointed out the first door on the right. "That was Bart's office," he said. "Door on the left opens into the guest room."

Abigail shone her light inside—sparsely furnished, with two single beds, their posts and headboards smashed, mattresses disintegrated into mounds of rotted down, a capsized chest of drawers, fireplace, wardrobe.

They went on, passing large picture frames that had fallen from the walls and lay in pieces on the floor.

"So what you got in that notebook that brought you to this wing?" Isaiah asked.

"In 1889, Packer hired an architect named Bruce Price to design this mansion. I had a breakthrough last winter at the New York Public Library, when I found Price's notes on the final floor plan. The original blueprints don't show this wing's true layout."

Lawrence opened the door at the end of the hall and entered, followed by Isaiah and the rest of the party.

Packer's bedroom formed the eastern extremity of Emerald House—twelve-foot ceilings and large windows still holding glass that in decent weather would've offered a jaw-dropping view of the basin and lake. The walls tapered to a fireplace at the narrow end of the room, spacious enough to roast six-foot logs.

Isaiah motioned to Abigail and the Tozers. "Ya'll sit by the bed and stay quiet." As Abigail sat down beside June, her headlamp brightened the head-board of Packer's bed. She noticed that a word had been carved into the wood, probably by some asshole with no respect for the past, just hoping to memorialize his girlfriend's name: LANA.

It felt good to get off her feet, but her thermal underwear had soaked through with freezing sweat. She unzipped her purple Moonstone parka and her pink fleece jacket.

"I have water in my pack," she said. "May I take it out?"

"Stu, ya'll searched their packs back in Abandon?"

Stu and the other masked man had sat down near the hearth, their ma-chine pistols trained on the captives.

"Yeah. Their packs are fine."

Lawrence stepped through an open doorway beside the entrance to Pack-er's room.

"What's in there?" Isaiah asked.

"This was Bart's closet."

"Motherfucker was livin the good life." They disappeared into the walk-in closet. Abigail couldn't see her father, but she could hear him knocking on the walls.

Lawrence spoke: "If we were to break through this one, we'd be in Bart's office."

"Well, hell, let's be sure."

"I've measured. There's nothing strange about the rooms on this side of the hallway. They match up perfectly with the original architectural plans. Now follow me." Lawrence and Isaiah emerged from the closet and walked back into the hallway. After a moment, Abigail heard Lawrence's voice again, indistinct and followed by more wall knocking.

She worked her arms out of the day pack's straps, reached in, and pulled out a Nalgene bottle, the water pumped and purified from the safe part of the stream that Scott had fly-fished the previous evening. The image of him dying in that hotel lobby felt like a stray ember behind her eyes.

The water tasted cold and faintly sweet, so unlike the lead-tainted piss that ran out of her tap in New York. As she drank, she tried to ignore the red dots that traipsed across her chest.

Lawrence and Isaiah returned to Packer's bedroom.

"This past summer, I made a thorough search of that guest room and found nothing," Lawrence said. "But I knew there was space between that room and Packer's room that was unaccounted for. I was getting ready to investigate Packer's room, when the Forest Service showed up. I didn't have a permit to be here, and the fine would've been huge. I had to sneak out of the lodge." He approached the enormous wardrobe to the right of the doorway, grabbed the side of it, tried to slide it out from the wall. "It's bolted down or something."

"We've got grenades."

"Wanna bring the whole wing down?"

He pulled open the doors, climbed inside, Abigail listening as he banged around. After a moment, she heard "Aha."

Isaiah smiled. "What I like to hear. What you got, baby?"

Lawrence's voice came back muffled. "Entire back panel"—he struggled with something—"slides out." A panel of wood flew out of the wardrobe and crashed onto the floor.

Isaiah was peering in now. "Would you look at that," he said. "You're a genius, Larry." Isaiah pointed at Abigail. "Come here. We may need you. It's a tight fit."

Abigail got up, crossed the floor. She stood beside Isaiah and looked into the wardrobe. With the panel removed, a black steel-hinged door was visible, three feet by two feet.

"Looks like some serious shit," Isaiah said. "Hope for your sake you can open it."

"Well, the bad news is this locking mechanism. Dates back to the 1860s. There are four locks, requiring three different keys." He touched the various keyholes. "Here's the pin tumbler lock. Here's the barrel lock. These two are bit styles."

"Ah fuck. We are gonna have to toss a couple grenades in here."

"Won't do anything. If this is the kind of door I suspect it is"—he rapped his knuckles on it—"it's made of ten layered one-eighth-inch steel sheets. But there's some good news, too."

"Pins and needles, Lar."

"See here? Three of the locks are already open. Only thing standing in our way is this bit lock, which has a turned bolt sealing the door."

"So what do we do?"

Lawrence faced Isaiah. "I'll be needing a guarantee."

"A guarantee."

"I spent the last ten years trying to find what's in here. Now, I'm willing to let it go—"

"That's a relief."

"—if I have your assurance none of us will be harmed. Give me that, I'll get you inside."

"That'll put your little heart at ease?"

"It will."

"Yeah, all right, Larry. You get me in there, you'll all walk out of these mountains."

"That's the truth?"

"You questioning the word of a marine?"

Lawrence let his pack drop to the floor. He unzipped the outer pocket, scrounged inside. After a moment, he withdrew something, held it up in the light of his headlamp.

Isaiah grinned through his mask at the long, toothed key. "Where'd you get that?"

"Found it in a safe in Bart's office last summer. I don't know for certain that this will open that bit lock, but it is the right type of key for it."

"And what do we think is in there?" Abigail asked.

"Summer of 1871, Bart Packer was broke and prospecting alone in the Sangre de Cristo Mountains. One afternoon, he got stuck above timberline in a thunderstorm. Found an overhang high on the mountain, took shelter there. He was waiting for the storm to pass when he felt an icy draft coming from behind. He turned around, noticed an opening in the rock, and crawled through it. When he got his candle lit, he found himself in a large chamber, and not ten feet away sat a headless skeleton clad in Spanish armor. Bart correctly deduced that he was looking at a conquistador, who'd most likely been in that cave since the 1500s. What lay beside the bones of this ancient conqueror was a pyramid of gold bars, ninety-one in all, twenty-two pounds apiece. That's about a ton of pure gold.

"When Abandon was in its heyday, it would've been worth six-hundred and sixty thousand dollars. Today, with gold trading at eight hundred and two dollars an ounce, Bart's ninety-one bars are worth over twenty-five million. Now, there may not be ninety-one bars in here. But even if he spent half of that, twelve and a half mil's a good payday."

"And you were just using this expedition as an excuse to find this gold?" Abigail said. "What were you planning to do? Sneak off with it without telling anyone?"

"No, of course not. Scott and I—"

"Scott knew?" Suddenly, that look between Scott and her father at the trailhead made perfect sense.

"—couldn't haul it all out ourselves. That's seventeen miles, and even if everyone carried as much weight as they possibly could, it'd take at least two or three trips. Besides, it's not just about the dollar value. Abigail, this was going to be a huge historical—"

"You son of a bitch. You selfish son—"

"Time to open that motherfucker, Lar."

Lawrence sighed, turned away from his daughter.

He took his time, delicately working the key into the lock.

The key turned and the mechanism clicked.

"It worked," Lawrence whispered. He grabbed the handle, and when he'd heaved open the steel door, Isaiah shoved him aside and climbed into the wardrobe, his headlamp shining into a secret room the size of Packer's walk-in closet—walls, floor, and ceiling made of stone.

"You're fuckin kidding me."

TWENTY-SIX

L arry, where are my gold bars?"

"I don't understand. They should be in there."

Isaiah shoved Lawrence out of the wardrobe. "Sit down!" he yelled at Abigail. "Not you, Larry." Isaiah backed Lawrence up against one of the giant windows.

"I'm telling you. They should be there. Maybe someone else—"

"You holding out on me?" Isaiah unsnapped the ankle sheath under his trousers.

"I swear," Lawrence said. "They should've been in there. I don't know—"

"Maybe that's the case," Isaiah said, then suddenly pressed the sharp, thin bone of his forearm into Lawrence's neck. "But how do I know? *Really. Know.* You aren't lying?"

"I swear to you I'm not. Please—"

"Words don't convince me, Larry, but you know what does? Pain. For instance." Isaiah gently removed Lawrence's glasses, dropped them on the floor, crushed them under his boot heel. "I'm gonna cut out your right eye—"

Abigail's stomach turned. *Not happening.*

"No, please—"

Isaiah leaned harder into Lawrence's windpipe, briefly cutting off his air supply.

"—and give you thirty seconds to rethink your answer. If you're still maintaining you don't know where they are, I may be more inclined to believe you. Know why?" Lawrence shook his head, eyes bulging. "Because right now you don't understand what real pain is. You think you do. You don't. But when I'm holding your warm eyeball in the palm of my hand, you're gonna have a much better idea. You'll know that I'm willing and fully capable of taking you apart piece by piece. This is not about torture. It's about me knowing in my heart that you're telling the truth."

"Isaiah, just listen. I need a minute to—"

"Sorry, Larry. This is the only way."

"Stop it, please," Abigail begged. "He's my father. He doesn't know."

"Yeah, well, we're about to find that out for certain."

Isaiah set the point of the dagger under the lower lid of Lawrence's right eye.

Lawrence struggled to cover his face.

"Hold still, goddamn it! Want me to accidentally push this into your brain?"

Abigail jumped up and lunged for Isaiah, but someone tackled her from behind.

She tried to fight him off, but he had her by the wrists in no time, his weight pinning her to the floor.

She stared up into that masked face, inches from her own, didn't smell vodka, reasoned it couldn't be Stu. What she could see of his eyes seemed strangely comforting, something familiar about them, so deep, burdened. *Because you recognize them.*

Abigail whispered, "You weren't killed. That was an act, for our benefit."

She jerked a wrist free and ripped off the man's mask, saw the scarred, bearded face of their guide, Jerrod Spicer.

"The fuck, Jerrod?" Isaiah said.

"You're with them?" Lawrence said, incredulous.

"She recognized my eyes." Jerrod got up, screamed, "Fuck! *How do we walk away now?"*

"You knew it might come to this," Isaiah said. "That was always a poss—"

"It's already come to a whole helluva lot more than you said it would. Why don't you take off your—"

Isaiah stepped back from Lawrence, ripped off his mask. "Happy?" Abigail's headlamp illuminated the face of a thirty-something black man she would've thought exceptionally handsome under different circumstances, his smooth-shaven features in perfect proportion—pronounced cheekbones, intense mud-colored eyes, dimples that caved when he let loose his broad and malignant smile.

Jerrod lifted off Stu's face mask, and the first thing Abigail noticed were the ringlets of Stu's curly black hair, then the week's worth of stubble, thin lips, sunken, red-rimmed eyes, saddest she'd ever seen. He'd been handsome once, but whatever monster was eating him inside had also sucked the life from his face, drawing it into an ax-thin blade of emaciation.

Jerrod took Isaiah over to the window. Stu got up and joined them. They whispered. Abigail looked at her father. He still stood against the window, knees shaking, crying, the floor wet under his hiking boots and a dark stream sliding down his cheek and into his beard, as if he wept blood. It took him a moment to muster his voice.

"There's one more place to look," Lawrence finally said.

They stopped talking. Isaiah walked over, crowded him up against the glass again.

"Larry, I sincerely pray for your sake you aren't fucking with me."

TWENTY-SEVEN

They made their way back to the stairwell.

"What's up here?" Isaiah asked as they ascended the second flight of steps.

"Servants' quarters." They reached the third floor, this level more devastated by the elements than the first or second. Up ahead, in the west wing, the gabled roof had caved, their headlamps showing snow falling through the ceiling. "We need to go up one more," Lawrence said.

They climbed, wood creaking, bowing where they stepped.

Abigail was the third to emerge into the cupola. She shone her light on walls lined with empty shelves, the books having long since disappeared, taken by vandals or reduced by time and moisture to wads of leather, paper, glue. Two chairs and a sofa had disintegrated on the floor. Half the stones had fallen out of the two hearths. Abigail edged toward an opening in the middle of the floor, peered down, her light beam shining to the ground level.

"All right, Lar. Where is it?"

Lawrence carefully moved over to one of the bookshelves and knelt down, the floor cracking. When he stood again, he held an eight-foot brass pole, severely tarnished, with a hooked end. He looked up. They all looked up, lights converging on a square door in the ceiling. Lawrence reached up, unlatched the rusted lock, pushed open the hatch. Snow fell through the hole into the library.

"You been up there before, Lar?"

"No. I always thought it was too dangerous. If the floor were to give way, it's a fifty-foot fall. But all things considered, I think it's worth the risk."

"How the hell we gonna climb up through that hatch?"

Lawrence pointed back to the bookshelf. "With that ladder."

Jerrod and Stu pulled the ladder out from under the long bookshelf, hoisted it up, and braced it against the opening.

"Doesn't exactly look like a Craftsman product," Isaiah said, grazing his gloved hand across a cracked wooden rung.

"I'll go up first. Test it."

"No, she will." He waved Abigail over. "What's up there, Lar?"

"I don't know. Maybe nothing."

"That wouldn't bode well for you, for any of you." He looked at Abigail. "Up you go."

She grasped the sides of the old ladder and began to climb, carefully easing her weight onto each rung. The fourth one snapped, but she caught herself. The tenth rung was missing. As she neared the top, snow collected in her hair. Then she scrambled out of the hatch, stepping onto the roof of Emerald House.

"Stay in one spot!" Lawrence shouted up at her. "I have no idea how stable it is up there!" She backed away from the opening, leaned against the wrought-iron railing that surrounded this small open veranda, snow blowing so hard into her face that she choked on it, had to cover her mouth with her hands.

Lawrence came up, then Isaiah, Emmett, June, and finally Stu and Jerrod.

Abigail rubbed her arms, and as she stood watching her father, it hit her: There was nothing on this veranda but an inch and a half of snow, and he looked nervous in the beam of her headlamp, like he was trying to pass off Monopoly money for true currency.

"Well," Lawrence said, kneeling down, inspecting a corner of the veranda, brushing the snow off the stone. "I'm just at a total loss, Isaiah."

Abigail gripped the iron railing. June and Emmett stood beside her, Isaiah with his back to her, near a skylight that had long since been liberated of its glass.

"*You're* at a loss," Isaiah said. The hood of his parka had fallen back, snow collecting in his black hair. "What exactly does *that* mean, Larry?"

"It means . . . it means I don't know where the gold is. I thought I did, but I don't. I'm horribly disappointed, believe me."

"Sorry to hear that."

"But it just isn't here. I don't know where else to look, and that's the truth. So here's what I'm thinking. We don't know a thing about you, so what if you three just leave us here, disappear into the night. We never see you again. You never see us. And we never say a word. Not even about Scott. We'll pretend this never happened."

"He's right," June said, staving off tears. "Emmett and I would just be so grateful to be home again. To put all this behind us. I'm sorry you didn't find the gold you were looking for, but can't this be over now? You men came wearing masks, which tells me that you didn't come into these mountains intending violence."

"We could just leave, Isaiah," Jerrod said. "Scott and Lawrence know more about me than any of us, but I'd be willing to walk."

Lawrence said, "Look, we could spend tonight in Packer's mansion, give you guys a chance to head out. I'm telling you, it'd be like this never happened."

Isaiah stared at the snow-dusted stone beneath his feet. "Stu," he said, "you got an opinion about this you'd care to toss into the hat?"

"I'm with you, man. Whatever you wanna do, I'm with you."

Isaiah nodded. He turned around, looked at Abigail and the Tozers, who were standing together on the east side of the veranda. He approached them, faced Emmett.

"I don't think I caught your name."

"Emmett Tozer."

"Cool if I call you Em?"

"Sure. June calls me that all the time."

"Well, Em." He pointed at Lawrence. "For this, you can thank that motherfucker."

He raised the machine pistol to Emmett's forehead, a red bead drawn between the man's widening eyes.

June screamed, "No, it's not his fault!"

The Glock coughed a burst of fire, and the back of Emmett's head blew out. He dropped to his knees, fell over sideways. In the low light, the blood looked like steaming oil as it blackened and spread through the snow.

June threw herself over her husband's body, shrieking his name.

Abigail tasted that salt and metal in the back of her throat again. *The worst moments of your life you never see coming.* She turned and spewed over the railing, knew as the bile burned her throat that she'd spend the rest of whatever life she had left trying to sever herself from this moment.

"You happy, Lar, you greedy motherfucker?" Isaiah said, his voice rising.

Abigail sank down into the snow. She could barely hear Isaiah speaking over the wind and June wailing, "Em, come back! Don't you do this!"

"Know what's gonna happen next?" Isaiah was in Lawrence's face now, Lawrence backed up into a corner of the veranda behind the hatch. "I'm gonna make that bitch get down on her knees, and you are gonna watch me put a bullet through her head. Then I'm gonna get—"

Lawrence cried, "No, don't. I'll—"

Isaiah grabbed his throat. "Don't ever fucking interrupt me! Then I'm gonna get this bitch"—he pointed at Abigail—"but I'm not shooting this one. I'm gonna take this knife and slowly cut her throat, let you watch her drain."

Abigail looked at Jerrod, noticed his legs quaking. Stu had pulled the bottle of vodka out of his backpack and begun to work off the cap.

"And then, if you're still maintaining you don't know shit . . ." Abigail made herself stand. She wiped her mouth. ". . . I'm gonna go to work on—"

"Isaiah!" Jerrod yelled.

"What?"

Jerrod started toward him. They met at the skylight, both men covered in snow.

"What the fuck?" He pointed at Emmett's body. "I did not sign up for this shit."

"What are you saying? You want out? That it?"

"I don't—"

"You know, you never had the stones to finish the hard shit, did you?"

"I don't want out. I just . . . You didn't say it'd be like this."

"Well, it is, so stop your fuckin crybabyin."

Isaiah lifted his machine pistol, started toward June, who still lay sobbing on top of her husband. "You watching, Larry?"

"I'll tell you whatever—"

"You can tell me after. Just wanna be sure you know I am not fucking around with you."

He stopped and put the gun to the back of June's head.

Lawrence pushed off the railing, lunged toward Isaiah, screaming, Jerrod and Stu running toward him, Isaiah swinging his machine pistol toward Lawrence, Abigail thinking, *I'm about to watch my father die.*

Lawrence's fourth step brought him past the skylight, and all seven of them suddenly occupied the same twenty-five square feet of floor space.

There was a deep crack, like a rafter fracturing, and the veranda of Emerald House caved in.

1893

TWENTY-EIGHT

The preacher and the Curtices reached Abandon at noon, having descended from the massacre at Emerald House in half the time it had taken them to hike up into the basin. Ezekiel hurried them down the desolate middle of Main and up a side street toward their cabin, his jaw set, eyes more intense than Gloria had seen them in a long while, enveloped in a slow burn.

The preacher said, "Zeke, I think we should alert the town to—"

"Ain't arguin with you about it anymore, Stephen."

"We've got vicious murderers roaming—"

Ezekiel spun around. "Do I come into God's house of a Sunday morning, tell you how to preach a sermon?" Stephen shook his head. "Don't counsel me how to proceed in matters a law."

"Zeke." Gloria grabbed his arm. "Look." The hillside above town was dotted with smoking cabins, half-buried in snow and tucked into groves of tree-line spruce, web-trodden paths branching from each one to the side street. Bessie McCabe staggered toward them along the path from her cabin, Harriet in her arms, neither dressed for the weather, wrapped only in quilts, Bessie's flour-sack underpinnings showing through, and no hat to be seen on mother or child as the snow gathered in their hair. Gloria could see that Bessie's face was flush with cold, the bruises on her left cheek turning purple and yellow around the edges.

"Everthing all right?" Ezekiel asked.

"Seen you comin up the street," she whispered, trembling.

"You're poorly," Gloria said.

Bessie looked downslope toward town, her eyes stormy with the weight of some damning choice. "I believe he's cut his wolf loose."

"Who?" the preacher asked.

Tears were running over her lips now. "My Billy." And Bessie's bare hand emerged from the blankets, grasping the bar of gold, snow falling on it, melting, making the yellow metal glisten. "He give me this this mornin, all wrapped up, like some Christmas present. Wouldn't tell me nothin of how he come to have it."

"Where's your husband right now?" Ezekiel asked.

"He left a few hours ago with Mr. Wallace."

"Know where they went?"

"Rode off toward the mine."

"You better come on with us."

"Why?"

Ezekiel leaned in, whispered in her ear for the sake of the child. "Packer and his ladies been murdered up at Emerald House."

The bar of gold dropped from her hand and sank into the snow.

"What you sayin, Mr. Curtice?"

"In a town of a hunerd twenty-three souls, they ain't much breathin space for coincidence."

"They killed 'em? Billy and Oatha—"

"Nobody knows exactly who done what yet. Now, was it just Billy and Mr. Wallace, or was there more men?"

"I think it's just the two a them. You gonna hurt him?"

"I'm gonna bring him in. Whether or not he gets hurt or kilt, that's his choice. He do that to you?"

Bessie brought her hand to the bruises, as if to hide them, eyes alight with shame.

"Daddy done it," Harriet said.

Ezekiel brushed his gloved hand across the little girl's cheek.

"I'm real sorry about that, sweetie. He ought not've."

Ezekiel squatted down, lifted the gold bar out of the snow, stood mesmerized by it, trying to disavow the shot of adrenaline it pushed through his veins, thinking if there was anything left in him of that man he used to be, he'd ride up to the mine with an entirely different purpose, caught himself half-wishing he'd stumbled onto an opportunity like this back in the old days.

He handed the bar to the preacher. "You better keep this. Well, come on, ladies. No point in y'all standin out here, freezin in them rags."

They walked up the street, then veered onto the path to the Curtices' little steeple-notched cabin, a barrel for a chimney pot, a root cellar on the south wall, and a sod roof that in the summertime sprouted sunflowers. At the front door, Ezekiel stopped, said, "Gloria, bring my rifle and the revolver for Stephen. We'll be needin a box a cartridges for each."

As the women went inside, Stephen said, "I'll not carry a gun, Zeke."

"You kiddin me?"

The preacher shook his head. "But I will ride up with you."

"The hell you gonna do if they start shootin?"

"I'm praying it won't come to that."

"You see the same thing I saw up on the roof a Emerald House? That look like the handiwork a men who talk things out? Hell, we'll have to get Doc now."

Gloria returned with the old Schofield in one hand, Ezekiel's sawed-off Winchester in the other. Bessie was bawling inside, Harriet whispering, "It's all right, Mama. It's all right. Don't cry."

Ezekiel took the box of cartridges, his carbine by the barrel, said, "Man a God don't want the revolver, but you hang on to it. Better pull in the latch-string and fort up. Don't go out. Don't open it for nobody. Billy or Oatha or some rough-lookin feller come by, you know what to do." She nodded. "Better go on, load up that Schofield now. Remember how I showed you?"

Gloria threw her arms around his neck, felt the sandpaper of his face against hers, caught that smell of his that still melted her knees. "You come back to me," she whispered.

He lifted his hat and pulled off Gloria's sealskin cap so he could kiss her forehead and tug at those blond curls.

"Always have, Glori. Always will."

TWENTY-NINE

The cabin of Russell and Emma Ilg stood a hundred yards north of the Curtice homestead and was unprotected by trees, so the snow had drifted to the roof on the windward side. Ezekiel followed the snow tunnel up to the front porch and pounded on the door.

When it opened, a man with disheveled sandy-blond hair and thick spectacles grinned at them. He wore a brown sack coat and matching trousers, and his enormous mustache was freshly combed and waxed. The scent of soap emanated from him, the sour spice of whiskey on his breath.

Over Russell's shoulder, Ezekiel saw Mrs. Ilg carrying a pot from her cookstove to a candlelit dinner table already sagging under its load of steaming graniteware.

A fire blazed in the hearth and balled-up pages of newspaper lay around the base of the spruce tree; their gifts—mostly homemade crafts—were lined up on the makeshift log mantel.

"Merry Christmas, Zeke. Stephen."

"Tell me you ain't fixin to eat, Doc."

"Yeah, in about five minutes. Something wrong?"

"I really hate to do this to you—"

"What?"

"You ain't roostered, are you?"

"Had a nip of whiskey in my coffee a bit ago."

"A nip."

"I ain't drunk, Zeke. What's the problem?"

Mrs. Ilg walked over, her silvering hair pinned up, purple evening gown flowing across the dirt floor in her wake.

"I'd rather say in private."

"Merry Christmas, gentlemen," Mrs. Ilg said.

Ezekiel and Stephen tipped their hats.

"Ma'am."

"Ma'am."

"Well, do we have time to eat first?" Russell asked.

" 'Fraid not."

"What's going on here, Zeke?"

"We're having to borrow your husband. I apologize for the poor timing. It can't be—"

"I've been cooking all morning. Can't it wait just an—"

"Honey, if they need me now, they need me now."

"Doc, we'll be waitin for you at the stables. Best bring your possibles and your rifle. Don't dawdle. We gotta light a shuck on this."

The livery had been erected a quarter mile north of town to save the residents from the persistent stench, but the wind, when it blew, tended to sweep in from the north, so it carried the odor of shit and trail-worn animals right up Main. In the boom years, the stink was eye-watering, even on the south end of town. But on Christmas Day in 1893, you couldn't smell the stables until you saw them.

Ezekiel struck out with the preacher and the doctor, the sheriff astride a moon-eyed bay gelding he'd purchased in Silverton that fall. They rode through Abandon and up-canyon toward the Godsend, the horses sinking to their knees, the riders' heads bowed, hat brims shielding them from the heavy slanting snow.

At the turnoff to Emerald Lake, they picked up the only tracks they'd seen—a ten-burro head-and-tail string led by two horses.

"Can you think of a reason somebody'd be quick-freightin up to the Godsend on Christmas when the mine's shut down?" Russell asked.

"Sure can't. And from the look of it, these poor animals are carryin some load. Probably sinkin past their stomachs."

They rode on, the sides of the canyon closing in, the blizzard diminishing their world until they could see only the tracks they followed. Another mile through deepening powder and Packer's twenty-stamp operation appeared in the distance, a multilevel mill built into the back of the canyon, flanked by the mine office, lower boardinghouse, and a blacksmith shop.

"Strange not to hear those stamps," Stephen said.

They stopped twenty yards from the mill, Ezekiel, already cold, beginning to shiver. "That's a concern," he said, pointing to where the tracks continued on, not toward the mine, as he'd anticipated, but up the south slope of the canyon.

"You don't reckon Oatha and Billy were foolish enough to drive that pack train up to the Sawblade?" Russell said.

"Well, unfortunately it looks that way, don't it?"

"That's desperate behavior. I don't like taking the dugway to the Sawblade in July, when the snow's gone."

"The hell they got to lose? They murdered five people last night."

"I'm fair tired of this snow, and I don't relish the chore it'll be getting our horses up there."

"Well, Doc, I don't, either. I'd rather be back with Glori at the cabin, sittin by the fire, sippin whiskey, but that don't appear to be in my immediate future." A great wedge of snow slid off the mill's sloped roof. The horses startled.

The preacher said, "Y'all think that slope could slide on us?"

"Yeah," Russell said. "I think it's entirely possible."

The three riders followed the tracks away from the mill. At the canyon's end, they paused, gazed up the smooth white slope, Ezekiel counting five switchbacks before the burro trail vanished into the roiling snow-swollen clouds.

"Two thousand feet up. Madness, Zeke. Pure madness."

"I know it, Doc, and you're slick-heeled. Hope that cremello a yours is clear-footed."

"Don't worry. She may be light in the timber, but she's lady-broke and she's got bottom."

Ezekiel spurred his horse on and the riders began to climb.

THIRTY

They followed the burro trail up the slope, snow clinging to their slickers and greatcoats and hats and the horses and rigs and rifle butt plates and every other conceivable surface, until they resembled a trio of ghosts conjured up out of the snow.

Ezekiel rode point, holding his saddle horn, head lowered to the storm. The other men didn't see it, but he smiled, even more immersed in the moment than when he'd emerged onto the roof of Emerald House several hours prior and witnessed the slaughter that had occurred there.

This last year, he'd existed in a state of numbness so complete, it felt like living death. In bed with Gloria, it would often be well past midnight, occasionally dawn, before he drifted into sleep, so intense were the memories of those exuberant, passionate, bloody Leadville years, his mind blazing back at full bore, trying to unblur the faces, invoke the familiar voices, and tears coming when he did, because they brought with them the fleeting sensation of freedom and his old swagger and the limitless potential every morning had once afforded him. He'd never lain in bed in Leadville, obsessing on the past. It had all been vivid rushing present. Fuck even the future.

One night, he'd recall a week spent specking with the boys near Crested Butte. Another, the rowdy drunken revelry of a Fourth of July celebration. Then he'd imagine himself sitting at a corner table in some bucket of blood, three in the morning, brimming with whiskey as the calico queens hung on his shoulders, watching the paling demeanors of his opponents on the final hand, when he pushed forward his pair of nickel-plated Smith & Wesson revolvers with their mother-of-pearl grips, upping the pot for the flush he held.

Sometimes, he'd just lie there retrieving faces—whores he'd felt tender toward, men he'd fought, men he'd loved, killed, buried—savoring them all, every face, repressed scent, lost sound, with a sweet and piercing nostalgia.

Gus, especially Gus, kept him up nights, Ezekiel's lips moving in the dark as he spoke for them both—father-son conversations of God and love, guns and horses. Once Gloria had woken, asked, "Who you talking to, baby?" And he'd lied, told her he must've been whispering in his sleep. He loved his wife beyond words, but Gus, only Gus, had filled that vacancy, destroyed the angry, restless boredom left in the wake of his outlaw days.

But this Christmas, with his head bowed as the sky hemorrhaged snow, his mind blissfully attended to the present, to keeping his horse on the mountain, to listening for slides over the sounds of wind and snow pelting the leather of his hat, and how his feet had grown cold in the calfskin-lined cowhide boots, and what it would feel like to draw a bead on Oatha and Billy, see what they'd stolen from Bart.

Ezekiel was as happy as he'd been in years.

He felt like the true translation of himself again.

An hour into the climb, they stopped to let the horses blow.

"How close you reckon we are?" Russell asked.

Ezekiel shook his head. He had no way of knowing for certain, since after thirty yards in either direction, the trail disappeared into mist. They pushed on again, the horses panting and snorting, pausing every few steps.

Then the slope began to level out. Ezekiel found that he didn't have to lean forward as much and the horses quickened their gait.

He finally halted his gelding, and the others came up beside him on his left, the Doc and the preacher still engrossed in the discussion they'd been having for the last four hundred vertical feet.

"I'm not saying you sull around, but you do strike me as a melancholic these days," Russell said. "Are you daunsy?"

"I'd not deny it."

"You sleeping peacefully?"

"Not often. My mind tends to race in the silence and I don't know how to shut it off. I have these terrible headaches."

Ezekiel studied the distance. His back ached. The burro tracks continued on as far as he could see, which wasn't far in the blizzard. He suspected the pass lay just ahead.

"Do you ever experience desperate thoughts?" the doctor asked.

"Desperate? You mean like ending myself prematurely?"

"That's exactly what I mean."

"It's a grave sin, Russ."

"I'm aware. Don't mean it ain't afflicting you."

"I have, on occasion, considered it."

"Recently?"

"Last night."

At this elevation, no trees could thrive, but glancing up ahead, Ezekiel discerned a badlands—vague profiles of rock formations and a small boulder field, drenched in snow and looming like a herd of Gothic monoliths. He turned to his compatriots. Their conversation embarrassed him, a subject he felt uncomfortable being made privy to, though that wasn't his reason for interrupting. It was merely to advise the Doc to slide his Big Fifty out of the rifle scabbard and keep on the eye in case they were dry-gulched.

Russell said, "You should come by my office, Stephen, let me examine you. Your gums have a blue tinge. Absent a full evaluation, I can't say for sure, but it could be lead—"

"Doc, I'm sorry to break up your conversation, but—"

The ball made a loud crunch as it entered Russell Ilg's head through his left eye, taking a large shard of his skull with it on the way out. Then came the thunderous boom that Ezekiel recognized as a big-bore six-gun. The lead ball had knocked Russell from the horse, but his stovepipe boots had caught up in the stirrups, so that he hung upside down, the contents of his skull dropping into the snow as his horse dragged him back down the slope.

Ezekiel dismounted. The snow rose to his waist. He grabbed the Winchester, yelled at Stephen as another report spooked the horses.

"Get off a there, man! *You* wanna *get kilt?*"

But the preacher sat stone-faced and frozen in the saddle, staring through falling snow at the two figures darting through the boulder field.

Ezekiel pulled Stephen's boots out of the stirrups and knocked him off his mount into the snow. "Get back down the slope and stay hid. Take Doc's rifle if you want and keep your head down."

A shotgun blasted, and Ezekiel's horse boiled over, neighing and rearing up on its hindquarters before collapsing.

He crouched in the snow, eyes peeking over the surface as the preacher crawled away, weeping.

Ezekiel scrambled from his dying horse.

After thirty feet, he stopped, gulped down several lungfuls of thin air. He cocked the lever of the carbine, sat up, sighted a rock outcropping forty yards upslope that he suddenly realized was the pass, torn white ribbons of cloud streaming over it, driving the snow sideways, making it impossible to see anything distinctly.

A lead ball zinged past his right ear.

He swung his rifle around, sighted the left edge of a small boulder fifty yards away, and pulled the trigger on a vaquero hat that had peered around the corner.

It disappeared and he cocked the carbine again and clambered to his feet, now fighting toward the boulder field through chest-high drifts, smiling and swelling with all the murderous joy of a boy playing war.

THIRTY-ONE

Ezekiel walked into the boulder field and hunkered down at the base of a broken pitch of rock. He reached into his slicker and pulled the box of .44–40's from an inner pocket of his sack coat, tore it open, and slid five cartridges into the loading gate.

With the wind subsided and his horse no longer braying, what struck him now was the silence, his senses heightened, everything distilled. The smell of wet rock and gunpowder. The sound of snow falling on his hat. His heart thumping like it meant to bust out of his chest. Burning cold spreading through the left side of his face.

He heard distant whispering, got to his feet, stepped out from behind the rock formation. What lay before him on the gentle downslope reminded Ezekiel of a snowy labyrinth—countless boulders of varying size, some no bigger than a barrel, others rivaling wagons and cabins, bunched together in spots, spaced out in others, and a million places to hide. For a fact, Oatha and Billy had deadwood.

Twenty feet ahead, he spotted what he'd been looking for—tracks in the otherwise smooth, unbroken snow. He waded through the powder, light-headed.

After three strides, he froze. From behind a table-topped boulder came an exhalation. He brought the carbine's butt plate flush against his shoulder as something edged out from the rock.

He nearly shot a rawboned burro with missing ear tips, buried to its neck and laden with an empty cantia. It stood watching him through large dull eyes.

He moved on through the boulder field.

It had stopped snowing, and that seemed to magnify the silence.

He came to the tracks. Two sets. The snow so deep he had to squat down to find which direction the boot prints pointed, now pushing forward again with what he knew was deluded confidence.

Behind any one of the hundreds of rocks, they were laying for him, and this would all be decided by dumb luck: who saw who first.

The sound of a block of snow calving off a boulder drew his attention, and when he turned back to the tracks, a slouch hat poked out of the snow thirty feet ahead.

The carbine bucked against his shoulder and he lunged behind the nearest rock as a shotgun exploded the silence.

The shooter had disappeared when he peeked around the corner, Ezekiel figuring he'd ducked back under the snow to reload.

He sighted the spot where he'd seen the hat. Had there been only one, he'd have felt at ease staying indefinitely, pinning the man down, waiting for him to lift his head again. But the prospect of a standoff made him nervous with two men in play.

As he debated what to do, he heard the unmistakable snick.

Perhaps five yards behind and a little to the left.

Thought he was dead.

No sound like the hammer of a six-gun going back.

"Y-y-y-y-you go on and, and, and, and, and throw that rifle away."

Ezekiel remained crouched in the snow, leaning against the rock.

"Swear to God. I-I-I got a bead drawed on the back a your head."

"All right." But Ezekiel didn't throw his carbine aside. He kept a firm grip on the forend stock, a finger in the trigger guard, and turned slowly until he faced the boy standing waist-deep in snow.

Ezekiel had hoped to see the revolver trembling in Billy's hand, but the enormous Walker Colt was steady and leveled on his chest like a small cannon. "That was some shootin back there," Ezekiel said. "Head shot from what? Fifty, sixty yards?"

"Told you, throw that artillery down."

Billy's face twitched as if someone had placed hooks in the left corner of his mouth and was yanking them with a string. Ezekiel found the boy's eyes, didn't like the jitteriness he saw, would have preferred two rounds of ice. At least you saw it coming that way.

"We're neighbors, Billy. Our wives are friends." As he spoke, Ezekiel let the carbine's barrel ease down. Another few inches, he'd take the boy's head off. "You got a nice family in Bessie and Harriet, and I believe that shot that kilt the Doc was a accident. Now, I can't speak for your partner, but your bark ain't this hard."

"Well, Mr. Curtice, guess you don't know me so good after all."

THIRTY-TWO

When Oatha Wallace arrived, Ezekiel was leaning back on a small shelf in the rock. He'd pulled off his fleece-lined gloves and unbuttoned his slicker and sack coat and vest, unclipped his suspenders, torn open the muslin shirt.

"Where's his rifle?"

"Somewhere i-i-in the snow yonder."

"He ain't got a sleeve gun, do he?"

"Naw, I checked."

Oatha stared at Ezekiel. "He's gut-shot."

"I-I-I-I tried to shoot him in the head, but—"

"Naw, that's fine, Billy. His horns is clipped. Lead ball from a Walker in the bread wallet. Helluva thing. Caught a case a the slow, didn't you, old buscadero?"

Ezekiel watched the steaming black blood leak through his fingers as he tried to put back the gray tube of gut that kept pushing out. He could feel blood running down his legs and into his boots. Some had streamed down the rock and melted a burgundy hole in the snow. He looked up at Oatha, at the boy who'd set him on his sunset trail, and when he spoke, his voice came broken and strained by ragged exhalations. "Bushwhacking, huh? So that's how you operate?"

"Whatever gets it done," Oatha said.

"How much y'all come away with?"

"They's sixty-nine bricks, twenty-two pounds apiece."

"But you done the math."

"Sure, I done it. Just over five hunerd thousand."

Ezekiel nodded. "Maybe you can buy this boy a new gun. That Walker must be forty years old."

Oatha grinned. "And some clothes, too."

Billy blushed. Too poor to afford a greatcoat or a slicker, when he ventured out into winter conditions, his only recourse was to clothe himself in every ratty, moth-eaten garment he owned, so his ensemble comprised layer upon layer of old shirts, threadbare hand-me-down sack coats two decades old, and a blue frock coat that had barely survived a house fire back in Tennessee, and still bore the black-fringed fire-eaten holes to prove it.

Ezekiel looked at Billy. "You've broke your wife's heart, son."

"Ain't ye son. I want his Justins, Oatha. My feet are cold."

"We'll discuss the man's plunder in a bit. You got even a jot a decency in you, boy?"

Ezekiel moaned, "Got-damn."

"Hurt as bad as they say?" Oatha asked.

"They wasn't buildin a high line."

A dense cloud had blown over the pass and begun its rolling descent through the boulder field.

"You wanna go on and tell me, then?" Ezekiel said. "Don't see what you got to lose now."

"Tell you what?"

"I know my brother left Silverton with you back in the fall. He wired me before he left. I know it was you, Nathan, and two other men. Then you come into Abandon three weeks later all by yourself, sayin they decided not to go last minute."

"And you called me a black liar."

"And I stand by the claim. Christ." Ezekiel winced.

Oatha tossed his double-barreled hammer shotgun to Billy, waded toward Ezekiel, and knelt before him in the snow.

"Nathan was your brother."

"My little brother."

"What the hell. Don't matter much now, does it? I didn't wanna ride with 'em, but they caught up to me on the trail to Abandon in early October."

"It was four a you?"

"That's right. Started snowin the second afternoon, and it didn't stop for a week. We'd only packed provisions for three days a travel and we was hungry by the time the snow quit. Didn't have no webs. Ten miles from anywhere. Six feet a powder on the ground. Imagine tryin to walk any considerable distance in this shit.

"We tried to hunt, but all the game had gone down to winter in the foothills. Never saw so much as a rabbit.

"We was camped at timberline in a stand a dead spruce, and come October's end, we was starvin. One man run off. Horses died and froze. Circumstances was dire. The other men had the look a death about 'em already. I weren't far behind. There was enough snow melted, we coulda walked out if we just had a little strength.

"One mornin, I took my shotgun, so weak, I could hardly stand. Ways out from camp, I fired it into a tree. Started yellin I'd shot a elk. They come a-runnin. Hootin. Hollerin.

"McClurg arrived first, and I shot him. Nathan realized what was happenin, what we had to do, but he didn't want no part of it. I was left with no choice but to kill him.

"I didn't cook your brother, though. McClurg was plumpest, least gant up. I roasted his ass. Had both sides. Got my strength up, stowed everthing in a old bear den, and broke camp next mornin. Walked into Abandon three days later."

Billy stared at Oatha, mouth agape, broken teeth showing, looking more than a little mystified. "You et a man's backside?"

"Weren't no face-lickin Thanksgivin dinner. I was starvin, Billy. And this don't concern you anyhow. Just thought the man deserved to know his brother's fate."

In the midst of a cloud, mist blowing past and a few stray flakes of snow, Ezekiel was overrun by a coldness that settled so deep inside him, he knew he'd never be rid of it. He was dying and he thought of Nathan dying, felt a strange connection to his brother in that moment, wondered if he'd felt this alone in that moment before Oatha murdered him.

Ezekiel's respiration slowed. He tasted blood in his teeth, felt it trickling from the corner of his mouth. He had a terrible thirst, and he trembled with cold as he looked up at Oatha.

"Don't stare at me that a way," Oatha warned. "Like you're lookin at some kind a damn deviant. You lost your brother. I lost all three a mine to the Federals at Malvern Hill. You didn't have to sit there with Nathan, tellin him about home while he's near cut in half, everthin pourin out of him. Sight like that gets stamped on your mind, you can fuckin forget about ever gettin shed of it."

But Ezekiel had already descended back into the canyon, to his little cabin, to Gloria. He saw her in bed, felt her grief, and all the memories of Leadville and the boys and whatever selfish strain of freedom he'd associated with them and had tasted today wilted into the sham they were. His lips moved, her name on them, and he loved her more, needed her more than he ever had, thought of all the things he'd not said, wondered if she knew them anyway, then reckoned not, because he hadn't known himself until this moment.

He heard a deep unsanded voice. Fought to make his eyes open.

When they did, the boulderfield and mist and men and snow had faded to gray, and a darkness whose identity he well knew had whittled down his periphery of vision, so his whole world seemed to blacken around the edges like a winter-killed rose.

Oatha was only inches from his face now, his eyes such a pale and clouded blue, some might have mistaken him for a blind man.

It took Ezekiel a moment to comprehend the words.

"That man Billy shot. He kilt?" Ezekiel could only nod, utterly stove up. "Who else knows about Bart?" The darkness was closing in. "Boy, you best find the strength to provide a answer."

Just me and Doc.

"Just me and Doc," he whispered, his lips barely moving.

"How'd you know to find us here? Billy's wife? Bessie tell you?"

Tracks.

"Your tracks."

"Yours and the doctor's wife know about all this?" Ezekiel shook his head. "Yeah, that tastes of a lie."

Gloria don't know.

"Well, I can tell you we damn sure ain't takin no chances on a couple a leaky-mouthed bitches, feedin off their range."

Gloria don't know a thing.

"H-h-h-he's sayin somethin, Oatha."

You let her be.

"Well, if he is, I can't hear it."

"I-I-I bet Gloria knows. No tellin who else she's told."

"We'll kill ever man, woman, and child in Abandon if that's what it comes to. You set to see this through, Billy?"

"Y-y-yes, Oatha."

"You sure? Ain't gonna try to crawfish out a this?"

"For a fact."

"Better go on and curl this one up then so we can sail away."

"M-M-M-Oatha, he's almost dead any—"

"I don't give a good goddamn how almost dead he is. I ain't quittin this spot with that star-toter still above snakes. Savvy?"

Ezekiel heard his death sentence, felt a glimmer of relief, the pain beyond anything he'd known, like someone had thrown liquid silver in his guts. He watched Billy pour a sixty-grain powder charge into one of the Colt's chambers, followed by a wad of paper. The boy used a small built-in ramrod to seat a lead ball.

Ezekiel spent his last thought not on the horror of what might happen to Gloria, or his own inconceivable pain, or all the things he would not ever see or smell or taste again. He spent his last thought on his boy.

The sound of Gus's laugh.

What it had felt like to cradle him.

The nape of his neck.

With the bore charged, Billy set about fitting a brass cap to the nipple in back of the cylinder.

You was the best thing. You and your mama, and I wished I'd knowed that when I coulda done somethin to preserve it.

Billy waded up to the rock where Ezekiel lay dying, leveled the nine-inch barrel between the man's eyes. Ezekiel barely heard the hammer thumb back, because the possibility of heaven had dawned on him, and he was thinking how sweet and unexpected a surprise it would be to arrive there after all this, see Gus, sneak up on his boy, tickle his ribs, throw him in the air. And that laugh . . . *Please, God, let me hear Gus laugh again if You're real and have any regard—*

THIRTY-THREE

O Lord God of my salvation, I have cried day and night before Thee. Let my prayer come before Thee.

The preacher lay shivering in a bank of snow at the base of the boulder field, so far beyond those innocuous, eloquent prayers he'd delivered to his congregation on Sunday mornings, beyond the decorum he'd always reserved for addressing his Savior. He could only manage a silent, desperate psalm.

Incline Thine ear unto my cry. For my soul is full of troubles.

In the distance, a horse snorted. Stephen raised his head, saw Oatha Wallace and Billy McCabe loping through the powder on their mounts, leading a train of burros down from the pass.

And my life draweth nigh unto the grave.

Stephen ducked under the bank and burrowed deep into the snow, taking the cape from his black greatcoat and draping it over his head to keep the powder from falling into his collar.

I am counted with them that go down into the pit. I am as a man that hath no strength.

The preacher sat motionless and buried, his back to the snowbank, watching Russell Ilg's mare wandering between the boulders.

Free among the dead, like the slain that lie in the grave, whom Thou rememberest no more. And they are cut off from Thy hand.

He heard the tinkle of harness bells on the other side of the snowbank, no more than ten feet from where he sat.

Someone said, "Whoa now."

He envisioned Billy and Oatha tugging at their reins.

"Reckon these are Ezekiel's?" Oatha's voice. They were studying his tracks.

"O-o-o-or maybe that horse yonder."

Thou hast laid me in the lowest pit, in darkness, in the deeps.

"Naw, that horse come from farther up. These here are the tracks of a man."

Thy wrath lieth hard upon me, and Thou hast afflicted me with all Thy waves.

"I'll climb down and check it out if ye want, Oatha."

Stephen closed his eyes.

Mine eye mourneth by reason of affliction. Lord, I have called daily upon Thee, I have stretched out my hands unto Thee.

"They was just the two a them, right?"

"Yeah, I think—"

"Think?"

"Th-th-th—"

"You little stutterin greener, you better—"

"They was just the two a them. I know it for a fact. And we saw the other'ns body back there."

"Well, all right, then. Naw, don't get down."

Oatha clicked his tongue and the pack train moved on. When he could no longer hear the harness bells, Stephen staggered out of the drift and brushed the snow from the wool of his coat.

He stood alone on the mountain, a hundred feet below the pass, listening to the wind and the sound of it pushing grains of snow over the surface like sand skimming a beach. He thought of home in the South Carolina low country, and the memory of it filled him with heartsickness in this frozen desolation.

Stephen found Russell's horse sheltering itself on the lee side of a giant boulder. He swung up into the saddle, quirted the horse on its snow-matted neck, rode upslope in the tracks of the pack train.

At the Sawblade, the wind blew steady and scaldingly cold.

It had scoured out the snow and built a cornice on the north side, allowing Stephen to dismount onto bare rock.

He followed the burro tracks along an icy ledge. Despite the dizzying exposure, he couldn't stop himself from peering over. He saw a red crater two hundred feet below—one of the burros had lost its footing, gone over, exploded in the snow like a viscera bomb.

The ledge ended at a recess in one of the jagged spires upthrust from the pass like a rotten canine tooth. He spotted an opening at knee-level in the back wall, a small claim hole just wide enough for a man to crawl through.

Stephen loosed the cloth buttons, reached into his coat. He thought he had a match in one of the pockets, but he didn't find it.

He approached the hole. It went back four feet, then opened into darkness. He crawled in, wriggled himself through the tapering passageway, then finally emerged, the ground solid beneath his feet, though he had no sense of the chamber's dimensions.

He extended his right foot. It struck something hard.

He removed his gloves, squatted down, reached forward, his fingers grazing the cold gold, bars and bars and bars of it, stacked upon one another in a cube that rose above his knees.

He lifted one of them, held it to the light that drizzled in through the hole, and as he stood in that semidark, staring down at the chunk of yellow metal, he considered the blood that had already been shed for it and wondered how much more was to come.

He thought of all the people in that haunted town two thousand feet below, how they'd endured this brutal wilderness and all its impositions—the cold, the thin air, the loneliness, maddening isolation—for just a fraction of what he held in his hand.

And in that moment, he no longer regarded the residents of Abandon and the thousand other mining camps scattered like bacteria through the West as people of ambition and courage. They were a cold, dirty, desperate, miserable lot. He saw them now so clearly. They had crossed the plains and made homes in these savage mountains and borne their myriad afflictions not because they were brave pioneers pursuing a dream. They had come for no other reason but that their ravenous hearts raged with greed.

The preacher crumpled down in the cave and wept.

STEPHEN.

At the sound of his name, he went rigid with fear.

THIRTY-FOUR

Stephen crawled out of the cave and walked back up to the pass.

Above him, the clouds had broken up, beams of afternoon sunlight passing through, bronzing random patches of forest, summits, ice fields with the strongest light he'd seen in days.

The mare stood waiting for him on the windswept rock.

As he reached her and put his foot into the stirrup, he heard it, though owing to the wind, he couldn't immediately determine from which direction the sound had come. He looked downslope, and with the mist clearing, he could see all the way into the canyon and a line of specks near the Godsend mine—Oatha and Billy and the burros on their way back to Abandon.

He heard it again—a faint howl.

Others joined in, each of varying pitch and duration, like a discordant symphony of owls and geese and baying dogs.

Stephen pulled his foot out of the stirrup and walked to the other side of the pass, stood bracing against the wind, shielding his face with his gloves.

At first, there was little to see. Clouds sailed toward him and over him—mammoth schooners. Fog swirling in the depths below, hiding the long, broadening valley, the lake several miles south, the open country beyond. He'd taken this trail to Silverton once before—much faster than the wagon road, though more dangerous because it required a steep descent along a series of narrow ledges that switchbacked down from the cirque.

Now he gazed at those ledges, observed that the wind had blown them clean of snow, traced their dwindling switchbacks with his finger for several hundred feet until it passed over something that, from his vantage on the pass, resembled a trail of black ants ascending out of the fog.

He stood bewildered, listening to the alien howls until another sound became prevalent—unshod horses pounding the rock.

Out of sheer amazement, he stepped forward and squinted down at what looked to be an entire town on horseback—women in print dresses, suit-coated men, some still wearing their filthy workclothes, and a hatless blonde leading the procession, poorly dressed for the conditions in a bright gold evening gown. As they drew near, he puzzled at their horses' hides, deco-rated with pagan hieroglyphs depicting wolves, bear, coyote, elk, eagles, trees, cacti, mountains, clouds, the arc of rivers, and as the riders rounded another switchback, facing him now, he saw that the woman in front wore the painted face of a heathen, and the gold gown was drenched in blood, the original owner's entire scalp having been stitched into the warrior's tonsured head, the curly yellow hair still pinned up in the fashion of the day, and around that heathen's waist hung a belt of sunburned noses and he appeared to be smiling, his bloodstained teeth filed down into razor points, and his horse's mane interwoven with the hair of numerous scalps still warm, still dripping, and those behind him equally outlandish, one rider naked save for cape and bowler, another so caked with blood that he seemed to be rusting, one in nothing but a blue bonnet, one in a shredded corset beaded with eyes, and they bore weaponry of every design and from across the ages—shotgun, rifle, revolver, knife, lance, bow, sword—some holding rocks still smeared with blood and brain, others wielding sharpened human femurs, one grip-ping a crude mace constructed of oak and leather and shards of quartz, and this parade of demons cackled and groaned, conversing in a strange, unholy tongue that sounded like some ancient form of necromancy.

"God Almighty," said the preacher.

The trail they climbed had no destination but Abandon.

2009

THIRTY-FIVE

Abigail thought she'd broken her back, but then she managed to lift her head and suck in a breath of air, realized she'd only had the wind knocked out of her. She lay on the stairs on her back, wood creaking all around her, threatening to give. Somewhere above, a man groaned. Dust and snow clouded her headlamp's triangle of light. Someone said her name. She looked down at her father sprawled a few steps below.

"You okay?" he whispered. She nodded. June wept above them, and Abigail couldn't determine if the source was grief or pain. She glanced up, saw she'd landed just below the cupola, her headlamp shining into the library, spotlighting the pale, terrified face of June, the woman clutching a bookshelf and standing on the only ribbon of flooring still attached to the struts. With the sky exposed, snow fell into the stairwell column of Emerald House. Abigail lay midway down the third flight of steps. There was a sudden crack, and she watched something break through the ceiling, her light catching on a flash of blue ski jacket streaking past, realized it was Emmett, his body dropping through darkness, crashing into the second flight of stairs, nearly hitting Jerrod, punching a hole through the steps, the second floor, finally slamming into the ground level as June screamed out from the library.

Stu yelled, "Quit moving! You're gonna break this section of floor, too."

Abigail shone her light down and across to the next flight of stairs, where Jerrod and Isaiah clung to the middle section, the top half having been severed from the third floor by Emmett's fall.

Lawrence snapped his fingers. Abigail saw him motioning for her to climb down to him.

She descended carefully, and as she neared him, he reached up, turned off her headlamp.

His mouth pressed against her ear, he whispered, "We're leaving. Step where I step and keep quiet." Lawrence stood slowly. The step he occupied creaked. As he and Abigail moved down toward the third floor, Isaiah's voice rose up from below.

"Stu, where you at?"

"Up here in the library."

"You hurt?"

"Fuckin ribs are killing me. You?"

"Me and Jerrod're scraped up, but we'll live. The other two with you?"

"No."

"*Laaarry?*" Isaiah purred his name as a beam of light swung through the debris onto the stretch of stairs where Abigail and her father had landed. "I'm not seeing you and the cute bitch." A red dot appeared on the third flight of steps. "Sound off, motherfucker."

Abigail could see the bright bulb of Isaiah's headlamp a few feet away. With the upper portion of the second flight of stairs destroyed, there was no way that he or Jerrod could reach the third floor, but they could sure as hell see them and shoot. He had only to turn around. Lawrence grabbed his daughter's hand, whispered in her ear, "Follow me."

They crept around the stairwell toward the west wing, just a narrow corridor of gray rotting wood that seemed to joggle with the motion of Lawrence's headlamp, the hall lined with doors, some closed, some ajar, most having rusted out of their hinges and toppled over onto the floor. Fifteen feet in, Lawrence stepped on a floorboard that squeaked. They froze, as if to retract the sound, Lawrence switching off his headlamp.

"That you, Lar?" Abigail felt blind, thought of all the scary movies she'd seen, horror novels she'd read, realized nothing even approached this level of fear. She could have dreamed no better nightmare.

"Tell you what," Isaiah continued. "You do the smart thing, come on back, all'll be forgiven. But you run? Better not ever let me catch your ass."

Movement on the second flight of stairs.

"He's coming," Abigail whispered.

"But he can't reach us from those steps."

She heard a noise, glanced back. It sounded like quiet microexplosions shredding the floor and the ceiling. "What *is* that?" she asked. "Is this wing about to collapse?" The little explosions moved closer: one here, two there. When Lawrence flicked on his headlamp and shone it on the floor, they both saw it pockmarked with tiny holes.

"Shit," he whispered. "He's underneath us, shooting up through the floor."

They ran, surrounded by the muffled *thunk* of rounds passing through the floor and ceiling, decayed wood raining down, the jingle of shell casings dropping on the second floor like handfuls of pocket change, then a pause, followed by an intense thirty-round burst just ahead. Lawrence pulled Abigail through a doorless doorway, pushed her against the wall, the room small, part of the servants' quarters, boasting only a ruined bed and a wardrobe.

"There's a stairwell at the end of this wing," Lawrence said. "We're gonna take it—"

"But they're right underneath us."

"And getting ready to find out that the end of the second floor's west wing is rotted out. They'll have to go back to the main stairwell. That's the only way down for them."

After another fury of machine-pistol fire, Lawrence said, "He's reloading. Let's go." Abigail followed him back into the corridor, their footfalls noisy on the old wood. She heard someone yell "Fuck!" and wondered if Isaiah had reached the caved-in portion of the second floor. Up ahead, the wing terminated into a sitting area—crumbling furniture and overturned bookshelves grouped around a hearth. Above it all, a chandelier drooped from the ceiling, and through the broken windows, snow streamed in sideways.

Four strides from the sitting area, Abigail's right foot went through.

"Lawrence!" she screamed, up to her elbows, both legs sticking out of the second-floor ceiling. He sprinted back as the wood under her elbows broke. She dropped, but he had a solid grip around her wrists. Abigail looked down past her dangling feet, her headlamp jolted on, shining through a giant hole. The floor cracked under Lawrence's knees.

"I'm about to go through," he grunted, straining to lift her, the machine pistol at work again, ripping through the wood behind Abigail.

"Hurry," she whispered. During a brief reloading silence, Lawrence pulled her up, and they rolled into the sitting area as a slew of bullets eviscerated the spot where Abigail had punched through. They scrambled to their feet, tracking through blown-in snow.

"It's over here," Lawrence whispered, leading her to the northeast corner of the sitting area. "I don't think he can get a clear shot at us in the stairwell."

"Is it safe?"

"Don't know." Lawrence took the stairs two at a time. They descended through the second floor, finally emerging onto the ground level, their headlamps blazing through a kitchen replete with giant washbasins, two fireplaces, a brick oven, a clay oven, and numerous cabinets, all surrounding a long butcher-block island. The windows had held their glass, so there was no snow or wind, only silence.

"Kill your headlamp," Lawrence whispered. They both went dark. Without the aid of light, Abigail couldn't even see her father standing a foot in front of her.

"This is good," he said, leading Abigail forward. "We'd see their light if they were coming down the main staircase." She heard a doorknob turn, hinges grinding.

"It's pitch-black. How can you see anything at all?"

"I know this mansion very—" Lawrence stopped.

"What is it?"

"I heard something up ahead."

"What?"

"Wood cracking under a footstep."

A long moment of silence elapsed, and then Abigail saw the sole point of light in all that smothering darkness. She said, "Oh God," and Lawrence looked down at his chest, touched the red dot moving in tiny circles around the North Face logo on his parka.

They lunged back into the kitchen as glass fell out of the French doors and rear window. Abigail never heard the shot. Lawrence's headlamp lighted up. He pulled Abigail toward the washbasins between the ovens, helped her climb onto the counter, footsteps pounding toward them.

"What do I do?" she asked. He pushed her through. Abigail fell outside into the snow. As Lawrence climbed through the windowsill, the French doors burst open, headlamp beams sweeping in a frenzy of movement over the walls of the kitchen.

"Come on!" she screamed, but they dragged her father back into Emerald House.

THIRTY-SIX

Abigail felt hands seize her, pull her back into the kitchen, jags of glass on the windowsill slicing through Gore-Tex, fleece, thermal underwear, skin, blood running down her left leg as she slammed into the rotting floor. Her headlamp passed over Jerrod and Isaiah, each man holding night-vision goggles, the barrels of their machine pistols steaming in the cold. Isaiah's foot swung through the dark and she heard the breath rush out of Lawrence as he doubled over on the floor. Isaiah knelt before Abigail, slid the knife out of his ankle sheath.

"No," Lawrence hissed, still struggling to breathe.

Abigail tried to get up. Then she lay on her back, the left side of her jaw throbbing and burning, Isaiah sitting on top of her, pinning her shoulders down with the heels of his boots. He unzipped her fleece jacket and pulled her thermal underwear out of her waistband, exposing her bare stomach—ridged like a washboard and heaving in the dark.

"Hold his head, Jerrod. You watching, Lar? I'm gonna cut a hole right here," he tapped Abigail's belly button with the knife point, "and reach in, start yanking stuff out."

When the blade touched her stomach, she went to another place, without sound or feeling. She imagined a Long Island beach, middle of summer. Isaiah's headlamp became the gentle sun.

Her father's voice brought her back. "I lied," Lawrence gasped. "I lied to you, Isaiah." Isaiah still pushed the knife, Abigail sucking in her gut, pressure and pain beginning to build.

"Hear what he's saying?"

"I got ears, Jerrod."

"The gold isn't here," Lawrence rasped. "I'll help you find it. I swear. Just leave her—"

Isaiah suddenly sheathed the knife, stood up, left Abigail shaking on the floor. He lifted Lawrence and slammed him into the oven, the professor's feet off the floor.

"What would you have done?" Lawrence said. "You spend years trying to find something, then someone sweeps in last second to steal it all from you. I couldn't—"

Isaiah rammed him into the brick again, dust showering down from the ceiling.

"Your ass better start making sense in a fucking hurry."

"That secret room in Bart's wing is where the gold *was* kept, until Christmas 1893. For a long time, I was sure the bars were in Emerald House. I searched every room, even scoured the south-wing rubble. I'd given up, when I found Gloria Curtice's diary. Something big was going down on Christmas in Abandon. She wrote that two men—Oatha Wallace and Billy McCabe—had murdered Bart Packer and his servants and made off with a load of gold. Apparently, her husband and some other men rode up toward the mine in pursuit."

"So fucking what?"

"So . . . when you're in a tiny town, dead of winter, and you've just stolen two thousand pounds of gold, you have to hide it."

"Look in my eyes, Larry, and you better have an answer to this. Where's the gold now?"

"I haven't found it yet." Isaiah simply dropped him, slipped a clip out of his belt, popped it into the Glock, and racked the slide. "No, listen. Oatha and Billy had already been prospecting together. They had this claim up at Sawblade Pass. Gloria mentions it in her diary, because Billy's wife had blabbed to her about it. It would make perfect sense. They stash the gold up there, and first chance they get, it's a straight shot down the mountain into Silverton. They're home free and set for life."

"Then it's gone, right? They would've taken it."

"Would have, yes. Except, remember, every resident of Abandon disappeared on Christmas Day, so they probably never got the chance."

"You telling me the gold's up at the pass?"

"I'm telling you I think that's where it is, but I haven't had a chance to explore up there since finding Gloria's diary. Scott and I had planned to do that during this trip."

Isaiah paced around the butcher-block island.

"Isai—"

"Thinking, Jerrod." Three more trips around the island, then Isaiah stopped and looked at his partner. "Go help Stu and that woman down from the library, and get them set up in the foyer." As Jerrod disappeared into the west-wing stairwell, Isaiah walked over to Abigail and her father, now huddled together at the base of the brick oven. "You know where this old claim hole is or not, Larry?"

"I think—"

"Motherfucker, let me hear the word *think* come out of your mouth one more—"

"I can find it. I know where to look, and I'll take you up there at first light, when—"

"First light? Tomorrow?" Isaiah laughed, then reached out, caressed Abigail's face with the back of his hand. "I don't think you grasp the situation, Lar. This is your daughter, right? Well, know this. If I don't have these gold bars in my possession *before* first light, you're gonna watch me do terrible things to your little girl before I go to work on you."

THIRTY-SEVEN

The storm wound up into such a flood of snow, they lost sight of Emerald House just fifty yards out from the portico, Stu and June staying behind in the mansion's foyer.

Within the hour, Isaiah, Jerrod, Lawrence, and Abigail had reached the mine, the professor leading them beyond the snow-blasted remnants of the mill to the canyon's end, where they started the long, steep climb to the pass.

Jerrod had roped Abigail to her father in an effort to impede an easy escape, and she was trying not to cry in the face of the surreal horror of it all—the throbbing gash above her left eye, the blood sliding down her leg from that deep cut on the back of her thigh—when a crushing realization sunk in: *We're going to die in these mountains.*

She could find no reason to believe these men would ever let them live.

Worst-case scenario—they don't find the gold bars, and we die horribly. Best case—they find the gold and we die quickly. Is that what I have to hope for? A bullet in the back of my head?

Lawrence put his arm around her.

She shoved it away.

Five hundred feet up, they stopped to rest, sitting in six inches of powder on a rock outcropping, Abigail between her father and Isaiah, watching the snowflakes swarm in the beam of her headlamp, all four of them practically panting in the thin air.

In a lull between wind gusts, Lawrence looked over at Jerrod, said, "So Scott told you what we were looking for up here? Was he gonna cut you in but you double-crossed him? That the deal?"

As Jerrod passed a water bottle down the line, he shook his head. "Month ago, I left Hinterlands, Inc. for the day, got to my Bronco, and realized I'd forgot my keys. When I came back in, Scott was on the phone, feet propped on his desk, talking to you about the logistics of transporting a ton of gold through seventeen miles of wilderness. It got my attention."

"So all of this, two people dead, 'cause you forgot your keys."

"Ain't life some shit?" Isaiah said. "Tell me, Larry. I did some research on this ghost town before I came out here, but since you the professor, what the fuck happened?"

"I don't know."

"But you got a theory or something."

"Yeah."

"So share that shit."

"No, I don't—"

"I ain't asking. What you think wiped this town out?"

Lawrence hesitated, said, "I figured an act of God."

"You mean something supernatural?"

"No, I mean I thought God wiped them out. Like Sodom and Gomorrah, fire and brimstone raining from the sky, the angel of darkness. Nothing else made sense."

"That's cold."

"Yeah, well—"

"But I like it. Read the Old Testament. Back in the day, God used to do that shit all the time."

Abigail took her drink of water, glancing at Isaiah. *Keep him talking. Make a connection beyond victim-captor. If you don't humanize yourself, you're dead.*

"Could I ask you something, Isaiah?" she said.

"Sure, we can friend up for a little while. You know, I'm actually a great guy. You met me under any other circumstance, you'd probably love my ass."

Strangely enough, she believed him, imagined meeting him at her local gym, developing a flirtatious banter on neighboring rowing machines.

"Were you and your partners in Iraq together?"

Isaiah swiped the water bottle out of her hand, took a drink, wiped his mouth.

"Force Recon."

"Desert Storm or—"

"Iraqi Freedom."

"I just wondered, because on the hike in, I noticed Jerrod has post-traumatic stress—"

"We all got that shit."

Jerrod turned, and she could see his eyes narrowed under the bulb of his headlamp, considered the possibility that she'd misread him, that he might be capable of killing her.

"Why would you talk to her about that?"

"Chill out, my man."

"You saw combat?" Abigail asked.

"Christ, Isaiah. Tell her to shut the—"

Don't shut down on me.

"Yeah, we got into some shit."

"What happened?"

"Our unit slipped into southern Iraq in the weeks leading up to the major offensive."

"Ize, not fucking around here. What are you—"

"Jerrod, my therapist says it's healthy to talk about it. Bad for you to hold this shit in."

"You're crazy." Jerrod got up and walked away.

"The navy had bombed hell out of a Republican Guard division about a hundred twenty-five miles southeast of Baghdad, in the city of Kut. We were sent in a day later with the objective of confirming that no enemy combatants or artillery had survived the attack, greasing the skids for the invasion.

"Our CH-forty-six set down on this ridge just before dawn, and soon as we touched ground, we started taking heavy mortar and machine-gun fire. As the chopper was lifting off, an RPG hit it. Boom. Game over. It's me and five men versus fifty Republican Guard soldiers. We're pinned down. Majorly fucked. Half our unit's killed in the first three minutes. Me, Jerrod, and Stu surrendered, and that's when the shit went down.

"Woke up chained to a chair in a room without windows and with concrete walls so purple, they looked like they'd been primed with blood. These two interrogators went to work on us for the next week. I could hear Jerrod and Stu screaming in the adjacent rooms. That was the worst part. Listening to them, knowing what was coming."

Abigail touched his arm, looked into his brown eyes. *Keep him talking.*

"What did they do to you, Isaiah?"

He smiled. "Oh, lots of things. Those were some ingenious motherfuckers. They had this metal cot wired to a couple car batteries—that was loads of fun. You noticed the scars on Jerrod's face? Did that with acid. My stomach looks like someone glued a bunch of spaghetti to it. They don't tell you when you sign up for the marines that you might get gang-banged by a bunch of towelheads. I told them everything I knew. Spilled all my secrets. Even made up some shit they wanted to hear. They were on the verge of flaying us when the good guys showed up. Team of Rangers got us out of there."

Abigail stared up at him, his face surprisingly calm and expressionless in the glare of her light.

"I'm sorry that happened to you," she said, "but I guess what doesn't kill you—"

"What don't kill you makes you a mean-ass motherfucker."

"Can I tell you something, Isaiah?"

"What?"

"It's nothing like what you experienced, but I'm afraid right now. Afraid when you get this gold, you're gonna kill me, because I've seen your face and know something about you. Will you tell me if that's what's going to happen, so I can at least begin to prepare for it?"

Jerrod returned, said, "Think we could end the therapy session, get the fuck up this mountain?"

"Hey, I needed to do this. Shari says I don't talk enough about it, so I'm practicing. You should unload, brother. Shit's empowering."

"You ain't right, man."

Isaiah grinned at Abigail. "Don't think Jerrod ain't holding his shit together. He's doing okay. Our man, Stu, on the other hand—sad, sad motherfucker. Just fell apart. Wife left him when he came back. Took his little girl. He lost everything. How many times he try to kill himself, Jer?"

"Three."

"And, as you probably gathered, he's a raging alky. I know this gold ain't a cure-all, and we still gonna be fucked up rest of our lives, but don't we deserve a little compensation after all we been through? Ain't like Uncle Sam could give a fuck."

"Can we go now? You need a hug first?"

Isaiah chuckled, shot Jerrod the bird. "Yeah, let's hit it."

Never answered my question.

Before Abigail stood, she noticed something at her feet, reached down, lifted the light, brittle skull out of the snow. She shone her headlamp onto the braincase of some animal, a horse perhaps, browned and cracking, filled with bits of rock and bone fragments that rattled inside like sand in a seashell, and she imagined some carefree hiker, a half century from now, holding her sun-bleached skull in his hands, speculating with his companions about her fate.

THIRTY-EIGHT

Lawrence and Abigail stood at thirteen thousand feet, already a foot of snow at the pass and the wind screaming beyond comprehension, so hard that they could lean into it at forty-five-degree angles and be held upright. They watched their captors trudge upslope, wearing those acrylic black masks again to shield their faces from the stinging cold.

Lawrence waved them over and shouted above the wind, "I wanna explore this side first! There's a recess in the cliff that looks very interesting!"

Isaiah gave a thumbs-up, and they worked their way over from the saddle to the base of the palisade, a series of broken crags that, from Abandon, resembled an old saw blade cutting at the sky. When she saw where he was leading them, Abigail grabbed hold of her father's arm. Accessible from the pass, a ledge traversed the escarpment. To her right—vertical snow-glazed rock that lifted beyond the range of her headlamp. To her left—a stomach-churning drop into darkness. She shone her light over the edge and watched snowflakes swirling and tumbling down through the beam, losing sight of them long before they reached the bottom.

Near the pass, the ledge was four feet wide—broad enough for Abigail and Lawrence to walk abreast. But it narrowed as it crossed the face of the palisade, and Abigail had to follow behind her father, hugging the cliff as with each step she punched through a foot of fresh powder.

The ledge went on and on.

It narrowed to three feet, then two.

Toward the end, the ledge sloped down just enough so that Abigail's boots would slide over the icy rock toward the edge if she lingered in one spot too long.

Suddenly, Lawrence turned and pulled her underneath an overhang, out of the snow, out of the wind, the rock dry. Abigail's face had gone numb, and she took off her gloves, pressed her palms into her cheeks.

"Listen, Abby," Lawrence whispered. "I'm gonna try to—"

Isaiah and Jerrod emerged from the ledge and ducked into the overhang. They collapsed onto the rock, their black parkas blanched with snow.

"This it, Larry?"

"This is the place I wanted to check out, yeah."

"Don't look like much to me. You ain't fucking around again—"

"How about that? Does that look like something?"

Isaiah aimed his headlamp at the back wall, the corners of his mouth lifting, his bright, perfect teeth shining their malevolent smile. "Now, that does look like some shit."

Isaiah got up, walked over to the opening in the rock. He squatted down, peered inside.

"How far's it go back?" Jerrod asked.

"About four feet."

"Can you see anything?"

"Nah, this tunnel slants down and to the left." He put his light on Lawrence. "You been in here before, Lar?"

"No. I'd planned to come up here on some downtime during our three days in Abandon."

Isaiah pushed back his hood and pulled off his face mask. From underneath the overhang, the wind sounded like a fleet of jet engines as it tore across the pass. "See, part of me's thinking that you might be a conniving motherfucker. You feel me?"

"No, I don't *feel* you."

"You're telling me that's an old claim hole?"

"Far as I know."

"Well, I'm all for sending your ass in first, but what if it's in fact a cave? And you just disappear once you get inside? Only one of us can fit through that tunnel at a time."

"Look, I have no idea what's in there," Lawrence said. "I hope for our sake it's a shitload of gold. Based on my research, everything I know about Oatha and Billy, I have a feeling that's exactly what we're going to find. But I'm not leaving Abigail, so you don't have to—"

"All right, tell you what. We'll send Abigail in. Jerrod, undo Larry's end of the rope and whip up one of your fancy knots for the lady."

It took Jerrod less than a minute to untie Lawrence and prepare a harness for Abigail.

"Second time you've done this," she said as he ran the rope around her thighs. "Remember yesterday?" He'd taken off his mask, and when he looked up, her headlamp shone on the crescent moon scars that ruined his face. In spite of everything, she found it impossible not to feel a flicker of compassion for what he'd endured in Iraq.

"She's ready," he said.

Abigail approached the opening and shone her headlamp inside.

"What's the story on there being bad air in there?" she asked.

"Guess you'll let us know, huh?"

She climbed in and wormed her way through the tunnel, arriving after ten seconds in a small chamber roughly the size of her studio, but with a much lower ceiling—just barely over six feet. Isaiah crawled through the passage now, and she moved away from the opening as he stepped down into the chamber. "Get your ass in here, Larry!"

They shone their headlamps over the bare rocky floor, across the walls, the low, jagged ceiling. Isaiah walked the circumference of the room, returning to the opening of the tunnel just as Lawrence emerged. He grabbed the professor by the scruff of his yellow parka and dragged him out into the chamber.

"Fuck," Lawrence said.

"Fuck is right. What the fuck, Larry?"

Lawrence struggled to his feet. He walked to the farthest corner and squatted down, carefully lifting the only man-made object in the chamber.

"What you got?"

Lawrence held up the scraps of an old burlap sack. "This is what the gold was carried in. Probably used a team of burros to bring it to the pass."

"So what's the good news? There a secret passage? I push one of these rocks and the treasure room opens up? Larry? I know you got some silver lining for me."

As Lawrence stood up and looked over at Isaiah, Abigail saw something in her father's eyes she'd not seen until now: fear, bewilderment, a hint of real desperation. "This *is* where they brought the gold. I'm sure of it. It was stored right here on Christmas Day in 1893. Now it's gone. So they must have come back and taken off with it after they'd murdered most of the townspeople. I feel more strongly than ever that it was Oatha and Billy who somehow wiped out Abandon in an unprecedented act of mass—"

"See, I don't give a fuck about all that."

"What else do you want from me? At this point, I've done everything I can." Isaiah closed the distance between himself and Lawrence. "I'm not jerking you off here, Isaiah. I could lead you on some wild-goose chase all night long. 'Oh, I think it's here. Well, maybe they hid it there. Okay, one more place to look.' I'm not doing that. This is the honest, stone-cold truth. Now that I know it's not here, I don't have the first fucking clue where the gold is. May not even be in the San Juans."

Isaiah just stared at him, and Abigail could sense the internal debate going on behind his chocolate eyes, knew their fate was being decided, thought how Isaiah's silence was so much more horrifying than his noisy stream of threats.

He knelt down slowly, deliberately, lifted the right pant leg of his waterproof trousers.

Lawrence was trembling now, his hands behind his back.

He left his gun outside with Jerrod, but not the knife. He's going to kill my father. Then murder me. What a perfect place to leave our bodies.

Isaiah unsnapped the ankle sheath, and as he grasped the knife, Lawrence's right arm swung out in a wide arc that ended in a muffled cracking collision with the side of Isaiah's head.

Isaiah groaned, fell over unconscious.

Lawrence staring at the fist-size rock still gripped in his hand, half-stunned, as if in disbelief that his arm had done this thing.

THIRTY-NINE

Lawrence knelt down and unclipped the sheath from Isaiah's ankle. He cut the rope that linked Abigail's harness to the overhang, and as he slid the sheathed knife into his pocket, Abigail ran her hands up and down Isaiah's legs, his arms, and around his waist before suddenly stopping. She unzipped his parka, reached into an inner pocket, and plucked out an olive-colored ball the size of an apple and weighing just under a pound.

A band of yellow nomenclature ran across the equator of the steel sphere:

GRENADE. HAND. FRAG. DELAY. M67.
COMP. B

She looked up at her father, their eyes going wide at the same time. She turned the grenade slowly in her hand, examining the safety pin, the lever.

"What's going on in there, Isaiah?" Jerrod shouted through the tunnel. "We happy?"

Abigail leaned forward, whispered, "You ever handled one of these?" He shook his head. "You know how it works?"

Lawrence touched the safety pin. "I know you pull this out, and as long as your hand is holding the lever down, I think it won't explode."

"You *think*? What's your knowledge based on?"

"You don't want to know."

"Tell me."

"*Rambo*."

"Isaiah!" Jerrod shouted. "You're killing me, man!"

Abigail said, "Well, he's gonna be coming through that hole momentarily. You wanna try to fight him with the knife you just took?"

"He'd kill me."

"Then we have to throw this grenade."

They walked over to the tunnel opening.

Jerrod's headlamp illuminated the rock midway through from the other side.

"Isaiah!" he shouted. "I'm coming in, all right?"

"No, Jerrod," Abigail said. "We're on our way out."

Lawrence motioned for her to yank the pin.

"You find the gold?"

"We didn't find it."

Abigail slipped her finger through the ring and pulled out the safety pin. "How long do we have?" she whispered. "Once I throw it? Is it five seconds, or three?"

"I don't know." Her hand had begun to shake, knuckles white from the death grip she had on the M67's striker lever, lines of sweat trickling down her forehead and into her eyes. She blinked away the sting.

"If it's five seconds, Jerrod might have time to throw it back in here at us," she said.

"Isaiah? The fuck's going on? Everything cool?"

Isaiah moaned again.

"When I let go of this," Abigail said, "we dive into that corner and cover our heads."

"Make a good throw. We don't want it rolling back in here."

"Isaiah! You okay?" Abigail realized she'd been holding her breath. "I'm coming in!"

Abigail cocked her arm back and let the M67 fly. They lunged into the corner, Abigail's face crushed into the rocky floor. Lawrence sprawled on top of her. She shut her eyes, listening to the grenade ricochet off the rock as it bounced through the tunnel.

She heard Jerrod say "Shit."

Two seconds of silence, then the ground shook and shards of the ceiling fell down.

Abigail said, "Lawrence? You okay?"

"Yeah. You?"

"My ears are ringing." She sat up, turned on her headlamp. The chamber had filled with a haze of dust and smoke. They got to their feet, moved over to the tunnel.

"I don't hear him," Lawrence whispered. "Think he had time to throw it over the edge?"

They heard something behind them, and both turned, their headlamps spotlighting Isaiah, who was trying to sit up.

"We have to go," she said. "We'll shoot him with Jerrod's gun." Abigail followed Lawrence back through the tunnel into thickening smoke. As she came out under the overhang, she could see that her throw had been perfect. Her headlamp shone on the rock, blasted black from the detonation, steel fragments everywhere—under her feet, embedded in the stone.

But no Jerrod and no blood.

"Where is he?" Abigail whispered, the words hardly out of her mouth when Jerrod appeared around the corner from the narrow ledge, walking toward them unscathed, a red dot moving back and forth between their chests, Lawrence and Abigail backpedaling toward the far edge of the overhang, snow blowing in, squeezing out the residual smoke.

"Isaiah!" Jerrod hollered at the opening in the rock. "Is he alive?"

Before Abigail could answer, Isaiah's voice boomed back.

"You got 'em?"

"Yeah."

"Motherfucker clocked me with a rock." Isaiah climbed out of the tunnel.

"I almost ate shrapnel," Jerrod said. "Missing anything? You didn't hear your M sixty-seven go off?"

"I was out cold."

"Yeah, I'm standing here hollering through the tunnel, and you aren't answering, and just when I'm starting to think maybe something's not right, this grenade comes banging through. Dropped right where you stand."

"No shit."

"I didn't know if it had been cooked off, so I didn't have time to throw it over the cliff."

"What'd you do?"

"Hauled ass around the corner and prayed to God that skinny ledge wouldn't break up underneath me."

Isaiah turned his attention to Lawrence and Abigail. He smiled, severe pain in his eyes. "Damn, Larry, cute bitch, you bad motherfuckers you. Almost took out a couple of marines. That would have been some shit. Ah, damn."

"You all right?" Jerrod asked.

Isaiah bent over, shook his head as if to gauge the pain. "I think he fucked me up serious. Put your light here." Jerrod inspected the side of his partner's head. "How's it look?"

"Nasty bruise. How's it feel?"

"Like a monster migraine."

"You've probably got a concussion."

"Where's my Glock?" Jerrod lifted the nylon strap over his head and Isaiah grabbed his machine pistol by its long magazine, staggered toward them, wincing with each step.

"Abby," Lawrence said, "do exactly what I say, right when I say, no matter how crazy it sounds."

Lawrence took hold of his daughter's hand, the backs of their boots only inches from the edge and Isaiah less than five feet away.

"Jump."

FORTY

Abigail raced feetfirst down a forty-degree slope. She'd lost her father's hand on impact, but she could hear him yelling at her from above. "Get on your stomach, Abby! Dig in! Stop yourself!" Fifty feet below, she saw where the slope ended and dropped over a cliff. Now she rolled onto her stomach, snow rushing under her parka in a spray of freezing powder. She kicked in her boots. "Your elbows!" Lawrence shouted. Abigail dug in her elbows, slowed to a halt, gasping, shivering. Glancing over her shoulder, she saw the cliff edge less than five feet beyond the soles of her boots, felt a queasiness in her stomach, her depth perception skewed by vertigo, right leg badly quaking—the only appendage keeping her on the mountain.

Upslope, Lawrence's headlamp shone down on her. "Climb back to me!" he yelled. "Make sure you've got purchase with each step." Her face ached with cold. She wiped away the powder and started to climb toward her father, taking her time, kicking steps in the smooth old ice under the new-fallen snow. As the adrenaline rush waned, her tailbone began to throb. Lawrence reached down, grabbed her hand, pulled her up onto a boulder.

"You in one piece?" he asked. His pack lay open in the snow and he was cinching the last strap of a crampon onto his boot.

"My tailbone kills. It's cracked, or worse."

"I busted up my right ankle."

"That was insane, Lawrence."

"We were dead otherwise. I knew it was only a thirty-foot fall. I just crossed my fingers and hoped the slope was steep enough and had enough snow to cushion our landing."

Abigail peered up into the darkness, spotted two points of light somewhere above, obscured by the blizzard. "Turn off your headlamp," she whispered. "I see their lights."

Voices tumbled down from the overhang, vague but audible: "Snow's coming down too hard and my beam's weak. How many clips you got left?"

"Two. Let's just spray the fuckers."

Lawrence whispered, "We gotta move right now. Follow me." It was only five steps upslope to the base of the cliff. They reached it, flattened themselves against the wall of rock, and waited. From above came the sound of slides racking.

Then the machine pistols murmured. Abigail could hear the bullets striking ice and rock a few yards downslope. It went on for some time—random bursts across the slope, one of which came within two feet of the cliff base where they hid. It finally stopped, everything quiet save the wind. Jerrod's voice: "Well, that was a waste of ammo."

Isaiah: "How you feeling, Jerrod? Strong and big-balled?"

"What are you talking about?"

"Your ass better be right behind me."

Something crashed into the snow thirty feet downslope.

"God*damn*!" Isaiah screamed.

Jerrod landed several feet beyond, shouted, "Fuck, I can't stop!"

"Jerrod, try to—"

"Fuck!"

"Stick your knife in the snow!"

"I can't reach—" There was a long, fading scream. Lawrence began to climb down, Abigail following close behind. They reached the boulder, turned on their headlamps. Twenty feet below, Isaiah clung to the slope's steepest pitch, struggling to find an edge on the ice.

"Wait here," Lawrence whispered.

"No, I'm coming with you."

Lawrence tapped his boot. "I've got crampons. You don't. Wanna end up like Jerrod?"

Abigail watched her father work his way down.

Isaiah smiled when he saw him coming, said, "Larry, you must have cantaloupe-size nuts. You'd have made a helluva soldier, because that jumping off the cliff shit was pure badass."

"Where's your gun?"

"The strap's twisted around behind my back. I can't reach it without slipping."

Lawrence squatted down by Isaiah's head, jammed his left crampon into the ice.

"I was thinking, Larry. Wanna call it square?"

"No, Lawrence," Abigail said.

"Man, I just wanna get the fuck off this mountain, home to my family. You understand."

"Give me your hand," Lawrence said.

As he reached up, Lawrence stomped his right crampon onto Isaiah's left shoulder. Isaiah's boots lost their purchase and he slipped down the ice along the same path Jerrod had blazed, making no effort to self-arrest, just staring upslope, his eyes never leaving Lawrence.

"You better hope this fucking kills me," he said, and disappeared over the edge.

FORTY-ONE

Abigail gripped her father's arm as they traversed the mountain, moving at a crawl on a fifty-degree slope, Lawrence taking his time to thrust the teeth of his crampons deep into the ice, since they bore the weight of two.

"I would have liked to have seen their bodies," Abigail said. "Just to be sure."

"Yeah, but way too risky to edge up to the cliff and look over. We might have joined them. Trust me, they're either dead or wishing they were."

They pushed on, Lawrence's dimming headlamp doing little to guide their way. After awhile, he stopped. They'd left the steepest stretch of ice several hundred feet back.

"This isn't good," he said. "We should've run into our old tracks by now. I was hoping to follow them back into the canyon. That's the only safe way down."

They went on, Abigail covering her face with the hood of her Moonstone jacket, unsettled by the disturbing numbness that had begun to diffuse through her cheek from a patch of burning cold under her left eye. Every step sparked a needle of white-hot pain that shot from the tip of her tailbone up into her throat. She'd begun to cry when Lawrence said, "Thank God."

Abigail looked up. Through blowing snow, she glimpsed a two-story building perched on the edge of a cliff. "What is that place?" she asked. "Are we back at the mine?"

"No, we're a thousand feet above it. That's the ruins of the Godsend's upper boardinghouse. Forty men used to live up here, so they'd have easy access to the mine's upper reaches, where all the richest ore deposits were located. Oatha Wallace lived here."

"So is it good that we found it, or—"

"It means I at least know where we are, and I can get us down to the canyon floor from here. Come on, let's get out of the storm."

The exterior of the boardinghouse stood in dire disrepair, the wood spongy and soft, the porch overgrown with moss, animals having gnawed partway through the support beams.

The ground floor was bisected into two rooms by a hall that linked the front door to the back porch. The west door frame opened into the kitchen and dining hall, its floor rotted through. All that remained were a couple of cookstoves, four benches, a barrel, and the remnants of a screened cage where the food had been stored to keep it safe from rodents.

Abigail and Lawrence picked their way through the debris of a fallen staircase and turned into the living room. The furniture—rustic handmade pieces—still survived, and aside from a hole in the northeast corner, the flooring was largely intact. As they collapsed before a stone fireplace in the back corner, Abigail said, "I think I have frostbite on my face."

Lawrence removed his pack, got up again, limped over to a table in the middle of the room, its surface gray with age, still encased in bark. "You didn't see me do this," he said, then lifted one of the chairs and smashed it over the table. He carried an armload of broken wood to the fireplace and went to work arranging it on the rusted grate. From the emergency kit in his pack, he took a bar of trioxane compressed fuel and a plastic matchbox. "This may catch the whole place on fire," he warned. Lawrence struck a match, held it to the fuel. Soon the fire starter glowed and then the old wood began to pop and hiss, flames licking up between the stones for the first time in more than a hundred years.

Abigail scooted up to the edge of the hearth and extended her hands toward the warmth. "Thank you," she said. Her father had taken off his parka, and he inspected her face by firelight. "Is it bad?" she asked.

"It's just the top layer of skin that's frostbitten. It may always be sensitive to cold, but no serious damage. That gash above your eye looks worse than anything."

Abigail stared into the flames, shadows playing on the warped-board floor, the raw, unfinished walls. The accumulation of everything was pressing down on her, a meltdown coming, though she knew she didn't have the luxury of falling apart just yet.

"What's upstairs?" she asked.

"Just a big room with a stove in the middle and twenty built-in wooden bunks."

A pile of rat-chewed paper lay in a stack near the hearth. Abigail picked up an old catalog, thumbed through the brittle pages. She saw an advertisement for a wedding dress with a check mark by it, wondered if the miner had ever gotten home to marry his love, or if he'd disappeared with the rest of Abandon. She noticed some writing on the nearest wall.

"Who would come up here and defile this place?"

"That's not vandalism, Abby." Lawrence crawled over and shone his light on the tiny scrawl. "Some of the miners wrote this. You can tell because it was done with pencil, and the handwriting isn't like ours. It's very small and fine, almost like calligraphy."

Abigail, too sore, too warm to move closer, said, "What's it say?"

"Well, this is just a column of numbers. Over here, someone wrote, 'John owes Bill two dollars.' Below that one, 'This is hell.'"

"What's that drawing a couple feet above your head?"

Lawrence stood. "How lovely. I haven't seen this one. It's a miner's Nellie. Someone sketched a woman's face. You see a lot of these in boardinghouses, since the men were so lonely up here. . . . Abby." He looked back at her. "I had no idea he was gonna kill Emmett."

"I know you didn't. But you and Scott did drag us all into this shit. You did do that."

"Look, the real reason I contacted you wasn't for this stupid ghost hunt. It was for the gold. The plan was to locate it on this trip, maybe take a few bars out with us, come back later for the rest. I wanted to share finding it with you."

"So you just used Emmett and June for their backcountry pass?"

"You have no idea how hard it is to get legal access to this box canyon, and they needed a guide anyway. Abby, I was gonna take care of you. Of your mother."

"The time when we needed you passed a lot of years ago."

"I know." Lawrence sat down beside his daughter. "What did your mother think of your coming out here to see me?"

"Furious at first that you'd . . . after all this time . . . I tried to make her see it wasn't a betrayal, just something I needed to do."

"May I share something with you?"

He unlaced his boots, removed his wet socks, propped his bare feet on the hearth. "I was having my morning coffee the day you arrived in Durango, and I had this vision. Least I think that's what it was. I was a few years older. A little slower. Little whiter. Through some unexpected windfall, I was living in a vast mansion up in the mountains north of town. The house had been built in an aspen grove near a river.

"It was early June, and around midday there was a knock at the front door. I walked through the foyer with a big grin on my face because I knew who it was. I was expecting them. This beautiful family stood on my doorstep—my daughter, her husband, their two kids, Molly and Larry. My daughter and

I . . ." Lawrence cleared the emotion from his throat, spoke more softly as he continued. "We embraced, nothing held back. I shook hands with her husband, and he called me 'Dad,' and my two grandchildren ran inside and tackled me to the floor. See, this family had come to stay for a while. They had a whole wing of the mansion to themselves, and it was one of those perfect Colorado summers. I taught Larry to fly-fish in the river, and Molly loved to swim, so some days it was just the two of us, and I'd take her pool jumping at Cascade Creek, swimming at Haviland.

"In July, when the wildflowers peaked, we all hiked up to Engineer Meadow, and the flowers were more spectacular than they'd been in years. I showed my grandchildren how to identify the blooms. We even picked a bouquet for their mother.

"The evenings were best. After the kids had gone down, we'd have dinner on the back porch. Candles, wine, lots of laughter, watching the alpenglow fade out on the Needles, and then came the stars, and you couldn't believe how many there were, and there was no bad history, no pain, and, Abby, you looked at me across the table like I was someone you loved.

"I came out of this vision or dream, whatever you wanna call it, overcome by a devastating emptiness, a sense of total loss. I've lived alone in Durango, in a two-bedroom Victorian on Third Avenue, going on twenty years now. I don't have close friends. There are acquaintances, a brother I talk to on the phone once a year on Christmas morning. Occasional dates, but no real love life. My work's been my life and love. I've demanded absolute freedom, lived on my terms, and I . . ." His eyes were welling up. "I'm just now, at fifty-two years old, beginning to understand what the price of my freedom is. And it's this. I'll never have a summer like that one I imagined a few days ago."

The fire roared now, its heat thawing Abigail's face, causing an itchy burn in her left cheek. "Lawrence," she said, "that's a real sad story. But there's something you're missing, and maybe if you figured it out, you might be on your way to changing some things."

"What am I missing, Abby?"

She looked at his purple right eye, the line of dried blood cracking down his cheek like old plaster. "It's still all about you. What *you* lost. What *you* won't ever get to experience. It's about *you* getting old, feeling empty. I was four when you left, and I didn't hear from you again until you wrote me about this trip. Not on birthdays. Not on Christmas. Do you know I believed I'd done something to make you leave us? That it was somehow my fault?"

"Abby, you have to know that—"

"And that in some deep and broken part of me, I still believe that? You left us. Mom never married. Practically holed herself up in that house for years, thinking you'd come back. Maybe if I'd had a brother or a sister, it wouldn't have been so god-awful lonely. When I got into Columbia, you know she had to come to New York with me? 'Cause I couldn't leave her in Baltimore? 'Cause she had nothing? No one? I didn't spend college in a dorm. I lived with my mother in a tiny Brooklyn apartment, through two suicide attempts, three commitments, every second spent studying or working so we could eat, so we'd have heat in the winter, waking up, middle of the night sometimes, hearing her talking in the dark as I stood at her door, realizing it was you she was talking to, like you were lying in bed with her. Like you loved her. Even speaking for you. Do you know what that's like? To hear your mother re-enacting the first time you two met? Fantasizing about a man who'd left her twenty years ago? Look, Mom's better now, and I'm a big girl, got my own life. This isn't about me crying for the daddy I never had. But I wish you could've been there with me, just one of those nights, seen what you turned her into."

Lawrence drew back. He got up and walked over to the empty window frame. Several rocking chairs creaked out on the back porch, pushed by the wind. Lawrence looked back at his daughter. Abigail stared up at her father. She wanted to see his face streaked with firelit tears. Wanted to catch just a glimmer of self-loathing or shame in her father's eyes, though it wouldn't have changed much. But it might've been a start.

Lawrence had gone hard. He scowled, as if deeply offended, and in the light of the flames, his face appeared faintly grotesque and very old.

1893

FORTY-TWO

Oatha Wallace walked into the saloon without bothering to shed his oilskin slicker or knock the snow from his stovepipe boots, tracking great clumps of ice and powder as he crossed the board floor. Lana Hartman sat at the piano, working quietly through the first movement of Beethoven's *Moonlight* Sonata.

The young deputy still snored in drunken bliss beside the stove, wrapped in a bearskin robe, a spittoon between his legs.

"First rattle out a the box with some irrigation," Oatha said.

Joss set up a tumbler and a glass of beer as he reached the bar.

"What are you doin here?" she whispered. "Thought you wasn't comin back 'til tomorrow."

"There was a big goddamn spoke in the wheel."

"What?"

"Unexpected company up at the Sawblade. We was followed by Ezekiel Curtice and that doctor."

"Russ Ilg?"

"Didn't catch the man's name, but we had quite a scrape. Billy shot 'em both, and that makes seven dead in less than a day. We need to quit the flats right now, while the gate's open."

Joss took out her makings, rolled a cigarette, pulled a punk from her prayer book—just a sulfur-tipped splinter of wood. She lifted her shirt, struck the match against the middle button of her canvas trousers, then lit the quirly, smoke ascending into the bleary light of the kerosene lamp above the bar. Oatha took up the glass and drank, chased it.

"He's fair sobered," Joss whispered, motioning to the deputy. "Wasn't gonna get him really stewed 'til tomorrow, like we discussed."

"You got that big bowie under the bar? One you almost shoved through my ear this mornin?"

Joss grinned, blew a stream of smoke into his face.

"That should get the job done."

"What about . . ." Joss cocked her head toward Lana.

"You ain't got all attached to that she stuff, have you?"

"You ain't touchin her, Oath. Let me just send her on home."

"Fine."

"What about Billy?"

"What about him?"

"He comin with us?"

"Sure, he's comin. Gonna try to straighten that balky bitch a his out first."

"And if she don't straighten?"

"Well, she knows, and he knows that won't stand."

"You reckon that scrub'll kill his wife? Just like that?"

"I think you might be surprised."

"I'm still gonna be the one to deal with him for goin rough on ol 'Bart. You ain't forgot that, have you?"

"Jesus Christ, kinky, cut the boy some—"

"*You* ain't got all attached to your pard, have you?"

"No, but Billy done all right today. Ain't no scissorbill. Boy's got some sand. Kilt both those men up there like it weren't nothin, shined, and he's payin a visit to their wives as we speak."

"And I give a solitary shit why?"

"Look, we'll need his help gettin out a town, loadin up everthin at the pass. Drivin the burros down the other side. You can 'dobe-wall him in the tall timber, 'fore we get to Silverton. Don't you worry those pretty black eyes."

"Condescend to me one more time."

"Christ, you're in a sod-pawin mood."

"And what if his wife and kid come along?"

"Well, I guess they won't see Silverton, neither."

"I want no part a killin that little girl."

"Then you'll have no part of it. Pour me another'n. Oh, fuck it, just give me the bottle." Joss pushed it forward and Oatha thumbed off the cork, swallowed two mouthfuls.

"I gotta say," Oatha said when he'd finished. "I'm consternated about the future a our association."

"And why's that?" Joss took back the bottle and drank.

"You know I love you, so don't go gettin your underpinnings in a big fuckin knot when I say this."

"What, goddamn it?"

"You're a little smoky. Men tend to buck out around you."

Joss smiled, whiskey running down her chin.

"What you think, I'm gonna make you come, Oath?"

"It's a reasonable concern, all things considered."

"Only thing to get you kilt by me is tryin to get me unshucked and in the willows. I see the way you look at me sometimes."

"Think I want up in the snatch of a mestiza?"

"Right. Was it a hard climb up to the pass?"

"Wasn't no holiday."

"Why the fuck didn't we do this in the summertime?"

" 'Cause you gonna be doin the strangulation jig down in Arizona. Go on, tell Lana to git."

"Lana!" Joss yelled over the piano. Lana stopped playing, stared down at her lap. "Lana, honey, I want you to go on home for the day. We gonna be closin up early. You ain't done nothin wrong. Your playin was real pretty."

Lana got up from the piano bench, walked to the coatrack, and slipped into her wool-lined cape, pulling the hood over her head.

"Lana," Joss said. The young woman stopped in the doorway, her back to the bar, head hung low. "You take care now, okay?"

Lana went outside. When the door closed, Joss pulled the bowie out of its sheath, set the knife on the bar.

She and Oatha looked over at the deputy, who was still snoring quietly.

"The key to your shackles is—"

"On that big metal ring on Al's hip."

Oatha tilted the bottle, took another long pull. Then he wiped his mouth, picked up the knife, scraped his thumb across the blade.

"I keep it sharp," Joss warned.

Oatha sucked a whistle through his teeth and licked the blood from the shallow slice. "I'll say."

"How you gonna do it?"

"Slip it in between his slabs. Then twisty-twisty."

Oatha moved soundlessly across the boards. He stopped at the potbellied stove, waited for a moment, letting his fingers warm, then stepped over to the deputy's left side, positioning himself so he'd have the best angle for a downward thrust.

He opened the bearskin robe, exposing the man's chest.

Al's eyes flittered under his lids, and Oatha wondered from what dream he was about to awaken.

His grip tightened on the handle.

As he plunged the blade, he heard something outside, the knife point stopping three inches above the man's heart.

Oatha glanced back at Joss. "The fuck is that?" he whispered.

He set the knife on the bar, walked to the door, cracked it open.

It was late afternoon, the sky clearing, and though the sun had already dipped below the canyon walls, he could see its long rays coppering the distant bladed rock at the pass, two miles south and two thousand feet above.

Stephen Cole tore down Main Street, hell for leather through waist-deep snow, his horse kicking up clouds of powder, and the Bible-puncher shouting as if the apocalypse were upon them, "They're coming! They're coming!"

FORTY-THREE

Gloria wet the nib of her pen in the inkwell. She sat in a chair built of bent aspen branches and wrote by the light of a shadowgee made from an old can of Towle's Log Cabin Syrup, cut in half and poked full of holes. It hung from a rafter over the beautiful oak table Bart Packer had given them, the candle inside dispensing just enough light for her to write without straining her eyes.

When she'd finished, she blew the page dry and left the diary open on the table. Gloria walked to the bedroom doorway. She and Ezekiel had been lucky to find a cabin with a plank floor, and they'd spent a weekend last September laying straw and blue denim over the boards. It wasn't carpet, but it wasn't dirt, and you could walk over it in socks without freezing your toes.

Bessie and Harriet slept on the iron bedstead, and watching the mother and child hold each other under the quilt, Gloria felt a flare of envy. She looked at the mail-order rocking chair in the corner by the window, at Gus's crib, which Ezekiel had assembled out of packing crates, some of her dead son's clothes still laid out on the tiny mattress—a burlap sack stuffed with pine boughs.

The front porch creaked. *Zeke.* Someone banged on the door.

Gloria hurried back to the living room, grabbed the Schofield from the bookcase, where she'd left it sitting near a few dime novels.

"Mrs. Curtice! Y-you in there?" Gloria edged to the door. "Need to speak to you straight away!"

Her husband's words echoed in her head: *Don't open it for nobody. Billy or Oatha or some rough-lookin feller come by, you know what to do.*

The door shook.

Gloria put her hand on the latch, said, "What is it, Mr. McCabe?"

"I come for Bessie and Harriet. They in there with ye?"

Bessie emerged from the bedroom in her flour-sack underpinnings, a blanket wrapped around her shoulders. She mouthed "No."

"They aren't here, Mr.—"

"N-n-now I don't know if I believe that. How about you open this door and let me take a look for my own self?"

"Now isn't the best time, Mr. McCabe. I'm sure you understand."

"Naw, Mrs. Curtice. I don't understand. But I'll give you ten full seconds to open this door 'fore I tear it off the hinges."

Bessie said, "We ain't comin home with you, Billy."

"Oh, y-y-y-you ain't, huh? Why don't you open this door so we can have a face-to-face conversation like adult human beins?"

Gloria said, "When Zeke gets home, we'll all talk this out."

"W-w-well, we might be waitin here quite a spell."

Gloria lifted the latch, threw open the door. The barrel of the single-action revolver touched the end of Billy's nose.

"You wanna elaborate on what the hell that meant?"

Billy smiled, his jagged teeth showing, but his eyes were skittish. His horse stamped in the snow. Even though his vaquero hat kept his face in shadow, Gloria could see that it was flecked with blood, and her heart fluttered.

"Why don't you go on and, and, and, and put that away. You ain't never shot nobody. You ain't about to."

"You don't know anything about me. Get your hand away from that gun. Where's my husband? He went up to the mine, lookin for you."

"I guess he didn't find me, did he?"

"You said, 'We might be waitin here quite a spell.' What's that mean, you runt? Ain't you man enough to stand by the words that come out of your mouth?"

"You do like I said and p-p-p-put that revolver away."

Gloria thumbed back the hammer. Billy's eyes widened.

"I don't know what's happened to you," Bessie said. "Your mind ain't right. You and Oatha kill those people like they say?"

"Now ain't the time, Bess. Go on and get Harriet and come on."

"Said I ain't goin with you, Billy."

His face went red and the corner of his mouth began to twitch. He turned as if to leave, then suddenly reached back and swiped the revolver out of Gloria's hand, almost like an afterthought, and swung the walnut stock into her face.

Gloria sat down in the cabin doorway, dazed, her nose burning. When she looked up, Bessie was crying in the threshold of the bedroom, blocking her husband's path to Harriet.

"Billy, just leave. Please. I'm scared a you and it—"

"Your hair's fallin out 'cause I can't put adequate food on our table. Know what that feels like for a man? They's risks and they's sacrifices in life, yeah? Well, I just made a few big ones, and now we're set like you can't even believe. That dream we talked about before I come out west? Remember? Well, it's here. We got it for the takin. Tired a goin to bed hungry? A not bein able to afford cake soap? A wearin fuckin flour sacks for clothes? S-s-savin all year just to buy a doll for Harriet? You want a new dress? You can have twenty of 'em. It'll take our baby girl all day to open her presents next Christmas. We'll go somewhere warm and buy a big house and Abandon won't seem like nothin but a bad dream. H-h-h-hell, we'll go back to Tennessee if you want. Get your mother, your brothers out a them shacks. Maybe I can take care a Arnold. You think they don't deserve that?"

Gloria struggled to her feet. She felt dizzy, her head swimming, blood and tears running down her chin, staining her white petticoat.

"What about Oatha?" Bessie asked. "I don't like that bunko."

"Fuck Oatha. We'll get our share, leave that son of a bitch in Silverton, shove out on our own steam, just you, me, Harriet, and our life could be so good if you can find a way to forget a couple days a poor behavior. C-c-can you do that, Bess? Then it's all yours. Everthin you ever wanted. We'll be a well-heeled pair a bums on the plush. Straight goods."

Gloria had begun to back quietly toward the kitchen. There was a knife inside the small wood box—a medicine chest filled with herbs and tinctures—sitting on one of the newspaper-lined shelves.

"Hey, Daddy," Harriet said. The little girl had climbed out of bed and she stood behind her mother, clinging to Bessie's legs.

"Hey there, darlin."

As she reached the kitchen, a board squeaked beneath Gloria, and Billy spun, drew his big Walker. "You do me a great favor and set down by the fire, Mrs. Curtice." Billy looked back at his wife. "You think I'm some monster, Bessie, but I ain't. Just willin to do more for my family than most."

"Billy, you say you done this for me, but look at my face. What kind a man beats on his—"

"Won't ever lay a hand on you again. That's a promise."

"I need to know what all you done before I—"

"And I'll tell you. Everthin. No more secrets. But right now, 'til we get out a this town, I need you to trust me. I love you and Harriet. You're my blue chips. That's the only reason I done any a this. Will you trust me?" Bessie looked over at Gloria. "Don't look at her. Look in my eyes. This is *your* crossroads. What do *you* want?"

"To be with the boy I fell in love with in Tennessee."

"You're lookin at him."

"Am I?"

"For a fact. Gonna be different after we leave. So much better."

"I wanna believe that, Billy."

Gloria said, "Bessie, you didn't see what your husband did to—"

"Shut up!" Billy touched his wife's face, and Gloria saw it happen—a softening in Bessie's eyes, walls coming down.

"Burn the breeze back to the cabin," Billy said. "I want you to pack what food we got, enough clothes for us to get to Silverton."

"We're goin now?"

"Can't stay in this bog hole."

"Bessie!" Gloria said. *"What are you doing?"*

Bessie reached down and took her daughter's hand. "I'm sorry," she said. "But he is my husband. I ain't got nothin else."

Gloria's eyes ran over. "Where's *my* husband? Where's Zeke?"

The McCabes walked onto the front porch.

Billy said, "Y'all go on. I gotta talk to Mrs. Curtice alone."

"About what?"

"Gonna trust me or not, Bess?" As Billy closed the door, Gloria stood up, the fire nothing more than a few orange coals.

"Is he dead? Will you tell me that before you shoot me down? Is that Zeke's blood on your . . . Oh God!" She'd noticed his cowhide custom-mades. "You're wearing his boots!"

"I can't shoot ye, Mrs. Curtice." Billy jammed the long barrel of the Walker down his pants and pulled a rusted buffalo skinner with a stag-horn grip from a sheath under his frock coat.

"Please," she said as he came toward her.

"Got no choice here. You set still, and we'll do this quick."

The front door opened. Billy tucked his knife into his coat, looked back over his shoulder.

"I thought I told you—"

"Something's happenin," Bessie said. "Oscar and Randall are ridin around yellin for everyone to come outside."

"What for?"

Gloria could hear the shouting now, saw two men on horseback loping up the path toward the cabin.

"Somethin about Indians. Come on, they're callin for you, Billy. Want you to ride up to the pass with some a the other men, help head 'em off."

2009

FORTY-FOUR

Abigail's watch showed 2:49 A.M. as the sprawling menace of Emerald House appeared through the falling snow. They'd killed their headlamps after leaving the switchbacks, and it had proved exceedingly difficult plowing their way through the basin in the total darkness of the storm. At the lake's edge, a hundred yards from the big Douglas fir trunks of the portico, they collapsed in the snow.

"I'm dying here, Lawrence."

"I know, me, too."

"I don't think I can walk much farther." Aside from her heart beating in her ears, the only other sounds were the lake lapping at the bank and the distant drone of wind tearing over the peaks. "I still think we should just hike back to camp, get my cell, try to—"

"I told you we won't get service in the canyon."

"But maybe up at the pass—"

"In this storm? Are you kidding?"

"Then let's just get the hell out of here, Lawrence. Go for help."

"It's twenty-seven miles back to civilization, and you just said you didn't know if you could walk any farther. In this weather, we wouldn't reach Silverton until Thursday morning at the earliest, and that would be hiking nonstop, hauling ass, assuming we didn't get lost or take a fall climbing down the icy south side of the Sawblade. Look, I brought the Tozers out here. Now that Emmett's dead, June's my responsibility, and I'm not leaving her in that mansion with Stu."

Oh, now you're responsible, when it might get us killed.

"Then what do you want to do?" she asked.

He struggled to his feet, reached down, helped his daughter up out of the snow.

"I want you to follow me and keep quiet."

They stole up to the west wing of Emerald House and Lawrence boosted Abigail into the same windowsill they'd attempted to escape through several hours earlier. Once inside, she watched her father hoist himself onto the sill, then gave him a hand stepping down into the kitchen on his sprained ankle.

Together, they slipped through the French doors and eased out into the corridor—just a gaping black hole that made Abigail temporarily forget the awful pain in her tailbone.

"I can't see," Lawrence whispered, "so just go slow, and make sure you don't trip on anything. We make the slightest sound, it's over."

"Is the floor safe?"

"Nothing is."

They proceeded with meticulous caution, testing the floorboards with every step to avoid a potentially fatal creak of weak wood.

The darkness never let up, and without the aid of headlamps, they had to trail their hands along the wall to ensure a straight trajectory down the corridor. Abigail followed a few feet behind her father, and she kept looking back over her shoulder, plagued by the unrelenting premonition that someone was creeping up behind them.

When Lawrence stopped, she said, "I don't like this. I wanna get out of here right now."

"Look." Thirty feet ahead, a dim splotch of light shone onto the marble floor of the foyer. "It's June," he whispered.

In the vicinity of June's headlamp, shapes began to materialize out of the darkness. Abigail could see Emmett's widow sitting on the floor on the other side of the staircase, her back roped to a timber that had fallen out of the ceiling, her hands pinioned, shoulders heaving with grief.

Abigail spotted Emmett's body, not ten feet away, at the base of the steps. It was impaled on a thick banister. She braced against the image, forced back the bile rising up her throat, made herself move on to the next moment. There was madness in the details, in the lingering.

Lawrence whispered, "Where's Stu?"

Abigail shrugged, quietly unzipped her jacket, and pulled a wallet from an inner pocket. She fished out a dime, knelt down. The coin made a soft and delicate purr as it rolled across the marble, spinning out just a foot from June's right leg.

The woman looked up, the bulb of her headlamp making it difficult for Lawrence and Abigail to see her.

"Hurry," June whispered. "He'll be back any minute."

FORTY-FIVE

They crept across the icy marble of the foyer, and when they reached June, Lawrence withdrew Isaiah's sheathed dagger from his ski pants.

"You okay, sweetie?" Abigail whispered, her words reverberating through the foyer like prayers in a vast cathedral. It was hard to see June's face with any clarity in the sole, fading light of her headlamp.

"My left leg's cut pretty bad," June said, on the brink of tears. Abigail touched her shoulder as Lawrence sat down and began sawing the knife through the climbing rope that bound June to the rafter.

"How long's Stu been gone?" Abigail asked.

"About ten minutes."

"We didn't see any new tracks leaving the mansion."

"No, he's still inside. He heard something up on the third floor, went to check it out."

"What'd he hear?"

"Sounded like wood breaking from down here. It was loud. What happened to you guys?"

"Isaiah and Jerrod are dead," Abigail said. "It was . . . Look, I'll tell you that story later. Does Stu still have night-vision goggles and a gun?"

"Yes."

Lawrence unwound the climbing rope and tossed it aside. "Can you stand up and turn around for me? I'll cut these off." The blade sliced easily through the nylon restraints. "June, I think it'd be a good idea to switch off your headlamp."

The three stood close together in sheer darkness.

After a moment, June spoke, her voice breaking, "I keep looking over there at him. Keep thinking he'll get up, come over to me. Or that any second, I'll wake in our apartment, reach over in bed, feel the warmth of him in the dark. But he's cold now, isn't he? Do you think I could go over and sit with him? Would that be all—"

"You hear that?" Abigail said.

"What?" Lawrence asked.

"Listen." From some remote part of the mansion came a sound like a muted jackhammer, and it took Abigail only a moment to place it. "Stu's firing his machine gun."

"That doesn't make any sense," Lawrence said. "Scott's back in town, dead. Isaiah and Jerrod are dead somewhere up near the pass. What the hell's he shooting at?"

The machine gun went quiet. High above, in one of the upper corridors, came the thump of slow, heavy footsteps. Abigail peered up—they all did—but there was nothing to see in that expansive vacuum of light. She reached down, grabbed hold of June's hand as the footsteps stopped.

No one whispered.

No one breathed.

Something crashed into the floor of the foyer, and Abigail and June nearly crushed each other's hands.

They stood in stunned silence, no one daring to move.

Lawrence finally turned on his headlamp.

"Dear God," June said. The light beam traced a widening lake of blood across the floor to its source—the destroyed head of Stu. He lay unnatural and broken on the section of marble exposed to the skylight, his face torqued away from them.

"You think Stu accidentally fell?" Abigail said. "Or jumped? Remember what Isaiah said about him? How he'd fallen apart since the war?"

"He drank half a bottle of vodka after you left," June said.

Lawrence shook his head. "Look, his gun's gone. Night goggles, too."

"So maybe he left them on the third floor."

Lawrence started toward the west wing.

"Wait!" Abigail whispered. She caught up with him. "You aren't seriously going up there?"

FORTY-SIX

Emmett's plunge had effectively destroyed the central staircase, so Lawrence and Abigail worked their way back toward the kitchen to the west-wing stairwell.

They climbed to the third floor and stood for a second time in that bullet-shredded corridor, Abigail feeling trapped in some kind of repetitive fever dream, coming back again and again to this nightmare world.

Their headlamps passed over the doors, the wood-paneled walls, the mounds of snow where the ceiling had failed.

Lawrence limped a few steps into the corridor, stood there listening.

They proceeded on, over the pockmarked wood where Isaiah had fired up at them through the ceiling, skirting that hole where Abigail had punched through and nearly fallen to her death.

They reached what was left of the central staircase.

"I don't hear a thing," Abigail whispered.

"Me, neither. Look at that." He pointed to where several dozen brass shell casings had rolled against the wall. "What was he shooting at?"

They walked on, their headlamps aimed toward the end of the east-wing corridor, an occasional snowflake drifting down through the ceiling, a speck of bright white in their light beams.

"Maybe he did jump," Lawrence whispered. "Got fueled up on vodka and freaked out when he heard something. Emerald House shifts constantly. It's full of noises. Or it could've just been an animal. Another coyote."

"Should we go back, then?" Abigail said.

"Yeah, I think that's a good—" Lawrence took a sharp breath.

"What?" Abigail whispered. "You're scaring me, Lawrence."

"Something just stepped out from one of the rooms at the end of the corridor."

She clutched her father's arm. "Where'd it go?"

"Toward the sitting room, I think. It was just a shadow, and it moved so fast."

"Okay, let's not do this, all right? This is stupid. Like in horror movies when people walk into haunted houses by themselves for no good reason. I wanna go—"

"This isn't like that, Abby. Come on. We have to see."

"No."

"Then go back down to the foyer and wait with June, but I'm not leaving until I—"

She tightened her grip on his arm, said, "I'm not going anywhere in this place alone."

"Then I guess you're coming with me."

Lawrence continued slowly down the corridor, Abigail clinging to her father like she was eight years old again.

They came at last to a decimated sitting area at the corridor's end, heard nothing but the wind moaning outside in low, dissonant tones like some demonic choir. Snow billowed in through the window frames, having already buried the bookshelves and even drifted into the fireplace.

As Abigail swept her headlamp over the ravaged furniture, the listing chandelier began to tinkle.

Lawrence was already turning to go back, but before following him, she shone her headlamp into the far left corner.

"Jesus Christ!"

"What?"

"Lawrence!"

A man crouched behind a rat-eaten divan, his knees drawn into his chest, rocking slowly back and forth and shivering with cold.

"*Are you with them?*" he whispered, and Abigail felt so completely paralyzed that her knees gave out and she sank onto the floor, trembling with pure fear, adrenaline raging, heart red-lining, even before she saw Stu's machine gun in his hand.

1893

FORTY-SEVEN

Molly Madsen sat in the bay window, eating the wedge of chocolate cake from the Curtices' Christmas basket and looking down at the commotion on Main Street. It had been years since she'd seen this many people out on the town at once—entire families webbing north through deep snow, many still buttoning their slickers and coats and pulling on their mittens, a ubiquitous look of fear and confusion on all the faces.

Molly heard footsteps out in the hallway, followed by a soft knock. She rose from the divan, crossed the room barefooted, and opened the door. A young blond woman stood in the hallway, enveloped in a white woolen cape.

"May I help you?" Molly asked.

Lana noticed that under the sheer bed linen, draped like a shawl over her shoulders, Molly was naked.

On many occasions, Lana had glimpsed her sitting in the bay window from the street below and thought her pretty. In proximity, Molly Madsen looked hard-wintered, pupils dilated from laudanum. Her five-year self-imposed confinement to room 6 had turned her skin the sun-deficient gray of a dead tooth, and though her pitch-black hair dropped to her waist, you could see her scalp on top, where her hair had thinned and become laced with silver. Seam squirrels—lice—crawled under the hair on her arms.

The room reeked worse than a bunkhouse—spoiled food, oranges, a hint of old perfume.

"You're the piano player," Molly said, and when she smiled, Lana saw her lips smeared with chocolate icing and bits of cake stuck between her rotting teeth. "Jack and I have so enjoyed sitting in the window, listening. The music carries quite well. It's a sure cure for putting me to sleep. Was that Beethoven you were playing this afternoon?"

Lana reached into her cape, pulled out a pencil. She stared at the tan-colored wood of the door frame, trying to conjure words that had for so long existed only in the safety of thought. She couldn't remember the last time she'd written anything, but it was easier to recall the letters than to amass the nerve to create them, with no words spoken, no direct communication with another human being in three years, since that Christmas night in Santa Fe.

Molly said, "Can't you talk?" Lana looked up, forced herself to make eye contact. Her gloved hands trembled as she pressed the pencil tip into the wood.

When she'd finished, Molly scanned the tiny writing on the door frame, said, "It's Engler. *Mrs.* Jack Engler. Why on earth would I come with you?"

Lana scrawled an answer, overwhelmingly strange to converse with another person, even like this. The piano had been her larynx for so long.

Something awful happening.

Molly read it, said, "Well, I can't leave yet. Jack should be here any moment, and what would he do if I was gone when he returned? I have to be here to greet him. Do you understand?"

A draft wafted through the hallway, blew open Molly's shawl, her nipples erect in the chill.

Lana wrote: *Leave note.*

"What if he didn't find it? He'd be distressed if I wasn't here. Jack's very protective. No, I think I'll wait in our suite. But thank you for the invitation. We'll come along when he arrives. Where is this ball being held?"

Lana shook her head, eyes welling up with tears.

"You know, I have the perfect dress for it. A rose-colored evening gown. Jack first saw me in it in San Francisco, knew instantly he had to have me. Would you care to see an albumen print of my husband? You've never seen a more handsome man, I assure—"

Lana tried to grab her arm to pull her out into the hall, but Molly withdrew into her suite and slammed the door.

FORTY-EIGHT

Lana refastened her webs in the lobby of the deserted hotel and went outside. The sky was a rusty red, the walls of the box canyon slathered in alpenglow.

Sounds of men shouting resounded through Abandon.

She waded out into the middle of the street, where a path had been beaten down in the snow, fell in behind a young family of four, followed them down Main, listening to the children complain of the cold, begging to go home so they could finish supper and play with their Christmas toys.

Glancing up a side street, Lana saw more people streaming out of the cabins, and someone yelled, "*Hostiles?*"

They passed the burned-out buildings on the north end of town, torched over a year ago in an autumn fire. The family ahead of her stopped. The father knelt down, drew his children into his arms.

"Why you cryin, Pa?"

"Ain't." But he wiped his eyes. "Gotta leave y'all for a spell."

"Where you goin?"

"Me and some a the other pas are gonna ride up toward the pass and stop what's comin, make sure don't nothin happen to this town and all the mas and children in it. But I'll be back 'fore you know it. Need you to listen to your ma for me."

"Yes, Pa."

"Yes, Pa."

He stood and embraced his wife, and as Lana bypassed them in the deeper snow, she heard the woman say, "I'm scared, John."

"Don't be, love. Just pray."

The web tracks branched off from Main and went up the hillside. Lana passed smoking cabins on the spruce-dotted slope, saw two Italians on horseback rousing families from their Christmas suppers, hollering for them to get dressed quick and head up to the chapel.

The church stood in the distance, one of the first buildings erected in Abandon, though after a decade of scant upkeep, it needed whitewashing, and the windows on the north side had been boarded up since a blizzard had blown them out in the winter of 1890.

A crowd was gathering on the steps, and as Lana looked up at the wood cross, black against the copper sky, it began to teeter and she startled, thought for half a second the world was ending.

Then the iron bell began to clang, faster and faster, and she saw the preacher, Stephen Cole, pulling the tolling rope, not with the leisurely announcement of a wedding or a Sunday service, but with all the ominous urgency of a warning, so hard that it shook the belfry and made the cross stand crooked.

2009

FORTY-NINE

He reached into his parka, pulled out a lighter and a pack of Kools.
"You wanna smoke?"

"That that menthol shit?"

"Of course."

"What the hell."

Isaiah slipped two cigarettes between his lips, lit them both, handed one to Jerrod.

"Ain't this some shit."

They sat perched on a four-foot ledge, midway down the icy head wall.

"You got the first-aid kit in your pack?" Jerrod asked, his voice straining with pain.

"Nah, it's in one of the duffel bags back at the mansion."

"Fuck."

"Hurts bad, huh?"

"Holy shit, man. A little morphine would really hit the spot."

"It looks bad."

"I haven't looked."

"No? You can see the bone—"

"Shut the fuck up. I don't wanna hear that."

It was snowing so hard, Isaiah had to cup the end of his cigarette to keep the ember dry. Jerrod took an aggressive drag, leaned back against the rock he'd slammed into feetfirst on his fall down the mountain. Both legs were stretched out, but the right one had rotated almost ninety degrees, so at a passing glance he appeared to own a pair of left legs.

"You think Lawrence is lying?" Jerrod asked.

"Did at first. Now I'm not so sure. I think he may be just as pissed as we are."

"So no gold."

"Nada."

"Fuck, this hurts, man. Talk to me. I gotta keep my mind off it. What were you gonna do, say we actually found it, managed to get the gold out of these mountains?"

"So, say it turned out to be twenty-four mil, right? That's eight apiece. Well, first off, I'm in debt over two hundred thousand. I was gonna pay that shit off, put enough aside to send the kids through school, set me and Shari up so we didn't have to work. Then after that, say I got four mil left to play around with. We were gonna build this tight palace, man. In one of those upper-class all-black suburbs of Atlanta. We'd already sketched a design. Shit. Home theater. Exercise room. Huge master bedroom. Twelve-foot ceilings. Big pool. Jacuzzi. Basketball court. Giant grill out back. Kind of place my kids would wanna come back to after they were grown and gone. Christmas or Thanksgiving, it'd be me and Shari, our three kids, about a hundred grandbabies running around. I'd have liked that."

"Shari knows what you're doing out here?"

"Me and Shari, we synced, man. No secrets. That's the only way. She's my partner in all things. So how 'bout you? Any big plans for your share?"

Jerrod tossed his cigarette over the ledge and groaned.

"Come on, baby, you gotta keep talking. Chase that pain away. You seen worse."

"No, actually, we have a winner." Jerrod closed his eyes, tucked his gloved hands into his armpits, shivering violently. "I didn't even need eight million," he said.

"You'd have stayed in Colorado?"

"No, I was gonna head up to Alaska. Last frontier, right? Find some land out in the middle of bumfuck. Where there wasn't even a road in."

"You Daniel Boone motherfucker, you."

"Maybe in the Chigmits, the Aleutians. Put a cabin on a big lake. Always wanted to get my pilot's license. I'd buy a little floatplane, and the only time I'd ever leave would be to go for supplies. Just live out there and fish and hunt. Forget about all the shit I've seen."

"I hear that."

"Nobody'd ever see my ass again." Jerrod gritted his teeth. "I never been so cold, man."

"Think Stu would've got his shit together with his share?"

"I think he'd have just drunk himself to death faster, and with better booze. Damn, man, this is getting worse and worse."

Isaiah flicked his cigarette away. He stood up, peered over the ledge, staring down into roiling snow and bottomless dark.

"How's it look?" Jerrod asked.

"Steep as shit. Can't even tell how much farther down it goes."

"We got a situation here."

"That we do, brother."

"You aren't hurt bad, are you?"

"Just my head and my pride, but they hurt like a motherfucker."

"You foresee any way of getting me out of here?"

Isaiah sat down, put his hand on Jerrod's shoulder, shook his head.

Jerrod nodded. "Afraid you might say that."

"Just don't know how we'd explain our way out of this one, partner."

"I'm sorry. I fucked that jump up." Jerrod wiped his eyes.

"You ain't gotta apologize for shit." A catch in Isaiah's voice, too.

Jerrod said, "Look, if it's gotta be this way, I can't just sit up here by myself, wait to freeze to death. Not in this kind of pain. You know what I'm saying?"

"I feel you."

"There's no other way? You sure?"

"I don't see it." Isaiah pursed his lips together and cocked his head, his brow furrowing up as his eyes welled. "Serving with you, man," he said.

"I know. I know. Same here. Let's just get this the fuck over with, huh?"

Isaiah took up his machine pistol and racked the slide. His eyes burned. He couldn't see, had to wait a moment, letting them clear, not wanting to fuck any part of this up.

"You wanna pray or something, Jerrod?"

"Wouldn't know what the fuck to say. Haven't prayed a day out of my whole life. God ain't a fool if He's up there, and I don't wanna insult the Man, particularly now."

"Anything you want me to take care of when I get out of here? Anybody you want me to go see, let 'em know, give 'em a message or—"

"Like who?"

"I don't know. Your parents." He smiled. "Your harem of bitches."

"Nah. Nobody'll notice."

"You ready, then?"

Jerrod drew in a deep breath, looked all around at the rock, the snow, the darkness, the cliffs, taking heed of this cold ledge where he was going to die. "Yeah."

"Love you, brother. Never said that to a—"

"You, too, man. You, too. Family, you know?"

"Yeah."

"Well, the suspense is killing me, so . . ." Jerrod turned away. He stared at the tip of his boot, thought how pretty the snow was falling on it, and what a strange last thought this was.

Isaiah raised the machine pistol, positioned the barrel a few inches from the back of Jerrod's head. He calmed himself, held the red dot steady.

Jerrod slumped over into the snow.

Isaiah fired another Kool, sat for a while, smoking, listening to the wind, watching snow pile up on the rock, on Jerrod. For the moment, it melted on his friend's warm face.

At length, Isaiah stood up. But he felt empty, something unfinished. He had a notepad in his backpack, and he pulled it out and found a pencil, sat hunched over the paper, shielding it from the snow. He scribbled down five words, tore out the sheet of paper, and slipped it into the pocket of Jerrod's parka.

Isaiah gathered up his things, then followed the ledge for thirty feet until it slimmed out into nothing. As he began the slow and treacherous descent into the canyon, he kept thinking of what he'd written for his friend, wished it could have been more, repeating Jerrod's epitaph in his head like a plain-song.

This man was a soldier.

This man was a soldier.

FIFTY

The man behind the divan stood up, the machine pistol quivering in his grasp.

There was a flash, Abigail thinking he'd pulled the trigger, the walls of the sitting area lighting up, the snow glinting. It went dark again. Muffled thunder rolled through the basin, shook the chandelier, the weakened floor trembling beneath her feet.

Abigail rose up slowly, her arms outstretched in deference to the weapon. When the lightning came again, she noticed the streaks of blood down the man's face, his eyes rimmed with black bruises.

"Are you with them?" he whispered again.

"With who?" Abigail asked.

"The men in masks. There were— Get back!" he yelled and Abigail saw the machine pistol shift to her father.

Lawrence said, "You see my hands, right? I promise you we aren't a threat. In fact, we're probably in the same—"

"I'll decide that." His eyes returned to Abigail. "What are you doing here?"

"We arrived in Abandon this afternoon, a team of six. Downstairs in the foyer is the third remaining member of our party. Tonight, while we were exploring the town, those men in masks took us hostage. They killed our guide and a man named Emmett."

"Tell me the names of the men who attacked you."

Abigail had to think for a moment, her mind edging into overdrive. "Isaiah. Stu . . . and Jerrod. Jerrod was also one of our guides on the hike in. But they're dead now."

"All?"

"Yes."

"How'd the other two die?"

"Isaiah and Jerrod fell off a cliff near the pass a couple hours ago."

"What were you doing up there in this storm?"

Abigail hesitated only a second or two. "Looking for these gold bars. Did you kill Stu?"

The man nodded slowly.

"What happened to you?" Abigail said. "Your face—"

"Is it bad?"

"Yeah."

"You two look pretty banged up yourselves."

The man lowered the machine pistol. He stepped out from behind the divan, walked into the beam of her headlamp, tall and very thin, though even through the bruises, he had gentle eyes, which Abigail instinctively trusted. His silver-and-black down coat appeared to have been ripped through the middle by a knife swipe, and his stringy brown hair lay pasted with sweat to the sides of his face.

"I'm Quinn," he said.

"Abigail." Though it was difficult to tell with all the bruising, she placed his age around forty.

Her father stepped forward. "Lawrence."

"Lawrence *Kendall*?"

"Have we met?"

Quinn smiled. "No, but I'm an admirer of your work."

"What are you talking about?"

"I've been in the history department at the U of A, Tucson, the last seven years. This ghost town's been my passion for a long time."

"Thought I was the only one. What's your last name?"

"Collins."

"Haven't heard of you."

"I've only published in my field, Colonial America and the Revolutionary War. Abandon's more like a hobby, I guess."

"Last great mystery of the West."

"Absolutely. But I just got tenure this year, so I'm hoping to get funding and support for a semester of real study. Maybe even a grant to come here for a summer."

"Good luck getting a permit for that."

"Yeah, my attitude's been, Fuck the Forest Service. I've been coming up from Arizona every year to spend time in this canyon, do a little elk hunting on the side. But it's a real thrill to meet you, Lawrence." Quinn reached out to shake his hand. "I've read everything you've written on Abandon."

FIFTY-ONE

They came upon June at the base of the steps. She was standing by her husband, one hand on the banister that had run through him, the other caressing his shaved head.

"Just us, June," Abigail said.

She glanced up at them, void of expression, catatonic.

"Who's that with you?" she asked.

"This is Quinn. He was being held here by Isaiah and Stu."

Quinn froze when he saw Emmett, brought his hand to his mouth, whispered, "Oh God. June, is it? I'm so sorry. Is there anything—"

"No, there isn't. I just need to be alone with him."

Abigail touched her arm, said, "Maybe you should—"

"No! Go!"

They left June with her husband and sat down nearby on the cascading staircase that flowed toward the large oak doors.

Abigail pulled three water bottles out of Lawrence's pack and rolled two of them across the floor to Quinn.

"Thank you." Quinn unscrewed the cap and ravenously downed the entire twelve ounces in one long gulp. Then he leaned back against the steps and gingerly ran his fingers across his face as if reading Braille, trying to picture how the damage had distorted it.

"Isaiah did that?" Abigail asked.

"Quite a violent streak in that man."

"So what, exactly, happened to you?"

Quinn opened the second bottle of water and took another long drink. "I arrived in Abandon last Wednesday morning. Wednesday night, very late, I woke to the sound of footsteps near my tent. Frightened me pretty bad. I called out, asked who was there. No one answered. Of course, I couldn't go back to sleep, so I unzipped the tent and crawled outside. There were two men in masks with guns standing there."

He shivered, as if just speaking about it rekindled the fear. "Isaiah and Stu brought me to this mansion. They kept demanding that I show them where 'it' was. I told them I had no idea what they were talking about. They said I was lying. They beat me. Tied me up and left me in one of the rooms on the third floor. Several times a day, they'd come back, ask if I wanted to tell them or if I needed another beating. I would always say the same thing: I didn't know what it was they wanted.

"Tonight, after working me over for a while, they blindfolded me and slapped a piece of tape on my mouth. Few hours later, I heard a ruckus on the floor below and voices I hadn't heard before. Suppose that was you guys. I managed to find an edge on the old chair they'd strapped me to, finally cut through the tape around my wrists about an hour ago."

"You made all that racket up there that caught Stu's attention?" Abigail asked.

"Yeah. I'd crept downstairs, seen there was only one of them guarding June, and I knew it was my only chance. When Stu came up, he was drunk, and I managed to overpower him."

Quinn sipped his water. Outside, the wind still made that strange unnerving sound like ghosts humming.

"So why'd you come to Abandon in the first place?" Lawrence asked.

Quinn smiled. "Well, why are you here?"

Abigail sensed something in the current between the two men.

Lawrence said, "I was giving June and her husband a tour of the ghost town. They're paranormal photographers."

"That's all, huh?"

Abigail realized what it was: distrust. These two historians sizing each other up, attempting to gauge how much the other one knew, what to let on, what to keep to themselves.

"What was it again that you were looking for up at the pass? I think I heard Abigail say something about—"

"All right, should we quit jerking each other off here?" Lawrence said. "Anyone who's studied Abandon in depth knows that a sizable quantity of Packer's gold has never been accounted for."

"And you've been searching for it."

It got quiet for a moment. Then Lawrence said, "Yeah. And you?"

Quinn nodded. "You an honest man, Lawrence?"

"Guess that depends."

"What if I were to tell you that I have something in my jacket that might be able to help us out?"

"I'd be interested."

"Interested enough for full disclosure?"

"Assuming it cuts both ways."

Quinn reached into his pocket, handed Lawrence a rusted key attached to a nylon rope.

"Where'd you get this?" Lawrence asked.

"Full disclosure?"

"Yeah."

"From an old man on his deathbed."

"What's it open?" Abigail asked.

"I've spent the last ten autumns of my life trying to find an answer to that. I know it doesn't open anything in this crumbling mansion or the ghost town or the mill."

Lawrence got up, limped over to the entrance of Emerald House, threw the doors open, stood watching the snow.

Abigail called out, "You all right?"

After a moment, he returned, stared down at them, and Abigail could hear the change in his voice as soon as he opened his mouth.

"There's almost two feet of snow on the ground," he said. "I know it's late, and we're all past the point of exhaustion, but with the snow dumping like this, an avalanche would make it impossible to find. We'd have to wait until next summer, when the snows broke. Besides, it's not safe to be in Emerald House with all this snow piling up on the roof."

Quinn stood up, said, "I don't understand. What are you getting at?"

"I might know what your key opens."

1893

FIFTY-TWO

Under calmer circumstances, Gloria might have noticed the sky—clouds striated with a thousand tones of orange, like you were staring up into the guts of an overripe peach, and some of them still bleeding pink curtains of snow.

But she couldn't see anything through the window of tears.

Someone yelled her name.

Gloria stopped, turned back, looking downslope at the chapel far below, the clang of its bell echoing through the canyon.

The last of Abandon's residents trudged up the web trail, the closest of them Emma Ilg, wrapped in a black manta, her purple gown bulging out of the bottom, encrusted with ice. Emma stopped below Gloria and hunched over to catch her breath in the thin air.

When she looked up, she said, "Have you seen Russ— What's wrong?"

Gloria shook her head, tears streaming.

"Billy McCabe and Oatha Wallace . . . know 'em?"

"Know of them. Why?"

Gloria went to pieces. "I think they killed our husbands."

Emma's ruddy face turned cold, rigid. "No. Don't you say that to me. Russ and Ezekiel are up ahead. They're trying to find us—"

"Listen to me, Emma."

"I will not hear—"

"Billy and Oatha murdered Mr. Packer last night and made off with his gold. That's why our husbands rode up to the pass. But it's been four hours and Zeke hasn't come back to me."

"How do you know they're gone?"

"'Cause Billy came to my cabin and was on the verge of killin me before—"

"You've seen them dead?"

"No."

"Then they aren't. My husband's up ahead."

"Please, Emma—"

"Don't speak another word to me!" Emma pushed her way up the trail, knocking Gloria down into the snow as she passed.

A ways up the mountain, a woman screamed.

"Al, get your fuckin hands off me," Joss said.

"Come on, they's children up ahead a you. Watch that mouth—"

"Don't tell me how to be. You got these wrist irons too tight. They're strangulatin my hands. And I need a brain tablet."

"I'll fix 'em when we get there *and* get you a smoke. Simmer down." Joss glanced up toward the end of the canyon. With the storm having passed, she could finally see the steep white slope two miles south that led up to the Sawblade. She squinted her eyes, trying to raise the black specks zigzagging down like a line of warrior ants, thought she'd rather go it alone, take her chances in Abandon, than holed up with this miserable bunch of pilgrims.

Near the rimrock, the trail had become an icy staircase, stomped down and smoothed over by the passage of a hundred pairs of webs.

"How you expect me to climb with no hands?"

"Haul in your neck. I'm helpin you, ain't I?"

Joss purposely tripped, and Al had to grab her under both elbows to keep her from sliding down the mountain.

"We're almost there," he said. "Can you climb ten more steps?"

As Joss struggled to her feet, her fingers grazed over the bowie knife jammed down into her canvas trousers, and she thought, *It will be such a pleasure to stick this in you, you stackwad cocksucker.*

Fifty feet back down the trail, Joss heard a woman scream.

"Where's Daddy?"

"He rode up to the pass with Mr. Wallace, honey."

"What for?"

"Don't you worry about that."

Bessie walked ahead of her daughter as they climbed the slope above town, her mind running in ten directions at once. The gold. The murders. Heathens riding down from the pass. They'd been delayed in getting to the chapel, because Billy had told them to go home first and pack for the trip to Silverton. But she was with him now, and despite everything, it felt right. He was her husband, after all. The Good Lord commanded that she obey him.

The trail steepened, and just ahead lay a series of icy steps that climbed the remaining distance up the cuesta to the rimrock.

"All right, Har, I need to hold your hand on this part." Bessie turned around. "Harriet!" she screamed. "Harriet!" She couldn't see anything downslope, standing high enough above town that a slice of the sun still lingered over the far side of the canyon.

"What's wrong, ma'am?" An Englishman leading his wife and two daughters stopped on the trail just below.

"You seen my daughter? She's yea high. Six years old. Curly black hair. She was right here with me not a second ago."

"No, I sure haven't seen—"

"Oh Jesus. Excuse me." Bessie tried to scoot by, but the big bearded Englishman stretched his arm out to stop her.

"Ma'am, now you gotta keep climbing. We're in terrible—"

"I've lost my daughter!"

"And someone's gonna find her and they'll bring her along."

"Sir, please step out of my way."

"You're holding up the line."

"Harriet! Harriet!"

As Bessie tried once more to step around him, he scooped her up, threw her over his shoulder, and continued up the steps toward the rimrock, Bessie flailing and screaming, the Englishman shushing her.

"We're gonna get everyone safely inside, and if she isn't there, I'll go find her myself. That's a promise."

But Bessie's desperate screaming drowned him out. She even surpassed the church bell until the mountain swallowed her.

2009

FIFTY-THREE

June whimpered, "I should've stayed with Emmett. He's all alone in that place."

Abigail walked with her arm around June, supporting her, and within earshot of the two professors. "I know," she said, "but we can't split up, and with the snow coming down like this, the roof of Emerald House could collapse."

They made a careful descent out of Emerald Basin, down the steep switchbacks to the canyon floor, Lawrence and Quinn talking shop while they fought their way through the snow.

Even though her tailbone was in agony, Abigail felt revived by a second wind as they passed their buried tents, the llamas standing together in a mass of fur and breath clouds. It was almost four in the morning when they entered the ghost town of Abandon, a pride of headlamps moving between the dark and snow-fraught buildings—some swaying in the wind, on the brink of collapse.

She caught a fragment of what Lawrence was saying: "... tempting, but my first priority is getting June and my daughter out of here."

As they approached the north end of Abandon, Abigail improved her pace, came up between the professors, said, "So where are you taking us, Lawrence?"

He glanced back. "Not much farther now. All will be revealed."

At the end of town, Lawrence turned and led them up the east side of the canyon. After a hundred yards, Abigail's headlamp shone on something through the heavy snow—that ruined church in the spruce, its iron bell capped with snow, its cross powder-blown and listing in the wind.

They hiked on, the snow rising almost to her knees. Soon they were climbing again, Abigail using her hands and feet now, the slope so steep that she had to kick her boots in to avoid slipping. At the moment she didn't think she could climb anymore, Lawrence reached back and pulled her and June up onto a wide ledge.

They'd arrived at the base of the rimrock. From here, the canyon wall rose vertically into darkness, and Abigail was on the verge of asking where they could possibly go from here when she saw it—behind Quinn, an opening to a mine shaft, seven feet high and wide enough for several to walk abreast into the mountain.

"How have I never seen this?" Quinn said.

Lawrence pointed to the rock around the opening. "Because of the way the rock overhangs, you can't see the shadow of the tunnel from the canyon floor. You'd have to stumble upon it by sheer dumb luck, like I did last year."

He turned and walked into the mine.

"Warmer in here," Quinn said.

"Most of the mines around Abandon stay a balmy thirty-seven degrees Fahrenheit year round. Refreshing in the summer."

Abigail and June followed them in.

The wind died away.

"How's your ankle holding up, Lawrence?" Abigail asked.

"Doesn't matter. I'm on pure adrenaline now."

Water dripped from the ceiling onto the hood of Abigail's jacket.

The air smelled dank, of water and minerals.

"What is this place?" she asked.

"They used to call it a 'shoofly,' " Lawrence said, his voice echoing off the rock and trailing away deep into the mountain. "It's just an entryway into the mine."

She shined her headlamp into the distance, where the tunnel seemed to narrow, and thirty feet ahead, Abigail saw their headlamp beams converge upon a small iron door.

1893

FIFTY-FOUR

Shadowgees had been placed every twenty feet on the wet, rocky floor, like luminarias for a subterranean party. Gloria hurried along the downward-sloping tunnel into the mountain, following the echo of voices in the darkness ahead.

The day hole narrowed, and she came at last to a small iron door built into the rock. A man she recognized as the Godsend's assayer manned the entrance, and he offered his hand, escorting her through.

"You can head on over that way with the others, ma'am, and do watch your step on this uneven rock."

Lanterns and candles and more shadowgees illuminated the rock in firelight, and as she passed into the main chamber, the whole of Abandon overwhelmed her in a hundred-strong chorus of weeping and shouting and voices in varying strains of panic—bawling, terrified children; mothers and fathers trying to comfort them, many failing to hold back their own tears; a handful of men barking orders, attempting to manage the chaos; huddles of roostered miners, cursing whatever breed of heathen dare descend into their canyon and making pronouncements of war and grandiose predictions of the hell they would unleash on any savage who breeched the iron door; and Emma Ilg, flitting from person to person, a manic fly, asking if they'd seen her husband.

Gloria found a spot along the wall between two distraught families, crumpled down on the cold rock, and buried her face in the sleeves of her woolen jacket. *Heathens are coming and Zeke is gone.* She kept repeating it to herself, as if verifying that the nightmare was real, crying harder and harder as the pandemonium lifted to a crescendo.

Someone touched her shoulder. She looked up, and for a split second, out of sheer will and hope, she thought she saw Ezekiel squatted down in front of her, and her heart ruptured for him.

But it was the shunned madam she'd met last night at the dance hall, a thousand years ago, shivering under her bright red capote, her burgundy curls dusted with snow.

"It's Rosalyn," the old whore said. "What's wrong, honey? Where's your husband? He ride up to the pass with the other men?"

Gloria shook her head, but when she tried to tell her about Zeke, the words froze in her throat. Rosalyn sat beside her, reached over, and pulled Gloria's head down into her lap. She pushed back the hood of Gloria's cape and ran her fingers through her blond hair.

A voice rose above the din. Children stopped crying. The rowdy miners hushed. Gloria lifted her head from Rosalyn's lap, saw all eyes on Bessie McCabe, who was standing amid the crowd, ripping out clumps of hair, and screaming Harriet's name, her voice filling the cavern, reverberating down the tunnels, firelit tears glistening on her bruised face.

Stephen Cole rushed through the iron door toward Bessie. He embraced her and they sank down together on the floor, the preacher cradling her in his arms like a baby, rocking with her, whispering, "Calm down, my child, calm down. We'll find her."

Joss spotted Lana Hartman across the cavern, sitting quietly against the wall, her eyes shut tight, lips moving as if in prayer.

"Al, I told you I gotta see a man about a horse."

They stood twenty feet from the iron door, and even in the weak, shadow-ridden light, Joss saw the boy's pale complexion flush.

"Can't you hold it a little while longer?" he whispered.

"Let me go on down that tunnel there, have my piece a privacy."

"You know I can't let you out a my sight."

"You promised you'd loosen these wrist irons," she whined.

"Hell, Joss. Hell." The young deputy reached into his slicker, worked the key off the big ring attached to one of the belt loops on his dungarees, and waved it in Joss's face. "Zeke Curtice'll put me in the boneyard if I let you run a blazer on—"

"Al." Joss smiled, watched how easily the boy's face disarmed, knew for a fact he'd take full advantage if he ever got the chance. "You're too close to the belly. Watch me squat if you want."

"Might have to, Joss," he said, then sighed. "Turn around."

Al lifted her black serape and unlocked the wrist irons.

"Bring a happy jack," she said, and Al picked one of the shadowgees off the floor and followed his prisoner into the empty passage.

2009

FIFTY-FIVE

As Lawrence rapped his knuckles on the iron, Abigail's headlamp shone on the surface of a door so overrun with rust, it resembled brown mold. It stood closed and locked by means of a thick crossbar held in place with a padlock the size of a small shield.

Quinn reached into his down jacket and pulled out the key.

"Full disclosure, Lawrence. How'd you find this place?"

"On my final day last fall, I climbed up the east side of the canyon to take a picture of the ghost town from above, and happened to stumble upon this mine. You have to understand—at the time, I was so absorbed in my search for Oatha and Billy's claim hole that I didn't think twice about this shaft. Besides, there are countless mines above Abandon. Figured it wasn't anything special. But if you found that key in Bart's suite, *and* it fits that lock . . . Shit, my heart must be going a hundred miles an hour."

"I know, mine, too." Quinn held up the key. "Shall I?"

"Absolutely."

Quinn slipped the key into the hole.

"Is it working?"

"Don't know yet. The mechanism feels pretty stiff, so I'm going slow. Don't wanna break it off." Quinn carefully turned the key. "I think it's working." He slid the padlock out of the crossbar and set it down. "Jeez, that's heavy. Help me with this, Lawrence." The two men lifted the crossbar out of the deep iron brackets and dropped it on the rock.

With the crossbar gone, the door was naked save for a small lever on the right side near the rock, which appeared to function as a doorknob.

Lawrence lifted the lever.

From inside came the rusted squeak of a bolt moving.

The door swung inward and clanged against the rock, a strong, cold draft sweeping in, the mountain sucking air deep into itself, as if trying to breathe.

"Unbelievable," Lawrence whispered as Abigail felt June's grasp tighten around her hand.

"Lawrence, when did you first come to Abandon?" Quinn asked.

"Nineteen seventy-nine."

"You've got me beat. Do the honors."

Lawrence crossed the threshold, Quinn following close behind. As she entered, Abigail moved her headlamp along the walls, saw a grouping of holes in a sweep of unblasted rock, the product of a day spent double-jacking more than a hundred years ago.

She heard Lawrence gasp, and she broke away from June and went to her father's side. "What's wrong?" His headlamp was trained on an alcove fifteen feet off to the right of the iron door, his dimming light illuminating a collection of tattered burlap sacks, ten in all. Lawrence unclipped his backpack, took a deep, trembling breath, then limped into the alcove and knelt on the rocky floor. He reached into one of the sacks. His head dropped.

"What?" Quinn said. "They empty?"

Lawrence chucked something through the darkness.

A brick of solid gold thudded on the rock at Abigail's feet. Then another. And another. She reached down, picked one up. The bar looked small in her hand, but it felt disproportionately heavy for its size, the yellow metal gleaming under her lamp, its surface marred with chinks and divots, cold as a block of ice.

"You're holding more than two hundred and eighty thousand dollars right there," Quinn said.

Lawrence wept.

Abigail went to him in the alcove, asked, "What is it?"

He shook his head. "Waited a long time for this."

Quinn had been rifling through the sacks. "I count sixty-one bricks," he said.

Lawrence closed his eyes as he did the math. "Almost eighteen million. God, my whole body is tingling. Look at that." His right hand shook in the beam of his headlamp.

Abigail glanced over her shoulder, saw June wandering off into another part of the mine.

"I'm gonna go check on her," she said.

Abigail struggled to her feet, walked over to June, found her staggering through the dark, shaking her head and muttering to herself.

"What's wrong, honey?" Abigail asked. "You okay?"

When June looked back, her face had gone pallid and chalky, her eyes sunken, the small woman as bloodless as a cadaver.

She turned suddenly and vomited on the rock.

1893

FIFTY-SIX

When Stephen Cole raised his left arm, the noise in the chamber began to wane. Soon there was no sound but the occasional squall of a child. He stood in the center of the cavern, taking a moment to regard the horrified faces—these men, women, and children of Abandon who sat huddled together along the walls.

"Would you close your eyes with me?" he said.

Hats came off. Heads bowed. Children were shushed.

"Father." Stephen Cole fell to his knees. "We come before You on this, the night of our Savior's birth, a greedy, wicked, corrupt assembly. It is a dark hour. We have provoked Your wrath and for that I fall on my face and beseech Your forgiveness." The preacher prostrated himself, his cheek against the cold rock floor. "I lift up the children to You, dear God. Children! I beg You." His voice unraveled. "I *beg* You. Deliver them. Let them not be afraid, and if it be possible, allow this cup to pass." The preacher's tears ran down into the crevices of the rock. He whispered, "What of grace? Oh, my Father, what of grace? But not as I, but as Thou wilt. In Your Son's holy name. Amen."

Stephen wiped his face and rose to his feet, dusted the silt from his greatcoat, replaced his visored felt hat. He approached the town blacksmith, a small, well-liked man named Mason Stetler.

"Mason," he said, "I leave the town to your care. You're capitan. I'm going out that door now, and I'm going alone. If you hear a knock in quick intervals of three, know that it's me, but don't open it for any other reason. Better paint for war."

"Mind your hair, Stephen. Got a shootin iron?"

"Yes."

Someone grabbed Stephen's arm. He turned, faced Gloria Curtice, her wet, probing eyes still grasping for a shred of hope.

Stephen shook his head and embraced her. "Zeke is with our Lord now," he whispered. "With your little boy. Be dreadnought."

Her knees failed. As Gloria collapsed, wailing on the floor, her anguish masked another sound that emanated from the nearby passage—loud but brief, a sharp cry of pain.

Stephen carried a shadowgee, an old Colt single-action Army, and a shotgun up the tunnel. When he stepped out onto the ledge, he extinguished the flame and sat down on the rock. It was a good, protected rincon. The sun had gone away and bled the clouds into a deepening blue that cast the mountains in a gray-metal twilight.

He gazed down on Abandon situated in the gloom of the canyon floor, lifeless and dark, wondering how those six men fared who'd ridden up to the pass.

He wasn't afraid, enwrapped instead in the clutches of the most peculiar detachment he'd ever known, as if he existed somewhere above himself, watching everything unfold apart from the fear and the anticipation.

Still, a part of him kept listening for gunshots, unsure if the crack of their reports could carry this far from the pass.

Soon it was full-on night. He grew cold, his head exploding now.

Down in the canyon, specks of firelight winked on.

He returned to himself. His hands shook.

As the procession of lights moved through the empty town, Stephen took two shells from the pocket of his greatcoat and broke the breech of the double-barreled shotgun, whispering as he slid them home, "Wilt Thou shew wonders to the dead? Shall the dead arise and praise Thee? Shall Thy loving-kindness be declared in the grave? Or Thy faithfulness in destruction? Shall Thy wonders be known in the dark?"

The scalp hunters were already to the north end of Abandon, and Stephen watched them turn their mounts toward the chapel, following the tracks of the fleeing townspeople. His lips moved again in the dark, "Oh, my Father, if it be possible, let this cup pass."

Joss emerged from the passage and took a seat on the outskirts of the cavern, her hands hidden under her serape, blackened and sticky with blood. If a saloon regular saw her, they might puzzle at Al's absence. A reasonable explanation would be required.

She'd just set about inventing that lie when the roar of a shotgun filled the passage outside the iron door.

Everyone made a collective gasp, children crying, Mason Stetler yelling for every able man with a weapon to come forward, almost two dozen springing up, crowding the iron door in a ragtag battalion.

They waited.

Joss counted five staccato shots from a revolver. Three shotgun blasts. Then silence.

Stephen dropped two shells into the shotgun and reloaded the revolver from his cartridge belt.

Two heathens dead in the tunnel behind him. Two on the brink.

He was unscathed, but his heart beat so fast, he couldn't think.

More lights approached, already to the chapel several hundred feet below. He could hear their horses snorting, the sound of hooves breaking through powder.

He took several steps back into the tunnel, his whole body quaking. He closed his eyes, tried to still himself.

The riders closed in on the rimrock.

He exhaled when he saw Oatha Wallace and Billy McCabe dismount. They waded through the snow and climbed up onto the ledge, stood just outside the entrance to the mine.

Oatha's claybank eyed the preacher warily, and as had happened on more than one occasion in the last week, Stephen saw the horse's brown teeth lengthen and sharpen in the firelight.

Oatha hawked his plug of tobacco into the snow. His lantern hung down at the level of his knees, his face and Billy's all gone to shadow and grotesque patterns of light, eyes shining, breath vapors clouding. Oatha wiped the tobacco juice from his chin with the back of his glove.

"You know somethin, Preach," he said. "I'm feelin a little red-eyed toward you."

"Why's that, Mr. Wallace?"

"Weren't no injerns up at the Sawblade. We rode around for—"

Movement in the tunnel drew Oatha's eye.

He raised the lantern, peered around Stephen, the firelight falling upon one of his fellow miners, John Hurwitz, dragging himself off a pile of bodies, whimpering, his blood running out ahead of him down into the mine.

"The fuck's goin—"

At close range, the buckshot excavated most of Oatha's face.

His knees locked, and he pitched backward over the ledge.

Billy had caught only a few pellets in the right shoulder, but as he reached for his Walker, the preacher blew a ragged, gaping hole in the boy's chest.

Billy sat down on the ledge. He cupped his gloves to catch the steaming handfuls that fell out of him, looking up at the preacher, struggling to breathe, eyes asquint with profound aggrievement.

Stephen threw down the shotgun and pulled the revolver.

"God save your soul," he said, and shot the boy between the eyes.

2009

FIFTY-SEVEN

Abigail patted June's back. "Feel better now?"

June shook her head and spit onto the rock.

Lawrence jogged over from the alcove, asked, "What happened?"

"She threw up."

"I didn't even think about the air. It might be bad. Abby, do you feel strange or woozy?"

June stood upright, wiped the sweat from her face, said in a voice that bordered on defiance, "It's not the air." She moved away from them, into the darkness, her headlamp flickering across the walls, the ceiling. From twenty feet back, Abigail could barely see her in the fading light of her lamp—just her legs and the illuminated rock around her boots.

June suddenly sank down onto the floor and convulsed violently, legs bouncing up and down on the rock, arms flailing as if in the throes of electrocution.

Abigail ran to her, dropped to her knees, tried to steady June's limbs, whispering, "Oh Jesus, oh Jesus. June, look at me."

June went still, her eyes open and glassy and staring straight up at the ceiling, mouth agape, chest heaving up and down.

"Talk to me," Abigail pleaded. "Please say something. I need to know you can hear me."

As Abigail reached out to hold June's hand, the beam of her headlamp struck on something. She froze. The blood in her veins and arteries and the oxygen in her lungs seemed to congeal. She made an involuntary sound, something like a mewl.

The hand of an infant had caught her eye, less than five feet from where she knelt, the bones clearly visible—brown and tiny and perfect, clasping the phalanges of a larger hand. She turned her headlamp away, but it passed over another skeleton, this one adorned with strands of long blond hair that had matted to the skull, and still boasting jewelry—a gold wedding band on the long, brittle phalange of the ring finger and a necklace dangling from one of the upper vertebra into the rib cage.

Lawrence said, "Quinn, you need to come see this!"

June and Abigail got up. They stood in the center of a large cavern teeming with the bones of Abandon—at least a hundred skeletons, most still intact, their clothes having long since disintegrated in the cold storage of the cave, moist enough to support the growth of a hairy white fungus that overspread portions of the rock like a network of capillaries. The skeletons were of every size and scattered throughout the chamber in a vast array of death poses, the scene reminding Abigail of some morbid sculpture exhibit. Her stomach was churning, and she wanted to shut her eyes to it, but she knew that would make little difference. This mine and its occupants would stay with her for the rest of her life, in waking moments, in dreams.

They drifted wordlessly through the crypt. Most of the skeletons were sprawled across the floor, as if they had lain down en masse to die. Abigail saw one curled up in the fetal position in a corner. Another lay beside a small boulder, its skull cracked, pieces of it on the rock floor, pigmented in proximity with the deepest burgundy shade of ancient blood. A pair of skeletons lay along the wall, their humerus and radius bones intertwined, having perished in each other's arms.

Abigail felt herself coming undone as the images of the dying townsfolk accumulated.

A skull resting in the lap of another skeleton.

On a pair of femurs, the leather binding of a pageless King James Bible.

Between kneecaps, a clear corked bottle still holding an inch of century-old whiskey.

Skeletons sitting up grasping shotguns and rifles and revolvers, the wood stocks badly rotted or gone altogether, others clasping bricks of gold with their browned finger bones.

A handful clinging to the remains of their children.

And under a rusted-out shadowgee, a skeleton with long black hair tweaked both her horror and curiosity at once. On the wide plates of its browned pelvis lay minute femurs and tibias and ribs, a skull the size of an apple, phalanges no thicker than matches, and when she realized these constituted the bones of a mother and its fetus, Abigail broke down.

Lawrence walked over and sat with her. "I know," he whispered. "It's a lot to take in."

"Guys?" June said. "Would you mind turning your headlamps off? I've got Emmett's camera with me, and . . ." She was crying again. "He'd want me to shoot this for him."

They switched off their headlamps, Abigail hating the darkness, not even the faintest presence of light to adapt to in this pure, unfiltered black. She gave June one minute, listening to the click of the camera echo through the chamber and the distant drip of water. She finally said, "Sorry, but I'm turning my headlamp back on. I'm too freaked-out to just sit here in the dark." She found breathing easier with her headlamp on. "You must be beside yourself, huh, Lawrence?"

"This is beyond anything I ever dreamed of finding. The gold and the entire town, in the same place, at the same time."

"It's gonna be amazing material. This'll turn out great articles for both of us."

"I don't know about you, but I plan to write a book." Lawrence stood up, offered Abigail his hand, but she didn't take it, just sat there staring at a coal-oil lantern capsized between two femurs. "Abby? You all right?"

"I don't know how to process it all. Everything we've been through tonight."

Lawrence hollered through the chamber, "Quinn! Come in here! *Have you seen this? We found Abandon! They're all in here!*" Lawrence tapped his headlamp. "Damn, my light's dying. Walk with me back to the entrance, Abby."

They crossed the uneven rock, working their way among the skeletons.

"There he is," Lawrence said, pointing to the bulb of light thirty feet ahead. "Hey, professor, you really need to come in here, see all the bones."

When Abigail's headlamp struck Quinn, he was zipping his backpack.

He glanced up at them, said, "I hope it's enough, Lawrence."

"What? The gold? Of course, eighteen million is plenty for every—"

"I'm not talking about the gold." Quinn shouldered the sagging backpack. "I mean knowing what happened to the town. You spent a good part of your life trying to solve that mystery, and I want you to know I sincerely hope it's a good consolation."

"For what?"

Quinn stepped into the passage. The door to the mine slammed shut in a thunderous concussion of metal on metal, and its echo seemed to last forever. Then came a sound Abigail had already heard once before—the squeak of that rusted bolt sliding home inside the iron door, then the crossbar dropping into the brackets, then that giant padlock locking back.

1893

FIFTY-EIGHT

Gloria and Rosalyn sat against the rock wall, holding each other and listening to the burgeoning chaos near the iron door, where twenty armed men had gathered after hearing gunshots in the passage. But that had been some time ago. The men were growing antsy.

Someone said, "Time we rain hell on some red niggers."

"Preacher said to wait until—"

"And what if that fire escape's already lost his hair? Considered that? Sounded like quite a powder-burnin contest out there."

"Mason, get up here and bring the key with ye! We done waitin!"

Gloria watched the unassuming smith push his way through the cluster of miners, heading to the iron door.

"What'd you say?"

She couldn't see Stetler, who was surrounded by the mob of taller men, but his voice rose above the bedlam, far deeper and louder than his size seemed to accord.

"Said we need the key to this door. I do believe that's the only way to open it from inside."

"You see a keyhole there, Will?"

"What are you talkin about?"

"Preacher asked for the key, and I give it to him. What's it matter anyway? This door only opens from the outside."

"The fuck you do that for?"

"He asked for it!"

"Jesus. He gets himself kilt, *how we gonna get out?*"

Stetler ran his fingernails over the rippled surface of his bald head, which glistened with rivulets of sweat.

A miner said, "We better find some bang juice and powder. Blow that hunk a iron off its hinges."

One of the Godsend's dynos said, "Y'all not see this door when we come in? It's a inch thick. Amount a powder it'd take to blow it open, be a long chance this whole damn mine didn't come down on us."

Gloria turned to Rosalyn, whispered, "I can't listen to them anymore. Will you stroke my hair if I put my head in your lap? Like you was doin before?"

"Of course, honey. Come here."

FIFTY-NINE

Harriet McCabe lay in the middle row of pews, hiding. There had been gun-shots a short time ago, but it was quiet now save for the wind. She thought about her mama. Her friend Bethany. Her new doll, Samantha, which she'd had to leave behind at the shack. She was thirsty, hungry, but more than any-thing, cold and scared.

The sun had gone to bed, and the wind made a long low sound as it pushed against the boarded-up windows, the tiny church swaying and creaking like the hold of a ship, icy air filtering up through the space between the planks.

She shivered under her mama's gray woolen cloak. Just across the aisle stood a stove in a gap between the pews, a stack of logs next to it, and she'd just decided to light a fire, when the chapel doors flung open. Harriet gasped, brought her hand to her mouth. The doors slammed shut, the plank boards groaning beneath the weight of approaching footsteps.

She rolled under the pew, watched a pair of arctics pass two feet from her head. Toward the front of the church, something thumped on the floor, and Harriet scrambled quietly to her feet, peered over the top of the bench. She saw someone in the shadow of the nave. The man was on his knees, facing the barrier separating the front pews from the stage, his arms lifted, hands open to the simple wooden cross mounted on the wall behind the pulpit.

When he spoke, she startled, his voice loud enough to fill the sanctuary, though faltering and brittle as sandstone.

"It is finished, Lord God. Your good and faithful servant kneels before You to say that Your will . . . has been done."

He suddenly fell over, his stomach flat against the floorboards.

Harriet thought he'd died, until he wept, softly at first, then outright sob-bing, pounding the planks with his fists. Harriet had seen her daddy cry once before, but not like this. She'd never seen anyone in such soul-splitting anguish.

"*Why?*" The word exploded—guttural, ragged, raw. He screamed it three times, so loudly that Harriet thought it might shatter the glass of those tall south-facing windows. He got back onto his knees, and when he spoke again, Harriet had to strain to hear the words.

"You say You love truth. Well, here's my truth. I don't know who You are right now. I don't understand how the Creator of love and mercy and compassion, the God who seared my heart in Charleston, can command His servant to lock a town into a mountain. Women! Children! How can a child give You such offense? Are You not the God I think You are? Of David? Of Christ? You are ultimate, whatever Your nature, but I need to know if I've been wrong about You. Correct my perception. You know I love You. That I chose a cimarron's life in Your service, over a woman who still haunts my dreams. If You love me, Lord, if You love me at all, infuse me with a peace that passeth all understanding. Because I need it now. I'm in a bad way. This is my deepest trench, and I may not see the morning. Don't draw back from me. I've destroyed myself for You, and I am so alone."

He bowed his head, and as he cried, Stephen felt something graze his shoulder. He spun around and fell back, bristling with fear. A little girl stood before him in the darkening nave, her curls pitch-black and her eyes aching with hunger.

"Why you sad?" she asked.

Stephen pulled his cape around and wiped his face with it.

"You buggered me. How'd you get out of the mine, Harriet?"

"I been here since long before you came, hidin from injuns."

"You shouldn't have left your mama."

Stephen reached forward, wrapped the cloak tighter around her small frame. "You're shivering," he said. "Let's see if we can remedy that." He stood up and took the little girl's hand and led her over to the stove. Inside, balled-up sheets of the *Silverton Standard and Miner* awaited a Sunday service that would never come. A wicker basket full of dried-out fir cones sat under the closest pew, and Stephen took a handful and arranged the kindling and shoved in two logs. One strike from his machero did the job. He left the iron door open, and soon the flames raged, sending out eddies of heat, throwing firelight on the walls, the cold plank floor, the vaulted ceiling.

"Scoot up close, sweetie. I want you to get warm."

Harriet extended her hands toward the open door and Stephen sat behind her, setting his hat on the floor, tying his hair up. He pulled a small bottle out of his pocket.

"Here, sip this tincture of arnica," he said.

She unscrewed the cap, took a swallow, handed the bottle back.

"What are all those dots on your face?" she asked.

"Nothing." Stephen wiped the sticky specks of her father's blood from his brow, his cheeks, his mouth. Then he reached into his greatcoat and withdrew the single-action army revolver, opened the loading gate behind the cylinder. Three cartridges left.

Is this Your will, God? That I shoot Your child in the back of the head. Because I will do it. I am your faithful servant, but please. Please. If there is any other way . . .

"I'm hungry," Harriet said.

"We'll get something in our bellies here in a minute."

He coughed to mask the sound of the hammer thumbing back.

"I got a doll for Christmas, Mr. Cole."

Stephen blinked through the tears. "What's her name?" He choked on the words as he put the revolver to the back of her head.

"Samantha. She has red hair."

He knew he'd be sick after, fought off the urge to jam the barrel down his own throat. *Is this Your will? Speak now or forever—*

"She has two dresses, and my favorite thing is to comb her hair."

When Stephen touched the trigger, it came—peace flooding through him, warm liquid light. "Thank you," he whispered, and slid the revolver back into his coat.

Harriet glanced back, said, "You're cryin again."

"It's okay. These are happy tears. God is so good."

Harriet cocked her head. "Where are all the injuns?" she asked.

"How old are you, Harriet?"

"Six years."

"I think you're old enough to know something. Last night, God spoke to me. He told me that His judgment was coming down upon Abandon, that I was to be the instrument of His wrath, His brimstone and fire."

"So there weren't ever any heathens?"

"No, although at times today, God allowed me to believe there were. He let me see the heathens when I was standing at the Sawblade. Let me believe the lie. Showed me how to use it."

"Then where'd everbody go?"

"Do you believe in God, Harriet?"

"Yes."

"Does your father ever get upset with you? Like when you're disobedient? When you don't listen to what he says?"

"Yeah, when Mama's gone, he hits my bottom real hard with the metal part of his belt."

"But that's his job to punish you when you misbehave. In the same way, God is the father of Abandon, and all the people who live here are His children. But do you know what?"

"What?"

"The people of this town were very wicked."

"Why?"

"They were greedy. Sinful. They didn't love God. Thought only of themselves and what they wanted. They were obsessed with gold, and some of them were very evil and did terrible things to others. They took what didn't belong to them. Caused incredible pain."

"That's wrong. You're supposed to be nice."

"Yes, you are. And that's why God decided to punish everyone who lived in Abandon."

"What about Bethany and Mama?"

"Even them."

"But they aren't evil, are they?"

"Listen, Harriet. We can't start questioning God. Why He chooses to punish some but not others. We might not understand, but that's our shortcoming. We can only love and obey Him."

Her bottom lip began to quiver. "I wanna see Mama."

"Come on, sweetie. Listen to me. God told me not to punish you. That He loves you. That your heart is good. He wants me to take care of you."

"What about Mama and Daddy?"

"You need to shuck that question. Don't ask it again."

Harriet turned away from him and stared into the flames. Stephen put his hands on her delicate shoulders. "Let's walk to my cabin," he said. "I'll build another fire and make us supper."

"Did God punish Samantha?"

"No, sweetheart."

"She's alone and scared at home on my bed."

Stephen stood up, so tired that he felt he could lie down on his pine-bough mattress and sleep for thirty years.

"We'll stop by your old house and get her."

Stephen helped Harriet up and took her by the hand. Then the preacher and the child walked out of the church together.

The night was clear, the moon full and rising.

Infuse me with a peace that passeth all understanding.

Pinpoints of starlight twinkled, among them the rusty bulb of Mars.

Abandon lay dark and silent in its canyon, and from high above, Stephen heard a faint sound like a distant stamp mill.

They were beating on that iron door inside the mountain.

2009

SIXTY

Abigail approached the iron door—no handle, no doorknob, no keyhole. Lawrence came up and pushed against it and yelled Quinn's name.

She tried to rein back the fear in her voice. "Did that just happen?"

Lawrence backpedaled, then ran at the door and drove the heel of his boot into the metal.

It made a clatter that resonated through the cavern and died.

He collapsed on the rock and squeezed his ankle, wincing from the pain. Around the door's perimeter, the rock had been worn down, chipped away. Abigail shone her headlamp over the surface of the metal. It was covered in marks of desperation—dings and numerous indentations, as if someone had assaulted the door with an assortment of implements. She saw bullet grooves, scattered dimples created by buckshot. In the middle section, a large swath of metal had been dented in, and she imagined only a boulder carried by a group of men could have made such an impression in the indomitable door.

June wandered over from the chamber. "What happened?" she asked.

"Quinn locked us in."

"Why in the world would he do that?"

"No idea."

June spent a moment pushing on the door. She suddenly screamed Quinn's name.

"Save your energy," Abigail said. "I think people have tried everything to break it down. Even ramming a boulder into it. And they, um, they obviously didn't make it out."

"Oh my God. We're gonna die in here like the rest of them." She staggered back and began to hyperventilate. "How is this . . . how is this—"

"Okay, hang on." Lawrence struggled up off the rock. "Let's everybody just take a breath. We can all get horrified and hysterical, but how's that gonna save our lives? We're still gonna be right here when we finally calm down, locked inside this mountain. So let's skip the part where everyone freaks out. Most important thing now is light. It's as important as oxygen, and it's running out. We only need one headlamp going. Turn yours off. I'll keep mine on." Two headlamps went dark. "All right. Backpacks. Let's find out what supplies we have to work with. I think I left . . . Fuck." Lawrence ran over to the alcove and swept his headlamp in the vicinity of the ten burlap sacks. "It isn't here. I left my pack near the gold, and now it's gone. I had some rope. Batteries. Water."

"Mine's gone, too," June said. "I left it by the door before we walked into the chamber. All I have is Em's camera."

"I still have mine," Abigail said. She unclipped her hip belt and knelt down on the rock and unzipped it as Lawrence provided light. "So, I've got . . . not much. Gloves. Hat. Notepad. Roll of film. Two granola bars. Matches. Two water bottles, but only one's full. Damn, I thought I had extra batteries."

"All right, let's sit down and talk this out. I'm turning my headlamp off for now."

They sat together in the perfect darkness, fifteen feet from the iron door. Abigail closed her eyes, took a few deep breaths in an attempt to slow her heart and settle her mind.

Lawrence said, "I know it's creepy in here, and we're surrounded by the remains of people who died because they were locked in this mine, but I would urge us to keep them and their fate as far from our thoughts as possible."

June wept softly. "I'm sorry," she said. "I'm sorry. I'm trying not to."

Abigail reached out, took hold of her hand.

"We have three headlamps, and the brutal truth is, if we run out of light before we find a way out, we will die in here. We should store the headlamps we aren't using in Abby's pack so they don't get damaged. We also have thirty-two ounces of water. That's barely more than a glass each. We'll drink in small sips, every few hours, make it last as long as possible. Hopefully, there's water somewhere in this cave. Who knows if it's fit to drink, but we may have to try. Same deal with the granola bars. We'll ration them out in little bites over time."

"How long can we survive once the water runs out?" June asked.

"Three days. Maybe longer, since heat's not gonna be an issue. So now we have an important decision to make. We can't just sit here and hope to be rescued, because even if search-and-rescue comes to Abandon looking for us, they sure as hell won't find us in here."

"Maybe we could get some rocks and chip away around the door," June said.

Abigail said, "That's one option, but I looked at the door, and it's my sense that *that's* the big mistake the residents of Abandon made. They tried to break down the door or to chip around it. But this is hard, hard rock in here, and I'm certain we'd die of thirst before we made any real progress. I bet that most of the people in here wore themselves out fooling with that door. Then all they could do was lie down in that chamber to die, with no strength left to go look for more water or another way out."

"And no more light," Lawrence said.

"Exactly. I mean, all the residents of Abandon couldn't break through that door. We have no chance."

"Then what's the alternative?" June asked.

Lawrence said, "Looks to me like this is a mine that, as the men were blasting and expanding it, encroached into a natural cave. I'm sure that door is not the only exit from this mountain. I know we're tired, but I think we have to get up right now, while we still have a little strength and food and water, and try to find another way out."

June said, "You're suggesting we wander blindly through a cave?"

"You see another viable option?"

"What if we get lost?"

"We're already lost. Pretend that door isn't there, that it's solid rock. Might as well be."

Abigail said, "It scares me to death, but yeah, I agree that's our only option at this point."

"Should we split up?" June asked. "That would increase our chances of finding a way out."

"Actually, it wouldn't. Because we're on the clock here in terms of light, we can only spend as much time looking for another exit as our batteries allow. If we split up, we'll be burning through our headlamps twice or three times as fast."

June said, "If anyone had ever made it out of this mine alive, you'd have heard about it. Right, Lawrence?"

He turned on his headlamp, and the others blinked in the sudden light.

"More than likely."

1893

SIXTY-ONE

It took eight miners to hoist the boulder—seven hundred pounds of solid granite that ignited back cracking and groans. They started in the chamber, fifteen yards back, freighting it slowly over the rock, carefully accelerating to a jog as they neared the iron door.

The collision was tremendous. The front third of the boulder shivered off and broke the feet of three men.

The surface of the door had barely caved.

The Godsend's cager grabbed a hammer shotgun leaning against the wall, sited up the door, fired a shell of buckshot.

As the metal sparked, other men drew their revolvers and rifles, hammers squeezing back, levers cocking, the mine exploding in a cacophony of gunfire and filling with an acrid haze.

When the shooting stopped, the door stood defiant, the metal covered in silver chinks but no real damage done, except for the young man who lay quivering on the floor, a hole through his cheek, blood frothing out of his mouth onto the rock in a pink geyser.

Voices rose up, growing louder, competing to be heard.

Stetler held up two shadowgees and hollered for silence, but no one listened in the swarm of shouting men.

"We're all gonna peg out now."

"Better save the lump oil."

"Keep chargin the door."

"Used to could go that way, but the shoot's caved in."

"No food, no water."

"Preacher left us in the soup!"

"Gonna run out a light!"

"Hobble your lips!"

"Don't know your ass from a hole in the ground."

"Shut the fuck up!"

Meanwhile, Bessie McCabe stood in the center of the chamber, screaming for Harriet again, screaming until she couldn't breathe, until she felt like she was suffocating on choke damp, the chaos only stoking the hysteria in her head.

She overloaded, spotted the small boulder, fell to her knees, and crawled toward it.

She heard the miners shooting again, babies screaming, someone praying nearby.

Bessie got up on her knees, found two handholds in the rock, and, with every ounce of strength and zero hesitation, slammed her head down into the boulder. She heard the crack before she felt it, and blood ran between her eyes. When she came to, the cavern was inverted and spinning. She struggled back onto her knees, located the handholds, and managed two more blows before losing consciousness again. The next time she came around, she knew she'd done the job. A crowd of revolving, blurry faces surrounded her, and their voices and the gunshots and weeping and shouting all blended into a steady rush like the noise of a waterfall.

Her head lay in a warm, expanding pool, and she knew it was her blood and hoped it meant the end, thinking only of her daughter now, praying the injuns hadn't gotten her, and that wherever she awoke, Harriet would be there, too.

As her brain seized, she went back almost ten months, to a February morning on the plains of west Kansas, she and Harriet aboard a Union Pacific train chugging to Denver.

Staring off in the distance, she'd seen them lifting out of the horizon like a bank of clouds, thought they were coming into weather until she overheard another passenger say to his companion, "Have a look at the Snowy Range."

And as she died on the floor of that mine on Christmas night, she relived with a sort of bewildered nostalgia all the excitement she'd felt, watching the Front Range rise and rise as the train steamed west, a dream and a dare at once.

She'd pulled Harriet into her lap and pointed out the window.

"That's where Daddy is and where we're goin. That's our future, sweet pea."

And she'd believed it, too.

With all her heart.

2009

SIXTY-TWO

Starting out proved simple enough. They took the only passage that branched off from the chamber, Lawrence leading with the headlamp, followed by Abigail and June.

They hadn't walked thirty feet before Lawrence stopped, said, "Well, guys, here we are. First choice of many." The main tunnel continued on, at least as far as his headlamp shone, but there was also an opening in the rock nearby. Lawrence knelt down, looked through the hole. "A snug fit, but it definitely goes somewhere."

"Don't you think we should stick with the larger passageways?" Abigail asked.

"I honestly don't—" He gasped. "There's a skeleton in here and a pair of wrist irons. This might have been a prisoner. Yeah, let's stick with the main passage for now."

So they continued on, soon leaving all signs of mining activity—holes drilled in the rock for dynamite, rusted cans of black blasting powder, empty carbide kegs, strips of railroad track, drill steels, support timbers—and emerged into a natural cave, ceasing to follow the path of any particular tunnel, moving instead from room to room, some smaller than a closet, others larger than that first cavern, and the rock formations becoming more alien the deeper they ventured. Stalactites hung down from the roof, spilling their corrosive solutions into drip holes on the floor. Abigail ran her hands over walls of breccia—fragments of rock, fossils of bone and prehistoric crustaceans cemented together in sandstone.

An hour in, they came upon a richly decorated grotto. Lawrence's headlamp shone up at the ceiling, where stalactites bunched together, row upon row, like sharks' teeth. In the center, they'd melded into a strange conglomerate that reminded Abigail of a chandelier. Against the nearest wall, they resembled a pipe organ. In a far corner, the long tentacles of jellyfish.

They wandered into a smooth-walled tube, the ceiling just a foot above Lawrence's head. As they progressed through the elliptical passage, the walls grew farther apart and the ceiling lowered. Soon they had to walk hunched over, then squatting, then crawling on their knees, and finally their bellies, dragging themselves through the flattener on their forearms, just sixteen inches between the ceiling and the floor.

They'd been moving along this way for five minutes when Abigail yelled, "I'm getting claustrophobic!" She couldn't see Lawrence's light, felt trapped in total darkness, the warmth of her own breath blowing back into her face when she exhaled against the rock.

Something grabbed her ankle, but there wasn't enough space to turn her head.

June whispered, "They're all around us, Abigail. They won't stop talking to me."

Lawrence yelled back, "I hear something up ahead!"

They pushed on, the ceiling scraping the top of Abigail's head, her left leg beginning to bleed again, the crawling murder on her tailbone. *I can't breathe,* she thought. Then, *Yes, you can. It's just in your mind.* She had to tilt her head to the side and flatten her shoulders in order to writhe her way through. *What if we get stuck? I can't even move my limbs enough to turn myself around. This would be a horrible way to die.*

June cried, whispering in the darkness behind her, and Abigail had started to tell Lawrence to just turn the fuck around when she heard it, too— white noise.

The bulb of his headlamp swung toward her. "You're almost there," he said. Where the tube ended, less than a foot of space remained between the floor and the ceiling. Abigail squeezed her way through, and Lawrence grabbed her by the arms, helped her find her footing.

"Where is this?" she asked. Lawrence turned and let his light run up the sixty-foot walls of an immense hall. "Oh my God." They stood at the edge of a subterranean lake, fifty feet across, two feet deep. On the other side, a four-foot waterfall plunged into a pool out of a fissure in the rock. The pool overflowed, fed the lake, the lake flooding into a hole that chuted the mineral water into the depths of the mountain. The hall resonated with the crush of the waterfall, and the sound made Abigail think of her favorite spot in Central Park—the fountain at Cherry Hill. If you sat close, it was loud enough to drown out the city noise.

While Lawrence helped June out of the tube, Abigail bent down to touch the inky water—freezing cold, barely the temperature of fresh snowmelt.

When the beam of Lawrence's headlamp passed over the surface, she saw that the lakebed consisted of white crystals. Tiny translucent fish swam among them, eyeless in the dark.

They sat on the rock shore of that lake, caught in eternal night, sharing sips of water and pieces of a granola bar. Abigail's head dropped and her eyes closed.

"Wake up, Abby. We have to keep moving."

She sat up, rubbed her eyes. "How long was I asleep?"

"Five minutes."

"Where's June?" He pointed to a breakdown on the far side of the lake, where a section of the ceiling had fallen. June crawled around on the rock.

"She's acting strange, huh?" Lawrence said.

"Her husband was murdered in front of her. You forget that?"

They followed the shore to the breakdown and joined June on the shattered rock.

"What I'm thinking," Lawrence said, "is that maybe these rocks and boulders are blocking the opening of another passage. Help me move some of this."

"No," June said. "Leave it be. That's a bad place."

"Sorry, but I don't see another easy way out of this hall."

Abigail and Lawrence began picking up the rocks they could handle, tossing them aside. As she worked to clear the scree, Abigail realized she'd already begun to lose her sense of time. It seemed possible they'd been in this cave for an entire day.

As she lifted one of the larger rocks and dropped it on the growing pile, the waft hit her.

Abigail stepped back. "You smell that? It's like . . . rotten eggs. Come give me some light, Lawrence. I may have broken through."

Lawrence moved one more rock, the opening now spacious enough for them to climb through. He shined the light inside, said, "Damn, it's just a tiny—"

Abigail shrieked.

Lawrence looked in again, jerked back. "Oh Jesus."

"Is she alive?" Abigail whispered. "She looks very alive." The breakdown had covered a recess in the wall, and inside, a young woman leaned against a flat-topped rock, her left arm draped over a colony of gypsum flowers, their crystal blooms curling between her fingers. She was naked, slender but curvy, her head resting in the crook of her arm, as if she'd just sat down and gone to sleep, her left hand coated in wax.

Lawrence whispered, "Beautiful." Her hair was long and black and her full lips still held color—deep maroon. She was pink-skinned, blood still in her veins.

"She must have just gotten trapped in there," Abigail said.

"No, I believe this woman was alive in Abandon in 1893."

"You're telling me this flawless corpse is a hundred and sixteen years old?"

"Look at the pile of clothes. Those boots. 'Custom-mades,' they called them. Those canvas trousers, the shawl. Look like the outfit of a modern-day woman to you?"

"That's impossible. There's no decay. She hardly looks dead."

"I know. It's the most incredible thing I've ever seen." He stepped back from the opening and inhaled a few clean breaths of air. "That rotten-egg smell?" he said. "Sulfur gas. Very toxic and probably what killed this woman. But it also preserved her, killing all the aerobic bacteria inside her and around her. That Christmas in Abandon, she was probably doing what we're doing now—just trying to find a way out. Maybe she saw this nook, decided to rest. Then the ceiling came down, entombed her, sealed her in. In an airtight environment, the sulfur gas had nowhere to go, so there's no decomposition. Kept her literally frozen in time. Look at her. That's the face of someone who lived and breathed in the town of Abandon. Bet she had a story to tell. God, she's lovely."

June suddenly screamed, "She's looking at me! She won't stop looking at me!"

Abigail said, "That woman's dead, honey. Been that way for quite a while."

Lawrence lifted a rock, placed it back in front of the opening.

"What are you doing?" Abigail asked.

"If fresh air gets in, she will decay. We should seal it back up, leave her as we found her."

SIXTY-THREE

They climbed out of the waterfall room through a blind shaft that accessed another passage, spent several hours moving through a network of tunnels that crisscrossed and dead-ended and turned back into themselves. For the first time, Abigail felt lost.

They stopped to rest in a room where the stalactites and stalagmites had merged together in the shape of hourglass columns. Abigail sat up against the cold calcite, staring at her watch—11:03 A.M. They'd been rambling through the cave for five and a half hours. She hadn't had any meaningful sleep for twenty-nine.

"I really need to rest," Abigail said. "I'm on fumes here."

Lawrence said, "These daylight hours are too precious to waste. There's no point searching for a way out at night. Suppose we walked through a room when it was dark outside that had a daylight hole. We'd never know. So we have to keep going until the sun sets."

"But that's another eight hours. I can't—"

"Abby, do you understand that we have maybe three or four days to find a way out? And that after that, without water, we'll be too weak to cover any ground? It'll be over for us then."

She rested her forehead on her knees and cried.

The constant motion of Lawrence's light beam wreaked havoc on Abigail's stomach. Or maybe it was this cold, deep, underground air, the jagged rock walls narrowing over the last fifty yards, the tunnel beginning to slope gradually down. Abigail thought, *Great, we're going* deeper *into the mountain.*

She instantly felt guilty for complaining to herself. Bad as things were, the last twelve hours had been infinitely worse to June.

"How you holding up?" Abigail asked. "We can rest anytime you want. Just say when." June made no response. Glancing back, Abigail said, "Everything all—" Even in the paltry shreds of light that slipped back from her father's headlamp, Abigail could see that there was no one behind her. "Lawrence, she's gone."

He stopped, shone his headlamp back up the empty tunnel. "How long?"

"I don't know. Those were the first words I'd said to her in ten or fifteen minutes."

"June!" Lawrence screamed. His voice ricocheted down the tunnel, stirred up a single echo, and quickly died away.

No answer.

"Well, come on," Abigail said. "We have to find her."

They jogged back up the tunnel. After a minute or so, Abigail thought she heard something.

"Lawrence," she said. "Lawrence!" He spun around. "I think I heard—"

A scream exploded from the bowels of the mountain. It ended abruptly, but its reverberations went on and on.

Lawrence said, "What the hell?"

"Was that June?" Another scream ripped through the cave, this one farther away. "She sounds like she's in agony," Abigail said.

They rushed up the tunnel as the screaming continued, arrived after two minutes of hard running at a split in the passage.

A woman's voice shouted, "WHERE ARE YOU?"

"I can't tell which one it's coming from," Abigail said.

"PLEASE, GOD, JUST KILL ME!"

"This way," Lawrence said, and he started into the larger of the two passageways.

"I'M SO THIRSTY!"

They moved through a series of grottoes, the screams getting louder.

"I'M STILL ALIVE! PLEASE! FINISH IT! KILL ME!"

Lawrence stopped.

"What's wrong?" Abigail whispered.

He shook his head. "Thought I saw something in that room up ahead."

"What?"

"I'm not sure. It moved fast. Forget it."

"I don't hear her anymore."

Lawrence shouted, "*June, where are you?* Help us find you!"

The cave seemed to hold its breath.

"I hate this place," Abigail said.

They worked their way through a forest of stalagmites interspersed with pillars of bedrock, coming at last into a stagnant room with feathery blue fungi clinging to the walls and moving in slow-motion waves, like underwater sea grass.

Three steps into the next room, Lawrence froze, and Abigail heard him whisper, "My God." As he sank down onto the floor, his headlamp shone on the expanding pool of dark blood that flowed out of June Tozer's head.

She lay on her back beside the small boulder she'd used.

"Everything's spinning," she mumbled. They knelt at June's side. Abigail took her hand, laced their fingers. In the poor light, only the volume of blood hinted at the extent of damage June had managed to self-inflict. She groaned, her lips moving, searching for the strength to form words. "I couldn't . . . stand it. They were all around me, trying to use me. Where's Emmett?" She tried to call out to him, but his name miscarried in her throat.

"He's not here right now," Lawrence said.

"I'll be with him soon?" she mouthed between wet breaths. "And Ty?"

"Who?"

"Their son," Abigail said. "Yeah. Ty, too."

"I wanna hear him laugh again."

"You will, sweetie." Abigail was crying, overcome by June's deathbed desperation—wishful thinking and unanswerable questions begging answers, any semblance of truth be damned.

"He's always been a little boy in my mind. You think he's grown up into a—" She choked, then coughed, a mist of blood sputtering through the gaps between her teeth.

"Try not to talk," Lawrence said.

"Will I still be his mom? I was for six beautiful . . ." She moaned, her eyes closing. Abigail placed her ear on June's sternum, listening for the rise and fall of lungs expanding, deflating.

"I'm so sorry." Lawrence wept. "This was my fault."

June's chest swelled, Abigail's head lifting.

Then it fell—down, down—one long exhalation, all air expelled, and never rose again.

SIXTY-FOUR

At three in the afternoon, Abigail heard Lawrence say, "There's light up ahead."

The two of them entered the largest cavern yet, more than a hundred feet across, filled with enormous spires that rose from the floor. A spring bubbled out of a crack in the wall, speleothem deposits hanging like curtains from the high ceiling. They stood in the luminous shaft that angled down, bathing them in daylight. Forty feet above, a chimney bored through the ceiling, and Abigail saw a distant patch of gray at the end of it.

"Never get there," Lawrence said. "Don't even get your hopes up." He walked over to the spring. "Abigail, bring your empty water bottle." She went to her father and dug the Nalgene bottle out of her pack. Lawrence held the plastic lip against the rock, and with the bottle halfway full, he strode into the middle of the cavern and held it up to the natural light.

The water was cloudy, sediment already settling on the bottom. He sniffed it. "Potent sulfur smell." He sipped the water, winced, and spit it out. "Very mineralized. Tastes bitter and acidic. Much stronger than the hot springs in Pagosa. I don't know if this is even safe to drink." Abigail gazed up at the window in the ceiling, beating back the despair. This was far worse than traveling through the dark zone, she decided. This was throwing it in your face, a glimpse of the unreachable—heaven from hell.

When they finally stopped for the day, a smothering depression had descended on them. It was suppertime, but there would be nothing more to eat than a nibble from the last granola bar, a sip or two of water. They would sleep in their damp and filthy clothes, in the cold, on a hard rock floor, and when they awoke, it would still be dark.

Abigail and Lawrence sat against the wall in a small room with a low ceiling, a space that resembled fifty other rooms they'd passed through during the last fifteen hours.

"We shouldn't have left her there," Abigail said.

"What could we do? Dragging her through the cave with us won't bring her or Emmett back, will it?" Lawrence switched off his headlamp.

Abigail, desperate to hear his voice, anything to break the uncompromising black-hole silence, said, "You've found the remains of Abandon and you now know how they died, but you still don't really understand what happened, do you?"

"Nope. And Quinn—if that's really his name—throws a new wrench into the equation."

"But knowing they all died in this cave?"

"My gut tells me that, like us, they were locked in here. Maybe by Oatha Wallace and Billy McCabe. But the fact that the gold was locked in as well kind of refutes that theory."

Sitting there in the dark, listening to him talk, Abigail felt shards of cold begin to prick her face, wondered if it might be the first sign of frostbite or hypothermia.

"Why do you think Quinn did this to us?" she said. "Any idea?"

"Beyond plain old greed? No. We should probably drink some water."

Lawrence turned on his lamp, reached for the bottle. At first, Abigail mistook them for dust motes in the light beam, then realized these white things were actually snowflakes.

"Lawrence?" she said. "It's snowing in here."

He looked up. "Oh my God, I saw the chimney when we first came in, but it was already dark outside. I assumed it was just another blind shaft." His headlamp spotlighted the hole in the ceiling, snow floating down through it, melting on the cave floor.

Abigail got up. "Lawrence, can you lift me up there?"

She straddled his shoulders and he stood slowly, his legs shuddering under the strain. "Scoot to the right. You're crushing me into the ceiling." Abigail peered up the narrow chimney, wondered how far to the surface, if it even stayed wide enough for her to get there. "Okay, let me down." Lawrence bent his knees, eased back onto the floor. Abigail said, "I think I can climb up there if you lift me a little farther up the hole."

"Well, I know I couldn't do it even if my ankle wasn't wrecked. And with no rope, only one of us can get out. How would you feel about going alone, trying to find help? I can draw a map on your notepad, get you back to the trailhead. You'd have to find the keys to Scott's Suburban. I'm not sure if they're with him or in his pack at the campsite."

"And I'll get my cell, try to call for help from the pass."

Lawrence sighed, relief enveloping his face like the loosening of taut cables.

"You should get some sleep before you go, Abby. A few hours at least."

The alarm on Abigail's watch seemed to beep five seconds after she'd closed her eyes. She'd slept for four hours on the cold rock, dreamless and deep. She turned onto her side and faced Lawrence. His breath warmed her face, and in that virgin dark, she caught his scent—a repressed relic from those precious years when he was Daddy, and not the remnants of aftershave, no superficial mosaic of man-made chemicals, but his core, lifeblood odor, and it carried her back even further than the smell of cut grass and school-bus seats and sno cones.

"You awake?" he whispered.

"My alarm just went off. Guess it's time. You weren't asleep?"

"Been thinking."

"What about?"

"Those gold bricks, the greedy people they've killed through the centuries, people they're still killing. But you and the Tozers didn't come into these mountains for greed. Emmett and June are dead because of me. You're in this cave 'cause of me. And I'm sorry. Beyond words, I'm sorry. It won't change a damn thing now, but I need to say it, need you to hear it. I know what a selfish no-good fuck I am. And what you said in the boarding-house? You were right, Abby. It's all about me. Always has been." He cupped her face in his gloved hands. "Take this with you," he whispered. "If you make it back to me. If you don't. My leaving . . . wasn't your fault. Or your mother's. I left because something inside of me was broken. Still is. I hurt people I love, who love me, and I don't know why. But my little girl, my beautiful, perfect little girl, I'm so sorry I hurt you, so sorry you got me for a daddy."

Abigail fought like hell against it—a realignment, the unraveling of an old stubborn knot.

With Abigail astride her father's shoulders, she was still a foot shy of any usable handhold.

"I'm just not far enough up the chimney," she said. "Push me higher." As she lifted off Lawrence's shoulders, her headlamp illuminated the closest jug, a few inches from her fingertips. "Almost there," she said, reaching out and grabbing the jug with both hands. "Got it."

Lawrence said, "Find a foothold."

Abigail's fingers had already begun to cramp, and her feet were scrambling for purchase.

"I can't find anything. Oh God, I'm slipping! I can't—"

"*Feel that?*" Lawrence yelled as he jammed the toe of her right boot into a crevice. "Let your weight rest on your feet now!" Abigail settled onto her legs. "Just take your time. Get your strength back up." As she caught her breath, Abigail shone her headlamp up the chimney. It appeared to narrow farther up, but the handholds were plentiful. She cinched down the straps of her day pack, then reached over her head for the next handhold—a crack in the wall wide enough to slide her fist into.

She pulled herself up and moaned, the pain in her tailbone excruciating.

"Remember to climb with your feet," Lawrence yelled up to her. "Otherwise, you'll tire out." She tested her weight on a big chockstone wedged in the chimney, decided to trust it, and made the next move, rested for thirty seconds, then made another. As long as she allowed her legs to bear the weight, her arms didn't cramp. She climbed through a ten-foot section filled with bombproof buckets. Then the rock became wet, then icy, then snow-dusted. The handholds dwindling. Suddenly, she had nothing to grab.

"I'm stuck!" she yelled. "No handholds!"

"Chimney the rest of the way up!" His voice sounded distant, like he'd shouted up to her from the bottom of a well. "Push your feet against opposite walls. Hold yourself up with the pressure!"

She stood perched on a thin lip, half an inch wide, legs trembling with the onset of a paralyzing weakness. "I'm gonna fall!" she screamed.

"Listen to me! Take your right leg, dig it into the wall at your back, and keep the ball of your left foot pressed hard into the wall facing you!"

She tried it, the soles of her boots slipping on the rock. Pushed harder, pain radiating out from her tailbone so intensely, she felt it in her fillings and nearly fainted. She finally regained purchase and inched her way up again, her boots jammed into the rock, taking handholds and footholds where she could find them, chimneying where she couldn't.

Snow poured down on her, and she heard the shriek of wind just above.

Abigail glanced down the chimney, Lawrence's headlamp just a pinpoint of light seventy feet below, thought of the night he left, all those years ago, her first concrete memory. And she wondered if, as her father watched her climb to the surface, leaving him stranded in the dark, it felt anything to him like it had to her the night she'd watched him walk out her bedroom door.

You marooned us in a deeper cave than this, and you never came back. How do you forgive that? You deserted a four-year-old girl whose world you made turn 'round. You made me feel worth leaving. How do I forgive that? If I don't come back, Daddy, no one will ever hear from you again.

Her head emerged into the blizzard as she scrambled out of the cave, nothing but a hole on a steep, snowy slope, rimmed by three feet of powder. She checked her watch—12:32 A.M. She'd been underground for twenty hours. Her fingers, arms, and legs were cramping, and she stood high on a mountain, wind howling, in pitch-black, whiteout conditions, with no idea where she was, or how to find Abandon.

1893

SIXTY-FIVE

The next morning, they took the air, walking together down Main, the sky midwinter blue, the sun lifting over the east canyon wall and the unshaded snow already too brilliant to look at.

The fires had gone out in the mercantile and surrounding hillside cabins, so the air smelled cold and crisp, rinsed of woodsmoke.

Harriet looked up at Stephen, squinting, though the bonnet gave ample shade to her eyes. She thought it strange to be with this young preacher who treated her like a grown-up, asked her opinion of things. This had not been her experience with Daddy.

"Where did God take the people?" she asked, and not for the first time since last night.

When Stephen stopped and squatted down, his webs sank another foot in the snow. "Harriet," he said. "I already told you I don't—"

Something had moved above them. He glanced up at the second floor of the hotel, saw Molly Madsen standing in the bay window, staring down at them. He grimaced as the ulcer in his stomach flared.

They fought their way through deep drifts blown against the brick building, finally emerging into the lobby of the hotel.

"Go play at the billiard table, Harriet."

Stephen removed his smoked specs and unlaced his webs, then climbed the stairs. In the dark hallway, he knocked on her door, and when she asked who was there, he replied, "Stephen Cole."

The door opened. The preacher blushed. Though colder in her room than in the hall, Molly had clothed herself only in a sheer chemise. She stood shivering, breath steaming through corpse blue lips.

"When I saw you on the street, I thought you were my Jack. I'm expecting him any moment now."

"May I come in? Build a fire for you?"

"Oh. Well. Yes, that would be fine."

Stephen stepped inside, laid his felt hat on the desk as Molly shut the door after him. Her suite smelled like a night jar, though it wasn't the filth that struck him as much as the loneliness. It had holed up in this room, over-spread the sad gingham walls, the chipped furniture, its wilting occupant. He knew Molly's situation—the abandonment and humiliation that had festered and atrophied into madness. He'd visited before, but always from the hall. She'd never invited him in, and in truth, he'd been glad of it.

"The furnace is over here," she said, leading him to a potbellied stove across from the bed. "Mr. Packer has always provided assistance of this nature. He's a dear friend and business associate of my Jack, though he hasn't come around lately."

Stephen counted enough logs stacked against the wall to heat the room for a day, maybe two. He balled up several sheets of old newspaper so brittle, they flaked apart in his hands. With the fire going, he said, "Why don't you come sit over here?"

Molly knelt before the open stove, her eyes glazing as she watched the aspen logs blacken in the flames. Stephen grabbed the dusty quilt from her bed and draped it over her shoulders, then unbuttoned his coat, eased down beside her.

"Molly," he said, "the town's been vacated."

"Everyone left? Even Mr. Packer?"

"Him, too, and I'll soon be leaving, so I was hoping I might persuade you to come with me."

"What if Jack comes and I'm not here? If no one is here?"

"We'll send word to Jack the moment we reach Silverton. I'll even pay for the tele—"

"But that isn't how . . . I'm supposed to be sitting in the window, looking down on the street. And then I see him walking toward the hotel, and he sees me up here in the window, and he doffs his hat and I smile and he runs up the steps and down the hall and—"

She lost her breath.

"It's okay, Molly."

"I will be *here* when my Jack comes to Abandon."

"Who'll bring you food and water? Wood for the stove? Who—"

"Jack will see to these things. He is my husband, after all."

"Molly," Stephen said, and the words tempted him: *You've been in Abandon ten years, this hotel for five, and you'll die in this room if you don't leave with me. You've got as much a chance of seeing Jack again as those sagebrushers did of making their fortune in this desperate town.*

Instead, Stephen stood. "Would you excuse me for a moment?" He left the suite and hurried down the stairs toward the lobby and the clack of ivory balls. The child had made a game of rolling them, three at a time, into the table's leather pockets.

The preacher slipped back into Molly's suite, found her basking in the heat of the stove, staring into the smoldering pile of embers. The room now reeked of wood smoke, a great improvement.

He sat with her again, said, "I was hoping you'd tell me of Jack?"

Her face enlivened, and as she spoke, Molly veered into sanity, Stephen catching peeks of the woman she must have been.

She narrated their first meeting in San Francisco and the ball, their courtship, the first time he kissed her, and finally the wedding, straying into the smallest details of the clothing worn, food served, floral arrangements, guests in attendance, everything as clearly recalled as if the event had transpired that morning. Stephen marveled at how thoroughly she described her husband's face, the tone of his voice, even the smell of him, so by the time she pulled out the crinkled albumen print of Jack, Stephen's mind had already formed an excellent likeness of the man.

Someone knocked at the door. Molly rose from the warmed floorboards by the stove, crossed the room, and asked who was there.

"Harriet McCabe, ma'am."

Molly opened the door, looked down at the little girl standing in the hall. "What do you want?"

Harriet's eyes cut to Stephen, back to Molly. "There's a man in the lobby asking for you."

Please God, let her believe the lie she so loves.

Molly staggered back. "His name?"

"Jack Engler, ma'am."

Molly flushed, glanced back at Stephen. He came to the door, said, "Harriet, I want you to go downstairs and tell Mr. Engler that Mrs. Engler will send for him momentarily. Hurry now."

As Harriet ran down the hall, Stephen closed the door.

Molly glanced at her chemise, which was stained and threadbare, a pitiful garment. She whispered, "He can't see me like this."

Stephen went to the wardrobe, threw open the doors. The dresses and gowns hadn't been worn in years; all were mottled with gray dust.

Molly chose a corset, much too small, but Stephen fit her into it as well as he could manage, hooked the two bones in front, and laced up the back. "Which gown?" he said. "I happen to like this blue—"

"Jack detests blue." She detached a peach-colored evening gown with plentiful ruffles from its hanger.

"A lovely choice, Molly." He pulled it over her head, helped slide her arms into the sleeves. As he swept the dust off her shoulders, he felt as if he were dressing an oversize child.

Her hands shook.

Stephen steadied them, said, "Don't be afraid. Your husband is down in the lobby because he loves you. He's come back for you."

He sat Molly down at the dressing table. Her hair hadn't been brushed in a long while—thin, oily, so tangled that he hesitated to run bristles through it. So he picked up the silver brush and slid the smooth backside of it down the length of her coarse black tresses.

Molly's reflection in the cracked mirror sent back the rubble of a woman, and Stephen prayed she didn't see herself as he did, that God might cause a beautiful distortion of the image her eyes received.

While he pretended to brush her hair, he considered Jack, wondered where this man lived today, and if he ever thought of the woman he'd deserted, this mad, pathetic creature of obsession, wished Jack could see what he'd done to his bride.

"You're stunning," Stephen said.

"I don't have any rouge."

He pinched her cheeks. "There. You're perfect now."

As Molly beamed, Stephen glimpsed the dignity she'd once possessed. He went to the door, cracked it open, yelled, "Harriet! Mrs. Engler is ready to receive her husband!"

Stephen shut the door. Molly walked over, her chest billowing beneath the shabby gown.

She stood three feet back from the door, Stephen behind her.

They listened to the heavy footsteps thumping up the stairs.

Molly glanced back at Stephen, grinning with all the giddy joy of a new bride, thinking of the first day she'd arrived in advance of her husband, in this fledgling camp called Hope.

And all the things she'd wanted to do, places she'd intended to see, children to bear, tore through her mind like an avalanche.

She'd waited so long.

Now he was coming down the hall, and Molly whispered "Oh Jack" as Stephen thumbed back the hammer, raised the revolver to the back of her head, and waited for the knock at the door.

SIXTY-SIX

In the evening, Stephen went for water, blessed with convenience in this regard, since the hillside behind his home boasted a spring. The cabin's previous occupant had raised a simple structure over the rock where the water surfaced, so it could be easily accessed in the winter months.

A lantern in one hand, an empty pail in the other, he webbed fifty feet up the trail, past the privy and toward the shed, the moon so bright that he could've left the lamp behind.

He stepped under the tin roof and traded the lantern for an ax that hung from a nail in the clapboard.

Ice had amassed around the lip of the flat rock where the water spilled over, and when he'd chipped it clear, he set the pail under the trickle and sat contentedly on a dry rock, blanketed, like all the others in this old tailings pile, with an orange flocculent mass.

He'd always assumed it was algae.

A solitary cabin glowed on the east slope above Abandon, though you couldn't see inside, since the windows weren't made of glass, but white cotton cloth soaked in tallow. It was a cramped, one-room, saddle-notched affair with a mud and stone chimney, a little porch out front, and a corrugated metal roof that stayed warm enough with a fire blazing underneath it to keep the snow from sticking. Inside and out, it was a spartan dwelling, severely lacking the touch of a woman.

Stephen pulled two enameled graniteware pots off the fire and hustled them over to the rustic table where Harriet sat waiting for supper. He eased down onto the deacon seat and lifted the top from the larger of the two pots.

Steam bellowed out. The slumgullion simmered.

He spooned a serving of stew into Harriet's bowl, then sliced her a piece of sourdough bread and lathered on several spoonfuls of wild raspberry preserves. One of his parishioners had left the bread and jar of jam on his doorstep Christmas morning. He dipped Harriet's tin cup into an earthen vessel he'd bought off a Navajo trader, filled her cup with water, then poured himself some Arbuckle's from a spouted pot, allowing himself a sip of coffee before ladling the stew into his own bowl.

He blessed the meal. It needed prayer.

The stew was horrendous—so wanting of salt and spice that it held all the complexity of dirty water with chunks of gristly elk meat and potatoes and cabbage bobbing on the oily surface.

But his new guest slurped it down without prejudice and even asked for more.

After supper, Stephen prepared Harriet's bed on the mattress he'd taken from the McCabes' shack earlier in the afternoon.

For pajamas, Harriet wore her underclothes, Bessie's peignoir—too long and bunched up around her feet—and a pair of drafty socks sewn from flour sacks. Stephen made Harriet turn away while he slipped a flannel nightshirt over his union suit.

"Would you like a story before we go to sleep?" he asked.

Harriet stood at the foot of his aspen bedstead, looking at the old newspaper that served as wallpaper, tacked to the logs.

"What would that be like?"

"You've never had a bedtime story read to you?"

She shook her head, and Stephen realized it owed to her parents' illiteracy. He got up from his mattress—just a bunch of burlap stitched together and stuffed with pine boughs—and walked over to the railroad tie mounted to the stone above the fireplace, the shelf serving as mantel and bookshelf.

He chose a scuffed, well-used volume, called Harriet over to her bed before the hearth, and tucked her in under the quilts. She lay between Stephen's legs with her head in his lap, and he read for ten minutes by firelight from *The Adventures of Tom Sawyer*.

He closed the book when he thought she'd fallen asleep, but as he tried to extricate himself without waking her, Harriet's eyes fluttered open and she said, "What happened to Miss Madsen?"

Stephen touched the back of his hand to the young girl's face. It was soft and cool. He gently wound one of her pitch-black ringlets around his finger. "Molly was very sick," he said.

"Like scarlet fever?"

"No, in her head. God told me to end her suffering, so I did."

"How did you?"

"Do you know how a gun works?"

"They hurt you."

"They can. I shot a bullet into the back of Molly's head so she wouldn't be sick or sad anymore."

"Did it hurt her?"

"It killed her body, but her soul never felt a thing."

"You gonna shoot me in my head so I go to Jesus?"

"No, Harriet. You've got a long and happy life ahead of you."

She closed her eyes.

Stephen ran his fingers through her hair until she fell asleep.

Harriet awoke. The fire was dying, and though her feet were cold, she could still feel the warmth of the flames on her face. The sound that had roused her from the dream came again. She sat up on the lumpy mattress, looked over her shoulder at Mr. Cole's bed in the corner against the wall. The preacher had buried his face into his pillow, and he made strange, sad sounds.

Harriet took her doll and got up from the mattress and walked over to his bedside. "Hey," she said.

Mr. Cole lifted his head off the pillow. Even in the low light of the cabin, she could see the wetness on his face, knew what it was.

"What are you doing up?"

"I heard you bein sad. Is the wet because everyone's gone?"

Stephen wiped his eyes and sat up against the wall, his long legs hanging off the bed, feet touching the freezing dirt floor.

Harriet climbed onto the mattress with him.

"I'm sad for a lot of reasons."

"Like what reasons?"

"Well, mainly because God told me to do a very hard thing, something I didn't think He was capable of. Or me, for that matter. But I did it, because we have to obey God. Always. And now, I um . . ." He wept again. "I feel like I don't know Him anymore. Like He isn't who I thought He was. And that's fine. He's perfect, whatever He is. That's my failure, to make naïve assumptions about His nature.

"Then the devil constantly tells me these lies, whispers in my ear that maybe it wasn't God who spoke to me. That it was actually him, the evil one. Or that this horrible winter, this town, the thin air, the greed—all that took my mind from me."

Harriet pried open the fingers of his right hand. "What's that?"

In Stephen's sweaty palm lay an ornate sterling silver hairpin. He let Harriet hold it. "It's a hairpin," he said.

"What's that?"

"A piece of jewelry a woman uses to hold up her hair."

"Why you got one?"

He smiled. "Fair question. It belonged to a woman named Eleanor."

"Was she your wife?"

"No."

"Is she dead?"

"No, Eleanor isn't dead. You know, you kind of favor her. She had black curls like yours. Dark eyes."

"Did she give you this?"

"We were picnicking on the beach late one afternoon. This was ten years ago, second-worst day of my life. I had taken her there to tell her I couldn't marry her."

"Why?"

"Because God told me to go to divinity school instead. To spend my life serving Him. It was a windy day and the wind kept blowing her hair loose, so she pulled out her two hairpins and stuck them in the sand. I swiped one when she wasn't looking. I suppose I shouldn't have. You know how you hold Samantha at night, and she makes you feel better? Safer?"

The child nodded.

"That hairpin is my Samantha. When I hold it, on hard nights, lonely nights like this, it makes me remember things about Eleanor—her eyes, the way she smelled, the sound of her laugh. And it makes me sad, makes me miss her, but it also reminds me that I was a very happy man once."

"You wish you stayed on the beach with Eleanor?"

Stephen gathered his hair and tied it up in a ponytail.

"No, Harriet, I don't wish that, because that would be wanting something in conflict with God's will. But I'll tell you what I do wish. Wish we could live twice, take a different path each time. That at the end of all this, when I finished serving God in the West, I could go back to that day on the beach, put a ring on Eleanor's finger instead."

"Maybe you can still go back."

"Eleanor's married to a lawyer named Benjamin. They live in Chapel Hill, North Carolina, with four children, last I heard."

Stephen lay back on his side, his head on the pillow, watching fire shadows move like black ghosts along the walls of his wretched cabin. He managed to cry softly this time, Harriet patting his back, telling him with the simplistic, heartfelt wisdom of a six-year-old that he would wake up in the morning feeling brand-new and happy again, how sometimes her daddy made her very sad and lonely and afraid, but that the feeling always passed, and that it would be the same way for him.

They slept in Stephen's bed and neither woke until just before dawn, and only because the fire had gone out, turned the cabin cold.

SIXTY-SEVEN

Lana Hartman had gone without food and water for two full days. She lay against the cold rock floor, watching the sole light source burn in the middle of the cavern—a miner's friend too weak to reach the gaunt and hollowed faces that lined the walls.

That first night locked in the mountain, the noise had been maddening—miners trying to beat the door down, quarreling, guns firing, children wailing. But most of the miners had left in search of water, and with the cavern quieted down, she now strained to hear the hushed voices—crying, prayers for deliverance, some praising God, others cursing Him, a pair of longhairs debating philosophy, theories concerning the soul after death.

Lana closed her eyes.

Sleep came in intermittent bursts of nightmare and fever dream. When she awoke, the thunder in her head had increased twofold, and Joss Maddox knelt beside her, stroking her hair. It took her a moment to latch onto Joss's voice.

". . . the worst of it. Wish Cole hadn't met with a skull cracker. Love to hear him defend the behavior of his lovin God. He cares so much for us, this is one antigodlin fuckin way a showin it. You're hurtin, and you ain't done shit to deserve this hard fuckin deal. If I could do somethin for you, Lana, swear to holy Christ I would.

"I come to ask if you'd go with me. I'm leavin this fuckin tomb, goin on into the cave, see if I can't find water, some way out."

Lana cut her eyes at Joss, the barkeep's face distended and malformed in the lantern light.

"That a nod?"

Lana moved her head again.

"All right. Here, let me help you up. Hope you ain't too weak to walk, 'cause I'm too damn weak to carry you."

Joss lifted the shadowgee she'd stashed with Al's body, lighted the candle, and set out with Lana into the cave. They progressed slowly, guided by candlelight, soon leaving the man-made tunnels and passing into karst terrain, traveling from room to room, Joss holding the shadowgee at head level to avoid walking into stalactites.

An hour out from the main cavern, they entered a small grotto. Water seethed out of the floor into a rimstone pool, and Lana ran to it, already on her knees and bringing a cupped handful to her mouth.

"Think you might regret that."

Lana stared down at the spring, tiny bubbles streaming up from cracks in the bottom, the surface appearing to boil. She touched her tongue to it, the water bitter and caustic, heavily alkalied.

"Poisoned them, don't you bet?"

Still, Lana almost drank it.

She watched the water slip through her fingers as Joss swiped extra candles from the two dead miners.

The hall echoed with the noise of the waterfall, the light too gentle to show its vast dimensions. They stood on the shore of a subterranean lake, its bed of white crystals shining under the rays of firelight that shot out through the perforated can.

The shadowgee clanged against the rock, and the women fell to their knees, bent down, put their faces into the water. Lana coughed up the first two swallows, but when she finally got some down, it was so cold and good, it made her head ache.

They sat on the bank, drinking until their stomachs bulged and Joss had to loosen the button on her canvas trousers.

She said, "Lana, you don't wanna know what I'd do to have one cigarette left in my dream book and some Mexican common doins—few hot rocks, menudo, bottle a mescal. Keep thinkin I hear someone bangin the angle iron. Tell you what—I'd swear off whiskey for a meal."

They wandered on inside the mountain, nothing but rock and shadows and firelight, Lana feeling certain that days must be passing for all their time in this underworld.

She was halfway through one of Haydn's concertos when Joss stopped, turned around, and said, "I think we better try to go back." The way her voice carried, Lana pictured them standing in a large cavern. "I don't have clue fuckin one as to our coordinates, but maybe Stephen came back after all or they got the door open. Hate for us to miss that blowout."

Lana shook her head.

"What?"

She reached down, touched her feet, grimaced.

"Oh, you're tired? Well, hell, I am, too. Maybe we should catch forty winks first. Let's find a decent spot."

They went a little ways farther, until they found a room where the rock was level.

"Your suite, Miss Hartman," Joss said. "Hope you find everthin to your likin. Here, we have some rock. Over here, some more rock. Oh, and here's some more fuckin rock. I hope you like rock."

Lana smiled.

"Ain't seen many a those."

SIXTY-EIGHT

The two women lay on the rock, nestled together for warmth and blanketed under Lana's woolen cape and Joss's serape. Lana's headache had eased since she'd filled her stomach with water, but the reprieve of pain only made room for the deep hunger.

Joss said, "We got three candles left. Hope that'll get us somewhere better'n this. I'm blowin us out for a while."

Lana heard a puff and the room went black.

It was perfectly silent, cold.

She felt Joss take hold of her hand.

"Believe this shit? I don't. Guess it beats turnin into a cottonwood blossom, bag over my head, rope around my neck, squirmin before a bunch a damn strangers. You warm enough? Squeeze my hand if you are."

Lana squeezed.

"Good." They were quiet for a while, Lana wondering if sleep would come more easily in the absence of psychotic thirst.

"You always been a mute? Squeeze once for yes, twice for no, three times for shut the fuck up, Joss."

Two squeezes.

"Just curious is all. Take no offense. You spoke recently? Like in your adult life?"

One squeeze.

"How long since you went quiet?"

Three soft squeezes.

"Three years?"

One squeeze.

"That sound you hear is the wheels turnin inside my head, wonderin what the fuck happened to you. Was you met upon by some horrific occurrence?"

One squeeze.

"Somebody hurt you three years ago."

One squeeze.

"A man?"

Squeeze.

"Cocksuckers, all. Was you a whore?"

Two squeezes.

"This the work a your husband or—"

One squeeze.

"Lemme venture a guess. . . . He caught you steppin out?"

"Two squeezes."

"Well, as our mode a communication would take about four fuckin centuries to unriddle this mystery, I'll leave it at this. You're a sweet human bein and for whatever reason you caught a rough shake, and I'm real sorry and I wish it hadn't . . ."

The ceiling glowed, both women gasping as the moon edged into view, nearly full and faintly yellowed, the color of ancient paper, their rocky prison shellacked with placid light.

"I shit you not, this is the first piece a luck I ever had."

The moon's brief framing in the chimney window ended, and it shrank away, continuing along its predestined path across the sky, stranding them once more in darkness.

Joss held the shadowgee above their heads and stared at the ceiling.

"You lift me, I believe I can scramble up that. Squat down."

Lana knelt and Joss straddled her shoulders.

"All right, raise me up slow like."

Lana stood, surprised by how light Joss was—barely a hundred pounds—and the weight soon lifted off her shoulders.

Joss began to climb, holding the shadowgee in her teeth, clawing her way up the rock, the candlelight dwindling.

Lana glanced around at the darkness on all sides.

"Fuck!" Joss had stopped, perched fifteen feet up the chimney, muttering to herself. Then she was moving again, but coming back down, the room rewarming with candlelight.

Her legs dangled through the bottom of the chimney.

She dropped to the floor, took the shadowgee out of her mouth, said, "Look here, Lana. Only one of us can go up. I want you to."

Lana shook her head.

"No? Wanna know what you got in store if you stay here? Whoever climbs up that chimney's gotta have the shadowgee to see, 'cause you can't hold no candle in your teeth. I'll leave you with three candles and two matches. No matter what happens, I'd say it's a long chance I ever make it back to this room, which means you gotta find the mine again, where everyone else is at. Your candle has the luxury a blowin out twice. After that, you might as well sit down and wait to die, in darkness and quiet like you never seen, and all alone, just you and your thoughts. Me? I'd much prefer to take my chances with whatever's on the bright end a this hole."

Lana shook her head, her chin twitching.

"I ain't lockin horns with you on this. You know enough about me to know I operate on the smoky end a the spectrum, so this ain't no easy offer to make. I would suggest you take me up on it 'fore the notcher in me rethinks the situation."

Lana pointed at Joss and turned her hands over, palms up.

"Don't worry about it. I've always survived. I'll get myself out a this, jam the breeze back to everyone else. Look, I done plenty a awful things, and not many of 'em ever keep me up nights, but leavin you here in the dark ain't somethin I care to haul around in my head, pokin at what few shreds a conscience I still possess. Savvy?"

She handed Lana the shadowgee and tied up her wavy black hair.

"Now I'm squattin down now, and I better feel your fuckin heft on my shoulders."

2009

SIXTY-NINE

It was more snow than Abigail had seen in her lifetime—waist-deep and still dumping. With the headlamp on, her visibility ended after ten feet. Without it, the world lay as dark as the cave she'd crawled out of.

Her options whittled to climb or go down, she chose to descend, and between the twelve-thousand-foot oxygen-deprived air and the energy it took to walk without snowshoes in a meter of powder, she had to stop every few steps to catch her breath.

The slope steepened.

A gust of wind knocked her down.

Twice, she banged her knees into blades of rock hidden beneath the snow.

A half hour out from the cave, the slope terminated at a cliff. Abigail knelt down, shone her lamp over the edge, her stomach knotting as she watched the flakes spiral into darkness. She had no idea how far it dropped, but she resolved that no way in hell would she be going that way.

Instead, she traversed a descending line along the edge of the precipice, her face going numb again, fingers freezing, light-headed from the elevation and the lack of food and water.

Soon she'd left the cliff behind, working her way down a small drainage filled with the murmur of a creek in the twilight of its season, trickling under the snowpack on its path to wider waters. She spied tall, slim profiles in the gloom below. She passed through alpine shrubland, winter-crippled timberline trees, then finally emerged into a forest proper.

The firs drooped under their loads of powder.

A branch caught her hood, snow raining down her neck. She ducked under a canopy of Douglas fir branches that dipped low enough to provide some semblance of shelter.

She pulled off her gloves, dug the ice out of her collar. It was so quiet in the forest, with only the creak of straining fir trees and clumps of snow sliding off branches. She was very thirsty, but she'd refused to take any water or supplies from Lawrence, recalled telling him she'd just eat snow. She scooped a handful into her mouth. Chewed the ice. Squeezed out several drops of water, then spit it out. Her head ached. She'd been cold. Now she was colder.

A howl erupted nearby. It rose slowly and faded slowly, with all the heartsickness of an elegy. She'd never heard that sound in the wild, and while it tripped all the primal fear triggers in her hard-wiring, she still found it lyrical and haunting and deeply sad.

It rose up again, closer now, and from someplace high above, perhaps that shrouded peak she'd descended, a collection of howls answered, their voices sweeping in a lonely cascade down through the forest. Abigail glimpsed something bounding through powder.

The wolf stopped thirty feet away, buried to its neck, ears flattened, hackles spiked, regarding her with its head cocked, as if in wonderment that a human had ventured out on such a night, eyes glinting in points of yellow fire, long incisors shining as it bared its teeth.

Abigail blinked and it was gone.

She got up, pushed on through the forest. After awhile, her watch beeped—3:00 A.M. She realized she'd been traveling downhill for some time, and that worried her. Abandon stood at tree line, but she'd gone well below it now, by as much as a thousand feet.

She turned back and ascended through the forest, taking the steepest line she could find, back up into deeper snow, thinning trees, using saplings to haul herself upslope.

Just before dawn, she passed through an odorless stand of trees stripped to their trunks—an ossuary of burned evergreens, this barkless, coneless, leafless, blackened wood mass-murdered some time ago by an electrical storm.

At timberline, she stopped to rest, beyond exhaustion, legs cramping, nauseated with hunger. She'd sweated out all her water and she made herself choke down a few handfuls of snow as the sky shifted from black into gray—the first progression toward dawn.

She sat shivering against a crooked, twisting runt of a tree, watching the gathering light shape out the wilderness around her. Snow came in spits now, and though the wind had slacked off in the forest, she could hear it moaning through the crags above.

Dawn dropped anchor.

She'd hoped to see the only landmark she knew—those jagged granite teeth of the Sawblade—but the cloud deck had decapitated everything above twelve thousand feet.

Then she saw it, a ways up the nearest slope—the tiny cross of Abandon's church puncturing the low gray clouds. She stood. The town itself lay just a quarter of a mile ahead. She could already see the other structures, and a tinge of pride coursed through her.

I found it in the dark, in the middle of a blizzard. Not bad for a city girl.

The possibility that Quinn was still out there flashed through her mind.

She turned off her headlamp and waded on into the box canyon.

SEVENTY

M ain Street lay empty, nineteenth-century wind chimes tinkling discordantly in the doorway of what had been the mercantile. Abigail stood between the saloon and the hotel, looking up at the bay window, that vantage point from which she'd first seen Isaiah or Stu through the red filter of Emmett's camera.

She studied the snow in the vicinity. With their tracks from Monday night now a day and a half old, there should've been no trace of them under four feet of snow. And yet she saw tracks, at least one fresh set, that moved into the hotel, then south toward the pass.

Abigail waded over to the entrance, stepped through the door frame. She banged her boots against the brick and knocked off the ice, then turned on the headlamp and swept it over the collapsed staircase, the archways, the front desk. Her last time in this hotel lobby, late Monday night, Scott Sawyer had been lying under the lounge's archway. Now the only sign of him was a dark stain on the floorboards.

She made a cursory inspection of the lounge, glancing under the billiard table, behind the fallen elk head, wondering if Quinn had found Scott, stowed him elsewhere.

If Scott had brought the keys to his Suburban with him on their Monday-night photo shoot, she could forget using his truck. It was seventeen miles from Abandon to the trailhead, another ten from the trailhead to Silverton. Twenty-seven miles. Farther than a marathon, in deep snow, at altitude, sleep-divested, and without food or water.

If my cell doesn't get service at the pass, that's what I'm in for. Might as well get going.

She heard a boot step on broken glass—across the lobby, in the dining room.

She rushed toward the doorway as a shadow darted out from behind the bar, footsteps coming after her, crunching over the shattered chandeliers, her heart slamming in her chest like a thing that wanted free. Before she reached the entrance, something grabbed her left arm and a gloved hand squelched her scream, dragging her back from the doorway, pushing her down behind the front desk.

Her headlamp illuminated Scott's face. "Scott? Oh my God, you're a—"

"Shhh. Someone was here just fifteen minutes ago."

"Who?"

"Didn't recognize them. I heard footsteps in the snow, so I hid behind the bar."

"How are you alive?" He raised his down vest, yellow fleece jacket, and thermal underwear top so Abigail could see where he'd duct-taped the knife wound closed to stop the bleeding, the right half of his abdomen bloated and inflamed.

"It hurts like hell, and I thought I was dead when they first stuck me. The blade nicked a rib, but it missed my vital organs. I faked it once those men in masks showed up. Hoped if they thought I was dying, maybe they'd just leave me tied up, which is exactly what they did. I came to consciousness last night, managed to free myself. I've been resting, gathering my strength to go out and look for everyone."

Well, they're all dead because of you and my father, she thought.

Abigail leaned back against the desk, could have fallen asleep inside of a minute.

"The three masked men?" she said. "Ex–Special Forces."

"Three? I thought there were only two."

"Your trustworthy assistant was the third."

"What?" Scott ripped off his headband, ran his fingers through his bleached-out hair.

"Apparently, Jerrod found out the real reason you and Lawrence had come to Abandon."

If he caught the edge in her voice, Scott didn't show it, just said, "So what happened?"

She told him everything except that they'd actually found the gold, and when she finished, Scott put his head between his knees and sat absolutely still and silent, though by the light of her headlamp, Abigail saw tears splattering on the floorboards under his face.

"I killed them," he said.

She put her hand on the back of his neck. "No, you—"

"No, I was their guide. They just came out here to see Abandon, take some stupid fucking pictures, and we used them for their backcountry permit. Jesus Christ."

"Scott, I know you're upset, but we have to go for help right now. Lawrence won't last long in that cave when the water runs out. Now, my cell's in my pack back at camp. If I get service at the pass, hopefully we can get somebody out here."

Scott looked up and wiped his face. He stood, limped off into the dining room, returned with his pack. He handed Abigail two Clif Bars and a Nalgene bottle. "The water's got two packs of Emer'gen-C in it. Get that in you. It'll help replenish the minerals and vitamins you've lost. You'll need a serious energy boost for what's ahead of us."

SEVENTY-ONE

They struck out south toward their campsite, choosing a route behind the buildings in an effort to remain unseen. Despite his wound, Scott moved quickly through the snow, and soon they'd left behind the row of false-fronted cribs at the end of town.

Up-canyon, Abigail spotted the boulder standing on the outskirts of camp. "I recognize that rock," she said. "The tents are just beyond it."

As they passed the boulder, Scott said, "Where's our stuff?"

He went out ahead of her, moving in frantic circles through the area where the tents had been. "I'm not believing this," he said as he dug in the snow. "Quinn must've taken our gear. Everything's gone. Even Gunter and Gerald."

"Who?"

"The llamas. Fucker better be packing a fucking arsenal if he touched my boys."

"You're sure the tents aren't just buried? The snow would've covered them, right?"

"See this?" Scott knocked the powder off the top of a pyramid-shaped boulder that barely jutted out of the snow. "Lawrence put his tent up right here, by this rock, so he could lay his things on it. Now all his stuff's gone. But cross your fingers and your toes." Scott waded over to another boulder, this one capped with four feet of snow. "I never set my tent up Monday night," he said. "I was too busy fixing supper, helping everyone else get settled into camp. I was gonna do it when we got back from photographing the ghost town. What I'm hoping is that by the time Quinn found our camp, enough snow had fallen to bury my big pack, which I left beside this boulder."

Scott ducked under the snow. A moment later, he popped up, hoisting his internal-frame Dana Design backpack like a trophy above his head.

Abigail worked her way over to him. "What do you have in there?"

"Everything. My tent. Extra clothes. First-aid kit. Sleeping bag. More bottles of water. A gas stove. Food. I don't think we'd have made it without this." He brushed the snow off his solid-black pack and loosened the compression straps.

"Please tell me you have a cell phone."

"Hate the fuckers."

"So we're hiking out."

"Seventeen beautiful miles." He dropped a big compression bag in the snow. "But no worries. I'll whip us up a meal before we go." He reached into the bag, emerged with two packets of Backpacker's Pantry freeze-dried dinners. "What's your pleasure? Paella with saffron rice and chicken, or turkey Stroganoff?"

Within the hour, they were on the move again, heading toward the Sawblade, swaddled in ashen clouds.

After a half mile, Quinn's tracks branched off from the canyon and climbed the slope toward Emerald Basin.

They pushed on, taking turns breaking a trail through the deepening powder.

By the time they reached the ruins of the Godsend, the drifts came to Abigail's chest.

"Let's take a breather," Scott said. They collapsed near the stamp mill at the foot of that steep white slope that swept up two thousand feet into the clouds.

"What happens if Quinn sees our tracks?" Abigail asked.

"Yeah, I've been worried about that."

"I mean, he will eventually see them, right?"

"Probably. And you're exhausted. I'm hurting. He won't have to travel that fast to catch us, and he has one hell of an interest in our never leaving these mountains. I'd feel a lot better if it was snowing like a bastard. We're target practice out here in the open."

"You got a gun in your pack?"

"Jerrod kept the pistol with him."

Abigail squinted down-canyon, subconsciously searching for a tiny figure plodding toward them through the snow. "I'll bet Quinn has a gun," she said.

"What we have to do is get as much of a head start as we possibly can. I was listening to my weather radio in the hotel last night, and it sounds like it only snowed above eighty-five hundred feet. If we can get down that far, we should be safe. He won't be able to track us. But as long as we stay in the snow, it's just a matter of time."

Abigail struggled to her feet, gave Scott a hand up. "Then let's get going," she said. "I'll lead for a while."

1893

SEVENTY-TWO

She used her thumb to pull the hammer back.

"Good. Now put your finger right here." He eased it onto the trigger. "No, don't squeeze yet. Not until you're ready to shoot something."

"I'm ready."

"What are you aiming at?"

"Our cabin."

The hammer snapped down on an empty chamber.

"Okay, now what if you wanna shoot it again?"

She worked the big hammer back.

"Perfect."

"This time, I'm shootin the chimney."

Snap.

"I think you've got it."

She heard harness bells ringing a couple hundred feet below, the burros growing antsy. The preacher took the gun from her and broke it open, dropped shiny cartridges into the chambers.

"This becomes dangerous now," Stephen said. "It'll be loud."

"Why you cryin?"

He gave her the gun, took a wipe from his frock coat, and dabbed his eyes. "Don't draw the hammer back 'til you're ready to shoot it."

Peering through snow-clad branches, she saw the mule skinner emerge from an empty cabin across the canyon.

"See him?" Stephen asked.

"That man's sold his saddle like Miss Madsen?"

"He's even more sick in the head. You wanna help him, don't you? Send him up to God with everyone else?"

"Uh-huh."

"You keep the gun inside your cloak until you get close. I don't want you trying to shoot him until he's as near to you as that fir tree."

"Will it hurt him?"

"No. Like Molly, he's already in great pain. You're making it go away. After the first shot, he'll fall down. You be real careful, and you pull that hammer back again, and you walk up to him and shoot him in the head."

The sick mule skinner shouted, "Anyone here?"—his voice so faint and lonesome, rising like a prayer from the canyon floor.

"I don't wanna."

"I know, but it's time."

"I'm scared."

"Nothing to be scared of, Harriet."

"You do it." She handed him the gun, but he shoved it back.

"God told me this chore falls to you, that you're His little angel of darkness, and He allowed me to save you for this very purpose. Do you see the perfection of His grand design? Please, Harriet. Go end that poor man's suffering."

"If I do good, you'll dope me with a sinker and some raspberry jam?"

"I promise."

"Mr. Cole, is God gonna give me new ones?"

"New what, honey?"

"Daddy and Mama."

Stephen stared down into Harriet's dark eyes. "I'll be caring for you."

"Bethany's daddy was the best I ever saw. She called him Papa."

Stephen blushed. "Well, I suppose that would probably be all right if you wanted to um . . . you know . . . call me that."

Harriet smiled. "Okay, Papa."

The little girl pushed through the trees and stepped out from the motte of firs. He watched her through the branches, webbing downhill, hands concealed in her cloak, just like he'd told her.

He looked over Abandon—the empty, smokeless cabins, the cribs, silent dance hall, his dark chapel on the opposite slope—and he couldn't stop the thoughts, remembering that first day he'd arrived here by stage, the town pure energy and motion, the new-sawn yellow boards of the buildings and the smell of fresh-cut wood, streets a soup of mud and shit and garbage, crowded with horses, buggies, pack trains, sidewalks jammed with miners, packers, whores, gamblers, con men, everyone trying to fill their wallets, eyes electric with a peculiar mix of misery, lust, and manic greed.

Who are you?

Stephen Cole.

No, who *are* you?

God's

No,

faithful

you murdered

servant.

an entire town.

A gunshot rolled through the canyon.

Thinking, *I am Your faithful servant I am Your faithful servantIamYourfaith-fulservantIamYourfaithfulservantIamYourfaithfulservantIamfaithfulfaithfulfaithful*

His head fractured with molten pain, and he fell unconscious before the second shot rang out.

SEVENTY-THREE

It was a twenty-one burro pack train, the first six animals loaded down with burlap sacks holding three quarters of a ton of Packer's gold, the next fifteen bearing stiff riders, all fastened to their mounts with one long mecate—Ezekiel Curtice, skin a plum shade of scarlet, burned from the cold and high-altitude sun, frozen straight through, an eviscerated Bart Packer, his four servants, Russell Ilg, Molly Madsen, the albumen print of her husband shoved down the front of her corset, Billy McCabe, a faceless Oatha Wallace, the still-warm mule skinner; and the four other men the preacher had murdered in the day hole on Christmas night.

It was dusk, the snow falling in big, patient flakes.

The preacher sipped from the tincture of arnica and prayed for the fifth time in the last hour that God might ease the awful pain in his head.

From his vantage, he could see the soft glow of his cabin across the canyon, where Harriet slept.

He slapped the rear haunches of the last burro. The animal brayed, and the pack train shuffled on into the mine.

Stephen dropped the shadowgees on the floor of the tunnel and pulled the key out of his pocket.

As he worked it into the padlock, the hair on his neck stood erect. *It's been three days,* he thought. *They must be dead by now.* He dropped the crossbar on the rock, lifted the lever, the bolt retracting, pushed the iron door open with the toe of his arctic.

When the noise of the rusty hinges died away, he listened.

Silence.

He knelt and lighted the rest of the shadowgees, carried them inside three at a time, setting the lamps on the rock around the door. Then he walked back up the tunnel to the end of the pack train and quirted them on.

The donkeys hesitated, reluctant to enter the mine. He slapped their bony rumps with the reata's braided rawhide. "Get on, now!"

They inched forward, carrying their cargo, the tunnel resonant with the clack of hooves on rock.

He drove the burros through the iron door and followed them into the mine. They bunched up near the entrance, huddled together and braying nervously.

Stephen went to work cutting loose the burlap sacks and hauling the gold bricks into a nearby alcove. Then he severed the horsehair rope that attached the dead to the burros and shooed the pack train out of the mine and back up the day hole. *It is finished.*

"There!" he shouted into the cavern. "All yours! For all time!"

He reached down to lift a shadowgee.

Fingers touched his arctic.

He shrieked, tripped, and fell as he moved for the door.

What crawled toward him in the firelight seemed neither man or woman, and barely human. Lipless and toothless, a dried-out shell of a person, it whispered words undecipherable, its inflated tongue lolling out of its mouth like a piece of jerky.

Stephen raised the lamp, and in that trembling firelight, he saw the throng of Abandon in the cavern, most dead, a dozen or so dragging themselves in his direction, beggars searching for crumbs of light. The one who'd touched his boot reached out for him, bulging, lidless eyes desperate for an end to their living death. Stephen wept as he backed into the tunnel and pulled the door shut.

He stood there for a moment, listening to a weak fist pound the iron on the other side.

Please, God, end their suffering. How does that glorify—

It stopped him mid-prayer—framed in that oval of charcoal light at the far end of the tunnel, a silhouette too tall to be a child.

SEVENTY-FOUR

Main Street lay empty, wind chimes gossiping in the doorway of the mercantile, where Lana barged inside, unsheathed Joss's bowie, and stabbed the blade into the first sack she could get her hands on.

The burlap split.

Flour poured onto the board floor.

She brought a cupped handful to her mouth, and despite the feeling that she was yamping from Jessup, the merc's owner, nothing had ever tasted better.

On her third mouthful, she spotted the jar of elk jerky sitting on the counter, made a break for it, using the knife to carve bite-size pieces, devouring five strips before her stomach offered the first rumble of satisfaction.

Lana stared at the fresh set of tracks through town, which looked too orderly to have been left by a herd of passing deer. She stood listening for any sound beyond the scrape of snowflakes collecting on her cape, cold and sore, having hiked all day since climbing out of the cave, through zero visibility and ungodly deep snow, just to make it back to Abandon.

She gazed up the east slope, searching for the mine where they'd all taken shelter Christmas night. What she saw instead, obscured by the falling snow, were figures near the rimrock.

Heathens.

She squinted, but instead of hostiles, her eyes sharpened the features of three burros bearing their riders into the mountain.

She post-holed north up Main, the snow coming to her waist, her feet mercifully going numb again, panting when she finally reached the chapel.

By the time she arrived at the base of the rimrock, the burros had disappeared into the mountain, the canyon fading toward a night she would never survive without roof and walls and fire.

When she caught her wind, she fought her way up the last of the burro trail, finally standing just inside the opening to the mine.

This warm passage smelled of trail-worn animals.

She heard water dripping.

Harness bells.

The clap of metal into rock.

Her eyes discerned movement in the dark, something coming toward her up the passage, and she'd started to retreat when the first burro moved by, out of the mine, back down the slope toward Abandon.

It took a minute for the pack train to depart the mine, and as the last burro ambled past, a man shrieked from someplace deep inside the mountain.

Lana ventured three steps into the mine.

A speck of firelight flickered a ways down the tunnel and a door slammed shut.

Someone knocked on it.

Someone wept and whispered and then abruptly hushed.

Water dripped.

Metal clanged into metal.

Outside, the jingle of harness bells dwindled.

"Are you real?" A man's voice, thick with tears, and something familiar about it—a refinement, the subtlest drawl.

Then footsteps pounded up the tunnel again, and not a hooved animal, but the softer squeak of boots on wet rock. Lana began backpedaling toward the opening, glancing over her shoulder into the snowstorm and the blue dusk.

"No, don't be afraid."

The footsteps coming faster now.

She knew this voice.

The preacher, Stephen Cole, emerged from the shadows, geed up, utterly wasted, gray-skinned, eyes bloodshot and black-ringed, hair unwashed, more like a creature sprung from the innards of the mountain than Abandon's spiritual compass.

"Miss Hartman, what are you doing out here?" He'd stopped just a few feet away, both of them close enough to the opening to be stung with the razor cold of stray snowflakes. "Weren't you in the mine with everyone else Christmas night?"

Lana nodded.

"A band of heathens rode through town just a couple hours ago. They're on the peck. Nearly raised my scalp. Everyone's still in the mine. I've been bringing food and water, extra candles. Packer's gold's in there, too. That's what all the burros were carrying."

It suddenly clicked. Stephen had hidden in Abandon since Christmas night, eluding the heathens, waiting for an opportunity to bring provisions to those who had holed up in the mountain. She felt a shot of relief and admiration, hoped Joss had made it back to everyone else in the main cavern.

"Come with me. We're not safe out here, particularly with night coming on."

Lana looked once more down into Abandon, nothing to see but snow and darkness and—

A single grain of light burned on the other side of the canyon—a firelit cabin.

When she turned back, the preacher had lit a shadowgee, and he stared intently into her eyes, offering his hand.

"Don't be ringey. You need to come with me right now."

She didn't take his hand, but she did walk beside him into the passage, and as they went on, candlelight glinting on the slickensides of the day hole, a strange thing happened. Her mouth ran dry and her heart raced, and as rays of firelight reached the iron door at the tunnel's end, she realized what it was—the preacher's eyes, his voice. *You need to come with me right now.* A predatory insistence bordering on desperation that she'd seen in another pair of eyes, heard in another voice three years ago that awful night in Santa Fe, and though it made no sense, she knew at some gut level that the preacher intended to kill her.

They reached the door and Stephen fished a key out of his pocket, slid it into the keyhole of a large padlock.

He turned just as she lunged at his back, the blade refracting shards of firelight. Stephen swung his arm down onto her wrist, and it might have knocked the bowie to the rock, but Lana had momentum and a ferocious grip.

The blade sank into his thigh.

The preacher screamed and Lana saw him reach into his frock coat.

Lana was running now, enveloped in darkness. She tripped on the uneven rock, fell as a revolver thundered. Her ears ringing, she scrambled back onto her feet and hauled toward that oval of dark gray in the distance, glancing back—flare of fire, another gunshot shattering the passage.

Ten seconds of hard running brought her out of the tunnel and into the early-evening light.

She followed the burro tracks under the rimrock, moving as fast as she could manage downhill toward Abandon, the hood of her cape blown back, snow pouring into her hair, down her neck.

It was the preacher's cabin glowing on the west slope, she figured. Had he lied about the heathens? Devised some way to murder the entire town?

On Main Street, Lana bent over, gasping, petered out, saw the preacher already halfway down the slope.

She looked south toward all the dark, empty buildings.

She could try to hide, but he'd hunt her all night.

North of town, she spotted movement, took a moment to realize it was just those burros Stephen had driven out of the mine, congregating at the livery.

Inside the barn, an albino, still saddled and toting a slicker roll, stood eating a bale of hay.

When Lana grasped the harness, the horse threw his head and whinnied, but she held firm and stroked his neck.

Her arctic slipped into the stirrup and she stood and swung her other leg over and settled into the saddle. She took up the reins and gave him a little kick, and he trotted out of the stable, halting under the overhanging roof.

The snow had let up and a bit of moon shone through between the clouds.

There was nothing left of dusk, and a voice whispered that she would die out there if she did this.

Gonna die here if I stay.

In the last light, she glimpsed the profile of a man hobbling out of town, heading toward the stables.

She dug the heel of her arctic into the horse's side and rode off into the dark.

2009

SEVENTY-FIVE

The wind was storm force at the Sawblade, blasting through the gap in streamers of freezing fog, the pass blown clean of snow. Scott held up a small yellow instrument with a digital display, locking arms with Abigail to keep her from blowing off the mountain.

They took cover on the lee side of the pass behind the palisade. Scott clipped a couple of carabiners onto the hip belts of their packs and short-roped them together.

He leaned over, shouted in Abigail's ear, "My Sherpa clocked that last wind gust at fifty-one miles per hour! Stay close!"

As they started down, Abigail couldn't help but think it a good thing the clouds had socked them in, so she couldn't see the sheer drop that awaited even the slightest misstep. Two days ago, she'd freaked out on this part of the mountain, been paralyzed by vertigo.

Despite the relentless wind, the rocky trail near the top lay under three feet of snow.

Scott led, Abigail close enough behind so she could touch his pack if she reached out.

They descended slowly, painstakingly.

Before each step, Scott stabbed the old ski poles he hiked with through the snow to probe the depth and check the ledge width, ensuring they didn't stumble onto a cornice. Abigail followed in his footsteps, trying to ignore how the oval of her face not protected by the hood of her Gore-Tex jacket was progressing once again from burning into numbness.

The wind let up the lower they went.

After the sixth switchback, Scott stopped to unclip their carabiners.

Where they stood, in the upper realm of the cirque, the wind had diminished to a soft, icy breeze. They'd dropped out of the clouds into a boulder

field, the snow having buried all but the largest rocks, the lumpy white terrain resembling a field of sugar cubes.

They moved on. Within the hour, they reached the timberline, and though
still post-holing in waist-deep snow, they had come safely down from the
pass and back into the trees.

The sense of relief was potent and long overdue.

In the late afternoon, they rested at eleven thousand feet in a pure stand of
Douglas fir. The cold front had pushed through, driven out the clouds, and
scrubbed the sky into high-gloss Colorado blue. They dug out a spot in the
snow, sat leaning against one of the old firs, eating gorp, sharing a bottle of
water.

"Drink as much as you need," Scott said. "I have a filter with me, so I can
pump more."

"I feel guilty drinking this," Abigail said. "Knowing my dad doesn't have
this luxury."

Scott broke open a pistachio, plucked out the nut meat. "You getting dehy-
drated isn't gonna . . . Lawrence is your father?"

"We aren't close. He left us when I was very young."

Abigail lifted the Nalgene bottle, and as she unscrewed the lid to take another sip, it twitched, the tree trunk between them went *psst,* a piece of bark
flew off, struck her face, and two streams of water shot out from the middle
of the bottle, one arcing into the snow, the other into her lap.

Abigail said, "What the—"

The delayed report of a high-powered rifle broke out above them in the
cirque.

Scott tackled her into the snow.

"How close?" she whispered.

"There was a three-second lag from when the bullet hit the bottle to the
gunshot. . . . If he's shooting one of the bigger cartridges, he's maybe . . . fourteen, fifteen hundred yards away. Just under a mile. Probably scoping us from
the ledges below the pass."

A bullet tore through Scott's pack, followed by fleeting silence, then a resounding gunshot.

"I don't know how the hell he's got us sighted up in these woods," Scott
said. "You run first. I'll be right behind you. Don't run in a straight line. Zig-
zag between the trees. Make yourself a harder target. Go."

Abigail scrambled up out of the snow, took off downhill through the firs.

After ten steps, she heard another gunshot, glanced back, didn't see Scott,
kept running, thinking, *The bullet'll hit you. You'll go down, might never hear the
shot.*

She came out of the forest into the little glade where they'd camped three nights ago, and on the other side, she ducked behind a tree. When she caught her breath, Abigail peeked around the corner, spotted Scott running toward her across the glade.

He stepped behind the tree, threw his pack down in the snow.

"What are you doing?" she said.

"I wanna see where this fucker is." He unzipped the top of his pack, jammed his hand inside, and pulled out a small black leather case, which he unsnapped.

He took out a pair of eight-power Nikon binoculars and lay flat in the snow.

Propped up on his elbows, so the lenses just barely poked above the surface, he brought the eyecups to his eyes, adjusted the focus knob, and glassed the cirque.

After a minute, he said, "There you are. Shit, I thought we were making much better time. You wanna see?"

Abigail got down in the snow with him and took the binoculars. Scott guided her finger to the focus knob. "First, find the pass," he said. She glassed the buttresses and couloirs of the cirque in the big sphere of magnification, then the jagged rock outcropping of the Sawblade, two thousand feet above and a mile away, the sharp rocks and snow glinting in the sun, a deep, shimmering quality to the condensed air.

"Okay, I've got it," she said.

"See the trail we took?"

"Yeah."

"Just follow it on down."

Abigail adjusted the focus, slowly glassing the ledges, tracing their steep descent down the back wall of the cirque. "I see him," she said.

"That's the guy who locked you in the mine?"

"Yeah, that's Quinn."

Minuscule among the huge broken crags, Quinn post-holed at a fast lope just past the fifth switchback in that silver-and-black down jacket. He toted a backpack and a scope-bearing rifle slung over his shoulder.

"Oh my God," she said. "He's almost down from the ledges." Abigail lowered the binoculars. "He's gonna catch up to us, Scott, and he has our tracks to follow."

Scott's face paled, and she wondered if it was from blood loss or fear.

He said, "We have to get down below the snow line."

SEVENTY-SIX

Abigail and Scott worked their way down through the trees at a lung-wrenching jog. The valley broadened. They passed into a forest of spruce and aspen. At ten thousand feet, the snow was only knee-deep. At nine thousand, just a foot lay on the ground. Abigail's tailbone felt like it had split, and she saw blood in Scott's tracks, his right boot squishing.

A little past six o'clock in the evening, they arrived at the alpine lake where they'd lunched on Sunday afternoon. The sun had slipped below the valley wall an hour ago, and a fleet of leaden clouds invaded from the west. Scott's Sherpa put them at 8,700 feet, but they still stood in snow to their ankles.

"How you holding up?" Abigail said.

He squatted by the bank. "Fucking agony."

"What can I do?"

"Nothing. We just have to keep descending. Think Quinn's stopping?"

They pushed on past the spruce-rimmed lake, down and down, faster than they'd moved all day, light dwindling, clouds thickening up, dark and without texture, an immense sheet of metal stretched across the sky. They tramped through occasional patches of bare ground. Then there were more bare spots than snow-covered ones. Then just tatters of wet snow on the tree-shaded north aspects. Then no snow at all, but only the naked floor of the forest—spongy and saturated from two days of cold November rain.

At dusk, they came into the aspen grove—slim silvered trunks as far as they could see, some marred with arborglyphs, carved graffiti from the old West.

Abigail hadn't noticed it before, but the aspens had eyes, hundreds of them all around her, mysterious dark bark scars from where old branches used to be, watching her from every side.

Scott collapsed. "We have to decide," he said, breathless, "whether to stop for the night or keep going."

"Could you even go on any farther?"

He shook his head. "I don't think so, but maybe you can."

"I'm not going anywhere at night and alone with this lunatic out here. Besides, I'm wiped out, too."

"Well, we're out of the snow, so we'd better find a place to camp." Scott struggled to his feet. "The valley's a half mile wide here. Let's get ourselves out of the middle of it."

As they headed east through the aspen, Abigail felt her stomach tighten. The imminent threat to her life notwithstanding, there was still something unnerving about being in the wilderness with night coming on and watching the sky lose its light above you, a sinking feeling rooted in the most basic of primal fears—the woods after dark.

They came to a stream. It flowed stronger than Abigail remembered, and it seemed two lifetimes ago that she'd watched Scott fly-fish this same watercourse two miles up the valley for their supper. "Stream's up," he said. "I'm gonna filter some water, since we can't camp here. First place Quinn will look for us is along this stream. We'd never hear him coming."

They climbed down into the gully and found a place at the water's edge beside a pool protected from the chaos of the main current and clogged with aspen leaves that looked like gold coins floating in the water. Scott dug the PUR filter out of his pack and inserted the two hoses into the bottom. He fitted the end of one with a bottle adapter and screwed it onto an empty Nalgene bottle. The other hose, he dropped in the pool.

Abigail sat beside him in the fading light, watching Scott pump the filter and holding the newly filled bottles between her legs. She kept looking back up the gully. Scott had been right. Streamside, you couldn't hear a thing but the chatter of water flowing over rocks. Approaching footsteps would be lost in the noise. When he'd topped off five Nalgene bottles, Scott disassembled the filter and packed everything away.

There would be no dry, easy crossing.

They forded the stream—fifteen feet across and thigh-deep in the middle, so strong that Abigail had to brace herself and lean into the current to keep her footing. The water had been snow less than an hour ago. Her legs burned and her lungs contracted from the freezing shock of it.

They climbed onto the bank and up the muddy gully on the other side, hiked several hundred yards over a forest floor carpeted with brilliant aspen leaves.

The air smelled metallic and stale. It began to rain.

Scott turned to her, said, "I see where we'll camp tonight," and Abigail followed him into a thicket of chokecherry, not much space between the shrubs, but enough to conceal a tent.

SEVENTY-SEVEN

Four nylon bags lay spread out on the ground, containing the footprint, poles, pegs, and the tent itself—a bright red Hilleberg. They unrolled the footprint in a cleared area between the chokecherry shrubs, and Scott unfolded the tent while Abigail took out the poles and locked them together. In the deepening darkness, as the rain set in, they slipped the three poles into the tent sleeves and staked out the guylines, Scott's hands shaking so badly that he could barely grip the pegs to jam them into the softened ground.

With the tent pitched, they threw their packs into the roomy vestibule, climbed in, and zipped themselves inside. Scott shivered uncontrollably, and he slurred his words.

Abigail said, "You have spare clothes in here?" He nodded. "Why don't you get in the tent and take off your wet ones." Scott unzipped the inner tent and crawled inside. While he stripped, Abigail pulled everything out of his pack, realized she didn't feel right, either—her motor coordination was disrupted and she had trouble focusing on the task at hand.

"I can't find your sleeping bag," she said.

"Bottom compartment." She dragged out the Marmot compression bag, tossed it in with the Therm-a-Rest and his bag of extra clothes. Then she unlaced her boots, pulled off her socks, all her soaked clothing, and climbed in.

Scott twisted shut the air valve on the Therm-a-Rest, laid his sleeping bag on top of it. He wriggled inside, said, "Get in with me. We both have hypothermia."

Abigail climbed into the down mummy bag and zipped them up. Scott spooned her. She could feel him shaking against her, their legs so cold, like malleable ice.

"I should really get us something to eat and drink," she said.

"Just stay here with me for a minute, get some body heat going."

They lay shivering together, listening to the rain patter on the tent. The sky detonated. Thunder shook the ground and decayed like a shotgun blast, Abigail thinking it sounded so different from East Coast thunder. In the West, it was deeper, right on top of you, and seemed to fade forever.

"Think we're safe in this thicket?" Abigail asked.

"As long as we stay quiet and don't turn on any lights. Fuck, I can't get warm."

Abigail turned and faced him. She ran her hand along the right side of his abdomen. It felt hot, swollen, and sticky. "Your wound's leaking," she said.

"My boot was full of blood. I'm hurting pretty bad again."

"I saw the first-aid kit in your pack. I'm gonna get it out, and you're gonna tell—"

"You think I'm dying?" he asked.

"No," she said, though she didn't know. "I think once we get some food and medicine in you, you'll feel a lot better."

She started to sit up, but Scott stopped her. "Not yet," he said. "Just stay with me. This is the worst shit I've ever been in. And I've been in some real shit. You believe in karma?"

"I don't know."

"Well, I think it's fucking me over at the moment."

"How so?"

"This trip isn't the first time I've gotten someone killed in the backcountry. I was involved in an accident on Rainier a couple years ago."

"What's Rainier?"

"*Mount* Rainier. The fourteen-thousand-foot volcano in Washington."

"What happened? Or if you don't want to talk about it, I—"

"Two years ago, me and a friend drove out from Boulder to do a mid-May ascent. It was stupid. Too early in the season to be on that mountain. Maria was a tall, gorgeous redhead. Strong. A solid rock climber, badass telemarking goddess. But she'd never done any serious mountaineering or glacier travel. She was inexperienced. I was cocky. Thought I could get her up the thing. And I did. We reached the summit cone, Columbia Crest. Had the time of our lives. But on a mountain like Rainier, all it takes is one mistake. A momentary lapse of judgment. And I made it. On the way down, Maria was jonesing to break out her skis. I knew it was a bad idea. Spring conditions. Variable snow. Everything from crust to corn. But I was feeling a little invincible after a perfect ascent.

"We were telemarking the upper edge of Ingraham Glacier. She was a much better skier, got out ahead. I'd told her to stay with me, that it was only safe to ski the top. Thing about Maria, she was always pushing it. She was fifty yards ahead of me when she disappeared. I think she never even saw it.

I stopped at the edge of the crevasse. Thing was huge, and it dropped down at an angle, so I couldn't see to the bottom. I didn't see Maria, but I could hear her screaming down there in the dark. There was just no way to descend into that crevasse. I mean, some of these ice fissures go down hundreds of feet. I got off the mountain fast as I could, flew back with search-and-rescue in a big Chinook helicopter. But it had snowed, covered our ski tracks. I couldn't even lead them back to the crevasse she'd gone into. Now all this shit's happening to us out here. I figure it's payback karma, and I guess I deserve it."

Abigail used Scott's Krill glow stick for illumination, since it put out a soft blue light, which would be almost impossible to see beyond the thicket. Scott talked her through firing up the tiny propane stove out in the vestibule, and as the water heated for their freeze-dried dinners in a slug-punctured pot, Abigail broke out the first-aid kit. She used a syringe filled with filtered water to irrigate the wound, then wiped it with iodine, applied the antibiotic cream, resealed it with several closure strips, and taped on a gauze bandage. Scott took three tablets of extra-strength Tylenol with his supper, and by the time they'd finished eating, Abigail could see in his eyes that the pain had begun to ease.

The glow stick lay on the floor of the tent, casting their faces in a weak blue light, which made them look cold and cadaverous.

They talked—about Maria, about Abigail's father—their painful memories a diversion from the fear. Abigail could feel sleep stalking her, waiting to pounce. She lifted a Nalgene bottle, took a long drink, the water excellent—pure and ice cold, tasting faintly of iron.

"Knowing what happened to you on Rainier," she said, "I'm surprised you ever went back into the mountains after that. Doesn't it feel like returning to the scene of a tragedy?"

"I never thought of it that way. These mountains, the West, they're my first love. See, I was born and raised in Jacksonville, Florida. A flatlander. Until I was fifteen, I'd never been west of Dallas. I'd seen the Smokies, the Adirondacks. But those are just big hills. Most exciting time of my life was the summer after my freshman year of high school, July of '93, when my dad rented an RV and took our family west.

"God. The day we drove across Kansas into Colorado. Interstate Seventy. The plains. The vastness of the sky. That high, dry air. Sinatra's *The Very Good Years* playing on the tape deck. Always think of that summer when I hear Frank's voice. He was our sound track for that trip." Scott's smile contained a measure of wistfulness.

"Never forget, I'm sitting up front with my dad and we're barreling west, an hour or so from Denver, when, way off on the horizon, I see what looks like a bank of clouds. I ask him what it is and he tells me that's the Front Range of the Rocky Mountains, and what looks like clouds is actually snow. Snow in July. I couldn't even imagine it. I'd only seen snow twice in Jacksonville. I wanted to be up in those mountains. On top of them. Needed to know every ridge, every crag. Next day, we drove up Mount Evans, one of the fourteeners. Me and my little sis had a snowball fight on the summit, and that was it. I was a mountain boy thereafter." Scott leaned forward and zipped up the mesh door of the inner tent. They climbed into his sleeping bag, turned off the glow stick.

"Tomorrow scares me," Abigail whispered.

"We're gonna head out early, while it's still dark. Just leave the tent here. We did good today. It's only another six or seven miles to the trailhead."

"You've got the keys to your truck, right?"

"Top of my pack."

They were quiet for a while, the sound of rain working on them like a tranquilizer.

"There's this part of me," Abigail whispered, "just wants to leave him in that cave."

Scott pulled her in close, their eyes shutting, both surrendering to the steady hiss of rain and far-off thunder.

SEVENTY-EIGHT

Abigail opened her eyes and looked at her watch—3:48 A.M. It was still raining, still pitch-black inside the tent. The sound of Scott unzipping the sleeping bag had woken her, and now he was crawling out of it.

"What are you doing?" Abigail whispered.

"I put it off long as I could stand it. I gotta go like nobody's business."

"Here, take this with you."

Abigail twisted the base of the glow stick. It lighted up and she tossed it to him.

"This is the worst part of camping," he grumbled, slipping into his fleece pullover. "When you absolutely, positively have to get out of your warm tent in the middle of a cold, rainy night to take a shit."

Abigail nestled back into the bag, asleep again before Scott got his boots on.

Abigail shot up in the sleeping bag. She'd been dreaming about wandering through an endless cave, room after room after room, and for a second, she thought she was still in that cave with her father, and that climbing up the chimney and finding Scott and being shot at had all been a dream.

The disorientation passed. She was tucked away in a thicket, somewhere in the lower reaches of that long valley, and, she realized, on the cusp of dawn, because she could just make out the tunnel-shaped walls of the tent and the bottles of water at her feet.

She rubbed her eyes, glanced at her watch again—4:58 A.M. A quiet voice in her head asked, *Why isn't Scott here?* She vaguely remembered waking some time ago. Then her mind cleared and it all came back. *It's been over an hour since Scott went out there to shit in the woods.*

Abigail put on her fleece jacket and her parka, found that her fleece pants and wool socks had mostly dried out. She dressed, unzipped the inner tent, and climbed through the vestibule, the door to which Scott had left open.

She poked her head outside—little to see in this first light, surrounded by chokecherry shrubs still holding on to most of their sunset-colored leaves.

Abigail pushed her way out of the thicket and emerged into the aspen grove.

The rain had stopped, the wind had stilled, and the light was so fragile that she couldn't yet tell if the sky was clear or uniformly clouded. She made a careful scan of the trees. She whispered, "Scott!" The only audible sound was the distant babble of the stream. The woods smelled of dead leaves, which made a deafening crunch under her boots. Her feet were already freezing in the damp socks.

She followed an old wash down through the trees, thinking Scott might have come this way to put some distance between the campsite and where he squatted.

Every few steps, she whispered his name. Her legs and tailbone were so sore from yesterday's trek, her knees gone to mush. She stopped. Listened. Looked back at the stain of the chokecherry thicket barely visible up the hill.

"Scott!" she whispered. "Scott!"

Fifty yards down the wash, something caught her eye—a shiver of blue light.

She jogged along the dry creekbed, came to the glow stick lying in the wet leaves.

She bent down and picked it up, trying to process what this meant and all the permutations of what might have happened.

When she looked up again, she saw Scott sitting against a whitewashed aspen covered in arborglyphs, his head drooped, Gramicci pants and thermal underwear still pulled down below his knees, and the front of his yellow fleece blacked with a half gallon of blood, spilled out from the dark slit that linked his earlobes.

She staggered back and collapsed on the bank, had to make herself breathe, her hands shaking, that voice now screaming in her head, *Get out of here right now, Abby.*

Somewhere nearby, leaves rustled. She stood up, looking from tree to tree to tree and at all the spaces between, misting now in the gray twilight, watched by all those aspen eyes.

Again, she heard the rustle of leaves. The noise had come from fifteen yards away, but there was no one there. This time, the sound of what she'd mistaken for footsteps originated a ways up the wash, and even as she stared in that direction, she realized they hadn't been footsteps at all, but the impact of thrown rocks.

The smoke of a menthol cigarette scooted by on the first breeze of dawn.

1893

SEVENTY-NINE

Gloria Curtice came back to consciousness from the strangest dream: The preacher, Stephen Cole, had driven a pack train into the mine, screamed, "All yours!" and, instead of saving them, locked back the door.

She opened her eyes, stared at the shadowgee in the middle of the cavern, her head resting in Rosalyn's lap.

The severe constriction of her throat made swallowing an excruciating proposition, and her tongue had become a foreign object in her mouth, an insensate strip of leather so swollen, it threatened to choke her. Her saliva had turned thick and foul-tasting, and between the riving headache and the stiffness in her neck, she didn't dare move.

In the eerie silence, everyone waited to see who would die next. Gloria no longer trusted her eyes to distinguish reality from phantasm. Some things, she knew had happened, and she clung to these last vestiges of sanity. She knew, that days ago, three separate parties had taken lanterns and struck out in search of water or another way out, and that none had returned.

She knew she'd seen the smith, Mason Stetler, accused of stealing a biscuit by six miners, themselves delirious with hunger and thirst; had watched three of them pin him down while the others hoisted a boulder from a pile of crushed ore and dropped it on his head.

She thought, erroneously, she'd imagined the schoolmarm, who had stripped naked in the middle of the chamber to perform vaudeville—juggling rocks, inventing songs of starvation and heathens, attempting senseless magic tricks, and closing the act with a bizarre dance that resembled a solitary high-speed waltz.

Likewise, the barber, who proclaimed himself the devil, welcomed everyone to hell, and commanded them to worship at his feet, only to be silenced by a half-dead miner who'd heard enough, drawn his Colt, and shot a hole through Lucifer's throat.

She felt certain the owner of the merc, Jessup Crider, had assumed a grim task when he'd addressed the living, that he'd actually stood weeping before them, speaking in a hoarse whisper, tongue so ballooned, he could hardly push the words through his teeth.

Jessup had said he'd been providing goods and services to the people of Abandon going on ten years and that he wanted to offer one last service. He had a carbine and two boxes of cartridges and any man, woman, or child who preferred to forgo this elongated death could come to him right now, and he'd not only spare them the agony but also the damnable sin of self-destruction.

Gloria had watched ten people drag themselves to a far corner of the cavern and sit shoulder-to-shoulder. They'd whispered last words to loved ones, last prayers, and then Jessup had walked behind them with a lever-action Winchester—one bullet each in the back of the head.

As ten streamlets of blood ran out and converged to fill a swag in the rocky floor, several people had gone and knelt at the edge of the pool, gleaming like black lacquer in the firelight, and lapped up the warm blood.

Some hours later, Jessup had extended the offer again, got twenty takers the second time. Gloria would have been one of them had she possessed the strength to lift her hand or to voice her desire.

Jessup himself had barely been able stand or even cock the Winchester's lever, and he'd given everyone ample warning that this was their last opportunity to make use of him.

When he'd seen to his customers, she'd watched him position the barrel of the carbine under his own chin.

Gloria knew that Jessup and his final act of kindness had not been an illusion of her disintegrating mind, because she would occasionally glance over at the thirty bodies slumped together on the floor, raging with envy that she was not among them.

She tried to escape into sleep again, kept telling herself that one of these times she wouldn't wake up.

This wasn't hell.

It couldn't go on forever.

EIGHTY

J oss heard the roar in the distance and smelled the water. Melted candle drippings oozed onto her left hand, but she didn't flinch, her fingers already coated with hardened white wax. She smiled because she recognized the sound of the cascade pouring into the subterranean lake where she and Lana had taken those first gorgeous gulps of water after leaving the main cavern. She might actually find her way back from here.

The flame quivered as she entered the waterfall room, and it would have extinguished in the draft, but she had it cupped with her right hand.

Joss climbed down the wet rock and knelt at the lake's edge, figured it had been at least a full day since her last drink. She held the candle in her left hand and bent over and dipped her face into the water, letting it siphon into her mouth. As she drank, several icy drops splashed on the back of her head, probably runoff from an overhanging stalactite, but, too engrossed in sating her thirst, Joss didn't distinguish the sudden hiss from the overwhelming crush of the waterfall.

When she lifted her head from the lake, she first noticed the odor of smoke, and then the black. Black beyond dreamless sleep or how she imagined death might be, like something had come along and snatched her eyes right out of their sockets.

She looked at her left hand, felt the candle in her fingers, saw only the faintest impression of the wick, fading from orange into amber.

"Calm the fuck down, Jocelyn. You got one match left."

She reached under her serape into the lapel pocket of her cotton dress shirt, felt her fingers graze the sliver of sulfur-tipped wood.

She took it out, held it in front of her face.

"You're holdin your life in that little splinter."

She'd performed this trick any number of times, even derived a measure of pride from it, to the point that six years ago she'd thrown out the piece of flint she kept in the prayer book with her papers and tobacco.

The move was simple—lift her serape and shirt, strike the match against the middle of three buttons that fastened her canvas trousers.

She set the candle beside her on the rock and lifted her shirt, reaching down in the dark, fingering the trio of metal buttons.

She held the match in her right hand and closed her eyes. Instead of being in a cave, she imagined herself chained up behind the bar in that beautiful saloon of hers, chewing the dog with Bart or Oatha, flirting with Zeke, glaring at that porch-percher Al, nooning by the stove. She conjured the aroma of whiskey, the cold rancid sweat of hardworking men. No big deal. No great importance attached to this match. Just time for a cigarette.

In the darkness, her hand moved, the match gliding toward her crotch. She was trying not to overthink it, but she noted she couldn't remember the last time she'd snapped a punk—this thought interrupted as she felt the match head graze the surface of the button.

Acrid bite of sulfur, then the match flared and the lake lighted up, firelight reflected in the water and the crystals, and she could have cried as she reached for the candle.

Her hand slid across wet rock—nothing there.

"The fuck?"

Already, the heat of the flame was descending toward her thumb and forefinger.

She leaned onto her right buttock, thinking maybe she'd sat on it, but no. Now, carefully, bringing the flame over to the rock, searching the contours, the crystalline veins—still nothing—edging her fingers farther down the match as the flame pursued, desperation setting in, and the heat building, nowhere for her fingers to go now, the fire blackening her thumbnail, her teeth gritted, her skin beginning to bubble, and the last thing she saw before the flame smothered was the candle, three feet from the bank, floating in the lake.

Again, the black, and, as if her brain sensed she'd seen her last light, disorientation flooded in.

"You ain't dead yet," she said, rising to her feet. She still had her bearings. She couldn't see it, but she knew that on the other side of this lake stood the opening to a flat tunnel she'd have to crawl through. From there, she'd take it one room at a time. No rush. No panic. She'd scream. Listen. She'd find them, or they'd find her.

Joss took baby steps along the rocky bank, arms outstretched. She came to a wall she couldn't feel the top of, but there were handholds, so she climbed, the waterfall getting louder, as though she stood above it now. And still she climbed, uncertain, just grasping in the dark, trusting her arms and legs to take her where—

Her right foot slipped, and she gripped wet rock, feet scrambling for purchase, her fingers cramping.

It hit her—a load of buckshot colder than Emerald Lake in June, with more properties of liquid metal than water, the current dragging her toward that hole that drained the lake deep into the mountain, kept the depth constant.

She came up gasping, lungs, heart, muscles, bones stunned, standing now in two feet of freezing water, stumbling on, no intended direction or destination beyond someplace dry.

After awhile, her knees banged into the bank and she crawled up onto it and climbed until her head struck a wall.

"Goddamn it!"

The way her voice blared back in her face, she figured she'd crawled into some kind of alcove. The air smelled fixed, and her hands shook so hard, she couldn't grasp the buttons on her cotton shirt.

She ripped it open, pulled her arms out of the sleeves, undid her trousers.

Her boots poured out several jars' worth of water apiece, and then she sat there naked, shivering in the black and colder than she'd ever been in her life, leaning against a flat-topped rock, sizing up her predicament, chuckle-headed with shock.

"Well, you got a Chinaman's chance now a gettin out a this hitch, you fuckin yack." She wiped her eyes, humiliated, facing death, and realizing she didn't have as much sand as she'd thought. This was worse than looking up a limb at the string party awaiting her in Arizona. No hiding from it—she was down-in-her-boots afraid, with not even a blanket to fill to calm her nerves.

She thought about Lana, wondered if she'd gotten herself back to Abandon, imagined that by now she'd freed everybody. They'd probably have a big meal of soft grub, outdoing even their Christmas Eve supper. But not her. She was done. Done being a saloonist, only thing she'd ever loved, never pour a shot of rotgut in that dog hole again, never taste whiskey, feel the sting of tobacco smoke inflating her lungs, never spread mustard with the rich, never exchange corral dust with the miners, never tell another bugged-up, bandbox, mail-order cowboy he weren't shit and to take his ready-mades and get the fuck out, never scheme with another picaro.

"*Got me, didn't Ye?*" she yelled. "Congratulations! You picked one fuckin helluva way to save me. *This funny to You? Wearin a big smile up there?* Let me tell You the straight goods. You think I'm gettin down on my knees now my leg's tied up and I'm feelin poorly, gonna beg You to spare me, make amends for my behavior and pledge everlastin loyalty, You got another fuckin thing comin. Thought it'd be like gettin money from home breakin my ass down in front a my unshucked self? Thought You'd steal my dignity while You kilt me? Well, fuck You! Don't know if You was watchin back there, but I saved Your child, Lana. Won my spurs, far as I'm concerned. *Why You hate me?* Tell You what. You all-powerful, all-knowin? We can call the shit even if You end me right now. Don't care how You do it, long as it's quick and—"

She didn't see it, but she felt it.

The alcove shook and filled with dust.

The waterfall went mute.

Her lungs burned, and within thirty seconds, the sulfur gas had killed her.

2009

EIGHTY-ONE

Abigail spun around, whispered, "No."

Isaiah stood between two scarred aspen trees, his breath pluming in the cold, moist air. He reached down, lifted his trouser leg, unsnapped the ankle sheath he'd taken from Jerrod, and slipped out the little dagger.

"Your boy over there never saw it coming. Cut his throat mid-shit. But I *want* you to see me coming. I want you to watch me carve up that beautiful ass."

Isaiah dragged on his cigarette, the ash cherry flaring and fading. Then he threw it down, blew out a stream of smoke, and started toward her.

Abigail sprinted up the dry creekbed as the mist thickened into rain, her lungs raw in the thin air. She spotted the chokecherry thicket in the distance, glanced back, tripped over a rotted log, plowing face-first through the soppy bed of the wash.

She sat up, dazed, sucking air as she wiped the cold mud out of her eyes.

Snow mixed with the rain—big flakes falling silently between the aspen.

Abigail clambered back onto her feet and ran up the wash, tree trunks chipping off all around her, bark exploding. Ten more strides, then she ducked into the thicket and dived through the open tent door. Scott's pack lay in the corner of the vestibule. She turned it over and unzipped the top compartment as brittle leaves crunched outside. She reached in, pulled out everything— bottle of sunscreen, map, wallet, small compression bag labeled "Scott's emergency kit," and finally the ring of keys.

She peeked out the vestibule through the chokeberries' foliage, bright as pyrotechnics in the dismal dawn.

All she could see of Isaiah was the pair of black leather boots just beyond the thicket.

"Why don't you come on out so we can do this?"

Bullets ripped through the tent. Abigail flattened herself on the ground, closed her eyes, clenching her hand around the keys so tightly, they cut into her skin.

"Get the fuck out here. Be ten times worse if I have to come in there, drag your ass out."

Abigail slid the locking mechanism up the drawstring and opened Scott's emergency kit.

It contained a whistle, a space blanket, waterproof matches.

"Bitch, I am counting to five."

Two packs of Emer'gen-C. A Clif Bar.

"One. Two."

And a Swiss army knife.

"Three."

She opened the blade, stabbed it through the rain fly, sliced a door in the fabric.

As Isaiah reached five and began pushing his way into the thicket, she crawled out the back of the tent and rolled under the shrubs.

She got up and accelerated to a dead run, turned back in time to see Isaiah emerge from the thicket and shove a new magazine into his machine pistol, the sound of her panting growing deeper, more frenzied, felt like she was drowning, short on air to fuel her legs.

She stepped behind a big aspen, light-headed, head pounding, trying to gasp quietly.

Isaiah shot by.

She watched him run down through the trees.

Ten yards. Twenty. Thirty.

He suddenly stopped, his back to her, head cocked, listening.

Abigail spotted a rock lying at the toe of her right boot among the roots. She picked it up, threw it as hard as she could, hoping it would make a diversionary racket in the dead leaves, that when Isaiah went to check it out, the noise of his footsteps would provide her cover to slip around to the other side of the aspen. With the thousands of trees in this grove, if she could only lose him for a moment, she had a chance.

But the rock skipped off a tree trunk and landed just five yards downslope of Isaiah.

He spun around and looked right at her, shook his head, half-smiling, as if miffed at a petulant child. With few trees between them, he had a clear shot. Kept her covered with the machine pistol as he jogged upslope.

Abigail sank down onto the roots, her hands shaking.

Isaiah stopped ten feet away, let go of his machine pistol, and unholstered the knife.

"Where's everybody else?"

She clutched the keys in one hand, the Swiss army knife in the other.

"We got locked in a cave," she said. "I was the only one who could climb out."

"Who locked you in?"

"This man pretending to be a history professor. Told us you'd been holding him at Emerald House for several—"

"Bullshit."

"It's what he said. He killed Stu. Threw him off the third floor of the mansion."

Isaiah's brown eyes dilated. "Why'd he lock you in a cave?"

"I don't know. I guess so he could have the gold all to himself."

"Shut the fuck up."

"I saw it. Touched it."

Isaiah came forward. "Where?"

"There's this old mining tunnel, and at the end of it, a locked iron door. You pass through, and off to the right in a little alcove, that's where all the burlap sacks are. We counted over sixty-one bars. Look, you've been lied to, so I won't be shocked if you don't—"

"How do you get to this tunnel?"

"Why would I tell you that?"

Isaiah knelt down, held the knife point under her left eye.

Abigail said, "And how do you plan to haul it out of these mountains on your own?"

Isaiah's eyes slimmed down into raging slits.

"You think," she whispered, "that what you went through in the war entitles you—"

He pushed the knife point into her lower eyelid as Abigail worked the blade of the Swiss army knife open with her thumbnail.

"I take what I want," he said, "because I have the big fucking balls to do it. You think people let shit slip away 'cause they're decent? Or moral? They don't take what they want 'cause they're spineless and gutless and terrified of God's retribution. Well, I'm not. I've already been to hell." Isaiah stood up. "Now get off your cunt and—"

He stepped back and sat down.

The report echoed through the aspen grove.

Isaiah dropped his knife and unzipped the black parka and his black fleece jacket and raised his T-shirt. Blood pulsed out of a small hole in the center of his chest and ran down his washboard stomach, pooling in his belly button, spilling over, diverting at his waistband. He looked up at Abigail as if it were her fault, then fell over into the wet leaves.

She ran her hands along his sides, felt a bulge in the left pocket of the parka. Working the zipper open, her hands closing on her father's Ruger, she transferred the revolver to her jacket, then slipped the machine pistol's nylon strap over Isaiah's head and stepped behind the tree as another round zipped past her ear and severed a sapling.

She swung out with a two-handed grip, and squeezed the eight-pound trigger.

Quinn stepped behind a tree as the Glock bucked, sprayed the forest, pushing Abigail back with the force of a high-pressure water hose, a stream of brass casings arcing over her right shoulder, flames shooting out the compensator ports, the machine pistol vacating the thirty-three-round magazine before it even crossed her mind to let up on the trigger.

She stumbled forward as the slide locked back, the gun impotent.

Abigail surveyed the aspen grove—no movement, no sound save for the hiss of rain and snow falling on the Glock's smoking suppressor.

She heard a soft whistle behind her, looked back, saw blood boiling and sucking back into the hole in Isaiah's chest.

She threw down the machine pistol and began to run.

1893

EIGHTY-TWO

*L*ana *standing by the living room window, staring through frosted glass at the crowd of carolers come to serenade her this Christmas night, their faces awash in candlelight,* Silent night, holy night, *a figure stumbling up the alameda toward the front door,* Darkness flies, all is light, *the choir faltering,* Feel free to get the fuck off my yard, *the carolers dispersing, Lana retreating to the Steinway, seating herself at the piano bench, thinking,* My playing soothes him, *perhaps some Brahms, the keys tinkling icily as the front door opens, slams, the meter quickening with her heartbeat as his boots pound the hardwood floor, his footsteps and the piquant waft of cactus juice moving toward—*

The stillness shook her from the dream.

Lana opened her eyes—starry and cold beyond reason, the horse standing in snow to its stomach, wind-broke and panting.

She was high above the timberline, between two promontories that seemed vaguely familiar, masses of rock and ice in black relief against the navy sky.

She realized she'd seen them two and half years ago through the dusty window of a coach that summer afternoon she'd first made the long trip to Abandon, though the wilderness had looked quite different then—greened out and only pockets of dirty snow in the shadowed mountain flanks. This was the crest of the main wagon trail, a twelve-thousand-foot pass between a pair of knobs collectively named the Teats.

Having slept with her head drooped the last several hours, she winced from a neck crick as she assessed the moon's position in the sky, estimating the hour to be approaching midnight. Thank God the horse seemed to know the way, although she wondered how much farther she could push this salado. But what was the alternative? Dismount, unfasten the apron straps, and spread out the bedroll? Star-pitch in six feet of snow?

Falling asleep on the way out of town, her feet had tingled with cold. Now they hung in the stirrups, disturbingly innocuous, a complete lack of sensation that she hoped was warmth.

Her hands ached, which she took for a good sign, balled up into fists inside the mittens to conserve heat. She had a suspicion it was lethally cold, but in the absence of wind, the thirty-below air temperature felt less pronounced.

Lana turned in the saddle, looked back the way she'd come—a smooth snowy slope bright as day under the moon, bruised only by horse tracks that more resembled the delicate indentation of a sandpiper's footprints on a beach.

Miles away, she could see the opening to Abandon's box canyon, the town itself hidden from view.

Again she traced the path her horse had taken, following the tracks five hundred feet back down the slope, across a narrow bench, then one last dip toward timberline, where at that moment one of the trees broke away from the forest and moved upslope.

Stephen Cole, she thought.

She attempted to gauge the distance—a mile, mile and a half at most.

He's following my tracks.

She looked at what lay ahead—it appeared as if the trail descended gradually over the next few miles, then dropped into the forest, where it paralleled the course of what she recalled was a river in the summertime.

Far, far on—ten, maybe fifteen miles beyond this drainage at whose headwaters she stood—something glowed in a distant valley.

Silverton.

It seemed impossibly far.

Lana darling. Could I steal your attention?

Her fingers rest on the ivory keys, piano bench squeaking as he eases down beside her, his breath heavy with a strange-smelling smoke and soured by tequila, maybe the better part of a jug, though she doesn't know for sure. He can hold the liquor of three high lonesomes.

Why are you dressed up like a sore toe?

It's Christmas, John.

Is it. *He unbuttons his claw hammer, rising slightly to straighten the tails.* I'm not back to stay.

She looks up at him, his eyes turned inward, dreamy with opium, pupils huge black disks reflecting the candles that line the top of the Steinway.

John, you aren't yourself.

Thank God for that. *He grins, something rote drunkenness rarely elicits.*

You went to that hop-alley den, saw your celestial. I can smell the smoke on—

This is engaging beyond all expectations, but they're holding up the game for me.

How much?

That grin again.

How much?

Down to my last chip, as they say, although it isn't really a chip in the conventional—

How. Much. Did you lose?

It would appear that Mr. Carson is now the proud owner of our casa.

What?

It was the worst streak of cards any man has ever drawn. Everyone at the table agreed.

You gambled our home?

Well. Yes. But all hope is not lost. The game took an interesting turn.

Lana tugged at the reins and pulled up just shy of the forest, the Teats looming under the brilliant smear of the Milky Way, and saw, not half a mile back, the rider progressing toward her.

She reached down and patted the horse's neck a moment before booting it on.

The forest dark save for when she moved across glades, the sky like ragged spiderwebs through the branches, the silk glistening with stars, and so quiet when they stopped, she could hear the pulse of the albino's tired heart.

She shifted in the saddle, the leather creaking.

The odor of the horse smelled strong in the cold.

She listened, heard nothing but the occasional clicking of her teeth, like Morse code in the night. She touched her heels to the horse and rode down through the spruce.

An hour later, she passed through a blowdown, the firs all bent over and tangled up in themselves like spilt matches and dusted with fresh snow, the horse threading its way through the felled trees like it had come this way before.

In the forest below, an elk bugled.

. . .

The moon low in the sky behind a mountain, the stars teeming, the horse wavering, Lana shivering under her white cape, trying to stave off a sleep that taunted her with the rhythm of the hooves breaking powder.

The horse would have crushed her, but it neighed two seconds before toppling, and Lana woke, just managing to drag herself away from where its hindquarters crashed into the snow.

She scrambled to her feet and wiped the powder out of her face, found herself standing among aspen, the snow to her chest and the stars obscured, yielding to dawn.

The horse lay on its side, blowing deep, snorting exhalations that weakened as she listened. She wanted to speak to the albino, give the animal some measure of comfort, but she could only squat by its head and stroke its great jowls until its heart quit beating and its big eyes traded their pained intensity for the empty glaze of death.

EIGHTY-THREE

Lana struggled on through the aspen, the numbness extending up from her feet into her ankles, her shins. Even her knees were beginning to burn.

She was passing through a glade and noting the first rumor of warmth in the sky when she heard the snort of a horse.

As she looked back, a branch snapped somewhere in the grove.

The cold was momentarily displaced by fear.

She bounded into the woods, ripped a spruce branch from a sapling, and doubled back into the glade, proceeding on, using the branch to sweep her new tracks smooth, reentering the trees after thirty yards, thinking if she could find a ramada, or throw together a brush shelter of some kind, maybe he'd pass her by.

The voice stopped her.

"Help!"

She turned and peered between straight white aspen trunks back out into the glade.

Where her tracks branched stood a gray-cloaked girl with long black hair, face as white as china in the dawn light, big black eyes shining. She recognized this child, having seen her in Abandon.

"Please, ma'am!" the child called out. "Help me!"

Lana hesitated, something urging self-preservation, telling her to just keep heading down through the aspen.

It's a child, for Godsakes, she told herself.

A tuft of cloud went pink above her as Lana waded back into the glade.

The child turned and watched her approach, trembling with cold. Lana stopped several feet away.

She gestured toward the woods, trying to ask where her horse was, but the girl didn't catch her meaning.

"You wasn't supposed to leave."

Lana mouthed, "What?"

Parting the manga, reaching into her cloak, the girl said, "God put you and all the other wickeds in it. Papa told me all about it. And he says I gotta send you back."

Staring down the bore of a large revolver, the child thumbing the hammer, Lana lunged, seizing the slender wrist with half-frozen fingers, the gun shoved up at the sky, the concussive shock of the report rattling her eardrums.

The gun disappeared in the snow and Lana pushed the child down, thinking, *He's coming,* and as if the thought itself held the power of incantation, he appeared, wrapped in a lambskin lap robe and moving at a single-foot rack out of the woods on a starred blood bay, the full-stamped saddle groaning in the cold.

He checked the horse by the strap and dismounted, limping toward her and grasping his leg where she'd stabbed him, his face wrenched up in some brand of agony.

The child sat up, crying, "She pushed me, Papa. She *pushed* me."

Lana knelt down in the snow, hands digging through powder, searching for the revolver.

Her mittened fingers grazed something hard. She grasped it.

The preacher five feet away.

She pulled on nothing but a root as his weight came down on her, the snow and the subzero cold biting every square inch of exposed skin. He turned her over, his eyes slitted mad, gums the color of blued steel, and he worked to pry her hands away from her face, his fingers wrapping around her neck, Lana staring up at the preacher and the purple sky and the child's inquisitive face.

"Go over by the horse, Harriet," he said.

"I wanna watch."

"Now."

As the child moved away, he began to squeeze.

What kind of turn?

Her husband smiles, his fingers pattering on the last two keys, right foot tapping the damper pedal.

You remember Mr. Sakey?

Yes.

I hear y'all swapped words two days ago.

Lana brushes a wisp of blond hair behind her right ear.

He bumped into me at the market.

And you called him a fucking capper, took him to task for—

He isn't your friend. He dragged you into all this, John. *Crying now.* It's 'cause of him. You aren't the same man you were before you made his—

You own a razor tongue, Lana. Ought to know better than to set it loose on a man like Sakey.

I have a truthful tongue. You lost our house.

I'll get it back.

He reaches into his jacket, pulls out a razor, sets it on the piano.

How? With what money? Think they're just gonna let you back in the game on credit? They're probably all laughing at you as we—

I told you. I still got one chip left, and it's better than any hard chink or banknote.

He shuts his eyes, and she thinks he's on the verge of losing consciousness, hoping he is, his arm reaching for the top of the Steinway, between candles, fingers closing on a fist-size geode, halved and inlaid with amethyst, a prehistoric egg with purple crystals that flash in the candlelight as he swings it at her head.

The world graying, purple and black spots blooming like supernovas, blotting out the sky, the preacher's face, Lana thinking, *I'm dying in this glade,* her hands tearing open his duster, his frock coat.

"It'll be over in a minute."

Her left hand caught in an inner pocket, fingers grasping a piece of metal.

John squeezing her throat, the world graying, purple and black spots blooming like supernovas, blotting out the ceiling, her husband's face, Lana thinking, I'm dying, *clawing at his eyes.*

I'm sorry, Lana. I have to get back in the game.

The murder of color, gray fading toward black, the preacher apologizing, his tears speckling her face, salting her eyes, and on the edge of perception, a distant *woomph,* trailed by mounting thunder.

I love you, Lana.

Oxygen-deprived panic.

Unconsciousness.

Dreaming, John, you need help.

. . .

The pressure on her throat subsided.

Stephen Cole stood up, color returning to the sky, to the man.

She coughed.

He looked away from her, eyes asquint.

It sounded like a barrage of gunshots, and then she realized they were aspen, snapping like firecrackers.

Her mouth full of warm, liquid rust, choking, and pain beyond her three miscarriages combined, like she's swallowed lava.

Lana sits up, light-headed.

Alone in the living room, beside the piano bench, walls candlelit, the front of her gown soaked with blood, which still pours from her mouth.

Lana sat up.

The preacher simply disappeared, exploding back in a wall of powder, and she moved, too, glimpsing sky and snow and sky again, somersaulting, the trees screaming by, saw the horse sawn in two by a jagged aspen, mushrooming into a pink cloud, Stephen Cole ricocheting off a boulder.

She reaches into her mouth and screams.

Everything stopped, the air fragrant with crushed spruce and freshly hewn wood, Lana surprised to see the sky, that she wasn't buried in snow.

She sat up, her heart pumping, slowly moved her arms to verify they still worked, ran her hands down the length of her legs.

She looked back up the mountain.

The slide had carried her a few hundred yards downhill, the debris path littered with forest carnage—curdled snow and spruce and splintered aspen.

She got up and listened for a long time, the key she'd taken from Stephen Cole still clutched in her left hand, watching for any sign of movement.

She thought about the child, buried somewhere nearby.

The cold rushed back.

She lifted an uprooted aspen sapling and began to stab it through the snow, slowly working her way up toward the glade, probing for the little girl.

But unto Thee have I cried, O Lord. And in the morning shall my prayer prevent Thee.

Stephen Cole lay cemented in snow and darkness.

Lord, why castest Thou off my soul?

He thought his arm wouldn't work because he'd been packed under several hundred pounds of snow and trees. This was true, but the reason he couldn't move a single appendage owed to the shattering of the bones in his arms and legs, the severing of his spine in four places.

Why hidest Thou Thy face from me?

He tried to call out for Harriet, but the snow had crammed into his mouth, gagging him.

I am afflicted and ready to die from my youth up. While I suffer Thy terrors I am distracted. Thy fierce wrath goeth over me.

It became difficult and then painful and then impossible to breathe.

He saw colors—violet and brown, columns of scalding light.

Thy terrors have cut me off. They came round about me daily like water. They compassed me about together.

He tried to pray for Harriet, for an end to any suffering, but his mind wandered to a windy South Carolina beach.

Lover and friend hast Thou put far from me, and mine acquaintance into darkness.

He was buried deep in sand, lost, running out of air, but he could hear her voice shouting his name.

And then the miracle happened: Something punched through, jabbing his chest, and he smiled now, because Eleanor had found him. She was digging him out, a shot of cold, fresh air streaming into his lungs, and he saw the sky and Eleanor staring down at him.

But she wasn't smiling. She looked angry.

He spit the sand out of his mouth and said, "Help me. Please, Eleanor. Please."

She began to bury him back.

2009

EIGHTY-FOUR

Abigail descended into a forest of ponderosa and Gambel oak, passed through curtains of mist between the trees, rain falling cold and steady, the air scented with wet pine. She'd been going for an hour when she came to the stream, fell to its muddy bank, and shoveled into her mouth handfuls of water so cold, her eyes ached.

Early afternoon, she walked out of the valley. The rain had let up, and what lay ahead looked familiar—a broad piece of open country surrounded by wooded mountains. Where the low dark clouds collided into the upper slopes, the conifers shone white with snow.

She spotted a ridge a mile away across the field. The map her father had drawn for her indicated that she needed to climb over it.

Though she didn't like the prospect of venturing out into the open, she caught her breath and went on anyway, running hard as she could through the knee-high grasses, praying a wall of fog would sweep through and keep her hidden. After a half mile, she ducked behind a boulder, sat down, panting and thirsty, the soles of her feet raw, warm blood pooling in her boots. She peeked over the top of the rock, looked back across the boulder-strewn field toward the opening of the ten-mile valley that climbed up to the Sawblade. Thunder boomed. She thought she heard a rifle report. Abigail prostrated herself, her heart beating against the saturated ground.

Out of fear and because of the mounting pain in her blistered feet, Abigail crawled the rest of the way through the field. It rained again, her knees and palms rubbing raw.

It took an hour to cover half a mile, but she finally arrived at the foot of the long ridge.

The moment she started walking again, she knew she should never have gotten off her feet. With every step, she reached a new level of agony, forced to trade off between walking on her heels and the sides and the balls of her feet, wishing she'd put some moleskin on her blisters last night when she'd had the chance.

Climbing up the mountainside, she fell into a rhythm—two steps, rest, deep breath, two steps, rest, deep breath, on and on. She thought that when they'd descended this slope during the hike in, they'd followed a path, but she figured it would be safer now to stay off-trail.

She came into a glade, saw that open country far below, boulders reduced to pebbles in a sea of dead grass. Something moved down there—the size of an ant from five hundred feet above, but clearly the figure of a man, halfway across the field, progressing at a tireless jog.

She hurried on. The mountainside became steep—snow on the trees and on the ground. She climbed into the clouds, colder and darker here, with intermittent bursts of snow. Fog enveloped the woods, thick as smoke, Abigail on her hands and knees now, the slope so steep, she wondered how the trees stood upright.

At last, she reached the summit of the ridge, socked in and snowing, clouds streaming through the treetops. She ran, moaning every time her feet hit the ground. Then she was heading down, digging her heels into the snow to slow her descent, a kind of controlled fall.

What had been a soft whisper that she mistook for wind grew louder. She came out of the clouds and the snow had disappeared and she recognized that whispering as a swollen stream. She could see it, a thousand feet below, winding through the canyon—chocolate milk streaked with white water.

She ran again, the noise of the rapids getting louder, her ears popping.

When she finally saw them, she felt for the first time in days that she might survive.

A quarter of a mile down-canyon, Jerrod's Bronco, the llama trailer, and the faded blue speck of Scott's Suburban stood parked where they'd been left four days ago, in a meadow by the road.

It was getting dark when Abigail picked up the trail two hundred feet above the road to Silverton. She followed it down five switchbacks before it straightened out, leveled off, and emerged from the spruce forest into a meadow.

She broke into a run, tears streaming down her face, and not only from the pain of her tenderized feet but from relief, too.

She collapsed in the grass on the driver's side of the Suburban, gulping lungfuls of air, every cell in her body screaming out in riotous protest at the last seventeen miles of abuse.

She looked across the meadow to where the trail entered the forest, her eyes slanting up through the spruce to the first switchback, then following it to the next bend.

Just before the third turn, she saw movement—a man jogging down through the trees.

She reached into the right side pocket of her parka. No keys. Left pocket. Not there, either. "What the hell did I—" She remembered, unzipped the parka and the breast pocket of her fleece jacket, jammed her hand inside, willing herself not to watch him come.

The third key she tried unlocked the driver's door. The rusted Suburban had been outfitted with knobby off-road tires, and Abigail had to step two and a half feet up to climb behind the wheel. She shut the door, slid the seat forward, and slipped the same key that had opened the door into the ignition. *If this were a movie, the car wouldn't start,* she thought.

The engine roared to life.

Through the front passenger window, she saw Quinn rounding the final switchback.

Abigail released the emergency brake and shifted into drive, her foot burning as she pressed the accelerator. The Suburban lurched forward over the uneven ground, rattling and rocking, the big tires rolling over rocks, through shallow ditches slicked with runoff.

She screamed when the bullet passed through the glass beside her ear, felt the spray of shards as they embedded themselves in the left side of her face, cracks spiderwebbing through the windshield.

She ducked and drove onto the road as another round chinked through her door and punctured the ashtray, the accompanying report drowned out in the noisy growl of the Suburban's 410 engine.

Where rocks didn't jut out of the dirt, the narrow road was washboarded. She looked down, found the off-road stick shift. *Good,* she thought. Scott had left the four-wheel high engaged.

Pain raged through her foot, up into her tailbone, raindrops plopping on the windshield.

Thunder dropped above the engine, clouds darkening, snow mixing in.

Abigail began to cry.

A half hour later, she flipped on the headlights.

Rain fell through the beams.

She kept looking in the rearview mirror, watching for another pair of high beams to punch through all that darkness, the Suburban jittery and bouncing like it might shake itself to pieces. She'd never driven such a rough road, and twice she took a turn too fast, nearly launched off the shoulder into the canyon.

After eight miles, the bumps smoothed out, and she could keep the speed at a steady thirty-five miles per hour.

A mile later, it turned to pavement, and she gunned the Suburban to forty-five.

Her ears popped.

She crested a hill, and below in the rainy gloom, a collection of lights appeared, and a green road sign flashed by:

WELCOME TO SILVERTON

POP. 473

ELEV. 9318

She veered through a hairpin turn, straightened out onto Greene Street, drove over a bridge that spanned all twenty feet of Cement Creek, and eased onto the brake pedal.

To her immediate right stood the San Juan County Courthouse, gold-domed and surmounted by a clock tower.

Ahead, streetlamps lined either side of Silverton's main thoroughfare, each illuminating spheres of slushy rain. It was a quarter past seven on a raw Thursday night, and with the buildings dark and scarcely a single occupied parking space as far as she could see, it seemed the town had already gone to sleep.

She drove a few blocks past rows of refurbished Victorian-style buildings that would have looked like something out of a Western, if not for their ostentatious paint schemes—Silverton Clinic, Fred Wolfe Memorial Carriage House, a Church of Christ no bigger than a trailer, Silverton City Hall, Wyman Hotel, Pride of the West Restaurant, Rocky Mountain Funnel Cakes and Café, Blue Raven Fine Arts, Outdoor World.

The saloons and brothels had long since been replaced with trendy coffeehouses, galleries, ice-cream, candy, and gift shops. There was even a photography studio where they would doll you up like a cowboy or a whore and take your portrait, so when you went home, you could show your friends you'd been in the real West.

The West for tourists, she thought. You could probably order an appletini from one of the bars and stand a good chance of not being shot between the eyes.

At the corner of Greene and Twelfth, Abigail pulled into a parking space in front of the Grand Imperial, a three-story white-brick hotel with lavender trim, red brick chimneys, and topped by a row of shed-roofed dormers.

She killed the engine, climbed down onto the street, and glass fell out of the window when she slammed shut the Suburban's heavy door.

Beyond the ticking of the engine and the splatter of icy rain, Silverton stood silent.

Looking through the windows, she could see into the lobby of the hotel, where a clerk read a paperback behind the front desk.

As she started toward the entrance, she heard the groan of a revving engine.

At the north end of town, headlights appeared.

1893

EIGHTY-FIVE

Milton wiped his mouth and shuddered. After a day of deadpan drinking in the Blair Street saloons, he'd just aired the paunches into a snowbank, noting bitterly to himself that he'd never touched liquor prior to coming west.

As he staggered up Twelfth Street toward the boardinghouse, even the glow from all that rotgut wasn't sufficient to ward off the loneliness or the early-evening chill.

The lights of Silverton had begun to wink on.

He passed a butcher shop, a grub house, a pharmacy, a Chinese laundry, and was thinking of his wife and son back in Missouri and choking on guilt, having had his thorn sucked that morning by a whore named Maribell, when he tripped over something and tumbled into the snow.

He sat up and scratched the ice out of his beard and shook his head in an attempt to right the spinning world. When at last he did, he found himself sprawled near the entrance to the Grand Imperial Hotel.

It took some doing, but he managed to regain his feet.

"Son of a bitch."

He stared down at what had toppled him—some bindle-stiff whore in a white cape, either drunker than he was or stone-dead, lying facedown in the filthy snow.

Voices washed out, distant.

"You a diploma doc?"

"I'm the best chance she's got of . . . This a whore?"

"I don't know. What's it matter?"

"I don't treat whores. Find Dr. Stout. He makes the rounds on Blair—"

"I'm not certain she's a—"

"You know how many dead prostitutes he's seen since Christmas Eve? Five. Had to pump the stomachs of seven. They all take to suicide this time of year. Morphine. Carbolic acid for the more desperate."

"She ain't poisoned. She's frozed."

"Or maybe she's poisoned *and* froze."

"She needs your help, whichever the—"

"Should it come to my attention she eats cock for her bed and supper, you can double the amounts on my fee bill."

"All right. She gonna die?"

"More than likely."

A man stood hunched over at the foot of the bed, chewing on a stogie, and even through skewed vision, she could see his smooth-shaven face glistening with sweat, his arm jerking back and forth, shirtsleeves rolled up, arms red to the elbows, the air pungent with the charred reek of friction—steel grinding through rotted bone.

"Goddamn it, she's coming to."

A washrag covered her face and she thought she would smother.

She came around, thinking of the little girl lost in the slide, and the first thing her eyes locked upon was a small man sitting at her bedside in a rocking chair and snoring, the wiry black hairs of his unkempt beard trembling with each exhalation.

She lay in a twin bed with a wrought-iron frame, positioned between two windows in a bare-bones room—hardwood floor and floral-patterned wallpaper adorned with three awful paintings.

The air held a red tint, and her eyes burned.

She felt feverish, her throat raw from the ether.

On the floor beside the rocking chair lay a Kelly pad and a washtub full of crimson water, out of which poked the handles of two knives and a bone saw.

She tugged at the cover and it slipped up her legs, her feet itching despite the fact that they weren't where they should be.

She glanced at the washtub, back at the bandaged, leaking stubs below her knees.

Her throat made a birdlike sound, and her eyes shone with tears.

A door opened and shut.

She wiped her eyes, glimpsed a tall, smooth-shaven man, his brown hair pushed high off his forehead in wavy, gravity-defying tangles.

He knelt down to inspect the bandages.

"I know this must be a shock for you," he said, glancing up. Lana felt a surge of modesty, realizing she wore only underpinnings. "You were found outside tonight by that gentleman"—he motioned to the small man still sleeping in the rocker—"unconscious in the snow. You're in room two oh three, on the second floor of the Grand Imperial Hotel in Silverton, Colorado."

He stood up, his white dress shirt specked with blood, forearms stained.

"I'm Dr. Julius Primack, by the way."

Lana's lower lip quivered. Last thing she recalled was emerging snowblind from a stand of aspen into a valley, seeing buildings in the distance, smelling wood smoke.

"You know that man?"

She shook her head.

"He saved your life, covered your medical expenses thus far. You have any money?"

She nodded.

"Reason I ask is because there's more work to be done. Your right arm's fine, but I need to take that left one off below the elbow."

She shook her head, began to cry.

"Mortification has occurred. You smell that? It's already begun to rot. I don't know how it froze so hard, but it did. I charge fifty dollars to amputate an appendage, and if you choose not to make this gentleman pay for the legs, we're talking a hundred and fifty dollars total. Can you cover that?"

Lana glanced down at her arms, her right a vital pink, her left the blackish purple of a ripe plum.

"Can you pay?"

She nodded.

"You haven't said a word. What are you, mute?"

Lana opened her mouth wide.

As the doctor leaned in, she saw that his face had been horribly scarred from some long-ago bout of smallpox. He smelled of stale cigar smoke.

"Maybe you aren't a whore after all. Where the hell's your tongue?"

Lana lifted her right arm, held her thumb, fore, and middle fingers together.

"You can write?"

She nodded.

He placed his ear to her chest for a moment, then sat up, flattened his palm against her forehead.

"Time is not on our side. That arm isn't off by daybreak, the infection'll hit your bloodstream. Then it won't matter what I cut off."

Dr. Primack walked over to a dresser and returned to the bed, where he eased down beside Lana and opened his satchel—a black pebbled-leather handcase lined with chamois and brimming with scalpels, a stethoscope, pessaries, a catheter, forceps, a splint, and various bottles containing tonics, bitters, and tinctures.

As he withdrew a brown leather-bound journal, the man who'd been snoozing in the rocker rubbed his eyes and sat up.

"How she doin, Doc?"

Dr. Primack shook his head and pulled a bottle out of the handcase, unscrewed the cap.

"Laudanum," he said. "It'll dull the edge on the pain."

Lana swallowed two mouthfuls, and then the doctor placed a Waterman fountain pen between the fingers of her right hand and opened the journal in her lap to a blank page.

"What's your name?"

She wrote: *Lana Hartman.*

"You live in Silver—"

She stopped him with a raised hand, wrote: *From Abandon. Preacher locked town in mine. Everyone dying.*

He stared hard into her eyes, as if attempting to discern whether the claim was valid or just the raving of a madwoman.

"You stretching the blanket for me?"

She scrawled: *I'm not crazy.*

The doctor sighed.

"Why'd he do it?"

She shrugged, wrote: *Went crazy. Locked gold in, too.*

He whispered, "How much?"

Whole string of burros to carry it.

Dr. Primack stood up, said, "Excuse me, Miss Hartman," and turned to the man in the rocker.

"Milton, could I speak with you in private?"

Lana craned her neck to peek out one of the windows beside her bed. The darkness was riddled and blurred with flecks of light like some syphilitic rash upon the town, the nefarious amusement of Blair Street and its salas and silver exchanges unrestrained even at this hour—pianos, dogs barking, aggressive laughter, breaking glass.

I'm not supposed to die in this town. Please God, she prayed.

The door opened and the doctor walked in, alone.

He came and sat down on the bed and repositioned the pen between her fingers.

"How long have they been locked in?"

She wrote: *Since Christmas night.*

"Do they have food? Water?"

She shook her head.

"Where is this mine, exactly?"

She was becoming light-headed, and twice the pen slipped from her grasp and she had to start over, make the words legible. She finally wrote: *Above town on west slope, I think. Sorry I feel so poorly. Bring my cape.*

Dr. Primack looked annoyed as he rose from the bed and lifted the ruined, sodden garment from the board floor beside the dresser. He brought it over, said, "Why do you want this?"

Lana reached for it, her right hand slipping into the inner pocket, grasping the key.

"What's that open?"

She wrote: *The mine. You have to get them out. There's children. Get the sheriff.*

"Of course." He took it out of her hand, stroked the key's long stem, its teeth. "I should operate immediately."

Lana was crying as Dr. Primack handed Milton the cloth, standing poised beside her left arm.

"I'll have it off in two minutes."

She stared at the finely serrated blade of the amputation saw dripping red water onto the bed, the collection of knives laid out on the sheets, the bottle of ether, the Kelly pad under her arm, the washtub glistening red under the electric light.

Though she was fading from the big dose of laudanum, her heart still reeled.

"Go ahead, Milton."

Here came the cloth, sharp bite of ether in the back of her throat, and then she floated in a warm gray sea, flanked by swirling voices.

"Damn, that was fast."

"Hold the cloth to her mouth."

"She ain't awake."

"Do what I tell you or get the fuck out."

Lana smiled, gleaming with morphine, and still in that same bed in that same room in the Grand Imperial, only now it was filled with the natural light of morning and noise from the street below.

She thought, *I've survived.*

Beautiful Dr. Primack stood at the foot of her bed, speaking with another man—round and gray-bearded, holding a bowler against his thigh, a shiny object catching early sunlight pinned to his black frock coat.

When she tried to lift her right hand to catch their attention, she felt the straps binding both arms to her sides.

She made a noise with her throat.

The men quit talking and looked at her. They walked over, sat on either side of the bed.

The older, bearded man ran his fingers through his thinning hair, his dirty nails leaving fleeting white trails in the ripples of his rosy scalp.

"Miss, I'm Sheriff Donaway, and Dr. Primack has explained to me the tragic predicament."

Thank God, she thought.

"He's had to take off both legs and arms, and arrangements are being made to transport you on the narrow-gauge to Mercy Hospital in Durango."

She looked up at Dr. Primack, who watched her with something that might have been mistaken for compassion.

The doctor turned back the cover so Lana could see the bloody, bandaged stubs below both elbows.

The morphine elation fading.

My right arm was fine. You told me it was.

"I understand this is most upsetting," he said, "but there was nothing I could do. Both arms had sustained severe damage. You'd be dead by now if I hadn't taken them off."

She opened her mouth. *Why haven't you told him about Abandon?* But it came out as little more than the ramblings of an idiot.

"Try to settle down, Miss Hartman," the doctor said. "You're in a fragile state."

They're dying.

"Please, Miss Hartman."

Why are you doing this?

"Can you give her something, Doc?"

"I sure can."

Dr. Primack hurried over to his hand case, which was sitting on the dresser.

She heard the words in her head as clearly as she used to speak them, but the room resonated with only an ugly, tongueless noise.

"Listen," the sheriff said, and he placed his hand on her shoulder. "Dr. Primack has also divulged to me your mental condition."

Bottles clinked in Primack's hand case.

"You're going to recover in Durango."

The doctor was coming back now.

"I have a connection with the asylum in Pueblo."

Primack unscrewed the cap, tilting the bottle's open mouth onto a white cloth.

"I'm certain I can get you admitted. They'll help you there, Miss Hartman. Make the life God has seen fit to afflict you with as dignified and comfortable as can be hoped for."

Look in his notebook. For Chrissakes.

"You're lucky to have fallen under the care of Primack."

She screamed and writhed, but the restraints held.

"Lana." The doctor spoke softly into her ear. "I want you to know I'm waiving my fee for the amputations. Now don't fight it."

The ether-soaked cloth descended toward her face.

"Just close your eyes and take a long, deep breath."

2009

EIGHTY-SIX

The lobby of the Grand Imperial stood accented by objects, the assemblage of which felt more like a cliché than a throwback to Silverton's boom years—burgundy floral-print wallpaper, tin ceiling, chandelier, a stodgy black safe near the front desk, a pair of wall clocks, a grand piano, a sculpture of four grinning outlaws on horseback firing their revolvers into the air, and a large-scale portrait of a whore hanging over one of two high-backed leather sofas that comprised the sitting area.

Abigail reached the front desk.

"I need help. Call the police."

"There's no police here."

"*What?*"

"Just a sheriff."

"Give me the phone."

"Are you a guest with us?"

"Are you *joking*—"

"The courtesy phone is only for guests of the GI."

Abigail placed the young woman at sixteen or seventeen. She sat behind an expansive antique desk, a horror novel clutched in her left hand. She was sucking a green lollipop that wafted a bizarrely scented amalgamation of apples and whiskey.

Abigail read the clerk's name tag. "Listen, Tracy. A man has chased me out of the mountains, and he's coming to kill me. Think we could make an exception tonight?"

The desk clerk laid the paperback down beside a keyboard and withdrew the lollipop from green-ringed lips, making eye contact with Abigail for the first time.

"Fine."

There was the screech of brakes, and, glancing in the mirror behind the desk, Abigail caught the reflection of the large front window that looked out onto Greene Street, saw an old beater of a Bronco slide into the Suburban's rear bumper—a slight collision that barely shook the vehicle.

"Is that him?" the clerk asked.

"Does the sheriff live in town?"

"Yeah, end of Fourteenth."

"Which way is that?"

A door slammed.

"Two blocks north."

Boots clomped on the sidewalk.

"Tracy, get down behind the desk and keep quiet."

Quinn stepped under the awning, and as he opened the door and started into the foyer, Abigail bolted up a carpeted staircase under a sign that read TO THE ROOMS.

She turned left, climbed twenty steps, already breathless.

In the lobby, a man yelled, *"Where'd she go?"*

She reached the second floor.

Left or right?

She went left, then right, heard footfalls racing up the steps behind her as she came to an intersection of corridors and stairs.

Left, right, or climb?

She turned left, sprinting down a hall—pink walls, white trim, white doors, squeakiest floor she'd ever encountered, past room 201, under a chandelier with two fried bulbs, room 202, then a series of black-and-white photographs of old steam engines, room 203, right turn, long, narrow hallway: 214, 215, 216, 217.

It dead-ended at a door with a sign under the metal handle: DO NOT OPEN. FIRE DOOR ONLY. WILL SET OFF ALARM.

Bursting through into icy rain, the alarm wailing, Abigail stood on a fire escape that overlooked a sparsely populated parking lot, the globules of slush glittering under the yellow streetlamps like jewels on the hoods and windshields.

She glanced back through the glass-paned door, didn't see him coming, prayed he'd taken a wrong turn in the maze of corridors.

She dropped to her hands and knees, lowering herself down the slippery ladder, and as her feet touched the pavement, the fire door banged open above her.

She crawled into the shadow of a nearby Dumpster. The ladder's metal rungs resonated under the impact of his boots.

He hit the ground.

From where she crouched, she could only see his breath pluming in the floodlights.

She reached down, felt the hard bulge of the Ruger in the side pocket of her jacket, but it was zipped in and she didn't want to risk the noise.

Ice pinged the Dumpster's metal lid.

Quinn stepped a little farther out into the parking lot. Abigail wondered if the shadow where she squatted was as dark as she thought.

He stood there for some time, motionless.

The floodlights cut off, and she couldn't see him anymore.

When they came on thirty seconds later, Quinn was gone.

Abigail got up and jogged through the parking lot, away from the illumination of streetlamps, the blaring alarm, into a dirt road cratered with puddles icing over.

Silverton at this hour consisted of cold and darkness and the isolated lights of little Victorian houses, some run-down and vacant since the mining bust, others polished up and slathered with bright paint by mountain-worshiping Yuppies.

She ran up Reese, blinded by sweat and freezing water that trailed down the back of her neck and along the curved ridge of her spine.

Somewhere in the dark, a truck engine mumbled.

She glanced over her shoulder, saw twin light beams slash through the pouring rain, the Bronco speeding up Twelfth Street.

She ran harder, splashing through puddles crusted with paper-thin ice.

A dog yapped at her through the window of a nearby house, and several blocks away, the courthouse clock tolled 8:00 P.M.

One street up, the Bronco bounced along a dirt road. She saw it streak between the houses, make a right turn onto Thirteenth, then haul ass for a block before initiating another hard right, the high beams now blasting head-on, accompanied by the roaring engine.

She dived off the street, her head just missing a mailbox, then flattened herself in wet grass against a chain-link fence as the Bronco screamed past, mud slinging into her hair, slopping down all over her clothes.

Abigail waited, listening to the engine dwindle up the road and the distant fire alarm and the deep, almost imperceptible static of the Animas River on the opposite side of town, running low in advance of winter.

When the Bronco turned onto another street, she struggled to her feet and wiped the mud out of her eyes and went on, soon crossing the intersection of Reese and Thirteenth, every footfall sending new shoots of pain up into her tailbone.

Another minute brought her to Fourteenth, where she veered left at an abandoned brick building and ran for one long block past decrepit white

Victorians and a double-wide into Snowden, another muddy road, rougher and more washboarded than Reese.

She looked around—just the faint drone of the fire alarm, like some psychotic mewling cat, and shards of house light, the air permeated with the rain-mellowed odor of wood smoke, and thirty yards on, at the end of a gravel drive, blades of porch light lying in triangles upon a Ford Expedition with a modest suspension lift, giant tires, a wench, and a light bar mounted on the roof.

Two blocks down, the Bronco turned onto Fourteenth, barreling toward her.

She wept from the pain as she staggered up the drive, passing the driver's door of the Expedition—gold-emblazoned with SAN JUAN COUNTY SHERIFF'S DEPARTMENT.

EIGHTY-SEVEN

Abigail reached the front porch of the Victorian—cherry, with yellow trim, Tibetan prayer flags strung between the gutter and a cluster of skinny aspen, a circular stained-glass window on the second floor, backlit with firelight, chairs in the yard fashioned out of old skis.

She pounded on the front door and, looking through the inset of curtained glass, saw a light flick on, heard footsteps crossing a hardwood floor that squeaked and groaned.

A bolt turned, a chain slid out, flopped against the door frame, hinges creaking, and there stood that petite, beautiful woman who'd hassled Scott over his fishing license four days ago at the trailhead, though no braided pigtails this time. No Stetson or parka. Just a woman in a pink satin nightgown and sheepskin slippers, hair pinned up with chopsticks, breath spiced with the faintest glimmer of vodka.

"Help you with something?" she asked.

Abigail's knees buckled. She sat down hard on the porch.

"What's wrong?"

Abigail couldn't speak, just pointed back toward Fourteenth, but there were no oncoming headlights, only streetlamps and darkness.

The sheriff squatted down in the threshold of the door.

"You were with that group headed out to Abandon. Last Sunday, right?"

"Yes."

"Your face is frostbit. What happened?"

"Please, just . . . get me inside."

The sheriff helped her to stand, then, with her arm around her waist, walked Abigail into the house and shut the door.

"Do the locks," Abigail said.

As the sheriff relocked the door, Abigail tried to unzip her muddy jacket, but her hands trembled too much to grasp the zipper.

"Let me help with that," the sheriff said.

"Thank you. What's your name?"

"Jennifer."

"I'm Abigail."

Abigail pulled her arms out of the sleeves, and Jennifer took the jacket and hung it from the coatrack. Then she guided Abigail through the foyer, past the staircase, and up a dark hallway into the kitchen.

"Here, sit down." She pulled a chair back from a small table and Abigail collapsed onto the seat.

"Could I have some water?"

"Of course." Jennifer opened a cabinet and took down a glass, filled it at the tap.

Abigail glanced around the kitchen, a peculiar mix of new and old— Sub-Zero fridge, granite countertops, an old gas stove salted with rust, an ancient faucet. On a wooden shelf above the sink, she spotted an array of empty Grey Goose bottles and antique bottles that a century ago had contained bitters and tonics, and a clear flower vase full of stained wine corks.

Jennifer set the glass down on the table and returned to the sink and filled a pot with water. Abigail caught a whiff of propane, heard the gas ignite. Jennifer sat down across from her.

"I know you're tired and hurting, but why don't you try to tell me what happened out there."

The heat from a wood-burning stove slithered in from the living room.

"They're all dead," she whispered. "Except my father, who's trapped in a cave."

"How'd they die?"

The cold had scrambled and clouded her thoughts, and she tried to decant the sequence of events, but the days and nights kept mixing and running into one another and reversing, like the warped memory of a fever dream, several versions of the last seventy-two hours emerging, until she couldn't separate with certainty exactly what had happened when and to whom and the horrible chronology of it all.

She shook with chills as she attempted to piece it back together, the events crystallizing and falling into order the more she talked.

But the version she told took a departure once they'd been locked inside the mountain. It was only a long-forgotten mine, and empty at that.

No bones, no gold, no revelation.

. . .

"Here, get this in you."

Jennifer set a big steaming mug of tea on the table before Abigail, who cupped her hands to the warm ceramic and left them there until her fingers burned.

"How long has your father been alone in the cave."

"Almost two days."

"How much water did you leave him with?"

"We ran out."

"I'll call search-and-rescue, get that ball rolling. Go on, drink your tea. You'll feel better."

Jennifer walked out of the kitchen, and Abigail heard the creak of her footsteps ascending the stairs. She raised the mug to her lips and sipped the tea—piping hot, peppermint with a harsh, bitter bite—wondered if the sheriff had sneaked in a bit of Grey Goose for good measure, hoped so.

Her feet ached. She set the tea on a place mat and reached down and pulled on the double-knotted laces of her left boot. The knot slipped. She tugged out the tongue and winced as she slid her heel out of the boot, the wool hiking sock cold, damp, and pink with blood.

Abigail loved her feet—small, feminine, exuding a slender, proportionate beauty her friends openly envied. These shredded, swollen blobs of flesh did not belong to her. They looked more like battered cod, blanched and translucent, with silver dollar–size blisters on her heels and ankles that peeled back, revealing raw skin the color of watermelon pulp.

She got up, had to walk on the balls of her feet to bypass the excruciating pain.

Being down there alone unnerved her, though she still caught fragments of Jennifer's voice upstairs. She took her mug of tea and limped out of the kitchen in search of a bathroom, came instead into a small office with a scratched-up desk, which faced a window. The desk barely provided the surface area to house its computer, printer, and fax machine.

Peering through the beaded glass, Abigail saw that the rain had changed over to snow.

Way off in all that darkness, a barb of red light slanted up and left through her field of vision and she thought she was hallucinating until she pegged it for the taillights of a car climbing the steep grade south out of Silverton toward Molas Pass.

Spider plants in need of watering hung from the ceiling, a pair of leather snowshoes from one wall, and her eyes fixed upon a framed photomontage beside them of jagged mountains under the heading COLORADO'S 54 FOURTEENERS.

She sipped her tea. Beside the desk, two unfinished pine bookcases almost touched the ceiling, but instead of books, they contained relics from the past—rusted railroad spikes, an old burro's shoe, pitons and a pair of crampons from the forties. Perhaps most fascinating, the middle two shelves of each bookcase displayed photographs of Silverton.

On one side stood framed photos of the present-day town and the buildings of Greene and Blair streets—the courthouse, city hall, the Grand Imperial— all set against the backdrop of mountainsides blazing with aspen and blue sky the purity of which could exist only above nine thousand feet in the Colorado Rockies, and there were photos of the Durango and Silverton Narrow-Gauge Railroad, the train having stopped to unload at Twelfth Street on a summer day, tourists leaning out of the gondola cars, smiling and waving, thrilled to spend a few hours in this romanticized mining town, to lunch in remodeled saloons and brothels, watch staged gunfights, have portraits taken in old-West costumes, children destined to return home with cowboy hats and six-shooter cap guns, tortured parents having to suffer their kids saying "Howdy, pardner" and "Get along, now" for the foreseeable future.

On the opposing shelves stood more Silverton photographs, these all in black-and-white, little windows to the past: a burro train standing in late-nineteenth-century Greene Street, the mule skinners staring dour-faced at the photographer. Soot-blackened miners and whores and suited gold and silver kings in a saloon, everyone raising beer glasses and tumblers, and not a smile to be found under all those handlebar mustaches. The railroad in winter, tracks framed by fifteen-foot walls of snow, and five bundled men with iced mustaches standing in front of a steam engine's cattle guard, shovels in hand.

But what caught her interest more than anything were the portraits of people long dead, their faces stoic, expressionless: a woman who might've been her age, carrying in her eyes the world-weariness of a refugee. A white-bearded gentleman, ragged bowler perched on his head, whose eyes betrayed their longing to cut loose a smile, despite having to sit still for the long exposure.

She considered all the photographs in her studio—family and friends at weddings, graduations, vacations, Christmases—and couldn't recall a single picture where someone wasn't smiling their heart out, thought how strange it would be if people in modern times never grinned for the camera.

Going solely on photographs, historians in the next century might mistake her world for a happy place, just as she'd always assigned misery and hardship to the past, prejudiced by a few grim portraits.

Abigail noted that she felt much better, the pain receding from her feet as she inspected the last portrait—a black-and-white shot of a young man with hair so unkempt that it struck her as contemporary, and for all its gravity-defying waves, might've run two hundred dollars, not including product, in a Manhattan salon.

The face that wild hair sat upon was handsome but uniformly pocked with tiny colorless indentations, so that he looked less like a live human being, more like a Seurat Pointillism.

The portrait's frame rested upon a brown leather-bound book, stiff and dry, so old that as she lifted it to her face and inhaled the smell, she couldn't detect even the faintest odor of tannins or glue.

She opened it to the first page, which contained six words handwritten in elaborate, perfect script: *The Journal of Dr. Julius Primack.*

EIGHTY-EIGHT

She thumbed the brittle pages, coming midway through to handwriting that looked different from the doctor's—smaller, less methodical, and nearly illegible, like it had been scrawled under duress.

There were eight lines in haphazard succession down the middle of the page, the first of which read *Lana Hartman*.

"You found it."

The sheriff stood in the archway adjoining the kitchen and the office, and Abigail couldn't exactly nail it down, but her posture evinced tension—Jennifer's arms hanging at her sides, knees slightly bent, her body coiled as if for a race or a fight.

And Abigail felt different—seismic shifts in the unavowed frequencies. She was edgy, a little nauseous, her awareness heightened, and she realized it wasn't that her body didn't ache anymore—she just cared less and less with each passing moment.

"You're a historian, too?" Abigail asked.

"You could say that." Jennifer walked into the office and stood beside Abigail at the bookshelf. "This guy"—she touched the portrait of the young man with the ruined face—"came out to Silverton from Chicago in 1891 with investment money. Lost it all on poorly chosen claims in less than a year."

"But he stayed."

"Julius had studied a little medicine in the mid-eighties, and since you didn't actually have to have a diploma to be a doctor where they were in high demand, he started a practice, kept prospecting on the side. If you read his notes"—Jennifer pulled the journal out of Abigail's hands, placed it back carefully under the photograph—"it becomes clear he was a very driven but very frustrated man."

"Why frustrated?"

"He became obsessed with finding some gold that went missing in Abandon, thought he knew where it was, that he had the key that would open this secret mine. But he could never find it. He went crazy, shot himself in 1924."

"Why do you have his picture and journal? Are you studying—"

"I'm his great-granddaughter. My brother and I are fourth-generation Silverton Primacks."

The sheriff slipped out of focus, and Abigail had to rub her eyes to bring her back.

"What's wrong?" Jennifer asked.

"I don't know . . . it's weird." It wasn't a bad feeling, just a sudden, blissful calm, and the only thing that unnerved Abigail was how fast it had bullied its way in.

Jennifer said, "That's probably the Percoset I crushed up in your tea."

Abigail's heart hammered so hard, she thought it would explode, then realized that the beating hadn't originated within her. Someone had knocked at the front door.

Jennifer had left the room.

Abigail looked down, saw a puddle and four pieces of ceramic on the hardwood floor.

She almost fell moving past the stainless-steel refrigerator, braced herself against the kitchen table, which turned over—place settings, her glass of water, and a vase of plastic lilies crashing to the floor.

She sat down on the tile.

In the foyer, Jennifer reached the front door and pulled it open.

A man loomed in the porchlight. Abigail knew him from somewhere. His shoulder-length brown hair was tied up in a ponytail, his silver-and-black down jacket dusted with snow.

He wrapped his arms around Jennifer, nothing remotely sexual or romantic in the embrace, the energy reflective of close friends or siblings.

He said, "We did it, Jen."

Abigail leaned against the refrigerator, her head humming as she watched Jennifer redo the locks.

The mosaic of pastel-colored tiles ensnared Abigail's attention, and the next time she looked up, that tall man stood at the sink, washing his hands.

Her eyes slammed shut, and when they opened again, her face lay pressed against the cold tile and the kitchen table had been righted and the sheriff and that familiar man sat across from each other.

". . . this storm, we won't be able to get back to Abandon until next summer. I told you it might come to . . ." His voice left audible trails, as if he were speaking in triplicate.

Abigail had been stoned before, drunk, even took Ecstasy a couple years back at an ill-advised rave in the Meatpacking District. This was nothing like that. She didn't feel euphoric, just tranquil and dreamy and wise. On some disassociated level, she understood the danger, but it was knowledge without emotion or investment, no more upsetting than hearing of a stranger's death on the evening news.

"I fucking hate this." The sheriff's voice.

Somewhere in the kitchen, a crow squawked nine times.

"This isn't the first blood spilled for those bricks. But we do this right? Finish it? Maybe it's the last. You thought of it that way?"

"I don't know if I'm wired for—"

"Remember what you said to me four days ago? 'There're people going into Abandon, and I think they're going for our gold.' You told me, 'Don't let it happen.' "

She went out of time again, wading amid thoughts jumbled and irrelevant and absurd, vaguely aware that she needed to bring herself down, untangle her mind from this exquisite high.

". . . four-hundred-foot drop off Peace Falls. There'll be no chance of anyone finding her until . . . Jesus, Jen, I told you to get her loaded."

Abigail tried to sit up.

"I spiked her tea with thirty milligrams of oxycodone."

If Abigail didn't move her head, she could actually bring their faces into focus.

"What'd she say, Quinn?"

"I couldn't tell."

This time, she got the words out, though they slurred against her thick tongue, sounded as muddled as everything else. "Why'd you drug me?"

Jennifer said, "Just to help with your pain. Nice, isn't it?"

"Lovely." Abigail stared at the man at the table, her mouth and eyes gone dry. "I know you."

"Yes, we've met."

Abigail managed to sit up against the cabinets, had to close her eyes to shut out the chaos of light and noise.

"In the mine?"

"No, Packer's mansion. But I did lock you and your father and June into the mine. More than a little surprised you found a way out."

"Oh, that's right." She tried to suppress a giggle. It all seemed so terribly funny. Then it hit her. "Jennifer," she said, "there were gold bars in that mine. I'll bet that's what your—what was he?"

"Great-grandfather."

"What he was looking for. I can show you— Wait." She pointed at Quinn. "He knows. He was there. He had a key. How does he have your great-grandfather's key?"

Quinn and Jennifer laughed.

Abigail laughed, too, her eyes catching on the clock above the sink, a different bird assigned to each hour.

It read 9:10 P.M.

Impossible. It had been hours since she'd walked into the office and looked at the Silverton photographs and Primack's journal.

"I need to get going, huh?" Quinn said. "Before this snow gets any deeper."

"I should go with you. I won't lie—I don't want to, but—"

"No, I'll take care of it. Abigail, wanna go for a ride?"

She thought about it. "Where to?"

"Just up into the mountains a little ways."

"Why?"

"To meet up with search-and-rescue, so we can get your dad out of the cave."

She smiled. "Know what I think?"

"What?"

"You don't mean the words you're saying."

"No? Then what do I mean?"

"Something bad."

Quinn stood up and reached down, grabbed Abigail's hands and pulled her to her feet.

"Help me get her boots on, Jen. Don't want her found barefoot."

"Actually, it doesn't matter."

"Sure it does."

"No, when people get hypothermia, start freezing to death out in the wilderness, they're often found half-naked. They go out of their mind, think they're warm, start stripping off layers of clothing. Just leave her boots here. I'll make sure they disappear."

"Can you walk, Abigail?"

"Of course I know how to walk."

She felt weightless on her feet, moving slowly and deliberately out of the kitchen into the hallway. At an ovular mirror, she stopped and regarded herself, leaning in close, her nose flattened against the glass.

"We could still not do this, Quinn."

"Stop now? After everything I've done? No payoff for any of it? That'd be the worst outcome. No, we're all in."

Abigail's pupils had been reduced to grains of black sand.

She turned away from the mirror and continued on toward the front door.

"Jen, this won't have been worth it . . . for Julius, for Grandpa, Dad, you and me, if we let the guilt crush us."

As Abigail reached for the doorknob, she saw her muddy jacket hanging from the coatrack. She lifted it off the hook, kept turning it around, searching for the armholes.

Quinn took it from her, held it by the collar, and Jennifer helped guide her arms into the sleeves.

"Would Dad have taken it this far?"

"Hard to say. We're doing this for all of them, you know."

Jennifer unlocked and opened the door and Abigail stepped out onto the porch.

Snow tumbled in the vicinity of distant streetlamps, and Abigail wondered how it could be snowing only in those select globes of light.

"God, it's beautiful," the sheriff said.

Abigail found the zippers and worked them open, shoved her hands into the pockets.

They helped her down the steps into snow not quite deep enough to cover the spear tips of the longest grass blades.

"We doing right here?" Jennifer said.

"If you can live with yourself, does it matter?"

"Can you?"

"I think so. We just have to forget a few days of questionable behavior."

They moved down past the grove of baby aspen and the sheriff's Expedition, gravel crunching under their boots and slippers and Abigail's bare feet, unfazed by the cold.

They arrived at the Bronco, Quinn already opening the front passenger door.

Abigail stopped at the grille, Jennifer beside her, snow melting on the warmed metal of the hood.

Quinn slapped the roof. "Come on. Get in."

In the right pocket of her jacket, Abigail's fingers touched something cool and hard. It took five seconds of feeling it to identify the object, and still she couldn't think of its name, only its function.

"Jennifer," she said, "you know, I forgot all about this."

"What?"

Abigail turned and pressed it into her satin nightgown, then faced Quinn, ears ringing as the sheriff went groaning to her knees, blood sprinkling in the snow.

"You didn't mean what you said about helping my father, did you? You just want—"

"Abigail, you're fucked-up on the meds. We're trying to help you and your father here."

Jennifer crawled back toward the house, and for a moment, Abigail wondered if maybe Quinn was right.

"You didn't mean to shoot her, Abigail. Now give me the gun. My sister's gonna die if we don't—"

It made a small black spot an inch below Quinn's right eye.

Blood ran down his cheek.

He reached up and scraped at the hole with his fingernails, like he'd been stung and was trying to dig out the stinger.

Abigail looked back at the Victorian house, where Jennifer had dragged herself up onto the porch and come to an impasse at the front door.

The sheriff cried out, "Oh God!"

"You just shot two people, Abigail Foster," Abigail told herself.

Snow slanted down through the porch light, Abigail figuring the full thirty milligrams of Percoset must be raging through her, because she was so stoned, so detached, her thoughts derailing and becoming unmanageable again.

She eased down in the gravel and stared at the prayer flags, frosted with snow and flapping in the wind, Silverton all hushed and still.

She was cold and itchy from the opiate, but she didn't care.

After awhile, she got up and staggered toward the porch, climbed the steps, stopping at the front door.

Jennifer lay on her back in a pond of black blood, her eyes open and glazed, her lips barely moving.

Abigail said, "Your nightgown's ruined."

Then she stepped over the sheriff and went inside.

EIGHTY-NINE

The sun had roused Lawrence Kendall from sleep on Wednesday and Thursday, but not on Friday. His third morning in the cave, a noise woke him, his eyes opening to pure black, his head lifting from the folded parka he'd used for a pillow the last three nights, fearing he was hallucinating again, but the sound held strong—the muffled yet unmistakable *whop-whop* of rotors chopping the thin air. He smiled, could have wept. Abby had made it out.

As he felt around on the cold rock for the last functioning light, he wondered why a helicopter would be searching for him after dark, but he instantly dismissed the thought as near-death confusion.

His fingers grazed the straps, and he slipped the headlamp on and twisted the bulb. He dragged Abigail's pack over to the granola-bar wrapper in the middle of the room, which marked the spot under the chimney.

Every time he'd slept, he'd dreamed of this moment, on the brink of deliverance, wondering if the smoke would make it all seventy feet up the chute to the surface, and, if so, whether he could generate a sizable-enough plume with what he had to catch anyone's attention.

As he unzipped Abigail's pack and grabbed the Doubletree matchbook and a handful of paper he'd already torn out of her notepad and balled up in preparation, his eyes fell upon the mound of snow nearby that had undoubtedly fallen from the surface.

The moment he got the paper burning, he'd fill the two water bottles with the snow, maybe have enough willpower to wait, let it turn to delicious slush in the cavern's thirty-seven degrees.

He gathered up the wads of paper and stacked them into a little pyramid before tearing out a match. It ignited on the first strike, the flame motionless in the stagnant room. He held it to the base of the pyramid, got seven pieces lighted before the match burned down to his thumb.

The helicopter sounded closer, Lawrence figuring if he could hear the rotors this well, it must be hovering right over the chimney.

All the paper seemed to combust at once, and the room flared with firelight as a dense cloud of smoke lifted toward the low ceiling, Lawrence picturing it just missing the hole and diffusing through the room, but this didn't happen.

In spite of his weakened state, he'd planned and executed perfectly. Like a vacuum, the chimney inhaled the smoke. Lawrence struggled to his feet, neck splitting, head pounding with dehydration as he stared up the chute, watching his precious smoke curl toward the surface.

Far up the shaft, something gleamed in the dimming beam of his lamp. It resembled snow, and the smoke had collided into it and stopped, hanging like mist in a hollow against the ice-plugged opening of the chimney.

The *whop-whop* of the helicopter blades pulsed as loud as he would ever hear them.

It was daylight out there, permanent night in here, and if he couldn't find his way back to the main cavern, he was going to die.

NINETY

Sunlight streamed through the tall windows with a brilliance that suggested the world outside had turned to glass. Abigail's head throbbed, as if someone had shoved a hot coal deep into the base of her skull, and with the woodstove extinguished, the living room was cold, particularly where she lay shivering on the futon by the window.

She had no idea how she'd come to be in this house. The last piece of memory that felt like solid ground seemed ages ago—driving Scott's Suburban away from the trailhead at dusk. Whatever came after had shattered against the back of her mind, and based on what few frames she'd glimpsed, she didn't want those memories reassembled. Her eyes watered with pain as she eased her weight onto her feet.

The nearest archway opened into a kitchen, and something about the table and the stainless-steel refrigerator and the shelf of bottles over the sink made her nauseous with fear—an inexplicable familiarity.

She limped into the foyer and pulled open the front door to cloudless early-morning cobalt, Silverton buried under a foot of new snow, spruce and aspen in the front yard sagging under the weight, the town silent save the murmur of a snowplow scraping north up Greene Street.

At her feet, a woman dressed only in a pink satin nightgown lay unmoving on her stomach, her skin tinged blue and powdered with snow, her bare legs smeared with blood.

"Oh my God."

"And then you shot them both," the woman said.

"Yes."

"Because you believed your life was in danger."

"Yes."

"Tell me again why you thought the sheriff of Silverton and her brother wanted to kill you?"

"You're looking at me like you don't believe me."

"It's not that we don't believe—"

"Then what?"

"Ms. Foster, we've got the sheriff and her brother dead here in town, and you're telling us there're six more bodies in the backcountry, most of which we won't be able to locate until sometime next summer when the snow breaks, and forget the small concern that none of this jives with the Jen Primack I've known and worked with for three years. Look, I know you've been through quite an ordeal, but for a small-time undersheriff in a sleepy town like Silverton, this is a helluva lot to choke down."

When Abigail awoke, they were sitting at the foot of her bed, whispering. She shut her eyes and eavesdropped on a debate concerning the merits of parallel versus telemark turns in champagne powder.

Silverton's size didn't warrant a hospital, so the undersheriff had put Abigail up in the Grand Imperial for the night and asked two nurses from San Juan County Public Health to check in on her every few hours.

She liked the undersheriff, Hans, a tall, lanky man in the neighborhood of thirty, who looked more like a snowboard instructor than a lawman—longhaired, bearded, and with a tattoo of a rock-climbing skeleton inked into the skin of his left forearm, just visible where he'd rolled up the sleeve of his khaki button-up shirt.

The special agent with the Forest Service made her nervous. She couldn't recall the redhead's name, but despite her rustic wardrobe, she managed to exude the cool, impassive confidence of a fed. And she'd hardly asked Abigail a thing, letting Hans lob questions while she leaned back in her chair in her muddy hiking boots, jeans, and down vest, not even bothering to veil her scrutiny and suspicion.

The special agent cut her eyes at Abigail.

"She's awake."

They dragged their chairs over into patches of afternoon sunlight that spilled in through the second-floor windows.

"How you feeling?" the undersheriff asked.

"All right."

Hans leaned forward in the chair, clasped his hands together.

"Search-and-rescue just got back a half hour ago. You might've heard the helicopter."

"They didn't find my father."

"They spent forty-five minutes hovering over the mountainside you think you came out on, with two men combing the area with binoculars."

"I told you: There was a chimney I climbed out—"

"I believe you, Abigail. Thing is, that's steep terrain up there. They spotted numerous avalanches, and they're thinking a slide may have swept down the mountain at some point in the last twenty-four hours, buried the opening to the chimney."

"So they've given up?"

"No, of course not. But there's another storm coming in tonight, blizzard warnings already up, so our window for finding your father is shrinking."

Abigail glanced at the special agent, could have sworn she caught a glint of compassion through the federal facade. "Maybe my father left that chimney room, tried to find his way back to the cavern where we first entered."

"Okay, even assuming he was able to find his way back, this morning an avalanche swept down that hillside where you say you entered the cave. So wouldn't the entrance be buried? And as you said, it was practically impossible to find in dry conditions in broad daylight."

Abigail shook her head, the tears coming. "He thinks I'm coming for him. Please. Fly me back there. Let me—"

"You honestly believe you can find it?"

"Tell me something, Hans. At what point would you quit looking for your father?"

1893

NINETY-ONE

Gloria's head lay in Rosalyn's lap, and she saw that lonely lantern still burning in the middle of the cavern, its flame a little lower than before. The pain had intensified into something like the worst aftereffects of drunkenness she'd ever experienced, her body begging for water as it slowly dried and wilted. *Still alive*, she thought.

Now only moans and soft bellows disturbed the silence, the whimpers of those waiting to die, wanting it more than a drink of water, worse than air.

She looked up at Rosalyn. "Hey," she whispered.

Rosalyn's eyes were open, but the old whore made no answer. She had died while Gloria slept, her mouth inflated by the gigantic tongue, eyelids cracked, blood rolling out of them and down her checks. Even while she'd been alive, the absence of water had allowed the mummification of her body to begin, the skin on her face shrinking, lips shriveling, gums blackened, nose withered by half, flesh leathered into the color of ashen purple, with livid streaks where the blood had pooled.

Gloria felt a glimmer of release that her friend had passed.

Again, she obsessed on water, imagined bending down on the shore of Emerald Lake, splashing her face on a bright summer day. She kept replaying the last drink she'd ever taken—snow melted in an iron pot over the fire in their cabin. She could still picture Zeke filling her cup on Christmas morning, remembered how the water had chilled the tin, how when she touched it, her fingerprints had appeared as ghostly, fading condensation on the metal.

The sound of weeping drew her attention. She could barely raise her head from Rosalyn's lap, but when she did, she saw a woman lying ten feet away against the wall of the cavern, touching the blond hair of a boy perhaps two or three years old. The woman had managed to pull him into her body and she kissed his eyebrows and his parched little lips and cried tearlessly. Her husband had died several hours ago and his body lay sprawled nearby on the floor.

The woman rolled her son across the rock toward his father and lay down between them. She held their hands and stared up at the ceiling, her lips moving, and she would not get up again.

Gloria closed her eyes. She thought about her husband and her son, wondered if they could see her dying in this cave.

Then she sensed him, opened her eyes, and across the cavern stood Ezekiel, dapper in that four-button sack coat, his Sunday best, and shining as if illumined by footlights.

Though his lips did not move, she heard his voice perfectly.

He said he was sorry she'd suffered, but that it was almost over, that he'd glimpsed the place where they were going, and there were no words for pain or loss there, and no past.

Our boy's there, he said, *and I'm told he's been askin for us. There's some kind a beautiful place waitin on our souls, Gloria.*

What's he look like, Zeke?

Like Gus, I suppose.

He ain't grown?

I don't know.

Will he always be a little boy, or will he grow up into a man?

I don't know the answer to that.

You go on to him.

I wanna wait for you, Glori.

You won't be waitin long.

June 2010

All right, we're back on the record oh nine CR one sixty-four, the *People versus Abigail Foster*. Let's go ahead and bring in the jury."

The woman occupied a table near the street, shaded by an umbrella, a copy of the *Times* spread out across her lap.

At the sound of approaching footsteps, she looked up.

"Would the defendant please rise?"

Abigail and her attorney stood.

"Madam Forelady, have you arrived upon a verdict?"

"We have, Your Honor."

It was all happening faster than Abigail had imagined. She felt dizzy, her knees trembling under her skirt, had to put a hand on the table to steady herself.

"Is the verdict to be returned a unanimous one?"

"Yes, Your Honor."

"How do you find as to count one of the indictment charging the defendant with murder in the second degree?"

Midday, mid-June on the steps of the San Juan County courthouse, and the sky shone spring blue, the scant deciduous trees of Silverton just beginning to leaf out, baby greens and yellows smudging this high valley where mounds of snow lingered under the eaves of Victorian houses. It had been the hardest winter in a decade, the snowpack still four feet deep above timberline on the north aspects.

Walter Palmer ended his cell-phone call with a curt "No" and looked at his client. "Wanna grab lunch, Abigail? Brown Bear Café, and I'm buying."

"I've got a flight to catch to New York." Abigail embraced him, this fifty-six-year-old, balding, pudgy lawyer with halitosis and no sense of humor who'd fought for her freedom as if it were his own, put a soft kiss on his cheek, and said, "Thank you, Walt. For everything. Best seventy-five grand I ever spent."

Twenty-four hours later at Alexandra, a café three blocks from her studio apartment, Abigail bent to kiss a woman with short silver hair who was wearing a cotton summer dress that showed off the constellation of freckles on her browned shoulders.

"You look cute."

She sat across from her mother, their table bordering the sidewalk of Hudson Street, a hot day in the city, the rectangle of sky between the buildings a washed-out summer white and the stench of the river draped like a dirty wet blanket over the West Village.

Sarah Foster said, "I ordered a bottle of wine. Best they had."

Abigail dropped on the table the stack of mail she'd collected from the post office.

"Mom, you didn't have to—"

"I know I didn't, but I did. Excuse me for wanting to celebrate that my daughter isn't going into the clink for thirty years. And you wouldn't even let me be there."

Abigail set her sunglasses on the wrought-iron table. "If the verdict had gone the other way, I couldn't have watched what that did to you."

Sarah took hold of her daughter's hand. "Always the protector. Well, it's all behind you now, Abby."

"Yeah, but you know the full story. For everyone else, not guilty by reason of mental defect doesn't mean you didn't do it."

"It's nobody's business."

"People wonder. They'll talk. Snow madness is what my attorney argued, what I said happened. That I went nuts for a little while 'cause of being stranded in the storm. Temporary psychosis and—"

"You know the truth. That's all that matters."

"Doesn't make it easy."

The waiter came, presented the bottle of chardonnay, filled their wineglasses.

When he'd left, Abigail pulled down into her lap the pile of mail rubber-banded together. As she perused the month's accumulation of magazines and past-due bills, she noticed the package from the mail-order film-processing company, and her face must have darkened, because her mother said, "What is it, Abby?"

Abigail tore open the envelope, withdrew a sheaf of photographs.

"Emmett Tozer shot a roll of film on the hike in, and his wife gave it to me our first night in Abandon. I guess I sent these in to be developed before I flew out to Colorado for the trial."

"Sure you wanna see those right now?"

The photos had been shot in black-and-white, and the first picture wrecked Abigail's stomach—a long downhill shot of the llamas, Scott and Jerrod, June and Lawrence, with Abigail bringing up the rear, every head hung as the party climbed a steep wooded section of the trail.

"This was the first day," Abigail said, handing the picture to her mother.

They worked their way through the bottle of wine, Abigail providing captions for each photograph until she came to a picture that closed her throat and sheeted her eyes over with tears.

Sarah said, "Honey, what's wrong?"

The ominous skyline of Abandon was a blur behind them, the low cloud deck expressed in a few dark strokes of gray, but their faces stood out in perfect focus—Lawrence smiling, not at the camera, but at Abigail, who was pulling away.

Abigail shook her head, laid the photograph on the table so her mother could see. Whispered, "I've never seen a picture of us together." She recognized herself in the way his eyes had gone to slits with his smile, saw Lawrence in the shape of her mouth. "I know you were angry that I went to see him."

"No, honey—"

"It wasn't a betrayal. I needed to see him, and it's strange to say, but all this shit I went through . . . meant I at least got to know him."

"And I'm glad you did, Abby."

"He was a broken man, Mom. What he did to us, it wasn't right, but he was so young."

Sarah was nodding now, and Abigail watched her mother push back the emotion.

"And he tried, Mom, you know? Asking me to come to Colorado, that was him trying. It couldn't have been easy."

Sarah lifted the photograph, stared at it for a moment, and when she looked up at Abigail, she was smiling through tears.

"He's looking at you here like you're someone he loves."

Abigail wiped her eyes, watched a man walk out of the watch-repair shop across the street. "Mom, I tried to find him. Three times we flew into that box canyon, but—"

"I know."

"—the snow was so deep, it had blocked—"

"Abby, you have to let all that go now."

"He died doing what he wanted, I guess. What he loved."

Sarah tilted the wine bottle, topped off her glass. "Where do you stand financially?"

"The lawyer wiped me out."

"If I had the funds to—"

"I know."

"Abby, I've been thinking." Sarah scooted her chair over and leaned in close, speaking just above a whisper. "It's summer now. Snow's melted in the high country, right?"

"In a month or so. Why?"

"What if you went back to that mine, took a few bricks—"

"No, Mom."

"Just enough to get you out of—"

"No."

"Darling, you're broke. Could you find the mine entrance?"

"Probably."

"So why suffer when you don't have to?"

Abigail leaned back in her chair.

"For hundreds of years, Mom, that gold's done nothing—*nothing*—but bring out the worst in people. Make misery and death. There isn't even the smallest part of me that's tempted to go back to that wilderness, into that mine, to get it.

"You know I'm not a superstitious person, but if anything in this world is cursed, that gold is. I couldn't be broke enough to resort to that. Now you're the only other person I've told about the gold and the bones. Not even my lawyer knew, and I expect the secrets of Abandon to die with both of us, so the awful history of that town can stay shut away."

Sarah had been biting her bottom lip. "Honey, that's noble of you, but it's gonna take you years to replenish your savings, get back on your feet."

"So be it."

"Are you sure? I mean, you've really decided this?"

Abigail finished her wine. "I jogged to Brooklyn this morning. Halfway across the bridge, I stopped and threw the key to that mine into the East River. So yeah, Mom, I'm sure."

They'd nearly killed the bottle of wine. Abigail was feeling pleasantly buzzed now, working up a good sheen of sweat just sitting in the city heat, no relief but when the buses roared by, and she thought about that snowy night in the boardinghouse with Lawrence and the vision he'd shared of spending a Colorado summer with her, with grandchildren he would never have. There was still anger. God, plenty of that. She didn't know how she'd ever be fully rid of it, but maybe there was space now for other things. Things that didn't keep you up nights, that didn't push good people away.

And she wondered where in that vast cave system her father had finally eased down to die, hoped he hadn't been scared, and that when he'd finally broken free of all that freezing dark, he'd found his way to that Colorado summer and the man he might have been.

If all time is eternally present
All time is unredeemable.

—T. S. Eliot, "Burnt Norton"

Through the grottoes and tunnels of this cold and silent underworld, he returns, impossibly, to Abandon's crypt.

The beam of his dying headlamp sweeps across the battered iron door—still closed, still locked.

She hasn't come.

The disappointment cuts deeper than he imagined it would, despite having warned himself she wouldn't anticipate his actually making it back to the cavern. *He* hadn't figured on it, assuming instead he'd run out of light and die of thirst, lost in the granitic entrails of the mountain.

He turns away from the barred exit and walks back into the cavern among the bones, fearing his light will expire at any second, wanting at least to see and choose his final resting place.

Lawrence doesn't procrastinate with the decision. He picks a spot along the wall beside a blond-haired skeleton wrapped in a deteriorated woolen jacket and slumped over on the rocky floor, the browned skull resting on the humerus of her left arm, Gloria watching the last flame of the last lantern sputtering in the middle of the cavern.

She wonders, *Am I the only one alive? No one else has made a sound in hours.*

The coal oil is nearly used up, the batteries almost dead, and they wait for the light to go away, each passing moment charged with the possibility they are seeing the last they will ever see of this world.

The flame recedes into the wick and the headlamp dims.

Lawrence pulls off his lamp, looks into the bulb, the light fading before his eyes.

Soon there is only the molten glow of the tungsten filaments, the lantern's wick, then nothing.

He breathes in slowly, out slowly, trying to soothe himself with the proposition that this is where he belongs, a certain justice inherent with being locked in the mountain to die alongside the objects of his obsession, but finding little comfort in anything but the knowledge that his daughter is safe, thinking it must be a sad testament that saying those hard truths to Abby before she climbed out of the cave was the single decent moment of his life.

Time limps by in the black.

They tremble with helpless terror, thinking it's death they crave, but they long only to be spared sitting alone with their fracturing minds, listening to death creep toward them.

Lawrence slides his arms out of the shoulder straps and unzips his daughter's pack, lifting out the water bottles he filled at the subterranean lake and standing them up.

He takes one, unscrews the cap, and turns the bottle upside down. When he's emptied them both, he throws the bottles out into the cavern, the plastic banging invisibly against the rock.

And Gloria and Lawrence gaze into the dark, thinking of a son, a daughter they will not see again, the images swarming and vivid, inlaid at once with such beauty and unbearable regret.

Chasing her little boy through an alpine meadow, sunlight caught up in his rusty hair, his high, small laughter resounding off the mountains as she tickles his ribs.

His little girl in his lap, turning the pages of some long-forgotten book whose words would crush him if he could remember.

Both, in their own way, thinking, *This is hell*—the absolute loss borne from all those slivers of perfection that passed unnoticed, unrelished.

In true dark, there is no gauging of time.

It moseys along and dawdles and hints at the horror of eternity.

At length, Lawrence folds the backpack into a pillow and settles down beside the bones of Gloria, whose shattered heart quits beating.